POOR SOULS

by

John William McMullen

WHISKEY CREEK PRESS
www.whiskeycreekpress.com

Published by
WHISKEY CREEK PRESS

Whiskey Creek Press
PO Box 51052
Casper, WY 82605-1052
www.whiskeycreekpress.com

ISBN 978-1-59374-716-0

Credits

Cover Artist: Jinger Heaston
Editor: Melanie Billings

Printed in the United States of America

WHAT THEY ARE SAYING ABOUT
POOR SOULS

"…The intention of this writer is to highlight the ordinary, and indeed the sinful, as being transformed by grace into something worthy of God. *Poor Souls* is a front-runner of the Catholic novel, though this is not immediately apparent because of its unpretentiousness.

So why does it haunt me and why do I want to hail it as an outstanding Catholic novel? Because the writer is an unswervingly honest professional with something pertinent to say, and because he says it with quiet sobriety without ever resorting to 'pious-speak'."
~~Reviewed by Leo Madigan for Fatima-Ophel Books

"…McMullen clearly demonstrates in this book the breadth of his knowledge of Church and seminary life and mores [by revealing] all the varying weaknesses and foibles to which humans are susceptible, whether layperson or clergy."
~~Reviewed by Frost at Twolips Reviews

"…There is a realism that made me double check the genre to make sure it wasn't nonfiction. You probably know the people in this novel.…"
~~Reviewed by Amanda Killgore for Huntress Reviews

"…Being a priest isn't always the easy way in life. And the inhabitants of the Poor Souls parish aren't all as Catholic as he would wish. But God will help him, God and many, many prayers. *Poor Souls* has taught me one thing, then it's that priests are human just as much as we are, but of course we knew that. It's a difficult decision to take and a bumpy road to follow, being a priest and staying one. *McMullen* has written this story in a humoristic way, it makes you wonder and laugh at the same time…a no-nonsense book, just the way I like it."
~~Reviewed by Annick for Euro Reviews

Dedication

~~To MG~~

Preface

My grandfather, John Louis "Moon" McMullen, once told me, "Life's too short to bitch. In life you can choose to die laughing or die crying." I choose to die laughing. If we cannot laugh at ourselves, then we are in worse trouble than I imagined.

St. Paul wrote, "God chose the foolish of the world to shame the wise; the weak of the world to shame the strong; the lowly and despised of the world, those who count for nothing, to reduce to nothing those who are something" (1 Cor. 1:27-28).

"If any of you thinks he is worldly wise, he had better become a fool" (1 Cor. 3:18b) for "We are fools for Christ" (1 Cor. 4.10).

John W. McMullen
Evansville, Indiana
29 June 2004
The Solemnity of the Feast of Saints Peter and Paul,
Super Apostles and Super Fools

Poor Souls

Chapter 1: St. Albert's Seminary

"Here I am, Lord."
– Is. 6.8

How does one explain the call to priesthood? I have no idea.

I grew up in the church—the Catholic Church. As a child, I recall invariably arriving late at church and Mother marching us down to one of the front pews. Observing the altar boys performing their religious functions—dressed in their black cassocks and white surplices, their black dress shoes barely visible as they knelt in humble adoration—I longed to ring the sanctuary bells.

At home, my younger brother and I played Mass; I was the priest and he was the server. It was the one time I had the upper hand over the baby of the family. We didn't use potato chips or crackers for hosts like other kids. We smashed a piece of white bread—turning it into a pasty piece of unappealing processed yeast—and used a cookie cutter to make it into a perfect circle. Reverently I raised the fake host above my head, closed my eyes, and said the words of consecration.

When I was about ten, my father caught us having Mass one day and asked me, "Martin, do you want to be a priest when you grow up?" Before I could reply he continued, "The priesthood's unnatural, son. Wait until they let priests marry, then become one if that's what you want to do with your life. But who the hell would run the cleaners?" Maybe that was when I first considered a call to the priesthood.

During high school, any thoughts of embracing celibacy went out the window, even though the Sisters and priest at my school encouraged us to pursue the vocation.

After high school, I went away to State College. One night during my senior year, I was at one of the local pubs having pizza and beer with a friend. He had just broken up with his girlfriend, and I had just lost the only girl I think I ever really loved. We were both drinking to get drunk; he was already there and I was well on my way.

He leaned over the table with swaying head and crossing eyes and asked me in a slur, "Martin, have you found your passion in life?"

"I'm through with passion. That's why I'm here getting drunk with you."

"I'm not talking about that kind of passion. I mean, you know, your *purpose* in life."

I knew that a business degree would serve me well in my family's dry cleaning business, but I had never asked myself that question. Was business my passion? Was managing my mother's dry cleaners to be my purpose in life? Would providing people with clean, starched, perfectly pressed shirts fill this emptiness, this deeply buried need to give my all, even unto death without counting the cost so that others might know Jesus? I had no idea.

My father lacked passion. He was seemingly trapped in a job that he merely performed as a duty to his wife and children—not to mention his father-in-law, Grandpa Buckner. Mother always said that my father was rescued from the curse of the steel mills by Grandpa Buckner. My father didn't see it that way. He was pressured by Grandpa to take the job after marrying my mother, thereby abandoning his plans of trying to land a job as a writer for the *Cainbrook Evening Press*.

Today the question was irrelevant. The roaring furnace of the steel mill was silent, the belching smokestack was crumbling, the paper was defunct, and my father was dead.

Yet, that evening's conversation in the pub with a drunk shifted my paradigm back to Catholicism, rekindling an interest in religion and faith. It was an epiphany of sorts, or at least I thought it was. I'm still not sure.

Things often happen like that. I admit that the party scene wasn't cutting it for me any longer. Whether to stop at that fifth or sixth beer or to just keep drinking until my troubles were spinning into oblivion was my usual dilemma and about as deep as my questioning went—until that night.

My friend followed his question with another. "Why the hell are we here?" With half-open eyes, he leaned over the table and suddenly swayed on his bar stool, retched and puked; he fell off the stool and landed in his regurgitation.

After that night, instead of being focused on what I'd be doing any particular night, I began to focus on what I'd be doing for the rest of my life. It was a profound thought for me. So much so, that I truthfully wonder if it was my own thought.

Nonetheless, after I graduated from college, I returned to my family's dry cleaning business, but I had never quite shaken that question about my passion in life. Might God be calling me to the priesthood? For over a year I wondered.

All I know is that I felt I had the call. I believe I had the call. I thought I had the call. I trust I had the call. But how does one explain the call to priesthood? I was reasonably content at the dry cleaners, but it seemed there was always something tugging at my heart telling me there was more to life.

The tugging persisted despite my frequent attempts to quiet it with a few beers, the sight of a pretty girl, or a weary night in front of the TV, remote control in hand, surfing the channels, and zoning out. Those things worked for a while, but the feeling that I was being called returned every time.

I had to make a decision. I would answer the call. Maybe it was one of the first real decisions in my life.

There was no flash of light, no voice like thunder, no spinning sun, no apparition of the Virgin, no bleeding crucifixes, no weeping statues, but only a whispering, subtle desire to rise above my individualistic routine to serve others as did Jesus, knowing that I could make a difference in the world.

Did I hear the call in the strains of Schubert's *Ave Maria* at Christmas Midnight Mass or Mozart's *Ave Verum Corpus* on Holy Thursday? Was the call in the seed of faith planted years ago at my baptism and nurtured along by the waters of daily prayer and the unleavened bread of weekly Mass? Was it in my high school retreat to the Allegheny Woods, where I was awakened in the middle of the night by the brilliant light of the full moon pouring through the cabin windows to stand silent under a starlit heaven listening for the voice of God? Was it in the film about Mother Teresa and her work among the poorest of the poor, or the faithful witness of my own pastor as he prayed Mass, celebrated the sacraments, visited the sick, and married and buried his parishioners?

One of my religion teachers once said that the act of making love and the accompanying ecstasy was the closest thing to the beatific vision. I had slept with only one girl. The only thing that remained was the feeling of love. Making love ended our relationship. I thought I loved her, but the morning after I was somehow emptier than before. Maybe it was just guilt, I don't know, but it changed everything between us. Then a week or two later I had the "passion" conversation with my drunk friend.

All the same, could the feeling of love, the kisses, the sexual intimacy, the very act of making love and the rush of bliss in dying to self have contributed to my call? Even in my sinful fornication, it seemed I had a foretaste of Heaven, and it made me long for more. Heaven, that is. My teacher said Heaven would be one eternal orgasm. That was something to look forward to.

My pastor at Our Lady of the River had long encouraged me to pursue the priestly calling. So, I decided to answer the call. The week before I left the dry cleaners and my apartment behind, he took me to dinner and gave me some advice.

"Now, Martin, let me forewarn you, son; I don't know what you're expecting to see when you enroll in the seminary, but let me tell you it's not going to be the 'Bells of Saint Mary's'. Bing Crosby was never ordained." I wasn't exactly sure where he was going with the conversation. "I mean it, son. Don't expect to see grim-faced men walking around in monk robes praying all the time. Just because these men are seminarians doesn't mean they aren't human. Once you're there, you might even think to yourself, 'what's he doing here?' Be careful not to judge. You'll meet some of the holiest men, but you'll also meet some of the most unholy men. I want you to know that before you get there. In all things, just keep an open mind. You may not agree with everything you hear or see, but whatever you do, don't forget why you're going to the seminary. I believe, as you do, that God is calling you to the priesthood. The Church needs holy priests. Never forget that."

He was quite right. As I prepared to finish my first year of seminary at Saint Albert's Priory, much of what he had said had been fulfilled. I had officially been a seminarian for the Diocese of Covert for nearly a year.

So, how does one explain the call? Christ's call to the fishermen seemed so simple. *Come, follow me. And they left their nets and followed him.* Why couldn't the call be as simple today? I had no idea.

Lord, I believe; help my unbelief.

Chapter 2: The Call

And so we intend to establish a school
for the service of the Lord.
— St. Benedict

I walked out of the seminary chapel into a cool sunny April morning. The gothic façade of the white limestone seminary building stood out against the cobalt blue sky. The chapel of Our Lady of Aquino and Our Lady's Grotto at the Priory of St. Albert the Great were both familiar from my childhood. The first time I had ever prayed here I was nine years old. My mother, Grandpa, and Grandma Buckner brought me here on a pilgrimage of thanksgiving following my recovery from rheumatic fever.

I made my way down the esplanade in front of the Priory and Seminary and entered through the double doors of the seminary building and up the stairwell. Class was about to begin.

My professor, the black-haired, forty-something Dominican-robed Father Joseph Kelley, had a lit cigarette dangling from his mouth, a large steaming coffee mug in his right hand, and a bundle of books under his left arm when he entered the classroom that morning to begin the day's lecture on *Theological Anthropology*. The black scapular over his front and back

9

contrasted with his stark white habit, as did his sandaled black-socked feet. Father Joseph flung his black scapular over his right shoulder as he feverishly scribbled notes on the black-board.

"God is everywhere," he pondered aloud, looking out over us but not making any eye contact. "Perhaps even in the depths of hell. Could it be that the flames of hell are the very same flames of God's love? Could the souls of the damned experience God's love as torture? Ah, that's the hell of it. They're all burned up, eh? But, then, 'dare we hope that all be saved?' as St. Paul wrote. Yes. Dare! For those who refuse God's love do so at their own peril. Yet, even then, we as believers must entrust them to God's tender mercies."

I doodled with my pen on my notebook page as he droned on about death, judgment, Heaven, hell, and purgatory. I needed another cup of coffee. Just then, a knock at the door interrupted class. It secured a welcome respite from such second semester metaphysical musings. Father Joseph would usually break in the middle of his two-hour class anyway so he could get a cup of java and step outside for a smoke. I was already thinking about which flavor of coffee I would get at the seminary canteen when Father Joseph suddenly returned to the room and bore down on my desk.

"Flanagan, the Vice-Rector wants to see you in his office." His nicotine-stained teeth matched his breath. "*Now.*"

I left my pen on my open notebook and stepped out into the hall. I wondered what Father Hugh would want with me. I stopped at the restroom before descending the stairs to the hallway of the Dominican Administration. What could he want? Purgatory and hell came to mind as I slid my hand down the stairs' handrail.

I'd never been to the Vice-Rector's office before, but I'd heard horror stories of a seminarian being summoned on suspicion of wrongful behavior and, within the hour, his belongings were out on Saint Dominic Drive and the fellow was thumbing his way back to Indiana or wherever.

When I arrived at the administrative offices, but before opening the oak door, I observed the reflection of Father Hugh's secretary in the open transom glass above the door. She was sipping a diet cola at her computer.

The secretary looked up from her computer screen and smiled as I slowly opened the heavy door. "I'm Martin Flanagan. Father Hugh sent for me."

"Oh." Her face fell as if she knew that whatever it was Father Hugh wanted to speak with me about would be unpleasant. "Have a seat in the hallway. Father Hugh is with someone right now." His door was closed with a *DO NOT DISTURB* sign hanging from the knob.

Great. I sat picking at my thumbnail, bouncing my right leg up and down as I thought of what Father Hugh might want.

Father Hugh was a narcoleptic and on occasion had dozed off even while celebrating Mass. Once when I was serving as his acolyte at Mass, his head had gone down during a tediously long homily with at least three good endings delivered by one of the new deacons. When it was time for offertory, I had to rouse him.

Waiting to meet with him, I thought about praying but couldn't find the words. I reached for my rosary, but realized I had left it on my nightstand. After a few restless moments, I looked up when the brass doorknob of the hand-carved ornamented door began to turn.

Father Paphnutius, the Dean of Students, emerged from the Vice-Rector's office into the hall. "Mr. Flanagan," he said with a slight bow of the head, his eyes unblinking and his face emotionless. "I didn't see you at vespers last night."

"Tuesday evening is our Diocesan gathering," I said as I came to my feet.

"But today is the twenty-ninth of April." His round frame inched closer as his black and white habit nearly touched the floor.

I gave him an empty look, unaware of any significance associated with the date.

"The twenty-ninth of April is the feast of Saint Catherine of Siena. Mystic. Second female to be declared doctor of the church. And a *Dominican*."

"Oh, of course."

"The Vigil was celebrated last night."

"I had no idea."

"God forbid that the theological and spiritual disciplines we strive to instill in our students are wasted upon the Diocesan seminarians." He had turned away and walked off before I could respond. But even if I had had time, Father Hugh would have prevented me. The Vice-Rector was standing in the open doorway.

"Mister Flanagan?" Father Hugh stood in the doorway. His white habit and black scapular were perfectly pressed and hung on his bony frame.

"Yes, Father Hugh," I started as I straightened up, still standing at attention.

"No ceremony."

"Ceremony?" I had no idea what he was talking about.

"You've never seen the film, *A Man for All Seasons*? It's based on Robert Bolt's play."

"No, I can't say I have."

"Deprived," he said, shaking his head in disbelief. "A deprived child, you are. Promise me that you *will* see it over the summer."

"Okay."

"No, promise me that you will."

"Yes, Father. I promise."

"Mister Flanagan," Father Hugh motioned me into his office like a shepherd to a wayward lamb. "Won't you please?"

Father Hugh followed me into the room and closed the door behind us. His study was immaculate and bright. Louvered white shutters faced the east and were open at forty-five degree angles, allowing the bright spring sunlight to stream through the windows and bask the room in an orange and pink glow. In the middle of the wall was an octagonal stained glass window of a human hand with its thumb and first two fingers upraised and the words *Ego te absolvo*. The red, yellow, green, blue, and purple shafts of light graced the wall of his bookshelves and Giotto and Raphael paintings. The room had a reverent silence about it.

Father Hugh walked around behind his desk. "Please be seated, Mister Flanagan."

I sank into a tan leather chair. My eyes followed a glorious beam of yellow sun that illuminated a vividly colored icon of the Blessed Lady; its gold frame accentuated the golden trim of the blue folds of her dress. An icon of Christ stood in place upon a miniature easel on the edge of the Vice-Rector's dark mahogany desk.

"So, Mister Flanagan—Martin Flanagan—how has your first year at Saint Albert's been?" Father Hugh sat down.

"Fine." What else was I to say? I was relatively content though nervous about being summoned to his office.

"*Fine*? I'd like to strike that word from the English language—it is such a lame excuse for an adjective." Hugh's eyes squinted in their tiny sockets.

"Really?"

"*Really* is as bad as *fine*."

I noticed Father Hugh's wire-rimmed, half-lens reading

glasses sitting on his desk near two wooden pens situated in an elegant stand.

"I know you've never been called to my office before, but weren't you called to the Dean's office last year for something?"

"No, Father."

"Oh, that's right. I'm thinking of the fellow from Connecticut. Or was he the one from Philadelphia? He was in the room across from you, wasn't he? You shared the quad lounge in Aquinas Hall. Brad something, wasn't it?"

"Greg. He was from Allentown."

"Oh, yes. Greg. He was a troubled lad, wasn't he?"

"I didn't really know much about him, you know." I told the truth.

"No, I didn't know." Hugh moved forward in his chair.

I studied a framed photograph of a younger Father Hugh in his black and white Dominican robes between a man and woman standing on the steps of an old gothic church. I presumed they were Father Hugh's parents.

"So, Mister Martin Flanagan, you tell me why I—Father Hugh, Order of Preachers, Vice Rector of Saint Albert's Seminary—have called you to my office."

"I have no idea." I looked away to the stained glass window.

"Don't lie to me, son." He stroked his chin with his right thumb.

"I'm not lying." I immediately regained eye contact with him.

"If you are, then I'll have to inform your bishop this morning."

I said nothing, not so much shocked at the threat of possible dismissal, but uncomfortable with confrontation with authority.

"Are you nervous, Mister Flanagan?" Before I could reply, he continued, "If you are innocent, then there is nothing to fear." He motioned to me with his right hand, his palm open.

"What have I done?" I wrestled with my memory as to recall any infraction I may have committed.

"Why don't you tell me how good of a tree climber you are?" He brought his hands together and tapped his fingers lightly.

"Trees?"

"Yes. Trees. Climbing trees."

"Okay, I guess."

"I see." Father Hugh reached for a clipboard on his desk and jotted down something before continuing. "How about climbing other things?"

"*Other* things?" I made eye contact with him.

"Yes, such as ladders."

"Yes, I can climb a ladder, but what has that to do with anything?"

"I am asking the questions, son. Relax." He made another note before speaking again. "All right, so you *are* thin enough to climb a ladder. Now what I want to know is how you were clever enough to get *the key?*"

"Key?" I had absolutely no idea what he was talking about.

"Yes, how does one go about getting *the key?*" He returned the clipboard to his desk.

"What *key?*"

"*What* key?" He chuckled. "Oh, you're good, Mister Flanagan," he leaned back in his chair and sighed. "Better than I was told."

"Excuse me?" I found myself perilously close to questioning Father Hugh's authority.

"Don't give me that." He moved forward again and sat on the edge of his chair. "You know good and well what key."

"No, I honestly do not know, Father." I sat erect.

"The key to the tower, Mister Flanagan." His voice was stern.

"Bell tower?" I inadvertently laughed. "Father, I have absolutely no idea what you're talking about."

"Yes. The bell tower. You may have noticed that we have a bell tower. Now tell me, without laughing, what the view is like, especially in the middle of a clear and starry night."

"I don't know. I wouldn't know. I get vertigo at those heights. I can't even ride the Ferris wheel at our parish fair."

"Oh, I do like your *modus operandi*. Vertigo does make for a handy alibi. Are you aware that *Vertigo* is one of Father Paphnutius' favorite Hitchcock films? Of course, my favorite Hitchcock film is *I Confess*. Perhaps *you* have something to confess?"

"No." I stared in his direction, thinking of his accusation that I had taken the key.

"Oh? Are we sinless?" Father Hugh chuckled.

"That's not what I meant, Father." I nodded slightly in humility.

"I know that," he said, smiling. "I do have a sense of humor, Mister Flanagan."

I sighed, briefly thinking the interrogation over.

"Humor me with the truth," he snickered, "and I'm liable to forget the whole matter."

"The truth is I don't know what you're talking about." I rubbed the knuckles of my left hand.

"We were talking about the bell tower. Have you forgotten?"

"I have no memory of it to forget."

"Yes, well, answer me this question: Did you sleep well last night without a pillow?"

"I slept with a pillow." What kind of a question was that,

I thought.

"Do you hear the bells ring at five a.m. each morning?"

"Not really, rarely ever. I grew up near a railroad yard. As a child I learned how to ignore noise."

"Bells calling men to prayer is not noise!"

"That's not what I meant."

"Did you hear the bells this morning?"

"No."

"Of course you didn't."

"I was asleep."

"Well, I slept through the bells this morning as well. And you do know why I slept in, don't you? And don't you dare diagnose me with narcolepsy!"

"I honestly am confused, Father. What are you saying?"

"All right, I'll make it simple. Did you or did you not *steal* the key to the bell tower, *climb* to the belfry, and *stuff* the bells with pillows last night?"

"No," I replied, holding back a laugh as I wondered who might have done it.

"Then who else is skinny enough?"

"You don't have to be skinny to climb the tower."

"Oh, really? How do you know?"

"Father, I don't know anything about this."

"Then who does? *Name names.*" He picked up his clipboard again.

"I have no idea." At that, I straightened in my chair and was ready to stand.

Father Hugh tossed the clipboard on his desk, sat back in his chair and sighed long and hard through his nose. "You don't, do you?"

"No, I don't." I relaxed and sighed softly.

Hugh took his eyeglasses off his desk and adjusted them on his head, bringing them halfway down his nose, seemingly embarrassed at his accusations against me. He picked a manila-colored file folder off his desk, opened it, removed the papers, and paged through them.

"You're from Covert."

"Cainbrook, actually. I'm studying for Covert."

"Oh, yes, yes. Born in Cainbrook. Attended *Regina Coeli* High. You attended State College. Majored in Business. Your father is deceased and your mother never remarried. Her family operates the Buckner Dry Cleaning chain. You have a brother who is estranged from the faith. Your pastor is Father David Gregory at Our Lady of the River. And your spiritual director is Sister Regina Claire."

"Yes." I was impressed with the minutiae. "That's me."

"Very well." He leaned forward in his chair and set down the folder before speaking again. "If you should hear who might be responsible for the bell debacle, you will let me know, won't you?"

"Yes, Father."

"Very well. Forgive me for thinking you were involved."

"That's all right," I said, but thought otherwise. "May I go now?"

"No, not yet. The actual reason I called you here is unrelated to the incident with the bells. I wanted to ask you some questions in confidence pertaining to a *PF* between Misters Rawly Huffhind and Matthew Tupps." Father Hugh's small round eyes narrowed to slits.

"*PF?*" I rhetorically asked, hoping to stall for time. Huffhind and Tupps' relationship was an open secret.

"A *particular friendship,* Mister Flanagan. You are familiar with the term, are you not?" I was. Huffhind and Tupps did spend a good deal of time together, though I had never explored the particulars of their friendship. I was too busy with my own life to worry about the few seminarians who made up *the girls' club.*

My flitting thoughts returned to a particular day in sacraments class when Father Hugh was covering the charism of priestly celibacy. One of the men had asked a question dealing with sexuality, and Father Hugh had spent a half-hour answering him. "I hope I have cleared up any questions concerning masturbation. Am I right?" Without waiting for a hand to go up, he continued. "Good. So, gentlemen, you transform your sexual energy into care for souls." Hugh's eyes were closed as he lectured at that point. "Your unavailability to one particular woman—"

"Or *man*," Matthew Tupps whispered loudly as he covered his mouth with his right hand. Tupps was a chubby, horn-rimmed bespectacled blonde seminarian from Des Moines.

"Excuse me?" Father Hugh looked up and removed his reading glasses, but no one said anything. He continued, "Your unavailability to one particular *woman* becomes your availability to all people. So offer it up, gentlemen." He gave a dramatic pause. "I have, and I have no regrets."

"What would you know, Father?" The voice of Matthew Tupps came forth again from the back of the room.

"Excuse me, Mister Tupps?" Father Hugh looked at him intently with his eyes wide open.

"You don't know what it's like," Tupps said with an expression of certainty.

"Excuse me?" Hugh now glared at Tupps. "What ever do you mean?"

"You sleep alone, Father."

"Why…don't you, Mister Tupps?" Hugh shot back.

"Most nights. Yeah." Tupps laughed.

"Class Dismissed!" Hugh smacked his hand down flat on the lectern and then made for Tupps. "Mister Tupps, you will accompany me to the rector's office immediately. Father Paphnutius will be very interested to hear you explain what you meant by that last comment." Hugh stared at Rawly Huffhind as he left the room. Rawly was a slender and tan Floridian.

As the men spilled into the hallway, one of them whispered loudly enough for everyone to hear. "Hey, Huffhind, looks like you'll be sleeping alone tonight."

Rawly bent over the water fountain, took a sip of water and rose up abruptly, eying me. "So, Flanagan, is Father Hugh in favor of masturbation or not?" Rawly turned and disappeared up the dormitory stairwell.

Then during the second week of January, Matthew Tupps celebrated his birthday at the town's pub and got drunk. After midnight, he staggered his way back to the seminary's residence hall and decided to take down the Christmas decorations that were still up in the seminary courtyard. He went to his room, draped a sheet around himself like a toga, and returned to the courtyard. In tears, he grabbed the dried up Christmas tree and carried it up the four flights of stairs in Aquinas Hall—only to throw it out the fourth-floor lounge window.

Many of the seminarians were awakened by the commotion as he began crying more and more, lamenting that Rawly Huffhind was in Mexico for the month of January and had missed his birthday party. Tupps then began throwing pillows, couch cushions, blankets and even a couple of folding chairs out the window. Some of the guys restrained Tupps and put him to bed.

"Mister Flanagan," Father Hugh's voice surprised me back into the present. "Do you know of any *peculiarities* about their PF? I mean, are they—*how* shall I put it—are they more than—let's say—*friends?*"

"I have no idea."

"*I have no idea?* You like that phrase, don't you? I rank it with the likes of *really* and *fine* and *nice.*"

"I'm sorry."

"Have either Misters Huffhind or Tupps ever tried to befriend you…let's say…in a…*queer* manner?" Hugh's lips puckered at the word queer.

"No."

"Do you know where they go on weekends? Some have said they usually travel together."

"No. All I know is that Rawly is from Jacksonville, Florida. Matt's from Iowa, but he's lived in California."

"Uh, huh. It does seem that both Mr. Huffhind and Mr. Tupps have been around. But do you know where these two go together?"

"No, but a lot of the guys go away for the weekend once in a while."

"They do, don't they?" He leaned on his desk and stared through me.

Though it was a loaded comment, I didn't elaborate on any of the rumors I had heard.

"If you hear anything about those two, you will tell me or the rector, Father Thaddeus, or Father Paphnutius, or your own vicar-general, won't you?"

"Yes, Father, but I'm not in the habit of trying to get people in trouble."

"Son, they're *already* in trouble! And it's my task to ensure that they don't entangle any innocent souls in their trouble, hence saving the Church from further scandal." I looked away, preferring to focus upon a hand-carved crucifix that hung on the wall to Father Hugh's left. "Don't allow these men to intimidate you, Martin Flanagan. Celibacy is a beautiful gift, and the priesthood doesn't need to be polluted with

Cretins or Corinthians."

"Corinthians?"

"I got the crucifix in Assisi." He ignored my question and focused on the crucifix.

"Nice." My eyes met his.

"Yes. I was there a month before the earthquake destroyed Giotto's frescoes in the basilica. Have you ever been to Europe?"

"No, but I do plan on going sometime before my ordination."

"Never have I found such peace as I did in Assisi. I understand art scholars are working to restore the frescoes there."

There was stillness between us, and the soft strains of violins and cellos came from the outer room's stereo speakers.

"Ah, Tchaikovsky's String Quartet, Number One. His *Andante Cantabile*. So sublime. Out of Tchaikovsky's tortured heart came incredible beauty."

I nodded slowly.

Father Hugh closed his eyes, following the melody in his eyebrows and tilting his head before speaking again.

"Did you attend our birthday celebration of Johann Sebastian Bach last March?" he asked.

"No, I was working on a paper for my sacraments class."

"I see. Bach was born over three hundred years ago. Have you studied music at all?"

"Sister Cecilia taught us music appreciation in high school. And I was able to attend an all-Tchaikovsky concert in college."

"The hundredth anniversary of his death was in 1993."

"That may have been the year," I said. "Did you know that Tchaikovsky disliked his *Nutcracker*?" It was one of the few things I remembered from Music Appreciation.

"Yes. And Maurice Ravel regretted writing his *Bolero*. I wonder if Christ ever regretted saying, '*The poor you will always have with you*'? Untold harm has been justified by those who take that one quote out of context."

"Or Saint Paul's letter to Timothy," I added in hopes of lightening the mood, "encouraging him to take a little wine, it being good for the stomach."

"Speaking of a little *wine* and a *sick stomach*, Mr. Flanagan, that brings me to my final point. Is there anything else you would like to tell me, or confess, before we part?"

"Nothing that I know of."

"Not even your little Saint Patrick's day outing with some of your friends that took you to The Leprechaun and The Paradise Inn in New Dublin?"

I was speechless as I wondered how he could have known about that.

"Is something wrong? Don't you know that a seminarian's excursions are not only monitored by your professors, but are also scrutinized by the faithful? Did you think your going to New Dublin would go unnoticed?"

"We had fried chicken."

"And *beer*."

"Yes, and beer, but we're of age, Father."

"It was during Lent."

"It was a *Tuesday* night, not Friday."

"I was told it was a Friday."

"It was a Tuesday."

"I don't care if it was Easter Sunday; do you deny drinking to excess?"

"We probably drank one too many pitchers."

"Pitchers? Then you were licentious!"

"Father, you make it sound as if we attended a bacchanal," I laughed.

"What happened afterwards at the hotel? I understand there were *women* in your company."

"Yes, the women were catechists and lay volunteers. Besides, Father Lee was with us."

"Oh, and I suppose that makes everything all right."

"He's a priest."

"Evidently you haven't read this morning's newspaper." Father Hugh opened his top right desk drawer and revealed the morning press. "Here. Read it. He and the principal of your *alma mater* have been discovered."

Priest Guilty of Two-Year Adulterous Affair with Principal of Regina Coeli Catholic High School.

Both Father Lee's and the principal's pictures were printed across the front page under the headline. I gave a cursory glance over the article. *Their two-year affair was known among some. It was not uncommon for her to accompany the priest on trips. Her husband, outraged at the revelation, states that on the morning he learned of the affair he found the priest and his wife together after morning Mass....*

My stomach roiled. "I had no idea."

"Your Father Lee has made life difficult for your poor bishop. He'll be cleaning that mess up from now till his retirement. This could ruin him, or worse, kill him. Did you know that *she* was with you that night?"

"Who?"

"The principal."

"Yes, but so was her husband. They were all together."

"And what have I always said? One thing leads to another. Concubinage isn't a likeable word. It's not a likeable thing. Let us not even think upon the matter further, lest we be guilty of entertaining temptation."

Slowly I folded the paper and handed it back to Father Hugh.

"Once your coterie arrived at the Paradise Inn," Father Hugh continued, placing the paper on his desk, "you danced, didn't you?"

"Yes, Father. I did." I knew I couldn't hide that from him.

"Have you forgotten that dancing is a non-negotiable? We have a rule about fraternizing with women if it gives the appearance of *dating* or *looking-for-a-spouse*. You know that! You're inviting disaster. Let's just pray you didn't dance with *that* woman." Opening the paper again, he pointed to her picture opposite Father Lee's. "You let women get too chummy with you and before you know it, you'll be throwing away your vocation."

Father Hugh looked at the newspaper in his hands again. "I guess things could be worse. At least Father Lee's indiscretion was with a *woman*."

I didn't respond as Father Hugh neatly folded the paper and returned it to the front drawer.

"Well, I have another appointment waiting, Mister Flanagan. So let's leave things as they are. Keep your eyes and ears open, and don't let me hear any negative reports concerning your behavior away from the seminary. Please know that I have put a recommendation in your file for an assignment at a parish."

"My diocese requires it. I'll begin this summer."

"Well, make good use of your pastoral experience—and no more dancing."

"Yes."

"Is there anything else you should tell me, Mister Flanagan?"

"I don't think so."

Coming to his feet, Father Hugh lowered his eyebrows and sighed. "That will be all, Mister Flanagan. Thank you for your cooperation."

"You're welcome," I said as I stood, "but I really didn't tell you anything you didn't already know."

"That's all right; you've been most helpful. I'll see you out. I'm sure you don't want to miss the second hour of *Theological Anthropology*." Father Hugh walked around his desk and over to his door, his face taut. "You're probably happy I didn't ask about a particular Christmas tree or about men who climb out classroom windows in the middle of a lecture. But as they say, I won't go there."

I moved toward the open door, feeling the blood rush to my face.

"Oh, and Mister Flanagan, I expect that our little conversation here this morning will be kept in the strictest of confidence."

"Yes, Father." I turned again to face him.

"Oh, I do have one last question for you, Mister Flanagan. Has your vocation director informed you of which parish you will be assigned?"

"No." I shook my head.

"Oh, I thought he would have told you by now."

My curiosity was piqued. "Do *you* know, Father?"

"I am not at liberty to divulge diocesan appointments unless directed to do so."

"Pardon my imprudence."

"*Impudence.*"

"Excuse my *impudence.*"

Father Hugh shook his head. "Oh, and Mister Flanagan, you should be more careful to whom you loan your pillows. One of our novices found one of yours stuffed in one of the bells this morning."

"Why do you think it's mine?"

"We don't think, we *know*. You, of all people, should know how we know from your experience in the dry cleaning business. The Priory's laundry service labels everyone's pillowcases and linen." Hugh paused, smiling. "Have a good day, Mister Flanagan."

With that, Father Hugh opened the door and I moved past the secretary's office and into the outer hallway. Rawly Huffhind was sitting on the bench waiting.

"Mister Rawly Huffhind," Father Hugh announced loudly, with a touch of anger, "in my office."

Rawly gave me a sneer as he brushed against me on his way into Hugh's office.

I made my way down the hall and up the stairwell back to class. Afterwards I went to Mass and then on to lunch. During lunch, all the talk centered on the news of Father Lee in Cainbrook, Father Hugh's investigation of the *particular friendship* between seminarians Huffhind and Tupps, and speculation as to who had stuffed the priory bells with pillows.

I excused myself from lunch, returned to my room, and looked at my bed. One of my pillows *was* missing.

Chapter 3: End of the Year

Fear is useless.
What is needed is faith.
— Mark 5:36

Before I left the seminary for my summer pastoral assignment, I met with my spiritual director, Sister Regina Clare. She kept challenging me to reflect upon my dysfunctional family background time and again.

"Many seminarians come from dysfunctional families; no wonder there's dysfunction in the Church," she said. "That's why there's so much secrecy. You grew up knowing how to keep family secrets, and you're so used to it that you don't know any different." The diminutive nun in her white Dominican habit commanded respect.

"The Church is a dysfunctional family. The bishops are harsh with their sons, the seminarians, but they need to look at themselves. Imagine the bishops arguing over the paragraphs on indulgences in the Catechism while the rest of the church is dealing with real issues like social justice, war, and human dignity, to name but a few. There's a whole lot of denial these days. Many of these dysfunctional men bring all that baggage with them when they come to the seminary." She leaned forward in her chair and gave me a probing look. "Tell me some more about your baggage, Martin."

Sister Regina Clare had her ways of making you talk. She'd look at you and stare in utter and complete silence, swiveling ever so slightly in her chair. Any response such as, "I don't know what to say" (one I frequently used) was met with short curt confrontations such as, "Oh, yes you do," followed by more silence and swiveling.

"Just tell me about the first memory that pops into your head. Don't edit your thoughts." Sister Regina stared and swiveled while I thought about what baggage from my past I could heap up and lay at her feet.

I closed my eyes and I went back in time to 1982. I was nine years old and actually near death, the doctors thought. My lungs were full of phlegm. It all started with a sore throat, but my father didn't think I was sick enough to warrant a visit to our family doctor. As it was, I was suffering from strep throat. Unfortunately, my condition progressively worsened, and the strep went into rheumatic fever.

As I hovered in and out of consciousness, suffering a one hundred five degree temperature, one of the emergency room doctors told my grandmother to quit praying because I was beyond hope. He was impatient and kept looking at his watch. It was evening. Maybe he had a date. He told the nurses to keep me comfortable and then told my mother to expect my death by morning. I recall him saying all of this while standing at my bedside. My grandmother gave the doctor a verbal flagellation.

Father David Gregory came to anoint me and give me the Last Rites that night. I remember him rubbing the holy oil on my forehead and in my palms. I resolved to live.

Something happened that night at Saint Luke's Good Samaritan Hospital. As I lay on the gurney looking up at the crucifix on the wall above my head, I felt as if Jesus was breathing in unison with me. Hallucinations are common with the medicine I was taking, but it seemed real to me. I was convinced that Jesus had taken my illness upon himself and he died from it, not me. I remember praying he would heal my parents' marriage as well.

As the firstborn son, I was named after my father, though I was not a junior. Sean was my younger brother by three years, yet in my father's eyes he could do no wrong. My mother doted on me in response, and it only made the animosity between my mother and father worse. Dad took Sean fishing and camping, leaving me home with the excuse that I was sickly because I'd had rheumatic fever. I would remind him that I had survived, as had he, but no matter, he left me behind with mother. Maybe I reminded him of all that he was—or wasn't.

Mother took my brother and me to church every Sunday morning to Our Lady of the River. My father wouldn't join us. Instead, he would get up early and go to the six a.m. Mass of an old retired monsignor who rejected the changes of Vatican II. My dad could get in and out in less than twenty minutes. It was the no frills Mass—no music, no singing, no sermon—nothing.

My father would join us for Mass on Christmas and Easter, but then he would complain for days afterwards about the length of the services. Mother would remind him that those two services were the longest.

The Diocese of Covert was slow to embrace the changes initiated by Vatican II. I can still recall hearing my father arguing in the 1980s that the church shouldn't have eliminated Latin from the liturgy or allowed the priests to turn the altar around to face the people. By the mid-1980s, some of the older parishioners had stopped paying their pew rental. *Pew rental.* I smiled at the thought.

I can hardly recall a time when my parents didn't argue. And change in the church wasn't the only thing they argued about. My father had left us a couple of times when I was six or seven. During my serious illness, my father and mother were separated, and he was staying at a roadside motel. Mother sat by my bedside and prayed the rosary, hoping for a miracle.

My parents were especially kind to one another while I was sick, however, and I remember praying that I would remain just ill enough so that my father could come back home. But my father didn't deal well with my illness and he would avoid me, rarely coming to my bedside. It was probably due to his own bout with rheumatic fever as a child that he couldn't face it again. He may have known what would happen. Rheumatic fever can greatly increase one's chances for having a heart attack later in life.

My father's father was dead. He had died of a heart attack when I was but four years old. My father's mother, Grandma Flanagan, hated our family and preferred to associate with her other children and their families. She never came to visit, and we never went to visit her either. When she died, my father went to the funeral home alone; he never shed a tear.

Mom's dad and mom, Grandpa and Grandma Buckner, are still alive, but they moved to Florida in the late 1980s. For me, Grandpa Buckner was a lot like God: he knew everything, ignored a lot, and corrected a little. Grandpa Buckner had started the family's dry cleaning business.

"You never have any idea, do you, Martin?" Regina Clare's voice startled me from my midday musings. "That's all part of it. You're damned if you do, damned if you don't. So, you simply choose not to make a move at all. When you were sick your parents bonded together but your father particularly avoided you. When you were healthy, your parents fought and often separated. Either way your father was absent. He relegated you to the role of the sickly one who couldn't participate in life's activities because it might hurt you. Of course, he was merely avoiding you so as to not deal with his own issues.

"If he had not died right as you began your adolescence, you might have rebelled against this in either a positive or negative way, either by getting involved in delinquent behavior or throwing yourself into the role of the family hero. But as it was, he died when you were fourteen. The lack of closure with that relationship right at the onset of adolescence left you in a state of psychological paralysis. The paralyzed have no feeling or ability to move. Would you say that describes you? A simple yes or no will do. No ambivalence, please."

"Yes."

"Very well." She smiled.

"So how do I get unstuck?"

"With God all things are possible. God can take the worst evil and transform it into good. Coming from a dysfunctional family isn't all bad. It can be an asset and even a blessing and strength. One with such a background can be capable of great compassion and empathy. Many of those in the helping professions come from dysfunctional backgrounds."

Sister Regina Clare smiled and our session came to a close.

Chapter 4: The Cookout

All that is necessary to be a saint is to want to be one.
God will make you what he created you to be
if only you will desire it and consent to let Him do it.
— St. Thomas Aquinas

It was the annual *Get-To-Know-Your-Seminarian Cookout* at Saint Thomas Aquinas Cathedral in Covert. I was unsure what to expect. I knew that the bishop and the vicar-general would be there, so I was a little nervous.

Father Samuel Good, the vocation director, was the host along with his associates, Father Xavier Lax and Sister Hildegard Hope. Father Lax was a short, chubby priest in his mid-thirties with thinning brown hair. Sister Hildegard was a Dominican in her late twenties or early thirties. She was always dressed in her traditional white religious habit and veil, and behind her back, she was called *Sister Sexy*. It seemed she was always with *Father Smells Good*, as some called him, owing to the scent of his ever-generous amount of cologne. They were a couple, but there was nothing inappropriate about their relationship; she was safe with Father Samuel. All women were safe with Father Sammy.

Father Samuel was a handsome six-foot blonde who drove a different luxury automobile every month and was never seen without his Roman collar. I had met with him at the diocesan chancery the week before. He reviewed my file but didn't mention the drinking and dancing incident at New Dublin. I certainly didn't mention it either.

"Just don't go into your parish assignment thinking that you're going to change the world," Father Samuel said as he stood next to my chair. "You're only a seminarian, and your role is to learn from your supervisor."

Father Wood was the new pastor at Our Lady of the Poor and Forgotten Souls in Purgatory Parish in Inglenook. I had never met the man, but I was to be assigned to Poor Souls as the seminarian-in-training.

It was a sunny and warm June evening in the upper seventies without much humidity when I arrived at the Cathedral rectory. The scent of pool chlorine and grilled burgers met me. Father Xavier Lax, dressed in a white t-shirt, blue jean shorts, and a Yankee's cap, was armed with a large spatula and was flipping burgers at the gas grill.

Father Samuel and Sister Hilda greeted everyone at the gate to the backyard deck and pool. Father Samuel had his black suit coat off, but his collared *Stadelmaier* Rabat vest covered the front of his French-cuffed shirt while his black and gold cufflinks glistened in the evening sunlight. My choice of a green polo shirt, khaki shorts, and topsiders was a happy medium.

I looked for Ernie Schaeffer, but then remembered that he had abruptly discontinued his studies for the priesthood. Of all the seminarians most likely to continue on for ordination, Ernie Schaeffer would have been the one. However, as one of the seminarians had remarked, "When you bring a date to one of your classmates' ordinations, I think someone's trying to say something."

There was a table with a vegetable tray and dip, apples and oranges, and a cooler full of cola, beer, and bottled water. Two men standing near the cooler drew me into conversation. "So, who are you?" asked a medium-built man with unusually curly red hair dressed in light blue shorts and a red short-sleeved shirt.

"I'm Martin Flanagan. I just finished my first year of theology at Saint Albert's."

"Good to meet you," the other man replied. "My name's Father Chris Studzinski." He was a muscular black-haired man in black running shorts and a sleeveless white weight lifting shirt.

"I'm Father Jack," the redheaded priest said, extending his hand. "Jack Ash."

"Or Jackass for short," laughed Father Studzinski.

"That's Father Jackass, Studly," Father Jack quipped. "We're supposed to be setting a good example for these guys so they won't think the priesthood's full of a bunch of guys who are messed up."

"How many beers does that make for you, Jack?" Studzinski asked.

"I don't know. Three? Maybe four? But who's counting?" His eyes were slightly bloodshot.

"Talk from the Bishop's Palace is that we ought not to drink in public." Studzinski nodded to Jack. "It sets a bad example."

"Yeah, we ought to go back to the way it was in the good ol' days." Jack laughed, holding his beer bottle aloft. "Go back to the rectory and get hammered by yourself. Boy, now *that* was healthy." He rolled his eyes and took a swig from his bottle of beer. "I'm sorry," he said in a feminine voice, "Father can't have Mass today. He's sick again."

"Monsignor Linguini's encouraging all his priests to enroll in a fitness program," Studzinski said.

"*His* priests? C'mon, Studzinski. That Bull—"

"Well, the bishop has named Linguini the chair of his *Wellness Committee*," Chris interrupted. "And he's encouraging us to take the pledge, you know."

"I liked Linguini better when he was one of us—*Father* Michael Linguini," Jack said. "I liked him even better when he drank. He was a hell of a lot nicer."

"Jack, that's an exaggeration," Chris Studzinski said. "Now be honest."

"Honestly? I'd rather have a bottle in front of me than a frontal lobotomy. Wouldn't you agree, Martin?" Jack took a drink of his beer and turned to me.

I smiled, not sure how to answer. "I guess."

"Oh, I like that. Very discreet. You'll fit in well," he nodded. "And speaking of frontal lobotomies, has the dynamic duo arrived yet?"

At that, we heard voices at the gate. Everyone turned.

"Ah, speak of the devil," Jack clicked his teeth. "Here he comes."

"The bishop?" Studzinski snickered.

"No. Linguini." Jack smirked. "Munchkin's not competent enough to qualify as a devil." Father Jack Ash reminded me of my Uncle Hoot, my father's other brother, after he had been drinking. He was the real black sheep of the family.

At the gate, two other seminarians and a prospective seminarian were introducing themselves to the bishop and the vicar-general.

"And this is my Vicar-general and Judicial Vicar for the Diocesan Tribunal, Monsignor Michael Linguini," the bishop nodded.

Linguini towered over the bishop as he shook the men's hands as if he were bishop. Linguini was nearly six and a half feet tall; a large man, though not disproportionately so.

Fathers Samuel Good and Xavier Lax made their way over

to where we were.

Father Jack opened another beer bottle and said, "Well, if it isn't Father Smells Good and his laxative."

I stifled a laugh; the priests did not.

Father Lax's face reddened as he reached in the cooler for a beer.

"Jack, you're so childish," Samuel replied as he nibbled on a carrot.

"That's *Father* Jack to you, Smelly—I mean, Sammy."

Father Samuel shook his head and rolled his eyes.

Father Lax waved his spatula at Jack and returned to the grills.

"Say, before the brass get over here," Jack said to Samuel, "what's going on with Father Hugh at Saint Albert's? I heard he went on a gay raid and kicked a few seminarians out."

"It was related to *particular friendships*." Father Samuel twisted open a bottle of spring water. "Two of the men were infatuated with each other."

"What was that line about worrying about the speck in your neighbor's eye while there's a beam in your own?" Jack looked at Samuel. "Father Hugh and his war on PFs," he snickered. "Some things never change." Jack exchanged glances with Studzinski, then turned to me. "So, what's the scoop, Martin? You spent the past year at Saint Albert's Hotel?"

"A particular friendship is a non negotiable and is thereby discouraged," I chose my words carefully, not interested in revealing any of the sordid details. "And so is dancing." The rules were long outdated, in my opinion.

"Oh, yes," Jack straightened his slouch. "Can't have any dancing now, can we?"

"The seminarians involved weren't interested in Martin," Father Samuel volunteered the information.

"Oh, well, Martin," Father Jack Ash began laughing,

"there's always next year."

My mind wandered as I thought of some of the tales involving Rawly Huffhind and Matthew Tupps. One night Tupps got drunk at Albert's Pub and sang *La Isla Bonita*, but changed the words. He was bawling and his eye shadow was all smudged.

I recalled my own birthday. I had gone to the pub for a burger and a beer only to discover that I was expected to sit upon an old toilet bowl dubbed *The Bishop's Throne* as the other seminarians carried me around through the pub.

On Tupps' birthday, the other guys carried him on the bishop's throne while he sang *It's Raining Men*. Rumor had it that Tupps had also been crowned Queen of the Priory at the underground Pink Triangle Ball.

At that Gerard Austin appeared, bringing me back to the present. He had the habit of doing that—appearing, that is. Some of the guys said he was capable of bilocation like Padre Pio.

Gerard Austin was also one of the seminarians studying for Covert. He had several aliases, Brother Hairshirt and Granola Man, to name a few. Gerard had seemingly been born *Old Church*, a veritable theological dinosaur. Underneath his uncombed hair and tattered black cassock, which was worn to a gray sheen in the knees and elbows, he was a stiff, unhealthily skinny man—more a scarecrow than a man.

Gerard stood there in his aged cassock and crusty sandals nibbling at sunflower seeds and chomping on an apple core. Gerard was the only person I ever knew who would eat the core. Every one of us grew silent for half a minute examining Gerard as if he was a holy relic from the Middle Ages. His austerity was bewildering.

His room looked like one of the *Who* houses after *The Grinch* had stolen Christmas. He had no bed, save that of a small pillow and a threadbare blanket on the warped, unpolished, scuffed wooden floor. The first day he arrived at the seminary he called maintenance and had them remove his bed. "We don't need beds and we shouldn't pamper ourselves with trifles," he announced as the maintenance crew removed it from his room. "We've lived in the lap of luxury for far too long."

Gerard did have one vice—an overindulgence in the number of rosaries. His collection topped two hundred.

My thoughts returned to the present when Jack Ash resumed the conversation. "So, why isn't Father Lee here?" Jack munched on a carrot.

"Give it a rest, Jack," Samuel said firmly.

"I just want to know the wedding date so I can go." Jack held an empty beer bottle aloft. He appeared to be looking for a trash can, but upon seeing none, he threw the empty in a potted plant near the pool. "Linguini can afford to hire a grounds-keeper."

I wasn't sure whether to laugh or not. Meanwhile, I reached in the cooler for a beer.

"You're so sacrilegious, Father Ash." Samuel clucked his tongue against his teeth.

"No, I'm not. That dumb-ass Lee ruined things for us," said Jack, reaching in the cooler after me. "Now I can't go to dinner or a movie with a woman without someone thinking I'm carrying on with her. What did he do? What's in this letter of his?"

The vocation director, Father Samuel, dropped his head.

"You got one, too, didn't you, Smells Good?" Jack laughed, twisting off the beer bottle's cap and flipping it onto the table with the vegetable tray. The cap landed in the dip as his beer foamed over the top of the bottle. "Double damn."

"Jack...." Samuel shook his head and glanced in my and Gerard's direction. "Not here. Not now."

"Ah, hell, why not?" Jack cackled, sipping the foaming

beer. "It's going to make the papers sooner or later."

Gerard gasped at his words and removed the apple from his mouth.

"What's the letter about?" Studzinski asked.

"He's getting married, dammit," Jack said. "Why are you the only lucky bastard to get an invitation to his wedding?" Jack plucked the cap from the bowl of dip and licked the dip off of it.

Gerard gasped again, his right hand over his mouth and his left hand reaching for his rosary at his side. "Father!"

"So soon?" Studzinski continued, ignoring Gerard. "I didn't think the woman was going to divorce her husband."

"She's not," Jack smiled, sipping more beer. "He's with a different woman now. And the rumor is that this new one's a tri-sexual."

"What's that?" Studzinski asked as he reached for a celery stick.

"She'll try anything." Jack flicked the bottle cap into the shrubbery next to the fence.

"Good God, man. Too much information," Samuel said. "I can't ever imagine them ordaining you today, Jack," Samuel smiled. "We don't need to hear this."

"Yeah, well, speak for yourself, buddy. At least I wasn't crowned *Queen of the Year*."

"Jack——" Samuel bristled as he motioned his right forefinger to his mouth in an attempt to shush Jack.

"Sammy." Jack shook his head and mocked Samuel.

I twisted the cap off my beer and observed Father Samuel.

"One of the newly ordained guys had *Hail, Holy Queen* as his opening hymn for his first Mass," Gerard Austin volunteered between bites of apple. "Then for a communion meditation he sang 'The Wind Beneath My Wings' to Jesus on the cross above the high altar."

"Oh, can you imagine the poor parishioners at his parish?"

Jack Ash leaned over in laughter.

"He used to wear sequined pumps," Gerard Austin continued as he reached for a bottle of bottled water.

"How did the seminary ever allow him to be ordained?" Father Chris Studzinski asked.

"Don't blame St Albert's. Father Hugh kicked him out." Gerard Austin finished his apple core in delight. "He applied to some seminary in California, and they went ahead and ordained him."

"What order was that?" Jack interjected. "The Sons of the Beaches?"

We all laughed. I took a sip of my beer and inconspicuously placed the bottle cap on the food table near three other stray caps.

"Well, anyway," Jack continued, "his ass will be in the news someday, you watch. Which reminds me of something else—what's this I hear about some visitors to Saint Albert's getting mooned by one of the seminarians?"

"One of the pretty boys, Rawly Huffhind," Gerard Austin said, "or *one of the girls*, as he prefers. He was sunbathing on the parapet of Aquinas Chapel getting ready for the *Queen's Ball* when the Prior came up with a group of pilgrims for Mass. They stepped out on the roof and got an eyeful. Rawly was in the buff. He didn't want any tacky tan lines. Some of the women nearly passed out, while the men wanted to hogtie him with their rosaries."

I also knew the details but resisted the urge to gossip.

"Speaking of someone's ass," Jack feigned a cough, "how are the bishop's bowels?"

"Oh, please. Jack, must we?" Samuel sighed and shook his head.

"Now, now, Sammy, stay out of this. I want to speak directly to our seminarians instead of having to speak through you. What are you, their interpreter? Don't they speak English?"

Observing the banter, I thought how much it reminded me of my own family and the arguments between my brother and me. In our family, relatives seemed to exchange barbs and insults as a sign of affection. Was it the same among the clergy? Was this part of the dysfunction that Sister Regina Claire had warned me about? None of the Dominicans at Saint Albert's had ever spoken to one another in such manner.

Gerard Austin had made his way to the bishop and vicar-general and was down on his knees in front of the bishop kissing his ring. The bishop motioned for him to get up.

"Oh, oh. What's the bishop eating?" Jack finished his beer. "If it's olives and cheese, look out for that spastic colon." Jack snickered, piling pretzels on a Styrofoam plate. "Just admit it. The old fart's got the shits, but he's too proud to wear the adult diapers. In the middle of my confirmation, he got up and ran out during his own homily."

Samuel Good cleared his throat. "It's called Irritable Bowel Syndrome."

"Yeah, well, whatever you call it, *Pretty Boy*, he was up and out in a heartbeat. But what made it worse," Jack nearly choked on a pretzel, "was that when the bishop ran to the john in the sacristy he forgot to turn off the cordless microphone." Jack was doubled over now, panting for breath. "So we heard it all go down, so to speak."

"Damn it, Jack, don't gloat," Samuel reprimanded. "If I remember correctly, didn't you once leave your microphone on while you were hearing confessions?"

"That's right, and don't think Linguini's ever forgotten it either, Smelly. Just you wait, you'll screw up one day and then we'll see who has the last laugh."

"Jack. The bishop's sick," Samuel spoke softly as he took a

drink of his water and placed the bottle on the table.

"You're telling me, but hell, give me a break. I've been sick, too. I'm sick of puny collections, whiny parishioners, bitching parents, diocesan politics, and news reports of pedophile priests. I didn't become a priest for any of that—and neither did you."

"Those are occupational hazards associated with the diocesan ministry, Jack, but everyone has his cross to bear," Samuel said as he nodded to me and adjusted his cufflinks. "Remember that, Martin."

"I'm nailed to mine," Jack said as he took a drink of beer. "Think of the continual increase in the diocesan budget. Does Monsignor Linguini—*and Clams*—honestly think he can raise that kind of money? Noodle Brain ought to be assigned to a parish. What's he do at the Bishop's palace all day? I think I'll tell Fettuccini Alfredo just what I think of Munchkin's parish tax."

"*Stewardship assessments,*" Samuel corrected him, tightening his lips.

"Stewardship, my ass. It's a *tax.* Admit it. It's the Bishop's Tax."

"It's a matter of semantics," Samuel said.

"I wonder how much money the diocese is shelling out for those three nuts the bishop shipped off to The Island of Misfit Priests?" asked Jack. "He's had those fruits in cold storage for years."

"Jack!" Samuel rolled his eyes. "You're mixing your metaphors."

"What?" Jack asked.

"Are they nuts or fruits?"

"Both," Jack replied.

"You really do want to get sent to Poor Souls, don't you?" Samuel said.

"Shut up," Jack snapped. "Lost Souls couldn't be worse

than my banishment to Our Lady of Roadkill at Possum Prairie."

Lost Souls? I listened intently as I drank some more beer, knowing that Poor Souls was to be my parish assignment.

"Are you sure?" Samuel glared at him.

"Samuel, you were at *Poor Souls* for three years. Maybe that's why the people there lost their faith." Jack finished his beer.

"Keep it up and the boss is liable to prove you wrong," Samuel raised his eyebrows.

"Oh, is that a threat? What are you, the eyes and the ears for the bishop?" Jack turned to me. "Don't listen to a thing he says, man. He's full of sound and fury, signifying nothing."

I avoided Father Samuel's gaze.

"So," Jack continued, looking in the cooler at the beer, "Flanagan, where's the boss sending you this summer?"

"The rest of the year I will be taking my pastoral course," I answered. "I've been assigned to Our Lady of the Poor and Forgotten Souls in Purgatory at Inglenook."

"Lost Souls? Crime in Italy! Good luck, you'll need it. You better hope that you don't lose your soul while you're there."

"Jack," Samuel Good interrupted, "he hasn't even moved in yet. Don't paint things as so black." Samuel cleared his throat noisily and glanced over at the bishop. "Jack, you're getting lippy. How many beers have you had?"

"Hell, I don't know. Studzinski's done asked me, but I don't count my beers." He curled his face at Samuel and turned back towards me. "So, Martin, I guess it won't be half bad—you'll be one of Father Robin Hood's merry men."

"Father Robin Hood?" I didn't get the joke—if it was a joke.

"Father Robin Wood. He can get the tightest of tightwads to give. Why else do you think Bishop Munchkin—?"

"Bishop Munchin," Samuel corrected him again.

"Munchkin, Munchin, it doesn't matter. We all know Linguini Tortellini and Mrs. Bishop, Sister Dymphna, make all the appointments in the diocese. Anyway, why else did Munchin agree to send him to Inglenook? Was it to pay off the diocesan debt? You know the folks in Inglenook are the stingiest givers."

"Jack, I'm so glad you're not given to conspiracy theories," Studzinski smiled.

"Look, you're not the one who had to endure the public humiliation of being removed as pastor."

At the words *removed as pastor,* I could only imagine what mischief Father Jack Ash could cause in a parish. He might well be the proverbial bull in the china shop.

"When the pastor openly declares that the patron saint of his parish was an angry misogynist," Samuel explained, pointing at Jack, "what else was there left for the bishop to do? Over a hundred people from St. Augustine's called the chancery demanding your removal."

Jack only smiled wide and nodded at me. "I hope you all are taking notes. It did get me out of there." I found myself laughing but wondered if I should.

"Say," interrupted Father Xavier Lax, "how 'bout those Yankees? Think they'll go all the way this year?"

"Who cares, X Lax," Jack said. "Don't try to change the subject. It's good for us to air our dysfunctions in front of these seminarians. Let's hope they're just as crazy as the rest of us so they'll fit in. It'd be a hell of a note if they're sane. If any of you think you're normal," Jack turned to me, "by the time you've been a priest for four or five years in this diocese, you'll be as nuts as the rest of us collared mutts. Why, Covert's even reserved a diocesan wing in the nuthouse. No, the Church is a corporation, and I'm a lowly grunt out working in some God-forsaken warehouse driving a dumb forklift."

"Martin," Samuel interrupted Jack, "have you ever met Father Robin?"

"No. Not yet," I said, refocusing my attention on Samuel.

"Well, I just saw him pull up. I'll be sure to get the two of you together so you can make the necessary arrangements for your moving in." Samuel patted me on the back.

"Sure. Thanks, Father." I was somewhat anxious about meeting Father Robin Wood.

Just then, the vicar-general and the bishop approached our group. "And who are these men guarding the watering hole?" the bishop asked as he caressed his pectoral cross with both hands. He was about my height.

Both the bishop and his vicar were wearing their formal priestly attire. All the other priests—except Father Samuel—were wearing sporty shirts and slacks, jeans, or shorts. This was only the third time I had ever met the bishop; the first time was at my confirmation and the second at the chancery when I met with him to talk about becoming a seminarian. In some ways, he didn't seem like a bishop. He wasn't tall enough and his voice wasn't all that commanding.

"Bishop, where's your pointy hat, stick, and cape?" Jack laughed. "I think these seminarians need to see you dressed in all your armor."

"Ah, yes," the bishop smiled ever so slightly. "The spiritual battle in which we are engaged requires all the armor of God, Father Jack."

Vicar-general Linguini eyed Jack and sucked in a deep breath before closing his eyes and dropping his head in an air of exasperation.

"I believe if you read the sixth chapter of Ephesians," the bishop continued, "you will note that our struggle with evil is not against mere flesh and blood but with the principalities and powers of Satan and this world's present darkness. Gird your loins in truth, cover your breast in a coat of holiness, and put on the boots of the gospel, holding up your faith as a shield, to quench the flaming arrows of the devils." The bishop looked at me. "My pointy hat—as Father Ash calls it—is the helmet of salvation, and every one of you has been given a sword—the fiery sword of the Spirit, the Word of God."

"Excellent, Bishop." Jack lifted his beer bottle.

The bishop took Jack's hand in his and held him by the arm before turning to the others and me. "My sons, I pray that you become *holy* priests." He then turned back toward Jack and whispered, "Don't get hammered." With that, the bishop and Monsignor Linguini moved on with Fathers Samuel Good and Xavier Lax dutifully following.

"Look at Linguini," Jack snickered. "He can't wait for the bishop to keel over so that he can wear the miter and swipe that crosier away and yank me out of active ministry once and for all." Jack laughed. "I'd like to tell him where he can stick that crosier."

Gerard Austin reappeared and stepped back into our circle; he reached for some cauliflower.

"So, Gerard," Jack asked, "aren't you hot in that cassock?"

"If our Blessed Lord could endure his scourging and crown of thorns, then certainly we can stand a little discomfort. St. Jean Vianney ate only a boiled potato every day and spent twelve to sixteen hours a day in the confessional."

"Do you expect *me* to stay in the confessional twelve hours a day?" asked Jack.

"Jean Vianney was a priest and he did it," Gerard quickly answered as he crunched the vegetable.

"Yeah, well, that was Jean Vianney. He was touched in the head."

"He's a saint!" Gerard raised his voice, his eyes wild. "And a *real* priest."

"And I'm not?" Jack laughed.

"He's the patron saint of seminarians and priests." Gerard stared at Jack.

"Well, then, he'd best be interceding for me. Until then, I'm no Vianney."

"You're right about that," Gerard sighed through his nose.

"And neither are you, Gerard. Besides, you're too proud of your humility."

"Monsignor Linguini has been——" Gerard began.

"When's the last time Pasta Pants heard confessions?" Jack argued. "He doesn't even have a parish. But he does drive a Lexus. So what saint is he imitating there, Gerard?"

"He's not a religious priest——" Gerard began again, trying to point out the difference between the diocesan and religious clergy.

"That's what I've said for a long time." Jack cackled, looking around at us as if awaiting applause.

"You know what I mean. He's not a friar. A diocesan priest doesn't have to take a vow of poverty."

"Then neither do you," Jack said. "So why don't you lose the cassock and hairshirt, and dress like the rest of us?"

Gerard, startled at the word 'hairshirt', adjusted the top buttons of his cassock as if to make sure his undershirt wasn't showing.

"See?" Jack pointed at him with his empty beer bottle. "He *is* wearing a hair shirt."

"It is an ancient form of penance," Gerard huffed in admission of the discovery.

"So is self-flagellation, but I won't ask you about that. I just remember some saint who said his neighbor was his hair shirt. That's good enough for me."

Gerard rolled his eyes, reached for an orange, turned, and walked away.

As I drank the rest of my beer, the verbal barrage between Jack and Gerard reminded me of the arguments my parents had when I was a kid.

"Watch this," Jack laughed and held his empty beer bottle up and lobbed it into the swimming pool.

"Nice shot, Jack," Father Chris Studzinski said. No one else had seen it. Jack reached in the cooler and opened yet another.

A wiry, mustached, black-haired man in his forties wearing round wire-rim spectacles, a white golf shirt, red jogging shorts, and blue running shoes approached. I assumed he was another priest.

"Hey, Martin," Jack said, walking towards the man, "here's your pastor, Father Robin Hood."

"Father." I reluctantly approached the priest and extended my right hand. In my left hand, I held my empty beer bottle. "I'm Martin Flanagan." I hoped he didn't think I was an alcoholic; there was no telling what Father Hugh may have told him about the St. Patrick's Day outing.

"Oh, yes. My resident seminarian," the dark-eyed priest extended his right hand for a shake. "Good to meet you. I'm Father Robin. Robin Wood." He grasped my hand firmly. "Now, forget everything the seminary teaches you about parish life," Robin smirked behind his mustache and glasses.

Again, I was unsure exactly how to interpret the diocesan priests and their sense of humor—or the lack thereof.

"Okay…" It was more of a question than an answer.

"Flanagan. You're from Cainbrook?"

"Yes."

Jack took my empty beer bottle and tossed it in the pool. I looked around to see if anyone saw him do it.

"I see. Good one, Jack." Father Robin paused without as much as a smile, stroked his chin, and looked at me. "So, Martin, what are your hopes for your time at Lost Souls?"

I caught the parish nickname again, but I didn't correct him. "I guess I look forward to the opportunity to get to know the people of the parish. That's one of the reasons I want to become a priest."

"People? I hate people. That's why I became a priest."

I said nothing at Father Robin's words until some of the others began laughing.

"Don't let him fool you, Flanagan," laughed Jack, "Robin only hates the people who won't give any money to the collection."

"Well, then, that would be just about everyone." Robin laughed to himself. "What do the people know about the Church? They don't believe in anything. No, I take that back. They believe in themselves, money, clothes, luxury cars, double mortgaged homes, and expensive schools and colleges with good sports programs."

I studied the faces of Fathers Robin and Jack, trying to determine if they were serious.

"Think about it, Flanagan," Jack continued. "They don't call him Robin Hood for nothing."

"Okay, enough, Jack." Robin put his left hand on my right shoulder. "You're spooking the poor creature."

"You mean *rich* creature. His family owns Buckner's Dry Cleaners." Obviously, he had inquired about my family background. I had long tired of the insinuation that our family was ridiculously wealthy.

"Martin, I wanted to introduce you to Father Robin," Father Samuel interrupted, coming from behind, "but I see you've already met."

"Oh, it's you again, Sammy," Jack said. "I thought I smelled something sweet."

"Jack. Please. Just think," Samuel pointed to me. "This man might be your pastor one day."

I had a difficult time imagining myself a priest, let alone a pastor with Jack as one of my assistant priests.

"Don't worry," Jack said. "I've pissed His Highness off so many times that I wouldn't be a bit surprised if he pulls the carpet out from under me. Of course, it wouldn't be Munchkin; it'd be Monsignor Spaghetti Brains. When he made me pastor of St. Cunegunda's, he told me he was so mad that he wasn't sure whether he should defrock me or else just name me the pastor."

"So, your assignment was a reprimand. Does your parish know that they are being punished along with you?" Samuel asked.

"Who gives a rip? They complain about me all the time," Jack said. "Next time I guess I'll get sent off to the Island of Misfit Priests where I can paint and write poems that express my feelings about my unfulfilled sexual needs. These islands are quite popular vacation spots these days. Nearly every diocese has one."

"Oh, yes, The Island of Sexual Dysfunction," laughed Robin. "Maybe you'll bump into Father Lee over at Cleveland."

"Oh, hell, he's not there," Jack explained. "There was no dysfunction with him. Everything was working quite well—too well. He up and left with one of the nurses."

"Jack, you're incorrigible," Samuel shook his head and clucked his tongue.

"I know. Linguini and Clams told me the same ten years ago."

"Did I hear my name taken in vain?" The resonant voice of Monsignor Linguini echoed off the brick patio. I wanted to step away, but it was too late.

"Yes." Jack turned to face him. He was ten feet away.

"You're amazing Jack," Monsignor Linguini said as he observed a beer bottle bobbing in the pool. "If I didn't know better, I'd think you were a complete and total ass."

"Why, thank you, Monsignor. I resemble that remark! That's what my father always said about me. But then that's what people say about you, too. Why, Monsignor, I guess we're two peas in a pod. If you're ever named a bishop, then that means I might even be named one. Say, there's still hope for me after all. Wouldn't it be something if I was named a bishop and you weren't?"

"*You...are...such...an...ass,*" Linguini said.

"Sampson slayed a thousand Philistines with the jawbone of an ass. Just think what God could accomplish through me, a total ass."

"Very funny, but not original," Linguini glared. "That's what St. Jean Vianney told his bishop."

"Hey," Jack cried aloud, "get Gerard Austin over here, I'm quoting St. Jean Vianney. Yes, perhaps that's where I've heard that before. You must admit, though, that it makes for a wonderful coup de grâce, doesn't it?"

"Jack—you'd best stop before I do something I might regret." Linguini stood biting his lip.

"What's that? Send me to *Poor Souls?*" He held his arm out. "Look, I'm shaking."

The vicar-general stopped, turned towards the men, and glanced at Jack. "*Will no one rid me of this turbulent priest?*"

At that, Father Xavier Lax took his spatula and pounded a pot, announcing that dinner was served.

How could Jack Ash get away with so much verbal abuse of his superiors? If I continued in the seminary, I knew I would one day join the likes of these priests. Did I want that? What was I about to do with my life?

Chapter 5: Cainbrook Visit

"A certain man had two sons...."
— Luke 15.11

After I left the seminary, but before I took up residence at Poor Souls' parish, I stayed at my mom's for the weekend. On Saturday, I met her at The Cainbrook Country Club for lunch where she gave me the Sean Report. That's what I called her usual update on what my brother Sean was doing.

"He's got a new thing again," she said as she fidgeted with her pearl necklace. Her brown hair was brushed back and flipped under in a pageboy cut.

My brother, Sean Patrick, had left home when he turned eighteen and moved in with a cocktail waitress from a so-called "gentleman's" bar. He lived with her during his final year of high school. As it turned out, she was married, but Sean got her pregnant. Her husband reentered her life and made her get an abortion. He threatened to kill Sean if he didn't leave his wife alone.

Sean had gone to Cainbrook College for a few night classes, but he quit mid-semester. Now the saga continued. "He was arrested shortly after Christmas on charges of car theft," she continued, nervously folding her cloth napkin upon her lap. "He also had a run-in with that woman's husband.

The two crossed paths at some bar and got into a fight. Now he's facing a charge of assault and battery." She put her head in her hands. "It's such an embarrassment."

I sat there staring at my mashed potatoes, conflicted within. I resented Sean for what he was doing; yet, he was my brother.

"I don't think he's ever gotten over your father's death." She paused, clearing her throat, making an excuse for his behavior. "Now he's living with a new woman."

Thanks, Mom, I thought. So much for the Sean report.

"To him, I'm Saint Martin the Hypocrite."

"Don't you remember when the two of you were altar boys?"

I did. When we did become altar boys in grade school, we usually served at the nine a.m. Sunday Mass for Father David. We were expected to be reverent and pious as we knelt in the sanctuary to ring the sanctuary bells at consecration or carry the thurible of smoking incense at benediction. Sean loved to give me his mischievous smile and try to make me laugh while he pretended to pick his nose. I could almost smell the incense thinking of it.

"You're not even listening to me, are you?" Mother asked, breaking me from my reverie. "Have you heard what people are saying about priests? Do you think they'll ever change that rule on celibacy? I know Sean isn't going to give me grandchildren—at least legitimate ones—but you could. Have you been following that story about Bishop Numbnoddle and those priests over in Wheatfield? I mean, seriously, I can forgive Father Lee—he was with a woman. I know she was married, but three of the priests in Wheatfield molested altar boys! Haven't you heard about it? Father David has been sick over it—literally. He went to the doctor the other day. Oh, Mother of God, I hope he doesn't have cancer. Sweet Jesus!

"One of our regular customers, Mrs. Quigley, actually asked me the other day if you were taking Pedophilia 101 in the seminary. You know Mrs. Quigley's husband died of cancer last year?" She looked intently at me. "Sean's ruining our family name, you know. Is that Father Samuel Good all there?"

Mother's stream of consciousness required great efforts at concentration. "What do you mean, Mother?" I asked, knowing full well where she was going with the conversation.

"Well, he just seems too good to be true."

"I just think that's how he is," I answered, picturing Father Samuel with Sister Hildegard in perfect propriety.

"Hmmm." She sipped her coffee and slowly put the cup down on the saucer. "He just seems a little light in the loafers, if you know what I mean. Others have said the same."

"I really don't want to talk about it. I'm too busy to keep up with who's in and who's out of the closet."

Her mouth hung open at the allusion to the proverbial closet before she continued talking about who had cancer and who she thought might have cancer. My mind wandered.

Sister Regina Claire's words from spiritual direction came to mind. "Why have you come to the seminary, Martin?" she had asked me in February. "Let's ponder the question, 'Is your family's dry cleaning business a metaphor for your life?'

"Why do you want to be a priest? Is it because the act of cleaning clothes is symbolic of cleansing souls? You grew up around steamed and starched shirts and pressed collars. Don't you see the influence? You prided yourself on providing people with the means of appearing their best. Is the priesthood a way for you to help people to look their best spiritually? Do you desire to clean people's souls and make them perfectly presentable? If so, think again. You can't do it for them. They must do it themselves—with the help of God's grace, of course. But you can't clean someone's soul for them. They have to be willing to let God do that."

"Do you think these are the reasons I want to become a priest?" I replied. "To dry-clean souls?"

"I don't know," Sister Regina Claire answered. "What do you think? I cannot answer for you. Only you can determine your motive for pursuing the priesthood. All I know is that one cannot become a priest to receive—you must be willing to give."

She sat silently, looking at me with a look that I had seen before. It was the look a lot of the Sisters would give immature, adolescent boys. It was also the same look the Sisters gave to a lot of the clergy.

"Are you all right?" she asked.

"No. It's just—I've never thought of any of that before."

"Yes." Sister smiled. "I know."

"I know, I know. You haven't heard a word I've said." My mother's voice regained my attention. She had been going on and on about many things while my mind wandered.

"You weren't even listening to me. You've always been bad about that. What are you thinking about?"

"Nothing, Mother. Nothing."

* * * *

After lunch, Mother stayed to play euchre with some of her female friends. I decided to drive to the cemetery. The gray, afternoon clouds hid the sun as I drove slowly through the stone markers. Many of the decorations from Memorial Day were still up. At the Flanagan plot, I stopped the car, rolled the window down, and waited a minute or two before getting out. A male cardinal was perched in a maple tree singing his song. Time seemed suspended in the peace of the cemetery.

Regina Claire's words returned. "Suppose the reason you entered the seminary was in the hope you would find a father. Are you searching for your lost father? There are lots of *fathers* in the seminary. If so, then know that you've got to have a better reason to become a priest.

"Or do you think by becoming a priest you will discover your father alive again? Since he died while you were in church, perhaps, subconsciously, you think you'll find him here. Then again, maybe you want to become a priest in hopes of making up for your parents' failed marriage. You know that the children of dysfunctional families often blame themselves for their parents' marital problems."

"Yeah, and our family put the *fun* in dysfunctional," I sniggered.

"When you were young your parents were having difficulty, were they not?" she asked.

"It was that way as long as I could remember."

"And your father died before any of the problems were reconciled, correct?"

She was right. The answer was yes. As I approached my father's grave, I noted that the grass was green and healthy under the shade of the large oak tree that overshadowed the plot. I stared at the etched death date of my father on his headstone: *James Patrick Flanagan September 9, 1987.*

I prayed an *Our Father*, a *Hail Mary*, and a *Glory Be* as the cardinal continued to sing his song.

I tried to feel something in my heart. Instead, I felt empty.

* * * *

When I returned home, I took a nap on the divan in the den until a Bible landed on my chest. It was Sean. "Wake up, sleeping bishop."

"Sean," I stirred, squinting in the sunlight. "What was that for?"

"Shut up, faggot." He was in a torn gray t-shirt, cut-off blue jean shorts, and white running shoes minus socks.

"Sean—"

"Have you found a homo-lover yet?" He winked.

"I can't believe you." I sat up.

"Screw you—why do you want to waste your life in a church full of queer-baits?"

I sighed noisily and rolled my eyes. "Lighten up, man."

"Oh, look, the baby's getting mad. You gay-assed son of a bitch."

"Sean, you just called mother a bitch."

"Who gives a rip?" Sean shrugged.

"You should." I backed off, knowing he was serious. "Did you come to see Mom or just to bum more money off of her?"

"I came to get some of my clothes."

I knew Sean didn't come home very often these days—unless he needed money. "I know she gave you money. She always does, and I know you'll never pay her back."

"Did mama buy your lunch today?" Sean mockingly whined.

"At least I eat *with* her when she buys me a meal. By the way, who's the woman you're living with these days?"

"You're just jealous," he sneered.

"Not really."

"Oh, that's right." He tapped the right side of his head with his right hand. "You only fuck men, right?"

I shook my head and looked down.

"Don't act stupid, pink-eye. I met him before. What's his name? Dick?"

"Are you talking about *Nick?*"

"Yeah—Nick the Dick. He's your bed-bud! You're still living with him, right?"

"Nick was my roommate at State College. In the seminary we don't have roommates."

"Oh, that's right," he laughed. "You have significant others, don't you?"

"I am *not* gay." I rolled my eyes.

"If you weren't gay, you wouldn't have to tell me. I know how you are."

"How do you know? You've written me off. The last time you came to see me at the seminary you only stayed an hour. You couldn't wait to leave."

"Why would I want to hang around a bunch of fags?"

"What are you afraid of? Those who are the most vocal against homosexuality are usually the ones who are the most unsure about their own sexuality."

"You're the one who's gay, not me."

"Why are you so obsessed with homosexuality? Would you rather be shacked up with a guy?"

"I'm going to kick your ass." He clenched his hands into fists as he stepped closer to me.

"I'd kick yours," I interrupted, trying to be funny, "but I don't know which of your ends is up." I realized that I was hitting below the belt, but I couldn't resist.

Evidently neither could Sean. He smashed my jaw with a quick left fist and hurried out of the den, knocking one of the paintings on the wall sidewise. The advantages of living on my own came to mind, as did the disadvantages of trying to have the last word in an argument with my brother. The painful thought was particularly centered on the right side of my jaw. What they say is true: *One can never go back home.*

Sean's overt virulent fear of homosexuality reminded me of some of the archconservative seminarians who paraded around in their cassocks lamenting homosexuality. They were just as vocal—though without the vulgarity—but just as suspect as some of the more flamboyant boys.

Mother entered the den in her stocking feet. She was winded as if she had run through the house. "What did you say to Sean? Why do you always have to pick on him? You know he's a good boy. Your father treated you like that. Why do you want to run Sean off? You're going to be a priest. Would Jesus treat Sean like you treat him?"

I lowered my head not wanting to get into an argument with her.

"You need to think about some things, Martin." She disappeared as quickly as she had appeared and went down to the kitchen. I heard her and Sean talking. She was asking how much money he needed for the week.

Chapter 6: Arrival at the Parish

"When you are at Rome live in the Roman style;
when you are elsewhere live as they live elsewhere."
— St. Ambrose's advice to St. Augustine.

I drove through pouring rain all the way from Cainbrook to Inglenook the day I was to move in at Poor Souls parish. After about forty minutes, the twin spires of Poor Souls appeared through the mist and clouds. I parked my car on the street in front of the red brick rectory adjacent to the church. The words over the narthex façade of the church read: Parish Church of Our Lady of the Poor and Forgotten Souls in Purgatory.

With my suitcase in my left hand and my breviary under my arm, I climbed the concrete steps and rang the doorbell. I could hear chimes ringing out the melody of Big Ben as I looked through the leaded glass on the left side of the door. A female voice called out, "I've got it, Father."

A slightly round woman with a toothy smile and graying, blonde hair pulled back in a bun opened the door.

"Good afternoon," she said, peering through the opening. "May I help you?"

"Yes, I'm Martin Flanagan. I'm the seminarian assigned to the parish. I'm here to meet with Father Robin Wood."

"Yes, certainly. Father Robin is expecting you," she said, opening the door wide. "Come on in."

"Thank you." The spacious foyer's black and white checkered marble floor was inviting.

"Cat, get out of the way," she raised her voice as a fat, golden tabby tried to squeeze through the doorway at my feet.

"Sorry, Father," she said as the cat mewed loudly.

"*Martin*. I'm only a seminarian."

"You look like a young priest to me."

The cat had now maneuvered its way between my legs.

"Cat, come here!" she said, scooping the cat up into her arms. "I'll show you to your room, Melvin."

"Martin." I corrected her again.

"Oh, excuse me. *Martin*."

"That's okay. Thank you…uh," I stammered as I entered the house.

"Oh, excuse my rudeness. I'm Hyacinth. I'm the housekeeper here at Lost Souls. Been here for twenty years." The cat squirmed in her arms and scratched wildly.

"Lost Souls?"

"I'm sorry. It's a bad habit. I meant *Poor and Forgotten Souls*." The cat jumped out of her arms and scampered down the hall. The rectory was an old home—marble foyer floor, hardwood floors, high ceilings, radiators, and a hand-carved banister leading upstairs.

"His Highness and his Henchman, Linguini, have pretty much forgotten this place," Hyacinth lamented. "Poor Father Boniface. He should have been named Monsignor years ago, but 'no, not on your life' Munchin told him."

There were French doors just to the left leading into a formal living room and to the right was a half-bath restroom.

The cat ran up to me again, but Hyacinth scooped it up in her arms.

"Cat! Shame!"

"I like cats." I reached over and petted the animal. "What's its name?" I was still pondering her frank reference to the bishop as *His Highness*.

"Cat." She paused. "His name is *Cat*."

"Just *Cat*?" Cat purred loudly and closed its eyes. Just to the left of my foot was a dried patch of furry cat vomit.

"Yes. *Cat*," Hyacinth replied. "The last movie I ever saw in the theater was *Breakfast at Tiffany's*. Audrey Hepburn was in it. Have you ever seen it?"

"No, I can't say I have."

"Well, Audrey's character had a cat named *Cat*. Just be careful where you step. He gets hairballs and vomits them up in the worst places."

"Keep that cat out of my room!" An elderly, balding, red-nosed, blue-eyed man with thick, horn-rimmed glasses suddenly stepped out into the hallway from one of the rooms down the front hall. He was wearing a blue bathrobe over his clothes and he leaned upon a wooden cane. "The thing's barfing up hairballs everywhere! He just threw up on my best sweater! Oh—" he stopped mid-sentence when he saw me standing in the doorway.

"So, are you the air conditioner fellow? What took you so long?" He scrunched his nose at me and straightened up.

I smiled at the old priest, for he *was* a priest; his robe was hanging open and the white collar of his black clerical shirt was sticking out of his left shirt pocket.

"No, no, Father Boniface," Hyacinth interrupted. "He's the new one *the Pointed Hat* sent here." She squinted her left eye at me.

The old priest named Boniface clutched a tan-colored breviary in his right hand as he fingered the top of his cane, rubbing the wood slowly.

"You're not a priest?"

"No. I'm a seminarian."

"But you're thinking about it, aren't you?"

"The priesthood? Why, yes. I just finished my first year of seminary studies at Saint Albert's."

"A priest knows when he's in the presence of another priest. Some doubt it, but I know. What's your name?"

"Martin," I extended my hand. "Martin Flanagan."

"I'm Father Williams," the priest said, placing the breviary up under his left arm. "Boniface Williams." As he grasped my hand, his handshake gave me a warm feeling throughout, reminding me of my Grandpa Buckner.

"I think I've heard of you," I said, knowing the name Boniface Williams was familiar in diocesan lore.

"All bad, I'm sure. Well, don't believe everything you hear, boy." He motioned me to follow, and we moved down the hall and to the left, where we entered the kitchen. The pale oak cabinetry matched the walls that were painted a flat pine yellow. Dark red flagstones covered the floor and aging yellow curtains framed the windows above the sink.

"Have a seat," Father Boniface said, pointing to the oval-shaped, metal-framed table and matching chairs that stood in the center of the room. I pulled out a chair and sat on its dirty white vinyl cushion as Father Boniface did the same.

"Father Boniface desegregated the diocesan schools, you know." Hyacinth smiled, standing at the sink.

"That's right, and the Conservative Catholics and the Ku Kluxers couldn't decide who would lynch me first. Bishop Collins removed me when the Black Panthers clashed with the Klan on the steps of the school."

"Which proves you're a hero," Hyacinth said, appearing to hold back unspent emotion.

"Oh, Hyacinth, stop it. She's always trying to make me

out to be a hero. Hogwash. I didn't do nearly enough. Besides, that's an old war story and this young man doesn't care to listen to an old man ramble."

"You weren't rambling," I said, peering into Boniface's eyes. His face was scraggy with whiskers and his neck marked with wisps of stray beard.

"Father Boniface, you're one of the best priests this diocese ever had!" Hyacinth exclaimed. "It's just too bad that the pointed hats can't recognize greatness except among themselves and their pet priests."

"Hold your tongue, woman. Don't let Linguini hear you talking like that or else you'll be excommunicated and I'll be defrocked for good measure—guilt by association."

At that, Hyacinth grabbed a newspaper and began pursuing a fly through the kitchen. The fly landed on the counter, but Hyacinth busied herself with flipping the pages of the paper.

"Just swat the thing, Hyacinth," Boniface said as he watched her carefully folding the paper.

"I will, I will, but I have to get the paper just right," she said, her tongue between her teeth like an artist at work.

"What are you talking about?" Boniface squinted.

"This is the diocesan paper and I saw Monsignor Linguini's picture in it this week, so I want to make sure I swat the fly directly with his face." Hyacinth raised the paper slowly in her right arm, only to swiftly smack the fly. She lifted the paper up and the fly was stuck to Linguini's left cheek.

"You'll burn for that, Hyacinth." Boniface left the kitchen and went upstairs. I found myself amused by the fly-swatting at the vicar-general's expense.

Hyacinth disposed of her paper flyswatter and dead fly in the trashcan underneath the sink. Suddenly a pot and pan fell off the counter, crashing loudly. Cat spooked and ran wildly out of the kitchen and through the house. We then heard the sound of the garage door clattering slowly upwards.

"Speak of the devil, Father Robin's back," Hyacinth said, turning towards a door at the far end of the kitchen that led to the garage. Hyacinth had no qualms letting others know her opinion.

As soon as Father Robin Wood entered the rectory, Hyacinth announced my arrival. "Your seminarian has arrived, Father."

"Oh, he has, has he?" Robin looked over the top of his wire-rimmed glasses with his dark eyes. He had a stack of books in his left hand under his arm and a brown paper package under his right arm. He was dressed casually in a yellow short-sleeve shirt and blue jeans. "That'll be all, Hyacinth."

She rolled her eyes and walked back towards the kitchen.

"Hyacinth, I can't find any of my undershirts!" Father Boniface called out from the top of the stairs.

"I'm going to iron them for you, Dearie," she answered.

"No wonder I couldn't find them," came the muffled reply.

"Father Wood," I looked at Father Robin and held out my right hand. "It's good to see you again."

"I'm Father *Robin*. Don't call me Father Wood. I'm not an old crusty pastor yet." Robin motioned me to follow him down the hall. His study was just down from the kitchen on the right.

"Father Robin," I replied, putting my unshaken hand at my side.

"Ah, much better," Robin smiled, flipping the light switch on with his shoulder, as he entered his study. "So, are you all moved in?"

"Pretty much. I didn't bring a lot."

"Yeah, that's what Father Samuel told me," he said, emptying the books and the package on a chair. "One of the seminarians was concerned that you might be suicidal."

"Suicidal?"

"Yeah," he looked at me. "He said you gave away a hell of a nice rug and some other stuff before you left for the summer."

"Oh, that," I laughed. "I had the option of storage, but since I didn't have that much, I just gave away some odds and ends." I tried to think who would have told. "Who told you that?"

"It doesn't matter." He looked away and walked behind his desk. "I see that you've met *The General*."

"You mean the old monsignor?"

"No, I mean *The General*. *General Hyacinth*. She's a tyrant, you know."

"I had no idea."

"You'll learn." He paused and looked at me again with his deeply penetrating black eyes. "And the old priest in the kitchen isn't a monsignor either." He then called the parish secretary, Susan Greene, into his office. He explained how he had brought her on as soon as he was assigned here.

For the rest of the afternoon, Father Robin told me all about the Inglenook deanery. Father Chris Studzinski was the pastor at St. Sebastian's and administrator of Immaculate Heart parish on the south side of town. St. Patrick's parish was the oldest in town, and Father Simon Frisbee was there. They still have pew rental. It took them until 1979 before they turned the altar around. And that was only because Monsignor Huffman died.

"St. Patrick has a beast of a Sunday night bingo," Father Robin explained. "One that I intend to slay if Frisbee gives me the chance. It's their golden calf. They even have to hire security guards, there's so much money being passed around. Can you imagine?"

I could. My home parish of Our Lady of the River in Cainbrook used to have Monday night bingo until Father David Gregory eliminated it. Some people left the parish over the decision; others hailed it as a victory for virtue.

"St. Paul's is north of town," Robin continued. "The bishop assigned Deacon Leonard Dill there to keep it as an active parish. Of course, the people of St. Paul's are supposed to attend Mass at Poor Souls. We're the largest parish in the deanery. Occasionally I say Mass at St. Paul's."

Father Robin had made plans for me to get together with Fathers Studzinski and Frisbee at the Red Lantern Inn, one of Inglenook's finer restaurants.

* * * *

At the Red Lantern Inn, Robin, I, and the two other pastors joined Greg and Teresa Blackstone for dinner. Greg was the CEO of one of the state's coalmines and his wife came from old Cincinnati money.

Greg Blackstone wore a white French cuff shirt, red silk tie, and a white Italian suit. Teresa Blackstone's bottle-blonde hair was stiff with spray and pulled back tightly off her ears. Father Simon Frisbee had large brown eyes and curly brown hair and was slightly overweight in his mid-forties, his clerical shirt quite snug. I had already met Father Chris Studzinski, the physically fit, thirty-something, athletic specimen of a priest.

Over martinis Greg complained to Father Robin, "The bishop's all over me for money again, Father."

"I think it's really Linguini. He's the one who can smell a dollar a mile away," Teresa said. She was dressed in a high-necked red dress with a diamond choker about her neck. "When will the bishop retire?"

"He'll submit his resignation when he's seventy-five,"

Robin answered as he reached for his martini.

"How old is he now?" she continued.

"Seventy." Robin took a drink from his tumbler.

"How long has he been bishop?" asked Greg.

"Since 1982." Robin returned his drink to the table.

"Crime in Italy!" Teresa exclaimed. "You mean we have him for five more years?"

"Most likely," Robin chuckled, "unless he dies before then. But whatever you do, don't give Hyacinth any ideas."

I shouldn't have laughed, but I did. I was quite surprised at how freely the Blackstones and Father Robin bashed the bishop and the vicar-general. I wasn't sure what Fathers Frisbee or Studzinski thought.

"What will become of Linguini when the bishop retires?" Greg meticulously arranged his silverware, aligning his spoon and knife on the linen tablecloth.

"That's up to the next bishop. He can be retained as vicar-general or return to diocesan ministry. But I doubt that would happen. He only knows how to pontificate."

"What's going to become of Bishop Numbnoddle over in Wheatfield?" Greg continued as he adjusted his tie and coat.

"Who knows? He's made himself quite a mess playing the old shell game."

At that, Father Frisbee took a draught of his dark German beer. His brown eyes met mine over the top of his mug. Father Chris cleared his throat and excused himself for a visit to the lavatory. Once he returned, I took advantage of the opportunity myself.

For most of the evening, the Blackstones swapped gossip of Church politics with Robin and the two other priests. I was bored with it all and was happy once the check arrived. I didn't ask Father Robin about any of the table conversation once we were alone in the car. I wanted to, but I didn't.

When we returned to the rectory, the priests planned to watch Monsignor Quixote, a movie that Father Studzinski had gotten from the library. "It's based on the Graham Greene novel," he explained.

I excused myself and prayed my rosary. Sister Regina Claire's words troublingly replayed in my mind as I deviated from the devotion. "You seminarians from dysfunctional families are all alike. You grow up learning to hide your family secrets, and you either mask your true emotions or deny them, and then when you become priests you go on keeping secrets and masking your emotions, living in denial.

"Your crazy Uncle Hoot was an alcoholic, but nobody dared admit it or say anything about it because someone might, God forbid, find out."

My guardian angel must have finished my rosary for me. When I woke the next morning, my rosary was still in my hand.

Chapter 7: Pew Rental and The Holy Bingo

"Martha, Martha, you are anxious and upset
about many things. One thing only is required."
— Luke 10.41

Simon Frisbee showed up early one morning at the rectory about a week after dinner with the Blackstones. His curly, brown hair was tousled and uncombed, and his clerical shirt was untucked. He nervously drummed his fingers on the kitchen table while waiting for Father Robin.

"Father Robin will be here as soon as he's finished saying Mass," Hyacinth smirked and straightened her apron. "I'd say praying Mass, but he just says it." She made her way up the back stairs, but called out from the top. "If *that one* needs me, let him know I'll be upstairs making the beds. And if Father Boniface wants his breakfast, come get me."

Frisbee poured himself a cup of coffee and inattentively paged through the morning press. Cat appeared at the door and purred loudly while staring at us.

There was an awkward silence between us as I tried several times to engage Father Frisbee in conversation. He was terribly distracted by something. Five minutes later Father Robin walked though the back door.

"Frisbee, there you are. We've got to talk."

"Yeah, I got your message." He pushed the newspaper aside.

I picked up my coffee mug and prepared to leave the two alone.

"Where are you going, Martin? You're part of my pastoral team," Robin motioned me with his index finger. "Get back here."

I returned and sat across from Father Frisbee while Robin sat at the head of the table. I had no idea what Robin desired to discuss.

"Where's the General?" Robin asked, looking at me.

"She's upstairs," I answered, glancing down at the newspaper headlines.

"Good. She doesn't need to hear any of this."

My eyes returned to his.

"Any of what?" Frisbee asked, his face taut.

"We've got to do something about St. Patrick's."

"You're telling me," Frisbee nodded, "but where does one begin?"

"Pew rental and the holy bingo, for starters," Robin adjusted his eyeglasses down his nose and looked over the lenses. "Simon, we need to eliminate them both."

"*We?*" Frisbee made eye contact with Robin.

"Yes, *we*." Robin nodded as he stroked the dark hairs of his mustache. "The bingo in the school basement is a wellness issue. After Sunday night bingo, the school children have to breathe the cigarette smoke the rest of the week. It stinks down there."

I swallowed, realizing I would likely be part of that *we*.

"*We* and what army?" Frisbee raised his left hand, looking about, nervously fumbling with the white collar about his neck.

"Very funny, but if they can do it in Cainbrook, then we

can do it here. Right, Martin?"

"Yeah, I guess," I answered awkwardly, knowing how difficult it was for Father David Gregory to dethrone the Monday night bingo king in Cainbrook, as the man who organized the whole event was called.

"The Sunday night bingo is our main source of revenue, Rob," Frisbee argued.

"I don't care. That doesn't make it right," Robin countered. "It's all about stewardship. The people need to learn how to tithe."

"I don't want to stir up any trouble." Simon Frisbee shook his head. "And they're certainly not going to tithe if we kill their bingo."

"Well, then, we'll sell it as a justice issue," Robin answered. "You're a priest. Get used to it. You're supposed to stir up trouble. Jesus stirred up trouble."

"I'm getting too old for stuff like this, Rob," Frisbee lamented, dropping his face into his hands.

"The other thing is that we need to get some of the laity involved as lectors and Eucharistic ministers."

"Rob, the parish council will have my head." Frisbee took a sip of his coffee.

"Then disband the damned council." Robin pointed to the table.

"What?" Frisbee nearly choked. "Just pulling the plug on the bingo bathtub will get me crucified!"

"There are precedents," Robin raised his eyebrows and took a drink of coffee. "Christ ran the moneychangers out of the temple. So can you." He pointed at Frisbee. "You heard me. And if I have to get rid of my own parish council here at Lost Souls, I will."

"What about your parish wacko, Martha Hart?" Frisbee asked.

"I'll turn the General loose on her." Robin laughed.

"No, I'm serious." Frisbee slapped his hand down on the table.

"Then they can leave for all I care." Robin squinted. "Pshaw!"

Who is Martha Hart, I wondered.

"Rob, if we're going to get rid of pew rental, we might as well get rid of the pews altogether."

"I couldn't agree more. They're old and uncomfortable and the partitions stifle any sense of community. So don't worry," Robin assured him. "I've already covered that. I've got a builder friend who's ready to dismantle the pews this Sunday night."

"Oh, God, no, Robin," Frisbee shook his head. "I can't go for any of it. When the bishop gets wind of it—"

"If we act quickly," Robin smiled, "he won't be able to do anything about it."

"But what if Linguini does?" Frisbee continued.

"It'll be too late. The old pews will already be torn out."

"Yeah, and I'll be shipped off to Bucktooth Nowhere," Frisbee pushed himself away from the table, "or worse. Possum Prairie."

"No you won't. I'm the dean. If he gets nasty, then I'll take the heat for it."

I was in no position to challenge the pastor. I couldn't tell Robin not to do it nor could I call the bishop and tell on him. What would they think I was?

"Do you have any idea what kind of a monster you're about to awaken?"

I wanted to ask the same question but didn't.

"Ah, there's nothing to it," Robin replied, his eyes bright. "Besides, can you imagine what that Gothic church with a beautiful white marble floor is going to look like without any pews? Why, the people will thank you. They'll think they're in a European cathedral. Once they see the difference, they won't want ugly pews cluttering up their beautiful worship space."

"Sure. Dream on, Rob."

"Oh, the tyranny of pews!" Robin stood.

"Rob, you'd do better to burn the place down." Frisbee laughed nervously.

"Say, there's an idea. I'll put it on my list. A nice fire *would* get rid of those god-awful statues, too, wouldn't it?" Robin pushed his chair in at the table.

"Not so loud," Frisbee hushed him. "The General will hear you." It sounded like Hyacinth was making her way down the back stairwell.

"Oh, she's as deaf as a post." Suddenly, Cat appeared at the foot of the stairs. Robin turned and saw him at the doorway. "Say, there's her damned flea-bearing feline vermin. Won't you guys help me get rid of it?"

"Rob, you're incorrigible." Frisbee shook his head.

"No, Jack Ash is incorrigible. I'm a deconstructionist."

"You're a what?" Hyacinth's voice penetrated the room as she emerged from behind the refrigerator with an empty clothesbasket in her arms.

"I'm sure you can provide any number of names for me, Hyacinth." Robin laughed, running his hand through his hair.

"You're right," she said as she turned and put the basket on the kitchen counter. "I ought to report you to Monsignor Linguini."

Rob smiled and waved her off. "You're not going to call him. Of that, I'm sure. You like him about as much as I do. It's one of the few things that we actually have in common."

"You mean you hate him about as much as you hate me." Hyacinth leaned against the sink and faced him.

"It's all the same" Robin grasped the back of his chair.

"Just leave my cat alone," she said as she pointed to Cat. "He's a beautiful animal."

"Martin," Robin said as he nodded to me, "I hope you're taking copious notes. This is all part of your pastoral training."

At that moment the back door buzzer rang. Hyacinth gawked out the kitchen window. "Oh, Father Robin. It's someone to see you."

"Who is it, Hyacinth?"

"Why, it's your girlfriend, Martha Hart." Hyacinth smiled, batting her eyes at Robin. "I know the two of you will want to be alone."

"Great. The parish wacko. Just what I need," Robin sneered.

The door buzzed again. Frisbee stood. "I'm out of here. I've got troubled parishioners of my own." He passed me and made his way through the house and out the front door.

"I'll get the door, Father Robin." Hyacinth stepped toward the door and smiled at me, seemingly enjoying every moment.

"No!" Robin cried out as he moved toward Hyacinth, but he was too late.

"Well, good morning, darling," said Hyacinth, as she opened the door wide. "Father Robin was just talking about you."

The big-haired, aging blonde entered the rectory. "Bless you, my child! Where is our dear pastor?"

"Here, Mrs. Hart," Robin stepped out from behind Hyacinth's shadow.

"Oh, do call me Martha." She gave Robin a slight, but reverent bow when she saw him.

"Martha, Martha, you are anxious about many things. What *didn't* you do during Sunday's Mass?" He pressed his thumb to the bridge of his nose, straightening his wire-rimmed glasses. "You were one of the greeters, you read the scripture, you took up the collection, distributed communion, and you even read the announcements. You should have preached."

"You *should* have her preach, Father Robin," Hyacinth interrupted. "She would do a better job than you. At least I know she would have something to say."

"Hyacinth," Robin clenched his jaw and turned, "doesn't the downstairs' toilet need cleaning?"

"Oh, yes," Hyacinth laughed, "that's the toilet you flush your sermons down, isn't it?"

"Hyacinth!" Martha's face went ashen. "You mustn't say things like that."

"Why not?" Hyacinth glared back at her.

"Why? He's a priest!" Martha whispered and looked at Robin.

"Really?" Hyacinth whispered back. "Oh. I couldn't tell." She laughed noisily as she went to the kitchen sink where she began washing dishes, making more noise than was necessary, clanking the glasses, cups, plates, and utensils.

I hurried to finish my coffee.

"So, Martha," Robin smiled and bowed slightly, turning his attention to the woman, "how can I help you this fine morning?"

"Well, Father, this morning before Mass I went to confession here—"

"I wasn't hearing confessions this morning, Martha," he said, adjusting his glasses.

"I know you weren't. That's why I've come to see you. It was that *man* again."

"*Again*? What *man*?" Robin asked. Hyacinth stopped what she was doing at the sink and listened. I stepped over to the sink to place my coffee mug in her dishwater.

"There's a man who's been hearing confessions," Martha said in a high-pitched whisper.

"See, Father Robin," Hyacinth said as she dried a coffee mug. "What did I tell you? Your idea of delegating your priestly duties to others has been taken to new heights."

"Stay out of this, General," Robin pointed to Hyacinth while keeping his eyes fixed on Martha's. "Go on, Martha. When did this start?"

"Oh, about two weeks ago," Martha answered. "I thought you knew. I told the parish janitor the last time it happened."

"He was probably drunk and forgot." Robin sighed and turned toward me. "Martin, do you know anything about this?"

"No, Father. This is the first I've ever heard of it."

"At first I thought it might be Father Frisbee, but then I realized it wasn't," Martha continued. "After Mass the man left the confessional and he got into an old, green station wagon and drove away."

Robin paused. "Well, if it happens again, come get me."

"Okay. And Father," Martha continued, "I baked some cookies for our young priest."

"For Martin? Well, that was nice," Robin answered, looking at me. "I'm sure he'll appreciate them. Won't you, *Father Martin?*"

"Yes, Mrs. Hart," I replied, walking nearer to Martha. "Thank you, but I'm only a seminarian."

"Oh. I thought you were a priest." The comment was flattering, but I was in no hurry to be ordained. *Once ordained, always ordained.*

"Martha," Robin continued, "I have one more question about the man hearing confessions. What's he like in the confessional? I mean, does he assign penances and the like?"

"I don't exactly know how to say this, Father, but it's like he really *is* a priest."

"See, Father Robin," Hyacinth called out from the kitchen sink, "if you'd hear confessions like you're supposed to, no one would have to do your job for you."

"Hyacinth. Please. Go make yourself useful and make breakfast for Father Boniface."

"Don't you think we should call the police or something?" asked Martha.

"No, not yet. Let me check into it first." Robin put his hands in his pants' front pockets.

Martha looked at her wristwatch and moved toward the back door. "Well, thank you, Father. I have to be going."

Martha left the rectory as quickly as she had entered. Father Robin walked over to the coffee pot and poured himself a cup while I walked up the back stairs. Hyacinth started to follow me upstairs, but turned back and spoke softly to Robin as if she didn't want me to hear. "Sounds like Bill's back."

"Yeah." Robin sighed. "Bill."

Chapter 8: Slingshot

God is closer to us than water is to a fish.
— St. Catherine of Siena

That Sunday, about eight in the evening, the builders were scheduled to arrive at St. Patrick's to tear out the pews. I reluctantly agreed to accompany Father Robin to the church. When we got there, Father Frisbee was pacing the floor, still uncertain about Robin's decision.

Father Robin took me to St. Patrick's school basement to show me *The Holy Bingo*. "Take a deep breath before we open these doors and go down, Martin. You won't be able to breathe once we're in."

We passed a police officer as we entered the school cafeteria. Every table was packed with serious bingo players. There must have been over five hundred people. Many of the people were smoking and dressed in t-shirts and ratty jeans, sitting behind their bingo cards armed with colored daubers as they played fifteen to twenty-five cards. I felt like an alien as I walked among the tables. Our Lady of the River's bingo was nothing compared to this operation. This was big business. "I-eighteen!" the caller said over the intercom.

"Bingo!" yelled a leathery-skinned woman wearing a black Harley Davidson shirt as she thrust her arm in the air.

"Damn it!" exclaimed a buxom woman in her sixties in a denim halter-top and a blue and white bandana; a cigarette dangled between her lips.

There was a collective sigh of anguish from the crowd as a well-dressed gentleman, one of the volunteer bingo workers, called out each number to verify the winning card.

"It's a sea of riff-raff," Robin whispered to me as we approached another police officer standing guard at the other exit. "Bingo is their eighth sacrament."

I noticed a sign on the wall: maximum capacity eight hundred persons—by order of the State Fire Marshall.

Robin turned to me. "Had enough?" I had; we hurried up the stairs. "You should see it when they have the week-long, twenty-four hour bingo marathon," Robin explained, holding the door open for me. We both inhaled fresh air. "They have to move the bingo to the basketball gym. They must pack in two thousand people or more."

When we returned to the church, the workers were just getting started. However, five or six parishioners happened by and before long, there was a group of about two-dozen holding a vigil outside the church on the front steps. Some of them were carrying signs protesting the pew removal. "*Save our pews*," and "*Chuck the Frisbee, not the pews*," were two of the more memorable. I felt particularly squeamish about taking sides in the affair, and I didn't have a good feeling where all this would end. This sort of thing certainly wasn't in my ministry's job description or in any seminary practicum.

* * * *

The next morning after Mass at Poor Souls, as I poured myself a cup of coffee, I looked out the kitchen windows and saw whom I thought was Hyacinth standing in the yard with a slingshot. It was. She was shooting at birds.

I opened the back door and called out from the steps,

"Hyacinth, what on earth are you doing?"

"None of your beeswax, youngin'."

I walked onto the freshly cut grass and nearly stepped on two felled crows. *Had she lost her mind?*

Hyacinth took the slingshot, reared back, and took aim at another crow high on a limb. She pulled back on the sling, releasing a rock. Another glossy-winged crow fell to the earth, hitting the grass with a light thud.

Cat scampered over to one of the felled birds, sniffed it, and batted the bird's head with its front paws before sauntering away from it.

"You're pretty good with that slingshot," I said, taking a sip of my coffee as I stepped over near her. "Where'd you learn to be such a good shot?"

"My brother and I used to pick off pigeons when we were kids." She bent down to pick up one of the downed crows in the dewy grass; she placed it in a black, plastic trash bag that was lying on the ground. I nudged the other large felled crow with my shoe. It stirred and took flight only to be quickly shot back down by Hyacinth.

"The crows around here are huge," I observed, looking at its bloody head.

"Yes, they eat out of the dumpsters at those fast-food places. These crows are healthier than some of the poor kids in town."

Many times flocks of the crows had flown over the church, their droppings falling like dirty snow.

"Oh, look, Martin," she pointed at one of the crows in the grass, "this one looks like the vicar-general, Monsignor Lasagna. And the one there on the sidewalk looks like His Highness, our bishop. Don't you think so?"

"I have no idea," I said, not wanting to agree with her comment.

"Do they teach you that at the seminary?"

"Teach what?"

"How to be totally wishy-washy and completely indecisive." I had no chance to answer before she continued. "Oh, never mind, just grab those birds and put them in the trash bag before Cat starts gnawing on them."

I put my coffee mug on the back stoop and returned to the yard to pick up the trash bag, incredulous that I was actually doing so. I grabbed two of the birds by the tips of their wings and tossed them in the bag. There was a dead pigeon a few feet from the crows, and I was about to grab it. "What about this one?"

Hyacinth came at me like a soldier. "Don't you dare!" she slapped my hand and snatched the bird up, flinging the pigeon several feet away. Walking over to it, she stared at it and exclaimed. "I wouldn't want it to be confused with my precious crows. These god-awful things are flying rats. What was God thinking when he created them? Bury it later. I wouldn't want Cat to eat it."

"What are you going to do with the crows?"

"Never you mind," she said as she snatched the black trash bag away. "Don't you have some prayers to say?"

"I prayed my office this morning before Mass." I grinned, knowing that she was trying to get rid of me.

"Well, then, open the door for me."

I retrieved my coffee mug, followed her into the rectory, and left her in the kitchen alone. Stepping into the hallway, between the kitchen and dining room, I peeked back in the kitchen to see what she would do with the birds. She was standing at the sink, feverishly plucking their feathers. I returned to the kitchen. "Hyacinth, what are you doing?"

"Nothing," she started, turning to face me. "Here." She reached for the meat cleaver on her butcher's block. "Chop their heads off after I've plucked out all their feathers."

"What?" The thought was disgusting.

"Just do it." She held the meat cleaver at shoulder's height.

I grasped the meat cleaver from her and raised it above the bird's neck. Hesitating at first, I whacked the head clean from the body of the bird on the cutting block. Blood oozed out on the block.

"Such a violent act against such an innocent creature," Hyacinth paused from her plucking and peered over at me. "Don't you think so?" She grabbed the severed head from the block and tossed it down the sink's drain.

"Yes."

"It reminds me of how Linguini treats people."

I ignored her baited comment. "Now what?"

"Do another."

Reluctantly, I raised the cleaver and severed the neck of another crow. This time it seemed easier.

"Are you going to cook these?" I scraped the head and blood off the block and into the sink.

"Not now. Maybe later. I'll freeze them for now. I'm waiting for a very special occasion. They're a Chef's Surprise for a very special friend."

"Just let me know when this special occasion is so I can eat out that day."

"I will if you promise me one thing," she said, still ferociously plucking feathers from the largest crow. "You can't tell anyone about my Chef's Surprise. Not even Father Boniface—you understand?"

"Yes, Hyacinth, but this is gross."

"Oh, and destroying church property isn't?"

"What?" I knew that she would somehow get around to the pew removal at St. Patrick's.

"Don't give me that. When did you and those two priests tell the people of St. Patrick's that their pews were coming out?"

"I didn't have anything to do with it."

"Oh, really? Well, I heard you were with *that one* last night when he had that construction worker and his drunken cronies come in and chop St. Patrick's pews to kindling wood. That makes you an accomplice!"

"Father Robin is the dean—"

"Never mind *that one*." She turned the garbage disposal on and pushed the feathers and bird heads down the drain. "But I will say one thing, tearing out the pews may very well turn out to be just the thing I need to welcome my special friend to Lost Souls."

"I don't understand."

"You don't need to. Just get out of my kitchen. Vamoose. Go bury that dead pigeon. There's a shovel hanging in the garage." The disposal whined with a loud grinding noise.

I opened the door to the garage, found the shovel, opened the overhead garage door and returned to the yard. When I got to the pigeon, Cat was rolling around in the grass with it between his paws. "Scat, Cat!" I said, nudging Cat with the shovel. Cat watched me duly bury the bird.

Walking back upstairs, I caught up on some of my reading before joining the ladies of the Legion of Mary for the recitation of the rosary at nine. Afterwards they treated me to an early lunch at the Pancake Palace.

* * * *

When I returned to the rectory about one o'clock, Father Boniface was grumbling. "What is it with the drains around here? The damned garbage disposal's clogged up again. And the downstairs' toilet keeps overflowing." I closed the back door and Father Boniface eyed me. "Martin, you haven't been clogging up the john, have you?"

"No." I could hardly keep from laughing.

"Well, then, what the hell's wrong with the drain?" I didn't immediately answer, wondering what affect bird feathers might have on the plumbing. Boniface didn't wait for an answer. "A few years ago I had a young associate who loved those damned all-you-can-eat buffets and I was forever calling the plumber to clear out the pipes. You're not eating a lot, are you?"

"No, I don't like those buffets."

"Me neither. They might as well have two long feeding troughs and just fill them with food and let the people belly up to the manger. Hell, forget utensils, people don't use them anyway." Boniface hobbled off, banging his cane on the floor.

A plumber arrived around dinnertime. He lectured Hyacinth about putting bird feathers down the garbage disposal.

Chapter 9: Dinosaur Confessions

I knew nothing; I was nothing.
For this reason God chose me.
— St. Catherine Labouré

"Father Robin," I asked, as we drank coffee before morning Mass. "Don't you think it highly amusing that Poor Souls is on Nottingham Lane and Inglenook is in Sherwood County?"

"Your point?"

"*Robin Hood.*"

"You'll have to do better than that." Robin returned his coffee cup to its saucer with a clank. "Are you insinuating that the old man in there is Friar Tuck?"

"No." I was surprised at his tone. "I'm sorry, Father. I was only joking."

"So was I," a smile spread across Robin's face as he shook his head. "Martin, if I told you that they took the word *gullible* out of the dictionary, would you believe me?"

"I have no idea."

"Never mind. It's almost time for Mass over at Immaculate Heart. Let's go before Captain Chaos tries to start without us."

"Who's Captain Chaos?"

"Deacon Leonard Dill. He's put the bishop in some pickles. He got up and preached one time when Father Chris forgot to go out there and celebrate Mass. Poor Leonard. He's a kind hearted soul that Bishop Collins ordained deacon back in the seventies," Robin sighed. "A lot of the people still won't receive communion from him."

"Why not?"

"He's married."

"What about the other Eucharistic ministers?"

"*Others?* There are none. Only *Father* can touch Jesus in the host."

"But *Deacon* Dill is validly ordained."

"But Deacon Dill has *sexual relations* with his wife and that makes him unclean in these people's eyes. He's *contaminated* with sex."

"That's crazy. Sex was God's idea."

"You're telling me. The whole idea that sex is dirty is contrary to Church teaching. I went to Immaculate Heart and tried to install some Eucharistic ministers, and one guy got up in my face and screamed at me, 'Pretty soon you'll be telling me anybody and their brother can touch Jesus.' And I said, 'yes, I am saying that.' The next week Linguini called me and told me to leave Immaculate Heart alone."

When Robin and I arrived at Immaculate Heart, Deacon Dill was sitting in the sacristy praying his breviary. He stood up when we approached him. Just as Deacon Dill stood, he passed gas, but as he did so, he coughed trying to distract us from the sound of the flatulence. It didn't work. And the odor was indeed foul.

On the way back to Poor Souls, Robin explained to me that the Deacon drank too much decaffeinated coffee. "That's why his gas smells so bad. But he does speak in tongues, you know."

"No, I didn't."

"Yes, he's one of those Charismaniacs."

"Charismatics?"

"No. Charismaniacs. Sometimes when he farts, he starts speaking in tongues to distract your attention. He even farts in tongues. You see, Martin, the Diocese of Covert is full of shit—the bishop craps his pants and the deacons fart, but we keep it all covert."

* * * *

When we returned to the parish, Hyacinth had dinner ready for us in the dining room. Father Boniface must have had one martini too many. He was spinning tales as Hyacinth moved in and out of the dining room with Cat bounding at her feet.

"Every year we hold the Parish Festival around the thirteenth of June." Boniface's blue eyes sparkled. "November second is the feast of All Souls, but it's too cold in November. Besides, Our Lady of the Lost and Forsaken Souls in Limbo, I mean Our Lady of the Poor and Forgotten Souls in Purgatory sounds lost, doesn't it? So I took the liberty of borrowing Saint Anthony's feast day for our parish since Saint Anthony is the patron saint of lost articles." Boniface pushed his black-framed glasses up his nose and laughed. "Maybe we ought to have our people pray to St. Anthony to help them find their lost faith instead of their dumb car keys.

"And while we're at it, we can get the priests to pray to him, too. So many priests these days are worried about *getting their needs met*. And if it's not that, then they're always worried whether the people are singing loud enough in church. Hellfire, you can't tell whether a man's holy or not by the tone of his voice. Sometimes those who pray the loudest are the worst hypocrites. Remember the Pharisee and the Republican?"

"You mean the publican?" Robin asked as he positioned

his wine glass above his knife and spoon.

"You mean what I know." Boniface shook his head and held his cane up in his right hand.

Midway through dinner, Father Boniface began telling another story, about one of the deceased members of the clergy, Monsignor Clarence Huffman. "One day I was in the sacristy here at Lost Souls, and I looked out into the church and saw that there was standing room only. People were everywhere, hanging from the choir loft, peeking from behind pillars, the doors wide open. It was the middle of winter, you see. I went out to see why all these people were here, it not being Christmas or Easter, you know. At first I got the big head, you know, thinking my preaching had improved and I was going to make converts like Saint Peter at Pentecost or Paul in Ephesus. Thousands of souls, can you imagine? Well, anyway, I noticed a lot of the folks squeezing into the church were parishioners from Immaculate Heart.

"I was worried that Monsignor Huffman might have dropped dead or something. He was Father Huffman back then—before he got the magenta. Anyway, one of the old parishioners from Immaculate Heart pulled me aside and told me that right before Mass was to start Father Huffman stepped out from behind the high altar, and genuflected, you see, but instead of stepping up to the altar, he turned around and announced, 'Your pastor's in a state of mortal sin! I can't say Mass this morning because I got drunk last night while playing poker. I've got to go to confession.' Then he told them that if they hurried over here to Inglenook, they could just make our ten-thirty Mass. Only Huffy didn't say Poor Souls, he said *Lost Souls*.

"When I went to preach my sermon I looked out and there was Huffy in his old ratty cassock and biretta leaning against one of the west pillars just outside one of the confessionals." Boniface twirled his cane in his right hand and stroked his scraggly chin's three days' growth of a beard with his left.

"I'll never forget old Huffy's funeral. For two days, the people made their way up the hill to Immaculate Heart. Thousands of people filed past his coffin. And it wasn't no fancy-schmancy casket, you see. It was a good ol' fashioned wooden coffin. His brother's a monk at Saint Bede's Abbey, and a couple of years before Huffy died he had the monastery's cabinet maker build him a coffin. Ol' Huffy used the coffin as a coffee table until he died."

Robin took a sip of his Merlot and seemed to be examining the wall above the fireplace's mahogany mantle. The cream colored paint on the walls was cracking in places.

"Oh, I remember the days when I had three associates here at Lost Souls," Boniface continued. "We'd sit around the table here, laugh, play cards, and swap stories. It was a wonderful time. We had each other. Things are different now. Perhaps they were simpler times. I'm not saying we can ever go back to the glory days, but you men best figure out a way to get these bishops to listen to you. Once they get that pointed hat and big stick, they change. I believe our Lord warned about men widening their phylacteries and lengthening their tassels. Oh, well, that's coming from a man who never made the rank of monsignor. I can't deny there were times when I desired the sash and the red-buttoned soutane, but now it doesn't matter. There are days when I wonder if the collar was worth it all." Boniface reminded me of my grandfather even more.

"People used to think that priests were different. In the seminary, they drilled it into our heads that we would experience an *ontological change* once ordained. Well, I sure didn't feel any different, except when I got pulled over for speeding or running a red light. The officer would see my collar, smile, and tell me to be careful. Boy, are those days gone. Nowadays the police may follow you around simply because you *are* a priest!

"I remember my first assignment. The old pastor made me feel like his shoeshine boy. He had me out there doing all the grunt work. At mealtime, he would serve just enough food. One time he thought my steak was bigger than his and during grace he walked over and traded plates. He yelled at the housekeeper for the mistake.

"I also had a ten o'clock curfew. He wouldn't give any of us parochial vicars—that's what associate priests were called back then. None of this associate pastor or co-pastor stuff. Anyway, he wouldn't give any of us the keys to the rectory. There were three of us, mind you. One night I stayed out late with a couple of priest friends and when I got back to the rectory around midnight the doors were all locked. I managed to knock loud enough on the back door for one of the other priests in the house to hear me. He came down and let me in the back door. Let me tell you, though, the next morning the pastor pounded on my door at five a.m. When I opened the door, he accused me of being a lush and a womanizer. He reported me to the bishop. Thank God Bishop Collins was an understanding man. Bishop Collins, God rest his soul.

"When Munchin was named his successor, I remember visiting Collins at the infirmary at Saint Albert's Priory. He had gone there to retire, you know. Munchin reversed everything he ever did. He took it hard. He told me he'd failed as a bishop. I told him he was a good bishop. And that he was.

"Speaking of bishops, I wonder who's running Rome these days. John Paul's a great man and all, but I think the Curia's wrestled control away from him.

"These new bishops don't stand for anything. Oh, they

get together and write these wonderfully verbose documents that nobody reads and then they go back to their dioceses feeling justified, but they haven't done a damned thing. They think the bureaucracy is the church! They're so far removed. Haven't they ever read Vatican II?" Boniface paused, looking at the fireplace and chandelier. He drank some coffee before continuing.

"Some of our priests run themselves ragged, burning the candle at both ends and in the middle. Then there are some who have no time for others, even those in need, and only go around talking about getting their own needs met, taking care of themselves.

"We had a young man here a few summers ago who was only interested in knowing who the parish heretics were. I suppose he wanted to beat them into submission with the Catechism. I learned later that he reported me to the bishop for not preaching enough on the fires of hell. But that's nothing. He wrote Cardinal Ratzinger at the Holy Office in Rome saying that the professors at St. Albert's seminary were all heretics. I was glad to see that the guy left our diocese. He's now studying at some ultraconservative seminary here in the states where they teach everything in Latin. Don't get me wrong, Latin is beautiful, sure, but who's your audience? They're out there training men for a pre-Vatican II Church that no longer exists. Good luck finding people who speak Latin. Who will they be ministering to? The Church is made up of human beings, not marble statues!

"At the other extreme we've got priests who vacation in Las Vegas, live at the casinos, gallivant about Europe, and golf at the most luxurious country clubs. Some of them only hobnob with the wealthy. And the bishop puts some of the guys up to it so he can keep—Oh, for heaven's sake, listen to me whimpering like a washer woman."

"Watch it, old man," Hyacinth called out from the kitchen, obviously listening to his every word. "*I'm* your washer woman."

"Regardless, I've thoroughly depressed Martin here," Boniface said, looking at me. "I'm supposed to encourage you in the vocation, not talk you out of it. But let me tell you, I know there are some guys in our diocese who can't wait to retire and get the hell out."

I found myself agreeing with much of what Boniface said. I had been sent to Poor Souls to learn about parish life and the priesthood; I was getting quite an education.

At that Robin excused himself, and Hyacinth began clearing his place at the table.

Boniface leaned towards me. "There are days when I ask myself, 'My God, what did I do with my life? Did I make a difference? Was my life one big hollow lie?'"

"How did you deal with celibacy?" I asked, curious as to how he negotiated a major, if not the main, drawback of the priesthood.

Hyacinth slowly stacked the plates and silverware and returned to the kitchen, but not before eyeing Boniface as if wanting to hear his answer to my question.

"I didn't." He paused, glanced at Hyacinth briefly and then back at me. "It dealt with me. I finally got too old to do anything about it. Everyday having to suppress my desire for a wife took its toll on me. I know. I was a downright bastard. I was in my forties when I became a pastor, and I became just like the old bastard I had to slave under at my first assignment.

"Only I didn't kick my young priests around, just the housekeeper. Every time I saw her was a reminder that I couldn't have a woman. It wasn't fair to her. I actually liked her. I liked her a lot." A trace of a tear shone in Boniface's left eye as he paused and looked away at the oil painting at one end of the room. "I loved her. But I was a priest." He removed his glasses and wiped his eyes. Suddenly Hyacinth reappeared in the dining room. Hyacinth quietly collected plates, bowls, and silverware from the table. Boniface continued to look down and away as she walked back to the kitchen.

Hyacinth smiled tenderly, showing her teeth as she returned with strawberry shortcake and coffee. Boniface smiled at her. I wondered whether the housekeeper of which Boniface had just spoken was Hyacinth. From the way he spoke, I had my suspicions. The two reminded me of an old married couple.

When Hyacinth sat to have her dessert and coffee, Cat hopped up on Boniface's lap.

Chapter 10: Reminisces

The saints and friends of Christ served the Lord
in hunger and thirst; in cold and nakedness;
in labor and weariness; in watchings and fastings;
in prayers and holy meditations; in persecutions
and many reproaches.
— Heb. 11. 37

The next week, I took time to visit Mother in Cainbrook. We went for breakfast at the Cainbrook Country Club. "Martin," Mother said worriedly as we sat outside on the veranda overlooking the lake and golf course, "have you heard about Bishop Numbnoddle and three of his priests?"

I had, though I said nothing. There was a scandal involving the three priests. A lawsuit had been filed which alleged that they had molested several altar boys.

"I can't believe it. They say that the bishop knew about the abuse, but instead of doing something he just moved the priests to different parishes."

I sighed and grew sick to my stomach.

"You'd best pay attention to what's going on around you, son. I was at the dry cleaner's yesterday and Mrs. Weaver— who at one time was a devout Catholic—asked me how you were doing at the seminary. She wanted to know if you were gay. Needless to say, I was irate. Are you sure the priesthood thing's right for you? Things are different than when I was your age. I sure hope you know what you're doing. Your father wouldn't have approved of your giving up a good career for the collar. But then who am I to judge? There were times I thought I was married to a monk."

She then proceeded to give me the Sean Report. He had borrowed thousands of dollars from her and was planning to move to Florida for some business opportunity. He had promised her that he would be back from time to time. I figured he was probably going to become a drug smuggler.

After breakfast I stopped by Our Lady of the River parish to see Father David Gregory, the priest who had anointed me when I was nine and suffering from rheumatic fever. Father David was a man of swarthy complexion; his father was black Irish and his mother was Italian. He was a complex man, on the one hand firmly orthodox, incorporated Latin into the liturgy, and yet he was involved in the charismatic prayer movement and had the spiritual gift of tongues. He was indeed an enigma to his fellow priests, as he was to me. There were those who considered Father David to be a theological extremist, guilty of an elitist clericalism, a veritable throwback to a rigid Tridentine Catholicism.

Father David's name had come up in a conversation with Father Robin recently. "You know him?" Father Robin asked me. "He's a dinosaur. Says Mass every day, hears confessions all the time cramped up in that box, and always wears his clerical collar and cassock. I suppose he sleeps in the damned thing. It's ridiculous. He thinks it's nineteen hundred. And he has no life away from the parish. It's unhealthy. Priests like him get us normal guys in trouble. The parishioners expect us all to be like him. There are people here who drive more than thirty miles to Cainbrook just to go to his Mass, you know."

I knew he was more complex than that. And I felt that I somehow owed something to the man. He had been my pastor for more than fifteen years, and I still believed that his prayers of anointing had saved me from death as a boy.

On more than one occasion, Father David had lamented what he called the "demystification of the liturgy" since Vatican II, and he bemoaned the fact that many priests weren't saying Mass daily. "A couple of our priests will only say Mass once or twice during the week. I can't understand these priests and their whining. They say they have no time for themselves. What did they expect? That's the nature of the priesthood. Our Blessed Lord had nowhere to lay his head so neither should we. Many husbands and wives have no time between their children and work. But many of our priests insist upon having almost a private life to the neglect of their pastoral responsibilities."

There was no question that Father David was devout. He rose at five every morning and prayed his office. He celebrated Mass every day of the week including Saturdays, a rare thing these days according to him. Monday was his day off, but he would have Mass first and then leave for the day.

Father David came to the door dressed in his black soutane, his rosary beads dangling from his right hand, and his black biretta was atop his head.

"Martin," he said as he opened the door. "I was just going to lunch. Won't you join me?"

"I had a late breakfast."

"No matter. We can talk." Father David shed his cassock and biretta and we got into his car. We went to his usual stop for lunch, the *Pigeon-Toed Moose Café*. The parking lot was badly in need of repair, with potholes large enough to swallow a small car. The door handles on the restaurant were greasy and the windows smudged. The décor was lost in the late sixties, the upholstery a gaudy orange and the woodwork a shellacked, shiny dark brown while the pungent smell of cigarette smoke permeated the place. Many of the customers watched us as we entered. There were paintings of Elvis Presley and Jesus on one wall, and across the room hung a photo of John Wayne.

"Look, Martin," Father David said. "Two kings and a duke."

An older blonde waitress took our lunch order. Her hair was in a kinky perm, and her gray uniform shirt was too small for her.

"So, Martin," Father David said, "what do they teach at Saint Albert's these days?"

"I read Augustine's *Confessions* this past semester."

"Ah, he was quite the libertine in his youth." David reached for the ashtray and moved it to his side of the table.

"We also had a course entitled *The Changing Priesthood*."

"I hope it wasn't taught by one of the dissident voices calling for the elimination of celibacy and the ordination of women."

"There are some moderates' positions—" I began.

"Yes," he interrupted, "but even then, many of the moderates and liberals who advocate optional celibacy are also in favor of artificial contraception and abortion. But, how can those who oppose the death penalty, war, and racism support abortion? Women have been sold the lie that in order to be free they have to kill their children. The true test of a civilization is found in its treatment of its most helpless and vulnerable members. You've no doubt had to deal with all the questions about Father Lee, but that's nothing compared to what happened in Wheatfield. At least Father Lee's indiscretion was with a woman and they were both consenting adults. But adolescent boys? Bishop Numbnoddle lost all his moral authority when he simply moved the abusive priests to other parishes in his diocese.

"What will become of the Church? If I didn't know the Church was founded upon the rock of the apostles and the faith of the martyrs, I would have left years ago. Meanwhile that liberal Cardinal of ours is giving the church away to the laity. I've seen whom they're sending to the seminary these days, and I've seen whom they're ordaining. My God, are we that hard up that we'll settle for any warm, male body?"

Rawly Huffhind and Matthew Tupps came to mind.

"They've already ordained a lot of men that they never should have. When I was in the seminary, men like that would never have been allowed to enter in the first place. I brought this up at our priest's retreat last year and thought some of the liberals would lynch me." He ran his left thumb under the front of his priestly collar.

"There are days, I tell you, when I don't even want to leave the rectory with my collar on, especially if there's a story in the headlines. I'm a marked man. All priests are. Nowadays if I say hello to the schoolchildren, I'm worried they'll go home and tell their parents that I tried to touch them. There are times when I even hesitate to look at them.

"God forbid if you try and use Latin or sing the *Agnus Dei*. If one of the conservative guys was to say a Latin Mass or have benediction after Mass, the Bishop and Vicar-General would descend upon the poor guy, and he'd be removed and sent off to some center for therapy. But if one of the faired-haired boys has homosexual relations with an altar boy, they'll just move him to another parish where he can do it again. It's the old shell game. Liturgical abuse is more serious than violation against the vows of celibacy. If you're *liturgically incorrect,* you'll be sought out by the rubric police, but never mind the real abuse."

No wonder Mother liked him; they both spoke in streams of consciousness. The waitress returned with our drink order, and I took a drink of my iced tea.

"Well," David said as he picked his cup of coffee up off the saucer and took a sip. "I just hope you don't believe everything you hear over at Poor Souls. Boniface is a nice man, but he was terribly liberal in his day. He put a lot of us on the spot with his social activism and anti-war protests and the like. The pastor there, Father Wood, is a young upstart. I'm not quite sure what to think of him." He pointed his fork my direction. "What do you think of him?"

"He's been good to me." I told the truth.

"Just do what Saint Peter did when the Lord bade him walk on water. Keep your eyes fixed on Jesus, son. If you don't, then you'll soon sink into the chaos." Father David reached for the pack of cigarettes in his coat, tapped one out, and lit it with his gold lighter. He took a drag, removed the cigarette with his right hand, and blew the smoke out the left side of his mouth.

"I can't understand Bishop Numbnoddle. He's one of the most progressive bishops in the states. He strains out the gnats of liturgical abuse, but allows this! He'll never regain his integrity! He should resign. Look at the predicament in which he's put all decent priests, not to mention bishops. It's enough to make you sick to your stomach. How'd they handle it at the seminary? I'm curious what they've said." He took another puff off the cigarette.

"Not much," I explained as I fiddled with my napkin and spoon. "The priests who are charged didn't study at Saint Albert's, so I guess there was a sigh of relief. We prayed for the church, but that was about it. It's a busy time of the year."

"Evidently not busy enough for some priests," he replied as he tapped the cigarette in the ashtray. "The authority of the church could be compromised. What are they teaching these guys in the seminary? Why would a guy want to molest young boys? Falling for a woman I could understand—even honor—but altar boys? Those who harm children—especially our own priests—need to go back and read Matthew: *It would be better for him to have a great millstone hung around his neck and be drowned in the depths of the sea than to harm a single hair of the head of a little one. Whatsoever you do unto the least ones, that you do unto me*, I believe is the phrase. What will become of the Church?"

Father David was speaking too loudly for my comfort, and I inconspicuously looked around to see if anyone was listening.

"The bishop here won't allow a wedding to be celebrated outdoors, even if the couple comes from devout Catholic families. On the other hand, if there's a couple that has been living together and rejects Church teaching to the point of securing a pre-nuptial agreement or an abortion, the bishop will turn a blind eye if they're getting married at the cathedral and the father of the bride drops a gold brick in the diocesan coffer.

"Oh, don't get me started. These bishops need to learn what real abuse is. I recall accommodating some of the elderly parishioners' desire for some Latin in the liturgy. After Vatican II, the older generation felt that the rug had been yanked out from under them with the elimination of the Latin liturgy. Boy, Vicar-general Linguini came down on me quicker than anything and accused me of *Liturgical Abuse.*

"Come on, who wants to get aboard a sinking ship? As long as these kooky bishops and vocation directors keep saying that there aren't any vocations, then there won't be any. It's a self-fulfilling prophecy. Stupid men. Sometimes I wonder if there are traitors in our midst, sabotaging good vocations. But if a man says *that* in the seminary I'm sure he'd be put on the rack.

"I'm convinced Bishop Numbnoddle doesn't want priests. And now this scandal, but no one wants to say anything. Everyone's in denial. I've said for several years now that because of the need for priests, they've been too willing to accept any warm bodied male." He smoked his cigarette and drank some coffee before speaking again. "Speaking of which, was I right about the seminary?"

"Right about what?" My mind was reeling from Father David's syllabus of errors.

"I told you that you'd encounter saints and sinners."

"Oh, yes. You were right."

"Well, just keep your head about you. Don't worry about what the other guys are doing or not doing. Keep your eyes fixed on Jesus. His is our standard of holiness. I'm sure the rector says the same thing. It's just a good thing that Christ promised that the gates of hell would not prevail; otherwise, the bishops would have brought the Church down ages ago.

"Well, enough of this. It's depressing. A few vocal dissidents have managed to taint everyone's opinion of the priesthood. Most priests are happier than most professionals. We must never forget that the world is charged with the glory of God! You do know Hopkins, right?"

"I'm afraid not."

"Gerard Manley Hopkins? Famous Jesuit Poet?"

"No, his name doesn't ring a bell." I was embarrassed by my ignorance.

"'The world is charged with the grandeur of God, but all is smeared...smeared with toil; and wears man's smudge...yet it will flame out, like shining from shook foil...'"

Father David crushed his cigarette butt in the ashtray and began reminiscing about his days in the seminary.

* * * *

Leaving Cainbrook, I was delayed by a train. The engine's horns moaned a lonely chord as I watched the freight cars pass by the flashing crossing gate. The sound and sight of the train took me back to the day before my father died. A train had stopped us on our way to my ballgame. He and I were together even though he and mother were separated at the time. My father and I started to get closer once I turned fourteen, and my interest in baseball seemed to trigger a change in my father's attitude toward me. That night he cheered me on like he had never before and after the game took me out for ice cream. With our mutual interest in baseball, it seemed that the two of us finally had something to talk about.

Once the train cleared the tracks, I doubled back and drove to the cemetery to visit his grave. I parked on the hillside, walked to his grave marker, and stood silently in the cemetery staring at his headstone. There was a fresh, red rose lying on it. I wondered who might have placed it there.

All I could remember was that late summer night at the ballpark when my father and I were together for the last time.

I wondered what might have been had he lived.

Chapter 11: Communion Calls

Keep death ever before you.
— Rule of St. Benedict

The next day I went to the Church mid-morning and knelt upon one of the prie-dieus behind the high altar. The silence rang loudly in the gothic structure. I grasped my rosary's crucifix and began praying. *I believe in God the Father Almighty, Creator of Heaven and Earth, and in Jesus Christ, his Only Son....*

From behind me in the sacristy, I heard the drone of a fly. I got up from the kneeler, walked through the apse doorway to the church sacristy behind the high altar, and stopped before the rocking chair where Father Boniface liked to sit and pray his obligatory priestly prayers. I put my hand on the back of the rocker and detected the fly in one of the sacristy's three half-oval, triangular-paned stained glass windows. The sun rendered the colored glass refulgent.

The buzz of the fly's wings brought back a memory of a time in my life when I wanted to free a trapped fly in a windowpane but couldn't because I was confined to bed. My untreated strep throat led to rheumatic fever. With an extreme temperature, I was experiencing hallucinations as I drifted in and out of consciousness.

When the doctor told Grandma Buckner that she should quit hoping for a miracle, she told him there was always hope. She prayed the rosary all the more. She prayed it so many times that she had rosary bead-burned fingers from beseeching the Blessed Virgin Mary's intercession to save me from death. That's the story my mother told me. When I was well again, I recall being brought to Our Lady of Aquino Shrine where the friars of St. Albert's Priory offered a Mass of thanksgiving for my recovery. Thanks to Grandma Buckner, the Virgin Mary, and her son Jesus, I was saved from death. I was convinced of this.

I'd love to find that doctor today and let him know that there was still hope. Preparing to make calls to the sick and shut-ins, I walked back to the sanctuary, genuflected before the tabernacle, and placed six Eucharistic hosts in my golden pix. The church's high altar was elaborately decorative; in the center above the tabernacle was a statue of a long-haired Jesus with flowing red and gold robes revealing his Sacred Heart. There were statues of Mary and Joseph above their respective side altars. Behind Mary's statue was a renaissance painting of her Coronation in Heaven; behind St. Joseph's statue was a painting of him looking up from his workbench in the carpenter shop, listening to the child Jesus.

I paused in prayer again before exiting down the main aisle, looking up at the hand-carved dark wood statues of the apostles along the walls—Peter, Paul, Andrew, James the Great, John, Matthew, Philip, Thomas, Bartholomew, James the Less, Jude, Matthias and Mary Magdalene. How interesting that Mary Magdalene ranked a spot along the wall. How did James, son of Alphaeus, feel about going down in history as James the Less?

* * * *

My first stop was the home of Viola Pitts. She was a thin,

pale, widow with stringy black hair and at least ten cats. The house reeked of animal urine and feces. I was amazed that a person could retain so much junk, for the house was cluttered with clothes, furniture, and a multitude of odds and ends, appearing as if she never threw anything away nor ever vacuumed.

Father Robin had described Viola as a bitter old spinster after our first visit there together. The visits were merely perfunctory: One Our Father and a Hail Mary, put the communion wafer on her tongue, and be done with it. At least that's how Father Robin had both described it and modeled it for me. Viola didn't seem to mind.

The next visit was with Mabel Marsh. She always wore a brown wig and her lips were smeared with bright red lipstick. The three times I had visited her, she had classical music playing and today was no different. Her house had a peculiar odor and one that I can't readily describe, but was nonetheless immediately recognizable when I smelled it: Aunt May. Sean used to say it was "old people smell."

As soon as I would arrive at her house, she would go into the kitchen and fix me a cup of tea. Then she would take me by the hand, sit with me on her sofa, and hold my hands while we prayed. She would often take the lead and pray out loud with prayers from her heart.

On this particular visit, just as I was about to read a passage of the scripture and give her communion, she interrupted me with more talk.

"I hope that I don't scare you none, son, but I'm into the charismatic prayer and all. You know our dear priest Father Bill Gallagher. God love him, he's dropped out now. They say he fell in love. When he was our priest here, he was on fire with the Holy Ghost. I still think of him. He was such a fine priest! It's too bad they don't let the men marry. It always seems we lose the good ones. It seems that some of the ones who lose their faith stay, and then the church is the worse for it."

Was this the Bill who was hearing confessions, I wondered?

"I don't mean to discourage you none, son. Just make sure this is for you. Life can be so lonely. I know. My cousin became a priest, but he joined some order out west. We rarely heard from him. He died two years ago in California.

"Well, I'm just glad you've come to *Poor Souls*—Father Boniface needs a good helper there. You'll make a fine priest. Martin, isn't it?"

"Yes."

"May I call you Marty?"

"That's fine. My grandmother does."

"Oh, listen to this lonely old widow woman chattering away, keeping you from your prayers and your other visits."

"Oh, no, you're fine," I said, feeling that somehow she was ministering to me more than I was ministering to her. "That's why I'm here."

"You're such a sweetie." Holding both of my hands, she brought them up to her lips and tenderly kissed them. "These hands are the hands of a priest." She closed her eyes as if to signal the time for prayer. I finished by giving her holy communion. A slow movement from a Mozart symphony sounded in the background as she saw me out the door. There was lipstick on my left hand.

My next stop was the local nursing home, where I visited two elderly women and Timmy Wimm, a disabled man in his late thirties.

My last destination was the residence of Henry and Rita Gordon. Henry was dying of colon cancer yet had chosen to live his last days at home with his wife. I had been there three times before with Father Robin.

When I arrived, Rita Gordon answered the door. She had dark curly hair that was too dark to be natural. She let me in the house, just inside the foyer. "He's sleeping. You can come back later." The sound of a news talk show was coming from his bedroom.

"Oh, that's all right. I also came by to see you, Rita."

"What for? Don't lie to me. I'm not the one dying. He is."

"I know, but it's got to be difficult caring for Henry, and you are one of our parishioners."

"Look," she said and pointed at me. "Mr. Gordon is well cared for. You just missed the hospice nurse. He's in love with her. He never talks to me anymore, but he'll talk her leg off, especially when she's in there giving him a bath or tucking him into bed. He lusts after her, you know."

I didn't exactly know what to say. "Well, thank God for your faith."

"I'm *not* a Catholic. I've always endured having to go to church with the old man, but I never converted. So there."

I stared blankly at her, taken aback.

"What's wrong?" Her nostrils flared a bit. "Cat got your tongue?"

"No, I just, uh, well...."

"I'll tell him you stopped by." She pressed me toward the door.

"Please tell him we're praying for him."

Just as Rita opened the front door to see me out, Henry coughed and called out from his bed, "Is that Father Robin from *Poor Souls?*"

"No," Rita answered.

"Then who is it, Dear?" His voice was strained.

"It's the young man from *Poor Souls*, but he was just leaving."

"But I want to receive communion." A tinge of despair colored his voice.

I stopped shy of stepping outside despite Rita standing behind me with her hand pressing the front storm door wide open.

"Bring him in, won't you, Dear?" His voice was a bit stronger.

"All right," she answered Henry but faced me with an emotionless stare. "Don't wear him out," she said to me in a low voice. "He's tired."

I followed Rita and together we moved towards the bedroom.

"Hello, my boy," Henry smiled. "I was just watching the news here. Looks like it's that time of the month again."

"How's that?"

"Time to go bomb Iraq. But if they really want to kick Saddam Hussein's ass, they'll have to do more than throw rocks through his palace windows. Boy, I thought Reagan could fool the media. Clinton beats him by miles. They call him Slick Willie, you know."

"Yes, I've heard that."

"Here, pull you up a chair."

"Thank you."

"Mack, isn't it?"

"Martin."

"Oh, yes, *Martin*. The medicine they're giving me makes me downright loopy."

I scooted a chair near Henry as Rita, clearly angry at my presence, walked out of the room.

"So, how are things at the parish?" Henry seemed genuinely interested.

"Pretty good, thank you, Henry. The Parish Festival went

well." I was watching the television screen as an angry Republican and a frustrated Democrat shouted at each other across an oak table.

"Is Hyacinth keeping you well fed?"

"Oh, yes, as a matter of fact, she is. She's quite the cook."

"Yeah, just look at Boniface. He's not starving."

Henry grew quiet when the talking head for the Republicans began blathering how President Clinton's failed policies had ruined Reagan's legacy. The Democrat roundly mocked him and the two began shouting at each other again.

Henry turned to me, "Hand me the remote over there." He nodded to his nightstand. "This is ridiculous. It's a wonder these folks don't stroke out arguing with each other. If they knew just how lucky they are to be healthy they wouldn't be so damned angry." I handed it to him and he fumbled with it for a moment or two, his thumb searching for the correct button to turn the set off. "There. Now we can pray in peace."

I opened my bible and read the reading for the day. It was a passage from the Thirty-Fourth Psalm: *This poor man called; the Lord heard him and rescued him in all his distress...the Lord is close to the broken-hearted; those whose spirit is crushed he will save.*

"I'm glad you read that," Henry said after a half a minute, exhaling slowly as if trying to relax. "I've been in terrible pain all morning." Henry's face twitched at the words.

I reached in my shirt pocket for the pix while praying the Lord's Prayer. As I held the host before Henry's outstretched tongue and said the words, "The Body of Christ," he suddenly began to convulse and retch.

I stood in disbelief for a moment as Henry moaned and breathed fast, loud, and hard. I returned the host to the pix not knowing what I could do. Rita's voice came from the kitchen, "Henry!" she dropped some pots and pans and ran in the room to find him shaking violently and vomiting blood.

"Do something, goddammit!" She grabbed me by the arm and shook me. I turned around looking for help; I didn't know what to do. "I told you not to bother him!" she screamed. "Oh, God, dial Nine-One-One, you sonnuvabitch!"

I moved for the phone, but I didn't know where it was. "Where's the phone?"

"Never mind, I'll call. You stay here with him! Don't let him choke!"

I took the end of one of the blankets and wiped Henry's mouth, clearing away some of the regurgitation. Henry's eyes were locked in his head, and his face was contorted in a frightful rigidity. I heard Rita crying into the phone to the police dispatcher. I began praying the Hail Mary aloud.

When Rita came back into the bedroom, tears filled Henry's eyes as his face softened, but a long, rattling wheeze of air exhaled from his lungs, and his chest and torso slowly rose up in an arc on the bed. Then it stopped.

Rita pushed me away from the side of the bed and screamed, "He's dead! You killed him! God damn you, you killed my husband! Had you not come, this would have never happened! God damn you!"

"I'm so sorry, I don't know what happened." I almost threw up.

"Get out of here! Call the ambulance. Do something!" she began pounding on Henry's chest and turning his face from side to side. "Oh, God, I knew something like this would happen!" I wanted to disappear.

I couldn't perform the Sacrament of Anointing, so I began to page through my breviary searching for the twenty-third psalm. A minute later there was a quick knock as the front door opened. The sound of a two-way radio squawked as a policeman entered the bedroom.

"He killed my husband!" She angrily pointed at me.

The police officer looked on suspiciously. "Ma'am, the ambulance is on its way," the officer assured her, looking at Henry and then me.

She then began crying uncontrollably, cursing and swearing that I had caused Henry's death.

"I'm so sorry, Mrs. Gordon," I apologized again, closing the psaltery.

"Just leave me alone," she screamed through her grinding teeth. "He doesn't need you anymore."

Once outside, I explained the entire matter to the policeman. The hospice nurse arrived, and she too explained Henry's illness and the inevitability of death. For weeks, his death had been imminent.

The hospice nurse asked me if I was all right. "Do you need to talk to a counselor?"

"No. I'm fine." I was no stranger to harsh words and outbursts of anger.

* * * *

Rita Gordon blamed me for everything. She told Father Robin. She told Hyacinth. She even called Father Boniface. I even wondered if she'd called the Bishop and Vicar-general. Father Robin advised me not to attend the funeral for fear that Rita might make a scene.

I did not attend.

Father Robin admonished me that a priest must minister not only to the dying but also to their relatives and loved ones.

Chapter 12: Rumblings

I do not seek to understand so as to believe;
I believe in order to understand.
– St. Anselm of Canterbury

The week after Henry Gordon's funeral, Martha Hart stopped me outside church after a Tuesday morning Mass. She was wearing a light green sweat suit. "He's back, Father."

"Martin. I'm a seminarian," I corrected her.

"Oh, that's right."

"*Who's* back?"

"That *man* who hears confessions," she said in a low voice and looking to see if anyone else was listening.

"Who is he?" *Bill*, I thought.

"I don't know, but I got his license plate number."

"You'd best give it to Father Robin."

"I was going to do just that." I reluctantly allowed her to follow me into the rectory. As we entered the kitchen, Father Robin was handing Hyacinth some of his clothes for her to press. Hyacinth set the hot iron on the ironing board in the corner of the kitchen.

"Martin," Robin said, glancing up out of the corner of his eye, "I saw that you got stopped by Mrs. Hart." Robin's face cringed and reddened as he turned around and saw Martha

Hart standing there. "*Well*, good morning, Mrs. Hart. It was good to see you at Mass. How may I help you?"

She handed him a slip of paper. "Here." It appeared that she was wise to his opinion of her.

Robin looked at it and then looked back at Martha. "What's this?"

"It's his license plate number."

"*Whose* license plate number?"

"That man in the green station wagon that has been hearing confessions. He did it again this morning—and I think I smelled liquor on his breath."

"If you knew it was him, then why did you go to confession to him?"

"I don't know. He's so caring" She glanced away from Robin. "Oh, not that you're not—"

"No, Father Robin," Hyacinth spoke up from her ironing, "it's simple: this man hears confessions and you don't."

Robin cleared his throat angrily, ignoring Hyacinth. "Mrs. Hart, why didn't you come get me instead?"

"I don't know. I'm sorry."

"Well, I'll look into this." Robin held up the paper. "Thank you for your concern. But if it happens again, come get me."

"Of course."

At that, Father Boniface came scooting into the kitchen wearing his slippers and robe. His cane thumped the red stone floor.

"Good morning, Monsignor," Martha said.

"Who're you?" Boniface said to Martha as he raised his cane.

"I'm Martha Hart." Her big blonde hair dwarfed her face.

"Oh, yes. By the way, I'm not a monsignor. Never was, never will be. Never mind me. Hyacinth, Dear, how about breakfast?"

"It's ready," Hyacinth announced as she put her apron on over her skirt. "Just have a seat."

Boniface sat at the head of the table as Father Robin saw Martha to the back door.

"Thanks for the information, Mrs. Hart." Robin opened the door. "I'll look into it." He returned, poured himself a cup of coffee, and walked out. "I'll be in my study."

"Martin, get a cup of coffee and join me for breakfast," Boniface said as he blew his nose.

I poured myself a cup and sat next to him.

"At least they haven't given me the boot yet and made me go live in the old farts' home," Boniface laughed as he perused through the morning's press.

"What's wrong with you, Boniface?" Hyacinth was warming his bacon and eggs in the microwave.

"Have you read the paper about that dumbass Bishop Numbnoddle over in Wheatfield? If one of his men was a hopeless alcoholic or a compulsive gambler, he'd been defrocked. If one of them had wanted a woman, he would have been damned before nightfall. If one of them had pilfered the collection basket, he'd be rotting in prison. But if your thing's adolescent boys, well, then, you get the best parish in the diocese.

"Hell, I've been a diocesan prisoner for years. My cell's upstairs. Look, here's my prison uniform," he pointed to his Roman collar through his robe. "I'm wearing prison blacks with just one stripe—right around the collar like some damned chained clerical mutt, strangling me to death. Oh, but there are no conjugal visits in this prison!" He laughed aloud.

Hyacinth seemed to stifle either a laugh or a sniffle as she placed the bacon and eggs in front of Boniface.

"It's okay, Hyacinth." Boniface looked at her. "I'm a bad one you know. And Martin," he turned to me, "if you let Linguini and the bishop know that you and I have these little chats, they'll arrange it with Saint Peter to confine me to Purgatory for half an eternity.

"Good God, son, there's a damned elephant the size of Massachusetts in the middle of the church dropping dung everywhere and no one's got the guts to say anything about it, especially these fair-haired company men we've got for bishops! All they want to do is scoop up the poop, but none of them have thought of removing the damned elephant! Bernardin was the one Cardinal honest about the whole mess and he's dead.

"Well, the chickens are coming home to roost, and quite honestly I don't want to be around when the dung hits the fan. In a way, I hope the whole damned thing comes tumbling to the ground, then maybe we can do church the way Christ wanted it.

"Munchin assigned one of the young guys to be the chaplain of Good Samaritan Hospital and then named him pastor of a parish thirty miles away. What the hell's that all about? It's his first pastorate. Talk about setting the guy up for failure. Look at what Linguini and Sister Dymphna did when they appointed Father Lee to be chaplain over at *Regina Coeli*. And it ain't getting any better, just ask Hyacinth."

"Leave me out of this, old man." She had returned to her ironing.

"Many of us knew that Father Lee didn't want the appointment to *Regina Coeli* for the very reason he's now gone. He knew that woman long before she was married. They were once in love, but old Munchin just had to send him to *Regina Coeli*. It didn't have to happen.

"You know that's why I'm not a monsignor. Bishop

Collins, God rest his soul, sent me here to Inglenook after Vatican II and by damned if he didn't retreat when some of the parishioners began to protest. He told me to turn the altar around and take all the statues out of the church. I'll never forget the day after I had them removed. I was going over to the sacristy for Mass and the sheriff stopped me at the door. He served me with a restraining order. I wasn't allowed to enter my own parish church! Can you imagine?

"You'd think I'd killed a man. The bishop got the judge to lift the order so I could say Mass that weekend, but half the parish didn't show and the other half that did show stared at me like they were praying me into tarnation.

"The other pastors in town told me to watch my back and said there was a posse ready to tar and feather me and run me out of town on a rail. I was as nervous as a long-tailed cat in a houseful of rocking chairs. I called His Highness, but he wouldn't take my calls. A day later, I received a letter, certified mail. It was from the bishop. He was ordering me to return all the statues to the church.

"It turns out that a group of the conservatives in the parish drove down to the Chancery and demanded that I be removed as their pastor. I should have figured as much. They were already gunning for me because of my liberal stance on civil rights and my protest against the Vietnam War. But the statues were his idea. Instead, I got blamed for the whole thing. I was young then. If I had to do it all over again I would—except for the statues. I'd leave them alone. I can laugh now. Imagine, though. They served me with papers."

Hyacinth began laughing out loud at the ironing board.

"What are *you* laughing at?" He dropped his fork and shot her a glance.

"In a world of justice, Boniface," Hyacinth turned toward him, "you'd have been named bishop."

"Oh, but I wouldn't have wanted it." He shook his head.

"I know. That's why you would have made a good one. In a world filled with good men, your gifts would have been recognized long ago."

"Thank you, Dear Heart, but you're not the one who gives out the magenta."

"You're right," Hyacinth retorted. "Linguini and Munchin would never have received it. What pathetic excuses for clerics—"

"Now, old Father Huffman—*Monsignor* Huffman. He got the magenta. I didn't. I made too much trouble. I embarrassed His Highness, you see. He said I embarrassed the church. My personal file was probably stamped: Damaged Goods."

"Why'd you ever stay in?" I asked, thinking about my own prospective priesthood.

"Because I believed I had the call and I believed in what I was doing. I hope you do. I could have gotten out. The Klan would have loved it. The Black Panthers would have loved it. Linguini would have loved it had he been around back then. Living the beatitudes is a delicate balancing act on the tightrope of moderation.

"It's just a miracle I got to stay here for so long. It's insane how they move the younger guys every five or ten years. They tell us priests we're supposed to create community. Well guess what? By the time a guy just starts to get things going and figures the parish out, the pointed hat comes along and wraps his crook around the guy's neck and yanks him up out of the parish and sends him to another one with the same orders to build community. No wonder many of the guys burn out after their third move. Some don't even make it to a third.

"Believe me, I'm too old to move now, but if he'd moved me ten years ago, it would have been my death sentence.

These wacky bishops don't have any idea what they're doing to their men.

"A lot of the bishops and priests are threatened by the laity because the laity is smarter than they are. They're threatened by women; threatened by good priests who minister well; threatened by the good priests who can't take it anymore and leave the active ministry; and then lastly, many priests are threatened by each other. If the rare priest comes along who dares raise a prophetic voice against the status quo, his brother priests will avoid him like a leper and his bishop will either muzzle him or send him off to Bucktooth Nowhere, or both."

Hyacinth took the coffee pot from its burner and walked over to the table to refill our cups.

"You can't go to some priests because they can't handle human emotion. They work at keeping themselves safe and distant. One pastor of mine, when I was a young associate, bragged that he could make all his communion calls to the sick at two hospitals and three nursing homes, and still make his usual rounds to the shut-ins of the parish all in one morning. He'd be back to the rectory well before lunch was ready. I went with him once. Boy, were those meaningful visits. God forbid anyone wanted to confess or spill their guts. The guy would go in, swish his hand in the air, make the sign of the cross, never look anyone in the eye, mind you, place the communion on the person's tongue, and be out the door before the person had even swallowed the host. Now that's pastoral. No messy human heartaches to deal with, just a clean spiritual visit which nourished no one. Of course, this is the same priest whose Sunday Mass lasted eighteen minutes. If that's all we have to do, we might as well have churches with drive-through windows. 'Yes, I'd like a Jesus host to go, and I'll have Precious Blood with that. Oh, and are you still giving out those glow-in-the-dark Mary night lights?'

"They always taught us that celibacy was to keep you free for others. Hell, who're we kidding? Many of the guys who are such big fans of celibacy are the ones who want to be free of any responsibility. I hope you're not one of them, Martin."

I drank some of my coffee and nodded.

"Oh, the priestly fraternity is tight. A real boys' club. I'd say men's club, but that would involve maturity, wouldn't it? Many of them are still boys. They've never grown up, still stuck in adolescence. They'll flirt with the girls. Maybe even go to bed with one, but they don't want anything to do with commitment. Sure, celibacy is easy for them. It's clerical distancing, they maintain. Bull—it's immaturity." Boniface sipped his coffee.

His words hit close to home. I thought of Sherry, my girlfriend in college.

"Look at what happened over in Wheatfield. Numbnoddle should resign over his shenanigans. Imagine playing the damned shell game with a pedophile priest. He might as well have played Russian roulette. I can guarantee that if the priest hadn't been a priest and had been a lay teacher in the school, he would have been drawn and quartered, his head would have rolled, and the winds of hell would still be howling. But because he was a priest, the bishop got his lawyers to placate the boys' families. Now that it's blown up in his face, the media is going to devour every priest, you watch. If you know a man's got a problem with boys, you don't move him from a graying parish to a parish with an all-boys' school!

"I have yet to hear Numbnoddle say he's sorry over the whole thing. Neither has the priest, for that matter. I'm afraid the only remorse they both might have is that they got caught."

"Father Boniface," Hyacinth interrupted him, "Am I going

to have to warm up those eggs again? Just eat. You're scaring the vocation out of the young man."

"No, no I'm not, Hyacinth. It's good to hear things from all sides. Saint Benedict taught that nothing burdensome was to be concealed from the novice." Boniface took another sip of coffee, paused, and glanced out the window before speaking again. "As far as the priests and their opinions on celibacy, neither the straights nor the gays want optional celibacy because they're all about self-preservation. Nah, whether it's the boys'—or *the girls'*—clubs, both are threatened by the presence of women, but for different reasons, you see. You ever notice that all the men who leave the active ministry and get married go for strong women? The other guys can't handle a strong woman.

"If you have a wedding Mass down at the lake, you'll get spanked for it. If you have a thousand people come for confession and you're the only priest and you grant them general absolution, you'll be beaten severely.

"Old Bill Gallagher, God love him, what a sweet man. When he was here, he'd be in that confessional for hours on end. Then he'd have the charismatic Masses. That was until Linguini made him stop. 'Too Protestant,' Linguini said. Well, it drove Bill to drink. He left for a wife. I can't blame him. She was a wonderful woman. But she died of cancer a few years back. Bill asked the bishop if he could come back to the active ministry, but he wouldn't let him. He was one of the diocese's best priests. They might as well have put a bullet through his head. Bill was born to be a priest. It's just that Bill also felt called to marriage. I wonder where he is these days."

"Bill?" I unintentionally said aloud.

"Yes. Bill Gallagher. Do you know him?" He looked intently at me and put both his hands around his mug.

"No, but I think I've heard of him."

Boniface paused before continuing. "Then there's that young priest, Father Todd something, he was just ordained and sent to Cainbrook. There's a story going around how he had a fling with one of the waitresses at the Pancake Place before he was ordained. So what? Even if he did, it's over. People won't let it die. Poor guy. He had a moment, you know. He's a man.

"No, there's no vocation shortage. If only the pope would just let all the priests who left to get married come back— why we've got two such men in our parish. They're leaders, but I can't let them do anything because they got married. Tainted love.

"Oh, I used to know, or think I knew, who the hell I was, but now I'm not so sure. I'm not so sure of anything anymore. One of the nuns here last year got mad at me during Mass because I called myself the priest. She said I was the president. I thanked her for telling me who the hell I was. Last year an upstart of a theologian told us priests on our annual retreat that we may soon come to be called *Sacramental Dispensers*. What the hell? Do I look like a vending machine or a stupid PEZ dispenser? This was the same guy who said we needed to start calling ourselves an *Icon—Facilitator— Gatherer*. How about just *priest*? What will I be called next year?"

"*Obsolete*," Hyacinth's reply came from across the kitchen.

"Oh, Hyacinth, what on earth are you ironing over there?"

"Father Robin's handkerchiefs."

"What? Why, the nerve of that guy."

"No, it's okay. I put extra starch in his underwear. Now, hurry up and eat your eggs before they get cold." She moved for the coffee pot, taking it in hand and turning around. "Here, have a warm-up on that coffee."

"He's going to try and get you moved out of here, I hope you know," Boniface warned.

"Let him try." Hyacinth leaned over Boniface.

"Ah, there's *The General* we all know and love."

I for my part was still curious about the priest named Bill Gallagher and kept my eye out for an older model green car with Illinois tag, seven—two—one—something. That's all I could remember from the piece of paper that Martha Hart had handed Father Robin.

Chapter 13: Memories Remain

Cupid is a knavish lad,
Thus to make poor females mad.
— *A Midsummer Night's Dream*, III, ii, 440

Later that week Father Robin invited me to the Red Lantern Inn where we joined the Blackstones for dinner again. The conversation revolved around the sudden news that a priest from another diocese would be joining the pastoral staff at Poor Souls.

"He's Father Kevin Murphy from the diocese of Wheatfield."

"He sounds like an F.B.I." Mrs. Blackstone wore a bright red, low-cut dress and pearl necklace.

"F.B.I.?" I looked at both Mrs. Blackstone and Father Robin.

"*Foreign-Born Irish*." Robin smiled.

"Is he?" I asked.

"No, he's American." Robin grinned. "But you never know."

"Why is he being sent to Inglenook?" Mrs. Blackstone asked.

"I don't know," Robin answered. "I asked Linguini the same thing, but he told me it was confidential."

"Oh, great. Numbnoddle's peddling his trouble on us now," Greg Blackstone huffed, straightening his red silk tie, and rearranging the cloth napkin on his lap. "I hope the guy hasn't got a thing for altar boys."

"Greg," Mrs. Blackstone bristled as she fingered the pearls about her neck.

"Oh, don't think that it hasn't crossed my mind." Robin sighed, taking a drink of his red wine. "And every parishioner is going to be suspicious why a priest from another diocese— especially Numbnoddle's Wheatfield—has been sent here."

I closed my eyes and thought of leaving the table for the restroom, tired of all the talk of priestly infidelity.

"Do you know this Wheatfield priest, Father Robin?" Greg drank from his beer mug.

"No, I don't. I've asked a couple of the other guys and they don't know him either."

"Well, the best thing would be for this Father Monaghan—"

"*Murphy*. Kevin Murphy," Robin said, returning the wine glass to the table.

"Well, he'd best come clean right from the start and tell the parish why he's been sent here." Greg ran his fingers along the top of the icy mug. "If he doesn't, the secrecy will only fuel the fires of suspicion."

"Oh, but Greg, that's how the bishops like it." Robin smiled sarcastically. "It gives them the upper hand. It's all about power."

"Yes, well, there are those in love with power in the corporate world as well." Greg sighed. "Let me tell you."

"When does this Father Murphy arrive?" I asked. "Maybe he's a good priest."

"Maybe. He's scheduled to move in over the Fourth of July weekend." Robin pointed at me. "And I'm going to assign him to you, Martin."

"Me?" I knew I should have feigned an illness and gone to the restroom.

"Why, yes. You can show him the ropes."

How could I do that? I wasn't even a priest.

"Don't worry," Robin said, observing the look on my face.

"Father Robin," Greg interrupted, holding his beer mug aloft. "Are you sure there is enough room for another priest at Poor Souls? There's Father Boniface, you, and Martin—"

"Don't forget *the General*." Robin rolled his eyes. "Once upon a time there were five priests assigned to Poor Souls at one time. Besides the priests' bedrooms upstairs, *the General* lives in the housekeeper's apartment above the kitchen. There's plenty of room. I've even thought of having all the priests in the Inglenook deanery live in community at Poor Souls rectory."

"How would that work?" Greg asked as he returned his beer to the table.

"I don't know," Robin stared at his wine glass, "but with fewer and fewer priests, it's a lonely life. Maybe community living would help rebuild the morale of our clergy."

"Do you think Linguini would approve of such an arrangement?" asked Greg.

"You've got to be kidding. He's part of the morale problem," Robin said.

The waitress returned to the table and Robin ordered another glass of wine for himself. I ordered a red crème soda.

The rest of the conversation dealt with other interests. The Blackstone's were flying to New York the next day to attend an opera at the Met. They invited me, but I couldn't accept. They invited me on their next trip and also offered me tickets to a Yankees' game in July.

Meanwhile, Father Robin put back one glass of wine after another.

* * * *

After dinner, Father Robin and I left the restaurant and walked to the car. As Robin drove off the parking lot, he began tuning the radio dial. He turned to a rock and roll station playing the Doobie Brothers' song, *Jesus is Just Alright*. Robin turned the volume up and sang along.

It was a side of Robin that I hadn't experienced before. As Robin drove, he made a turn in the opposite direction from the rectory and church. John Mellencamp's song, *Pink Houses* came on the radio. Robin turned the volume down and turned to me. "Martin, have you ever been in love?"

"Yes." I was thinking of Sherry, my girlfriend in college.

"Was it serious?" Robin asked.

"Sort of. We dated through college. On our first date, we went to see *Carousel*. She liked me and all, and I liked her, but we broke up senior year." I didn't tell him everything about our relationship, especially that Sherry and I had slept together.

"*Carousel*? Then you remember: *If I loved you...*" Robin began singing it.

"I liked it better on stage."

After a moment of chuckling, Robin became serious. "Did you love her?" he asked.

"Yes."

"Do you ever think of her?"

"I am now." I recalled the night Sherry and I made love. I thought we loved each other, but our night of lovemaking ended everything between us. We had been dating on and off through college. We had never slept together and the night we did, we didn't sleep.

Our date night started off at Saturday evening Mass. I met

her at the church closest to the campus and afterwards she offered to drive to a restaurant for dinner. A few hours after drinks, we were dancing. By midnight, we were back at her apartment where I spent the night. The next morning we were both sober and things seemed different. I felt empty inside. Maybe it was the hangover.

Sherry didn't say much except that she was hungry and wanted to step out for breakfast. She drove us to a small, family style, hole-in-the-wall restaurant where we ate breakfast. We hardly spoke and she barely looked me in the eye. It was awkward. Afterwards she dropped me off at my car, which was still parked at the church from the night before. When I stepped out of her car, ringing church bells greeted me. I had forgotten it was Sunday morning. We kissed goodbye. I tried to act like everything was all right, but we both knew it wasn't. I told her I'd call her. She drove away, and I watched her until her car was out of sight.

As I unlocked my car, families walked past me heading to church. A long triangular shadow of the steeple cast across the street; the shadow of the cross covered my car. I looked up and the eastern sun was eclipsed by the cross-tiered steeple—the silhouette of the cross against a bright blue sky. For a moment, I interpreted the shadow as a sign from God and thought about going to confession. The thought passed and I opened the driver's door, started the car, and drove away.

I never called. Sherry tried to reach me, but I didn't return her calls. It wasn't too long after that my roommate told me Sherry was dating someone else. About a month or so later, my friend questioned me about my passion and promptly puked on the floor of the pub.

My memory of Sherry's last kiss faded into an approaching stop sign. Father Robin slowed the car to a stop at the intersection. Billy Joel's *Uptown Girl* was on.

"Intimacy's a scary thing," Robin said with a soft smile as if reading my thoughts.

"Do you ever get lonely?" I asked, taken off guard.

"I don't have time to get lonely." He sniggered. "Hell, I don't even have time to pray. I used to be a pastor. Now I'm an indentured business manager." Robin paused at the stop sign, tarrying longer than necessary before going on. "I, too, was once in love. Nancy was her name. Nancy Higgins. She was a beautiful woman. She was one of my sister's best friends from college. She wanted to get married. I did, too, but I also felt called to the priesthood. I'll never forget the day I first told her. I took her to a coffee house and told her I had decided to become a priest. I didn't actually say that. I simply told her I was entering the seminary, but to her it was all the same. It was like that scene in *The Cardinal* at the café."

"*The Cardinal?*"

"It's a movie about an American priest who becomes a Cardinal. As a young priest in Europe, he takes a leave of absence for a year and in the process, he falls in love with a woman, but he decides to remain a priest. Later he sees the woman at the same café where they had gone after they first met. When she notices him, he's wearing his Roman collar, and she runs away in tears. The movie's based on the novel. I can't recall the name of the author.

"When I told Nancy that I was thinking of priesthood, she looked at me across that table as if I had died. She never wrote me once while I was in the seminary.

"The next time I saw her was at my ordination. When she came through the receiving line afterwards, she knelt for my blessing and upon rising, she whispered to me that she should have worn black. Then she kissed me one last time. I haven't seen her since.

"I told God that this better be good—the priesthood and

all. I still think of her. Last week my sister called and told me that Nancy and her husband are getting a divorce."

Through the windshield, I saw the twin spires of *Poor Souls* coming into view. *Send Her My Love* by Journey was now playing on the radio. Robin sang along in a wine-induced karaoke rendition. "*I still recall a sad café…*

The song ended just as he drove the car into the driveway. Had it not been so comical it might have been poignant.

"Well, here we are." Robin reached for the garage door opener and maneuvered the car inside.

We made our way into the kitchen from the garage, and Robin poured both of us a glass of water from the refrigerator. Handing me the glass he said, "Oh, I almost forgot to tell you. I saw Bill Gallagher today. *Father* Bill, I should say. He's the guy who's been hearing confessions, but for God's sake, don't tell *the General*. Bill was one of the associates nearly twenty years ago under Boniface.

"While Bill was here, he went on a leave of absence. He fell in love with Sister Cunegunda. She was one of the nuns over at All Hallows. When they announced that they were going to get married, the bishop got wind of it and suspended Bill from the priesthood. After Bill got married, Linguini had Munchin excommunicate him.

"Cunegunda died of cancer a few years back and Bill's been trying to reenter the active ministry, but the bishop won't let him because he—as Linguini phrases it—*contracted marriage*. Bill isn't working, and I'm afraid he's back on the bottle. Cunegunda was so good for him. He gave up the juice when she came into his life. So, if and when he should come around, we'll be offering him hospitality. He's looking for a place to stay."

"Sure." I nodded, eager to meet the ever-elusive Bill. "*Shelter the homeless*, I believe is the command."

"Very good, Martin. You're all right," Robin said as he poured the rest of his water in the sink and opened the liquor cabinet and poured himself a glass of whiskey. He walked out of the kitchen and down the hall to his study. "Good night, Martin."

"Good night, Father Robin." I retired upstairs for the evening, taking the glass of water to my room.

I recalled the words of Mabel Marsh from that week's visit. "The only unforgivable sin is blasphemy against the Holy Spirit. And can you believe that these men who run our church say that the Holy Spirit can only call unmarried men to the priesthood? Who are they to tell God that he can't call married men or women to the priesthood? I've also been reading the New Testament. Did you know that there were female deacons—deaconesses—in the early church? But the bishops tell us that only unmarried men may be ordained. In my old age, I've had time to read some theology. Can you tell?"

I shook my head in bemusement as I got into bed, turned the bedside lamp off, and covered myself in the sheets and comforter.

The solution to the priest shortage seemed relatively simple to the faithful.

Chapter 14: Parish Life

Nothing is small in the eyes of God.
Do all that you do with love.
— St. Thérèse of Lisieux

Poor Souls was a graying parish. During the first month at Poor Souls, I had gleaned a lot about the downtown parish. It was no longer made up of first, second, and third generation Irish, German, and Italian immigrant families. Like many of its counterparts throughout America, the nature of the Catholic neighborhood, ghettos in places, was quickly disappearing. Many of the parishioners had moved out of the parish boundary and had built new homes in the suburbs. A portion of the traditional industries had closed and, though some people still claimed Poor Souls as their parish church, many had moved on to greener pastures, figuratively and literally. The median age of a Poor Souls' parishioner was fifty, and the younger members were not only drifting away geographically, but spiritually as well. The devotion and faith of the previous generations were gone.

Many of the teenagers were no longer coming to Mass. Instead, they opted for the more contemporary services of the non-denominational churches, which were seemingly springing up everywhere. "The music and preaching are better,"

Boniface admitted. "It's like they're going for dinner and a show. The truth is that many Catholics don't feel fed or nourished by their pastors."

I had only heard gunshots in the neighborhood once since I had moved into the rectory. Boniface assured me it was nothing out of the ordinary, just a drive-by shooting or a drug deal gone sour. "Pray for them," he said. "Say an Our Father and a Hail Mary when you hear gunfire. Leave the rest to God. If it's real close stop, drop, and take cover."

A lot of the children were growing up in broken homes. "It's different from when I first came here thirty years ago," Boniface told me. "Back then the children came from traditional two-parent homes—a mother and a father—and the family all came to church together, week in and week out. Nowadays, I'd bet nearly half the kids have experienced a divorce in their immediate families, and I'm lucky to have sixty percent of the parish attend weekly Mass. Over a third of the parish only comes to Mass at Christmas and Easter. It's a serious issue that the bishops haven't even begun to address."

These were some of my reasons for wanting to become a priest. I wanted to change things. I wanted to love people so they could love God.

Chapter 15: Red Crème Sodi

The Lord desires so much to be with us
that in receiving Him in the Eucharist
we become members of His body, and
with all sweetness He pours Himself out.
— St. Albert the Great

Next Monday, after Mass and breakfast, I asked Hyacinth, "Who's in Bill Gallagher's old room?"

"You are," she said as she glanced out the kitchen window. "Poor Bill. I hear he's back on the bottle again. Sister Cunegunda—I mean Jacquelyn, I never could get used to her not being a nun—she got him off the juice, you know. Behind every good man stands a woman."

She turned from the breakfast dishes and stared at me as I sipped the last of my coffee. "What?"

"Oh, nothing." Her face was sad. "It's terrible the way the diocese treated him, especially after Cunegunda died. Don't get me wrong; I was sad when Bill left. We were doubly surprised when we heard that Cunegunda was leaving her religious community. It wasn't too long before folks put things together."

I got up to pour myself another cup of coffee. Outside the window, a blue jay was perched on the bird feeder.

"Martin," Hyacinth said as she wrung out the washcloth over the sink.

"Yes," I said as I returned the pot to its burner.

"I hope you think things through long and hard before you get in too deep." The wrinkles in her peachy face became pronounced in the light from the window.

"Too deep?" I asked, though I knew what she was trying to say.

"Must I explain everything for you? I meant before you get too deep into the priesthood. Just promise me you'll think things through before you make that final commitment."

"I plan on it, Hyacinth. In my short time here I've been given a lot to think about."

"No. Promise me. I don't want you to turn out, well, you know, like *that one*."

"Now, come on, Hyacinth, Father Robin isn't all that bad—"

"You're right. He's worse. A real robber baron. Imagine tearing out all of Saint Patrick's beautiful pews." She stopped drying the mug she had in hand and looked out the window at a pair of cardinals perched on a limb.

"They were happy, they say." Hyacinth sighed, returning to the subject of Bill Gallagher and Sister Cunegunda. "Folks around here said that their getting married meant they were excommunicated and all. My sister over in Wheatfield said that Cunegunda went to Mass every Sunday at Saint Peter's Church.

"When Sister Cunegunda, I mean Jacquelyn, came down with the cancer and all, some of the people here said it was a punishment from God for her breaking her vows and marrying a priest. They also said Bill's relapse into booze was his punishment. But he was always an alcoholic. Sister Cunegunda kept him dry. Boniface thinks that if the bishop had allowed him to return to the ministry after Cunegunda died, Bill would have stayed off the liquor. He'd never been so happy. She changed him. Even after she was gone, Bill was a different man...." Hyacinth's voice trailed off as she resumed her dishwashing only to turn around again. "Just promise me one thing, young man," she said, angrily pointing a dish scrubber at me, "if you fall in love with a woman before you're a priest, don't lead her on. Either marry her or break things off right then and there. And if, God forbid, you fall in love with a woman after you've become a priest, well...well...I don't know what to tell you." Her eyes glistened as she turned away to dry another mug.

I nodded in agreement with the feeling that Hyacinth was speaking from personal experience. And I could think of only one priest: Boniface.

Hyacinth opened one of the cabinets to put away the dry mugs. I saw her from behind the cabinet door wiping her eyes with the towel.

Just then, Boniface walked in and looked at her. "Good God, woman, what the hell did *that one* do to you now?"

"Nothing." She shut the cabinet door and wiped the sink with the towel. "Your breakfast was ready twenty minutes ago." She leaned over the sink and spoke.

"I got stopped by that woman, Martha...what's her name?"

"Martha Hart?" I answered.

"That's it! Then I had to plunge the damned toilet again," Boniface huffed and tapped the end of his cane on the red flagstone floor. "I can't understand it. It was working fine until Father Robin came here."

"Well, there you are; that explains it." Hyacinth turned. "He's full of you know what. I'm telling you, he's still flushing his sermons down that toilet."

"No, no, that can't be it. He never writes out anything. He just preaches from his heart."

"You mean his backside."

"Hyacinth!"

"Boniface!" She opened the cabinet above the sink and pulled down a mug. "I only say what you think."

"Well, yes, but not in front of the boy."

I worked to keep a straight face.

"He'll be all right," she said, pouring coffee into the mug. "Here's your coffee." She turned and handed Boniface the mug and went to the stove. "Now, how about some scrambled eggs and ham?"

Hyacinth served him while he continued talking between bites. "I've got to make a few phone calls. This Martha woman tells me some folks are real upset about Father Lax's Mass last night." Boniface turned to me. "Were you there, Martin?"

"No. I went Sunday morning at eight and left with the youth group afterwards. We went to the State Park for a hike and a swim in the lake. When I got back about four o'clock, I was so exhausted that I fell asleep and didn't wake up until seven. How do parents do it?"

"Ah, the joys of celibacy." Boniface took a sip of coffee and glanced up at Hyacinth. She looked at him but said nothing as she moved toward the stove.

"Father Robin is attending a funeral in St. Louis and that young priest, Father Lax—" Boniface started to explain.

"Ex-Lax." Hyacinth cackled at the stove, looking out the window at the pair of cardinals swaying on the limb.

"Yes," Boniface said, "*Father Francis Xavier Lax*. Robin got Lax to cover last night's five o'clock Mass. It seems he couldn't find the altar wine, so he used red crème sodi instead." Boniface dropped his knife and fork, spread his hands on the edges of his placemat, and reached for my left hand.

"Now, Martin, my boy, how hard is it to figure out where we keep the altar wine?"

"I have no idea. The cabinet is clearly labeled *Altar Wine*."

"Precisely. And even if you didn't have wine, why the hell would a guy use bright red crème sodi. Crime in Italy, if you're in a real pinch, use a little bit of grape juice or apple juice and no one will be the wiser. But red crème sodi? And for God's sake, don't offer the chalice to the entire congregation. Martha told me he filled four chalices with the stuff. Who would be dumb enough to consecrate red crème sodi?" Boniface coughed out a sigh. "And that guy's your vocation director?" He stared hard at me.

"He's one of the *assistant* vocation directors. Father Good is the director."

"Oh, yes. Father Samuel smells good, doesn't he?" Boniface laughed so hard he wheezed and triggered a coughing spell. His face grew redder and redder with each cough as he covered his mouth and hunched over his cane.

"Are you all right, Boniface?" Hyacinth tossed her spatula on the countertop and hurried to him.

"Yeah, yeah." He coughed. "I'll be fine, but if I cough up a lung..." he coughed again, "...do call the bishop..." he wheezed and coughed, "...of course, *after* you've called the ambulance."

"Stop that."

"Red crème sodi." Boniface laughed and coughed with tears in his eyes. "*Jesus wept.*"

I knew I shouldn't laugh, but I couldn't help it.

Chapter 16: Bubby and the Birds

*"Many souls desire to fly before God gives
them wings. Patience gains all things."*
— St. Teresa of Avila

Later that afternoon, while I was reading my breviary in the downstairs sitting room, I heard Hyacinth call out. "He's here!"

"Who?" I got up and went downstairs to the kitchen.

"Father Kevin Murphy. Go help him move in."

"Sure." I moved toward the front door.

When I opened the door, I saw a rusty yellow Volkswagen van parked up on the curb in front of the rectory. All of its doors were open. A small–framed, black-haired man wearing a priestly collar emerged from the back of the van. I went out and met him on the front sidewalk. He was carrying a draped birdcage, and a small, white Maltese dog followed him, nipping and yipping at his heels.

"May I help you?" I asked, observing the amount of junk in the van.

"Oh, thanks. Here." He handed me the birdcage and shut the van's back door. "Careful, they're asleep." I took the cage in my left hand and extended my right hand. "I'm Martin Flanagan. I'm the seminarian here at the parish."

He snatched a New York Mets cap from the passenger seat of the van and put it on his head. "Father Murphy," he said as he shook my hand with a firm grip. "Father Kevin Murphy." He reached inside the side of the van for two scuffed brown suitcases and pushed the doors shut with his right foot.

I led him up the sidewalk to the rectory steps.

"I haven't met Father Wood yet." He followed me through the front door and up the front stairwell.

"Today is his day off," I explained. "He should be back late tonight or early tomorrow."

The dog began nipping at my ankles, its teeth clicking together as it snipped at me; it had a noticeably exaggerated underbite with jagged teeth protruding from its lower jaw.

"Bubby's so sweet. She just wants to play." Kevin gently kicked at the dog. "Bubby! Bubby! Come here to Papa Murph!" The dog's toenails were painted a gaudy bright red.

"Oh, that's okay. I grew up around cats."

"Cats?" He laughed. "Don't put cats in the same category with dogs. I learned to shoot a gun by killing cats." Father Kevin informed me of his sport with such ease. "Of course, we only shot strays." Kevin chuckled, evidently noticing my shock.

"Oh." What else could I say? Just as I led Kevin through the upstairs hall to the guestroom, I saw Cat skitter out of his room and thump down the back stairwell. "This will be your room, Father."

"Thanks, Marvin—"

"*Martin*. Martin Flanagan."

"Martin."

"Father Robin cleared out one of the downstairs offices for you." I directed him to the office next to Boniface's.

Kevin made several trips to his van and carried in clothes,

boxes of books, a net full of soccer balls, a pair of shin guards, and several full-length garment bags full of liturgical vestments. When Kevin brought the final box of books to his new office, he came out in the hall with an odd look on his face. "What is that smell?"

I looked at the downstairs restroom. "It might be the toilet. The drain clogs and overflows now and then."

"Oh, does it now? Well, that will have to be remedied." He stopped and inhaled, smelling the air again. "It's not sewer gas. Worse. What I smell is cat."

"It *is* cat. The housekeeper has one."

"I didn't know. She shouldn't have." He then turned, made his way up the stairs, and retired to his bedroom without another word. He had evidently not seen Cat while we were upstairs.

Father Kevin's dog, Bubby—if that was the dog's name and not simply a term of endearment—made a lot of noise scratching on his bedroom door.

I returned to the kitchen where Hyacinth stood at the ironing board pressing Robin's handkerchiefs. "Well? What's wrong with him?"

"He has a dog and some birds," I explained.

"Why'd Numbnoddle dump him on Munchin?" Hyacinth asked. "And why'd Munchin put him *here*?" She kept ironing throughout the exchange. "There's got to be a story."

"I don't know. I didn't ask him. He just got here." I was uncomfortable with her asking the questions with Father Murphy upstairs.

"When Boniface gets back we'll find out." Hyacinth lifted one of the pressed handkerchiefs and folded it.

"Where is Boniface?" I asked.

"Monsignor Kelly came by and took him downtown to the Knights of Columbus for martinis and poker with a couple of their old cronies." She straightened up and looked at me. "This new priest best keep his dog and birds away from me and Cat. We're not running a zoo here, Martin. Does *that one* know this priest-on-loan has pets?"

"I have no idea."

"I knew you were going to say that." She sighed as she folded one of the handkerchiefs. "Just know that I can't be responsible for birds that become catnip."

Through the kitchen window, I saw a police car in the driveway. "Hyacinth," I pointed. "Look." The police officer was standing at the back door and pressed the buzzer. Hyacinth turned her iron off and walked to the window. "What now?"

The police officer looked in the rectory door window and knocked.

Hyacinth answered the door while I stood off to the side. "Good afternoon, officer," she said. "May I help you?"

"Perhaps. Do you know whose van is parked out in front of the house here? It's parked illegally on the yellow curb, too close to the hydrant, you see, and the vehicle has expired tags."

"It belongs to Father Murphy." I stepped forward. "He's from Wheatfield."

"Aren't we in the Diocese of Covert?" The cop tilted his head and looked at us out of the right corners of his eyes.

"Yes, but his bishop has sent him here for a while."

"*Wheatfield.*" The officer squinted at me and rubbed his mustache with the fingers of his right hand as if conjecturing. "Is *Father* Murphy here?"

"Yes, he's upstairs."

"Could you please send him down?"

"Right away, officer." I disappeared up the back stairwell and knocked on Kevin's door. Bubby began barking wildly.

"Father Kevin? Are you awake?"

"Yes." The dog was now jumping up and down, its toenails clacking loudly against the door. Kevin opened the door as if roused from slumber, his hair disheveled and the white plastic tab collar missing from his black clerical shirt.

"Father Kevin, a policeman's downstairs in the kitchen and would like a word with you about your van."

He seemed unaffected by the information. "Tell him I'll be down in a moment."

I returned to the kitchen and nodded to the policeman. "He's coming down." Hyacinth caught my eyes with hers, raised her eyebrows, and puckered her lips. Bubby came clacking down the back stairs. The policeman shook his head at the red nailed dog. Suddenly Father Kevin was standing in the doorway of the kitchen.

"Father Murphy?" The officer looked up.

"Yes."

"Reverend, I need to have a word with you."

"Sure. Let's go to my office." Kevin pointed down the hall.

"If you'll excuse us," the policeman said as he turned to follow Father Kevin.

"I just arrived here this afternoon…" The rest of Kevin's words were lost to the hallway as Bubby bounced along after him.

"Okay, not only is he in trouble with his bishop," Hyacinth said, returning to her work, "but he's in trouble with the law."

A few minutes passed before Kevin led the officer outside to his van. We nosily went to the sitting room and peered out the front windows, observing the officer examining Father Murphy's vehicle. The two talked at length. As the two continued speaking, Monsignor Kelly and Father Boniface drove up.

"Oh, God." Hyacinth sighed as she stared out. "Monsignor Kelly's probably had half a dozen martinis, and Boniface probably kept right up with him." Hyacinth doubled her fists in worry, and I observed her fingernails pressing into her palms as she rubbed her knuckles against her upper teeth. "Hurry, hurry," she spoke softly as she watched Boniface lumber out of Monsignor's oversized, red, 1960s Fleetwood Cadillac with winged taillights. He staggered out of the car and wielded his cane like an errant sword as he maneuvered to the sidewalk.

The policeman turned from Kevin and stared at Boniface. Then he glared at the old Monsignor behind the wheel of the luxury automobile. As soon as Boniface was in the clear, Monsignor Kelly gave a wave, pushed on the gas, and jerked the car away from the curb. The policeman shook his head as if pitying the priests.

Meanwhile Boniface negotiated the stairs and stepped into the rectory singing, "*I'll take you home again, Kathleen—*"

"Get in the house, old man," Hyacinth sternly said as she opened the door. "You're drunk."

"No, I'm not. What do the police want?"

"They have a warrant for Father Robin's arrest. He's been charged with destruction of church property. I hope they lock him up and throw away the key."

"What?" His eyes were wide open. "Are you serious?"

"Unfortunately not. It's that Wheatfield priest, Father Murphy," Hyacinth answered as she closed the door behind him. "Father Murphy parked his van in front of a hydrant and he has expired tags. You're just lucky that cop didn't arrest Monsignor Kelly for drunken driving and you for public drunkenness."

Chapter 17: Immaculate Dung

"Do not let your left hand know
what your right hand is doing."
— Matthew 6.3

On Tuesday morning, I was in the living room reading when Fathers Boniface and Robin came out of the secretary's office. The French doors were halfway open, and I found myself eavesdropping on their conversation as I visually examined the frayed, cat-clawed, yellowing sheer curtains that hung on the windows of the double doors.

"That's what I said. Red crème sodi." Boniface slowly enunciated each of the syllables in the words *red crème sodi*.

"Red crème soda?" Robin repeated Boniface's words before laughing. "Doesn't he know that won't work?"

"Jesus, Mary, and Joseph, how should I know? If he's a priest, then certainly he learned in the seminary that he is only to consecrate wine."

"What are you talking about?" Father Kevin came into view on the stairs, bouncing a soccer ball in his hands. He was fully dressed in his priestly garb, except for shoes. His black and white argyle socks stood out.

"A bit preppy, aren't we?" Robin smiled as he and Boniface stopped at the foot of the stairs.

"I'm on my way to the university. I'm helping coach their soccer team."

"Oh," Robin replied as the three priests stood upon the foyer's black and white marble.

"An alcoholic priest is allowed to use grape juice during Mass. With his bishop's permission, of course," Kevin said knowingly, as if trying to engage them in conversation about the talk of red crème soda.

"Yes, yes, that's right," Boniface nodded. "Bishop Collins tried to get Huffy off the liquor once and had him use grape juice in his chalice. He did. Once."

"Say, Father Kevin, you received a package this morning from the Bureau of Motor Vehicles," said Robin. "I put it on your desk with another letter."

"Good. It's probably my new tags."

"And you can park your van in our driveway or in the school parking lot. I noticed you parked down at the corner. You might block the view of the intersection."

"I'll move it," Kevin said, studying the soccer ball.

"Soccer, you say?" Boniface twirled his cane in his hand.

"Yes. I've always played," Kevin replied, again bouncing the ball in his hand.

"I thought the Irish played Gaelic football," Boniface said.

"Some still do," he replied, twirling the ball on his right index finger, "but the rules vary."

"I didn't think there were rules in Gaelic football," Boniface chuckled.

Just then, Bubby came yipping down the stairs with Cat hissing at her heels. Bubby's red toenails tapped upon the marble as she lost her footing and slid into the front door. Cat, with his back and tail arched upwards, cornered Bubby for a moment against the front hall radiator before they both skidded away into the kitchen. Cat mewed loudly and Bubby yipped. Hyacinth's voice was loud. "I ought to put anti-freeze in your water bowl, you ugly mutt."

"Father Kevin," Robin interrupted with a stifled laugh. "Did I know you were bringing pets?"

"Bishop Numbnoddle didn't tell you in his letter?" Kevin held the ball still.

"I received no letter from your bishop. Our vicar-general merely informed me to expect your arrival."

"Is there a problem with my pets?" Just then, one of the birds flew down the stairwell from the second floor.

"I'm leaving." Boniface ducked and grabbed his cane as he made for the hallway toilet.

"Well," Robin continued speaking. "I'm allergic to birds. You cannot allow those canaries of yours to fly around the house."

"They're not canaries—they're cockatiels. Australian parrots," Kevin said like a schoolmarm teaching a pupil. "I must have left my bedroom door open."

"Well, the dander from their Australian feathers is messing with my American allergies. Today I found bird droppings on the banister."

"It's not my fault Cosmas has learned how to open his cage door."

"Don't say I didn't warn you," Robin said. "Look at the way Cat is terrorizing your Baby—"

"*Bubby*," Kevin corrected him again.

"Whatever." Robin shrugged. "*The General* might turn her tiger loose on your birdies. I once had an aquarium, but Cat went fishing. I'm sure the baby sharks put up quite a fight before that flea-infested feline ate them."

"Is Bubby bothering you?" Kevin placed his soccer ball under his left arm.

"No more than Cat's smell from her litter box in the upstairs john." Robin sighed noisily from his mouth and shook his head.

"I told Hyacinth to pick up some air freshener." Kevin nodded.

"It'll take more than air freshener. That cat of hers stinks to low hell. Bubby only adds to the stench. I'm allergic to both cat and dog hair. Just pray I don't trip over your Bubby and fall down the stairs."

"I'll do what I can," Kevin promised.

"Yes, well," Robin continued, "whatever, the place still stinks like an elephant's cage."

I thought it best not to mention that on the way downstairs I had stepped in a fresh splotch of furry Cat vomit hours before.

"Which reminds me," Robin turned to Kevin, "can we get together this week and work out a schedule for the summer?"

"Sure."

"I'd like for you to preach at all the masses next weekend."

"Really? Are you aware that the Ku Klux Klan has a rally planned next weekend here in Inglenook?" Kevin asked.

"I think I may have heard about it, yes," Robin replied, his eyes closed.

"It was in this morning's paper. May I mention it in my sermon?"

"You're on your own there, Father Murphy."

"Thank you. I'm on my way to the soccer field if anyone needs me."

"Just let the secretary know when you'll be back," Robin said.

Father Kevin agreed and went upstairs.

Robin turned to me in the sitting room. "Are you taking notes?"

"I was reading the *Lives of the Saints*."

"Were you now? Join me in the kitchen," he said with a smile.

I got up and walked through the house to the kitchen. Robin had me sit at the table while he poured himself some coffee. He turned to me and held the pot aloft. "Coffee?"

"No, I've had two cups already." The morning paper was on the kitchen table and I read the headline: *Ku Klux Klan to Rally Local Citizens to Their Cause Next Week*.

Robin came to the table and set his coffee and cereal bowl down. He picked up the paper briefly and glanced at the headlines. "Damned neo-Nazis. Go get 'em, Murphy!" He tossed the paper aside.

"We're meeting at the Red Lantern at three o'clock this afternoon," he said between spoonfuls of cereal. "You can ride with me."

"Who's *we?*" I noticed that the coffee pot was nearly empty but the red light indicated that the burner was still on.

"Fathers Studzinski and Frisbee and the two of us. We're having a deanery meeting of sorts."

"What about Father Kevin?" I knew it was customary to include all the priests of a deanery at a deanery meeting.

"For all we know, Father Murphy is a plant put here by Linguini." He laughed. "Murphy's coaching his soccer team tonight, anyway."

I wondered if Robin was keeping something from Monsignor Linguini.

"Bubby, Bubby, come to Papa Murph!" the voice of Kevin echoed through the house along with the sound of Bubby clacking through the front hall. The dog obeyed, and the front door opened and closed.

"Something's got to go—either me or the animals." Robin shook his head and left the room with his coffee mug.

I walked to the counter and turned the coffee pot off.

* * * *

When we arrived at the Red Lantern that afternoon, the hostess seated us in one of the back rooms. The sun shone in on the bright, pastel colored paintings. Fathers Simon Frisbee and Chris Studzinski arrived soon after, and we ordered off the menu.

"So, Father Simon Frisbee," Robin said with a smile, taking a drink of his red Merlot, "what do you think?"

"I don't know, Robin." Simon busily folded and refolded his napkin. "I've looked over your proposal, and this is even bigger than the bingo issue. Linguini will blow his stack once he sees this consolidation plan."

"That is *if* he sees it," Robin replied, sipping his Merlot. "By the time he hears about it, we will have already implemented it. It'll be too late for him to do anything about it."

"What are you saying, Robin?" Frisbee asked as he looked around the table.

I wanted to ask the same question. Robin gave a glance in my direction, but made no eye contact as he returned his wine glass to the table and refused to answer Frisbee's question.

Father Chris Studzinski leaned in and put his mug of dark German beer down on the table. "Robin, don't get me wrong, but only the bishop can close a parish. You know that."

"We're not exactly closing St. Sebastian's. It will still be a chapel."

"But," Studzinski countered, "doesn't each parish still have to retain its own records and financial—"

"Don't worry about all that. We'll all live at Poor Souls. We'll pay to have that dump of a rectory at *St. Patrick's* remodeled for office space."

"But what about *Immaculate Heart?*" Father Simon Frisbee

asked.

"Yes, what about it?" Robin retorted. "Have you ever heard of rental property?"

"You can't just rent out a rectory," Frisbee said. "What if someone were to fornicate in it?"

"It probably wouldn't be a first—but let's cross that bridge when we get there. First thing's first. We'll reduce St. Paul's to a chapel and make Poor Souls the main church in the deanery."

"Then what about Sister Precious Blood?" Frisbee continued with his concerns. Sister Precious Blood was the last of a group of disaffected cloistered nuns that had lived in the old convent at St. Paul's.

"Her order is going to recall her to the motherhouse. She's getting too old to live alone anyway."

"Are you sure you know what you're doing?" Father Frisbee's brow ruffled.

"Yes, I do. We'll call it *the Inglenook Catholic Community*."

"Have you asked permission?" The question was out of my mouth before I knew it.

"Why?" he calmly answered. "The bishop wouldn't give it; but once we make the changes, the bishop will thank me. Besides, I've already mentioned it to Linguini, and he rejected it out of hand."

"I didn't mean to challenge you," I said awkwardly.

"Well, perhaps you should have," Robin answered with a smirk, "but admit it. You did challenge me."

"I guess I did," I answered without thinking.

"Someday, Martin, you will have to stand on your own. You're too ambivalent and wishy-washy. Be either hot or cold. If you're going to err, err boldly. The lukewarm are vomited out."

I didn't know if he was insulting me or teasing me.

* * * *

The next morning at breakfast, Boniface was complaining to Hyacinth about the diocesan budget. "You're just stirring up the hornet's nest," Hyacinth said as she put away the ironing board. "How can Linguini and our dear Chancellor, Mrs. Bishop, live with themselves?"

I sipped my coffee. I had nearly forgotten that some people called Sister Dymphna "Mrs. Bishop."

"The diocesan employees can be terminated at any time without recourse. *Without recourse!*" Boniface lamented. "Where's the justice in that, Martin?"

"I have no idea," I answered, trying to avoid having to give an answer.

"I'll ask you again, Martin: Where's the justice in that?"

"It doesn't sound like there is any."

"My point exactly, son. At the turn of the century Pope Leo XIII wrote *Rerum Novarum*, and in the 1980s the U.S. Bishops wrote a pastoral letter, *Economic Justice for All*. I guess the fine print read, 'Justice for all—*except diocesan employees*'."

"Okay, Boniface," Hyacinth called out as she began feather dusting the dining room buffet table and china cabinet. "Come up for air, Old Man. Don't discourage the poor boy anymore."

"Woman, mind your chores." Boniface leaned away from the table towards the dining room, his right arm resting on his cane.

"I am minding my chores," she said coldly, slowly dusting the cabinet.

"Saint Benedict said that the realities of religious life shouldn't be kept from the newcomers," Boniface argued.

"Yes, but he also said to avoid extremes," Hyacinth replied. "Otherwise, rubbing too hard to remove the rust, one may break the vessel."

"Now how would you know that?" Boniface looked stunned.

"Listen, just because I'm a woman doesn't mean I don't know a thing or two. One must give the strong something to yearn for, but the weak must not be given cause to run away."

"Well, glory be to God, I have a theologian for a housekeeper." Boniface hesitated before changing the subject. "Hyacinth, if you hear anything about this man dressed as a priest in the confessional, you will let me know, won't you?"

"Sure, but I think I know who our mystery man is," Hyacinth said as she stopped dusting and entered the kitchen.

"You think so?" Boniface nudged me.

I was about to reveal what I knew concerning Bill Gallagher.

"I'll bet you I know." Hyacinth aimed the feather duster at Boniface as she walked over to him.

"It does sound like Bill, doesn't it?" Boniface closed his eyes, nodding. "After Cunegunda died, Linguini wouldn't lift the excommunication. The last I heard Bill was living in his car. Why the pope just doesn't—"

"Not *this* pope," Hyacinth quickly interrupted as if she knew what Boniface's next words would be. She sighed and rolled her eyes as she returned the feather duster to the broom closet.

"Father Boniface—" I was about to explain to them Father Bill's dilemma, but the doorbell rang at the back of the house.

"I'll get it." Hyacinth straightened her dress and went to the door.

Martha Hart entered. "I must speak with Father Boniface."

"He's in the kitchen," Hyacinth said. "What's wrong?"

"I *saw* him."

"Saw *who?*" Hyacinth asked as Martha made her way into the house as if it was her own.

"Father Boniface, I saw the man who's been hearing confessions," Martha triumphantly announced as she entered the kitchen. "He's a priest. Or at least he dresses as a priest."

"What are you talking about, young lady?" Boniface squinted at her.

She repeated the tale to Boniface. I wanted to tell Boniface what I knew but I didn't want to do it in front of Martha.

"The duties of a priest do include hearing confessions." He chuckled.

"Yes, but this priest—if he really is a priest—never says Mass. I see him only in the confessional. But that's not all, Monsignor—"

"*Father,*" Boniface corrected her.

"*Father.* That's not all. I followed him this morning after Mass, and he's staying at the rectory at Immaculate Heart. But there is no priest at Immaculate Heart. I called the bishop's office this morning—"

"Oh, that should clear the air," Boniface said with a roll of his eyes.

Suddenly Father Robin entered the kitchen from the garage. "Hello, Mrs. Hart. What brings you here?"

She repeated her story.

He looked at me and patted Boniface on the shoulder. "Well, Mrs. Hart," Robin began, "sometimes a visiting priest will receive permission to stay in a rectory." He smiled cautiously. "I'm sure there's some explanation."

She mentioned her call to the chancery, and Robin dismissed her with the assurance that he would contact the vicar-general's office.

Once she was gone, Robin leveled with Boniface. "She's right, Father Boniface. I gave Bill Gallagher permission to stay at Immaculate Heart."

"I figured. Why didn't you tell me? I may be an old fart, but I'm not an invalid." He poked his cane into the floor.

"I know, I know." Robin patted Boniface on the shoulder again, looked at Hyacinth and me, and motioned us out of the kitchen.

Hyacinth and I closed the door behind us. She took my right arm in her left. "It's high time *that one* leveled with Boniface as to what's going on around here. Father Robin's trying to send him away, isn't he?"

"I have no idea."

"I don't like the way you said that," she said. "And did you know Bill was back?"

"Sort of—but I don't know him. I've never met him."

"Why didn't you say something?" She picked up the two throw rugs at the back door.

"I tried," I answered honestly.

"Evidently not hard enough. What else do you know that you're not telling us?" She went outside to shake the rugs.

Chapter 18: Shelter the Homeless

*"Let him among you without sin
cast the first stone."*
— John 8.7

Robin told Fathers Chris Studzinski and Simon Frisbee that he had put Bill Gallagher up at *Immaculate Heart*. "If Linguini gets wind of this," he warned, "then we're all dead meat."

"*We?*" Frisbee asked as we sat at the kitchen table drinking coffee.

"Yes, you're all my accomplices." He laughed as he looked at the two priests and me. "I called Linguini today and told him the priest Martha Hart had seen down at Immaculate Heart was our visiting Benedictine missionary."

"What Benedictine missionary?" Simon nearly spat his coffee.

"The one from Latrobe. He happened to be passing through Inglenook, and he needed a place to stay."

Father Chris Studzinski suggested another option. "You could've said it was Father Kevin Murphy."

"No, Linguini knows Murphy is staying here. Besides, Linguini might call Murphy. The next time I see that Martha woman I'll tell her about our Benedictine missionary."

"Benedictines aren't missionaries, Father Wood." The voice was that of Father Kevin Murphy entering the kitchen from the back stairwell.

"Well, well, well, Father Murphy." Robin forced a smile. "Aren't you a Benedictine monk?"

"No. Whatever gave you that idea?" Kevin was dressed in his soccer uniform.

"You look like a monk."

"I wouldn't know. However—not to change the subject—I am working on my homily for Sunday. Did you want to hear any of it, Father Robin?"

"No, I'm sure it's fine." Robin nodded from behind his coffee mug.

"Have you read this morning's paper?" Father Kevin asked, addressing no one in particular.

"Hell, I haven't read this morning's office," Robin said, referring to his obligatory priestly prayers.

Just then, Bubby came panting in the kitchen. The Maltese dog's underbite and jagged teeth made me laugh.

"There's a big story on today's front page how the Ku Klux Klan is planning to recruit Catholics in the area," Kevin explained.

"That's ridiculous." Robin sneezed and glared at Bubby.

"Here it is," Father Chris Studzinski answered, as he pointed to the article on the front page, skimming over it.

"I plan on letting the Klan have it from the pulpit," Father Kevin announced.

"Don't get yourself shot, man." Robin took another drink of coffee.

"Shouldn't we be doing something to show that Catholicism is diametrically opposed to the philosophy of the Klan?" Kevin asked us.

"What you're going to do will be plenty," Robin said as

he put his mug down. "Trust me. I venture you'll handle them single-handedly."

Suddenly Cat pounced on Bubby and clawed her. Bubby pooped on the floor. Kevin blamed Cat; Hyacinth blamed Bubby; Kevin blamed Hyacinth; Hyacinth blamed Kevin; Robin blamed Kevin and Hyacinth; and Boniface, just coming down for breakfast, blamed Noah for putting dogs and cats in the Ark.

Hyacinth shooed everyone out of her kitchen so she could clean.

Chapter 19: Bottled Truth

*Use discretion so that the strong have something to yearn for and
the weak have nothing to run from.*
— St. Benedict

I attended the weekend masses to hear Father Kevin
preach. He became furious in the pulpit and decried the Klan,
conjuring up images of Klan rallies, cross burnings, and Negro
lynchings. Kevin shared personal stories of his own family
members who had been the target of anti-Irish, anti-Catholic
hatred in the 1920s and 1930s—the Klan torching a family
business and terrorizing the children of Irish American Catholics.

He quoted Saint Paul: *That is not what you learned when you
learned Christ. I am supposing of course that he has been preached to
you in accord with the truth of the gospel.* "And I say to you here
in Inglenook, that if you join the Klan, then you join the ranks
of the anti-Christ and the devil and his fallen angels! No true
Christian, let alone a Catholic, can be a Klansman. The two
are incompatible!" His tone was dissonant, and his pulpit
pounding caused the speakers to crackle and pop.

Kevin went on to say that he would attend the rally to
protest the Klan's presence. He also invited any Catholic to
join him and his Jewish, Arab, and black friends in their
peaceful protest. I watched the congregation from the rear of
the church. There were a few men who left halfway through

the sermon. Once Kevin's tirade was over, several others left as well.

On Monday morning, both Father Robin and Susan, the parish secretary, began fielding calls about Kevin's sermon. Robin came in the kitchen after the morning Mass. "Father Kevin, what on earth did you say during your homily? Some of the parishioners are livid."

"What? Are they unaccustomed to hearing the gospel preached? Does the truth hurt? If that's the case, then they best find another parish."

Robin didn't say anything and returned to his study.

"What?" Kevin asked, looking at me as if I had said something.

"I didn't say anything," I replied, uncomfortable with his style of confrontation.

"Well? What do you think, Flanagan? You're Irish, aren't you?"

"I'm an American."

"What kind of an answer is that?" Kevin's face reddened, and the veins of his neck were visible. "Don't you stand for anything?"

"Well, yes," I agreed in order to avoid conflict rather than affirm my principles.

"Well, then, act like it. There are some things in life which are worth getting your ire up over."

Kevin angrily left the room. I pondered his words, lamenting my disengaged attitude. Sister Regina Claire's words returned to me. "You often agree with others thinking you'll avoid conflict, but instead you're creating more and more interior conflict within yourself. What will happen if there's too much conflict bottled up inside you?"

I didn't want to think about it.

* * * *

That Wednesday, Father Robin Wood returned from the print shop with a stack of bulletins for the weekend masses. He pulled one of them out and showed me the front cover. "Here, Martin. What do you think?"

I observed the page. It was a montage of all the parish churches in the Inglenook Deanery. I read aloud, "The Catholic Christian Community of Inglenook." Below the heading, it listed the different parishes. A large picture of Poor Souls was in the middle of the bulletin.

My God, he did it, I thought. I couldn't decide whether to go along with it or raise an objection and create conflict.

Kevin Murphy came in from his afternoon soccer practice around the same time. He was in his uniform and carried a soccer ball. "What's this?" he asked as he studied the bulletin's cover.

"These are our new parish bulletins."

"I didn't know."

"We discussed it for some time on a deanery level."

"Have you discussed it with your bishop?"

"Oh, yes. And the vicar-general." Robin had answered truthfully, but he failed to inform Kevin that the bishop and Linguini had denied him permission to consolidate anything. "Plans are set for all the priests to live here at Lost Souls. The rectory at St. Patrick's will be converted into office space and meeting rooms."

"*Poor Souls*, Father. Poor and Forgotten Souls in Purgatory," Kevin said as if he knew that Robin wasn't being completely honest. Then I realized that I wasn't being totally honest either.

My silence was a sin of omission.

* * * *

On Thursday afternoon, as I was reading in my bedroom, Father Robin knocked on my door. He was dressed in a white, short-sleeved golf shirt, green sports coat, and khaki slacks. "Martin, have you ever attended the symphony?"

"Once."

"You need some culture. I've got tickets to a concert this evening. Can you be dressed and ready to leave in fifteen minutes?"

"Sure."

"Good. I'll be waiting downstairs in my office."

I freshened up and put on a button down shirt, casual slacks, and a tan coat before meeting him in the driveway. We stopped at the *Red Lantern* for dinner before leaving Inglenook.

It was a two-hour drive to the university where a visiting Russian composer was to conduct Antonin Dvorak's *From the New World.* I had never heard the piece. The symphony hall was an old theatre from the early nineteen hundreds and had been newly restored; the interior was elegant and ornate, baroque in style.

The opening overture was Rossini's *Barber of Seville.* All I could see was Bugs Bunny giving Elmer Fudd a most unneeded haircut. I worked to keep from laughing out loud.

The thought of the cartoon took me back to Saturday mornings at Grandma and Grandpa Buckner's house. My brother Sean and I would stay at their house on Friday nights, and every Saturday morning we would awaken to the smell of hotcakes, freshly brewed coffee, and frying bacon. After breakfast Sean and I would lie in front of their large, color television set and watch cartoons.

The *New World* symphony gave me a chance to reflect. I closed my eyes and let the music wash over me. I imagined leaving Europe as an immigrant and arriving in America. Encountering this music for the first time is indeed like going away and encountering a new world. The melodies of the wind instruments hovering above the lush strings took me far away from Poor Souls—and partisan church politics. Indeed a new world.

The slow second movement of the symphony took me back home. I was in the ninth grade and I had gone out for baseball. It was one of the first times that my father seemed as if he was actually interested in me. Mother and Father were separated at the time; father was staying at an old roadside motel outside the city limits, and Sean and I were living at home with mother.

One night in late September, I had a baseball game. I had already struck out twice in the game when I got up to bat for the third time. I was so nervous. We had men on first and second. My legs seemed numb and my mouth was dry. The outfield lights were in my eyes and the pitcher, twice my size, hurled a nasty fastball. I called time-out in the batter's box several times before I was finally ready for a pitch. I took the first two pitches as strikes. On the third pitch, I swung away in hopes of sending the ball to the moon. The bat hit the ball squarely, sending it to right center. I almost forgot to drop the bat when I ran toward first. I couldn't believe the rush I got as the coach sent me on to second base for a double. Both runners scored. But the best part of that night was that my dad was there to see me get the hit. As I rounded first base, I saw him on his feet along the third base side. He was flailing his arms and cheering me on. I think it was the first time that I felt I had a real dad like the other kids. One like Sean had always known.

After the game, he took me out for a chocolate milkshake. I don't remember any of the conversation. All I remember is his smile. His smile was for me.

I remembered going to school the next morning at Regina Coeli High School. We always went to Mass at Our Lady of the River across the street from the school. As my class was about to leave church, Sister Beatrice called me to her pew. I wondered if I was in trouble. Did I slouch on the kneeler? Did she think I had gum in my mouth? Had she seen me talking during the offertory song?

"Martin, walk with me." She looked as if she was holding back tears as we walked over to the pews in front of the statue of St. Joseph. "Martin, I have some sad news for you, son," she said as she sat down and motioned for me to sit as well. "Your father died of a heart attack this morning. Your mother is on her way to pick you up."

I thought I was going to throw up. I looked at the statue of St. Joseph holding the child Jesus. It reminded me of a picture of my father holding me when I was about two. I stood up and walked away from the front of the church. I didn't have anything to say to Sister Beatrice. When Mother came to get me, I didn't say anything. I didn't say much to anyone.

I don't remember much else. It all seems like a blur. I don't even remember the funeral except the fact that all our relatives were there, and we had a ton of food left over afterwards. I do remember getting to meet my cousins, Tammy and Tommy, from Wisconsin. They were about my age, and we spent time going in and out of the funeral home. Every time we'd want to go out or come in, one of the undertakers would open the door for us. This kept me occupied so I didn't have to go look at my father stretched out in his casket.

The rosebush that my dad and I had planted together in the spring had died later that summer. Was it an omen that he would soon also die? We'd had a conversation while planting it. I had nearly forgotten about it, but the melody of the orchestra's strings and brass brought it to mind. He told me that if I ever went away to be a priest that I should do it because I wanted to do it, not because someone else thought I had a vocation. "You've got to do what's right for you." Why he brought up the priesthood, I'll never know. I wasn't even thinking of priesthood at the time. I had just discovered that the more I looked at girls, the fewer and fewer cooties I actually saw.

After he died, I do remember being angry. I was angry with Mom for being separated from him. I was angry with my dad for dying and leaving me alone. I was angry with Sean because he seemed unaffected by Dad's death. I was also angry with God for taking my dad from me just when we seemed to be growing close. Of course, at the time I didn't recognize that I was angry with God. I mean, seriously, you can't be angry with God. Right? God is God.

Yet, lots of people are angry with God. It's sort of in His job description. He gets blamed for most natural disasters. They're called "acts of God." Why not "acts of Satan?" God must be trying to tell us something, some say after a tornado or earthquake.

Some people disbelieve in God and are untroubled by such unbelief. Others believe in God, but are angry that he exists, and still others are angry that he does not exist.

Why am I studying for the priesthood? I'd asked myself the question a hundred times. If I were to go on to become a priest, I want to be the kind of priest Christ's apostles were— the kind of priest I believe Christ desires for the Church, men wholly committed to the life. But the way the church wants me to be and live as a priest, isn't always the way I think a priest should be or should live.

Do I want to be the kind of priest that the church demands? Will I ever be able to be the kind of priest I felt called to be in our current church environment? *Birds have nests, foxes have dens, but the Son of Man has nowhere to lay his head.*

I wish I could remember my father's face. Perhaps I should have looked at him in his casket more than once.

The crescendo of Dvorak's *Ninth Symphony* did something to me. I'm not for sure what or how to describe it. It was as if I had been riding the wild waves of a stormy ocean and had been washed up on a craggy shore. There was a resolution to the theme, but then again there wasn't.

Somehow, the music seemed a metaphor of my life. The symphony seemed unfinished.

* * * *

After the concert, Robin took me to a hole in the wall pub called *The Irish Wolfhound*. "I figured someone with a name like Flanagan would like a place like this."

Irish ballads and jigs played in the background while Robin encouraged me to sample the *Guinness* and several other beers from the Emerald Isle. Robin for his part imbibed in Irish whiskey.

"We'll come back in October when the symphony performs Puccini's opera *La Boheme*," Robin promised. "I'd advise you to enjoy your freedom now. Once you're ordained, you'll have no free time. In ten years there will only be twenty functioning priests in the diocese and, if the bishop's lucky, half of them will be sane."

The trip back to Inglenook seemed long. I slept some in the car as Robin listened to a classical rock and roll station on the radio. It was well past two a.m. when we arrived back at the rectory.

It was a good thing I had no appointments on Friday.

Chapter 20: A Bum's Ring

"Lord, when did we see you hungry and feed you,
or thirsty and give you drink?"
— Matthew 25:37

The following Sunday afternoon I was in the church sacristy preparing things for the five o'clock evening Mass when Father Boniface hobbled in, leaning upon his cane. He sat down in the old rocker and peacefully rocked back and forth before Mass.

A girl about ten years old walked into the sacristy and said to Boniface, "I'm your server, Father."

He smiled at her and reached for his cane. "Let's go pray." After Mass, I accompanied him back to the rectory. Hyacinth had prepared dinner and called us to the dining room.

I noticed the cracking plaster and wondered when the room had been painted last. A painting of a sailing ship reflected in the mirror above the fireplace. We prayed, and just as we were about to eat, the doorbell rang.

Boniface looked up. "Wait a minute—it's got the sound."

The doorbell rang again.

"What sound?" I asked, listening intently though not detecting any difference in the sound.

"Listen." Boniface leaned back in his chair, his right hand in the air pointing up with his index finger.

The doorbell rang again.

"It's a bum's ring." Boniface sat up straight with a straight face. "I'd know it anywhere."

It rang yet again.

"I'll get it," Boniface said, scooting his chair back on the parquet floor and grabbing his cane. "Come with me, Martin. They don't teach this in the seminary." He turned back to Hyacinth. "You'd best put out another plate, Dear."

Boniface moved toward the front door as the doorbell was now buzzing, no longer ringing. His cane tapped along the way.

"Yeah, it's a bum. He keeps his finger down on the button until the ringer's ready to burn off the wall. That way he knows you'll have to answer to get him off the buzzer."

As Boniface opened the door, the buzzing stopped. The scent of burnt electric wire filled the hall.

A man with a black mustache and beard, and wearing a dark blue sock cap and soiled brown fur coat, stood in the doorway.

"Good evening, Sir." Boniface opened the door wide. "Welcome to Poor Souls. How may I help you?"

"I was just wondering if you might have enough money for me to get a cup of coffee," he said as his eyes looked off to the left through the French doors into the front room.

"Now, if you're hungry, son," Boniface answered him, "then you're going to need a little more than a cup of coffee. Now, you come on in here and have dinner with us. We were just getting ready to sit down to eat. You came just in time."

"Oh, no, I can't do that," the man stuttered, looking up at the ceiling lamp.

"I insist. We have plenty. Join us." Boniface took him by

the arm and ushered him into the foyer.

"Let me take your coat," I offered my hospitality as Boniface shut the front door.

The man hesitated and shook his head, "I'd rather not."

I smelled something rancid; it was the man.

"That's all right." Boniface led him through the hallway to the dining room. "Hyacinth, we have company."

Hyacinth returned to the dining room with a casserole of steaming potatoes and carrots. She stared at the stranger as Boniface put him at the head of the table. As Boniface pulled the chair out for the man, Cat awoke and jumped away from his nap on the chair.

I sat to the man's right as Boniface sat to his left.

After Hyacinth finished setting the table, she brought out a platter of pork chops and sat next to Boniface. Boniface made the sign of the cross and said the blessing. However, before he was finished praying, the stranger had already begun eating.

The stench from the man was so intense that I could hardly take a bite of food. By the time I did take my first bite of potatoes, the man was finishing his second helping. Then he took three of the pork chops and voraciously consumed them, gnawing every bit of meat from the bones.

Boniface had taken only a small portion of potatoes and carrots and was buttering his bread.

"Boniface," Hyacinth whispered, "you didn't get any pork chops."

"It's all right." He smiled, taking her hand in his. "The man's hungry."

She looked across the table at the man. "Are you a member of our parish?"

"You talking to me?" he answered with a mouthful of potatoes.

"Yes," Hyacinth replied with a highbrow look.

"No." The man continued chewing.

The table was quiet as the man finished eating. I looked up at the painting of the sailing ship and wondered if its hull would have smelled as bad as our visitor.

Boniface broke the silence. "Well, Hyacinth, how about that cup of coffee our friend here came for in the first place. There's nothing like a good cup of freshly brewed coffee after a delicious meal."

Hyacinth went into the kitchen and returned bringing coffee for the stranger. She offered him cream, but he shook his head, took a couple of sips from his cup, and suddenly pushed away from the table and stood.

"Leaving so soon?" Boniface asked.

"I really don't like coffee in the evening. It keeps me awake." He then turned and glared at me.

"So, you really didn't want a cup of coffee?" Hyacinth stared at him.

"Why lie?" He turned toward Boniface but looked away and avoided eye contact. "I really want a beer."

"Oh, I can't help you there." Boniface chuckled. "I don't have a liquor license."

I muffled a laugh as I adjusted my napkin and glanced at the man. There were bits of potatoes stuck in his beard.

The man started for the door, and Boniface stood to see him to it.

Hyacinth clicked her teeth and looked at me before Boniface returned to the table, laughing. "What's so funny, Boniface?" Hyacinth clanked her knife and fork down on her plate. "You didn't get to eat."

"Oh, but he did."

"Like a possum in a trash can," Hyacinth continued, "and he smelled like one, too!"

"A possum or a trash can?" Boniface asked as he continued to chuckle to himself.

"Both." Hyacinth looked at the man's empty plate. "He ate like a king." Boniface was still chuckling. "What are you laughing about, old man? Are you tired of my cooking?"

"Oh, no, it's nothing like that," he answered. "I was just thinking of the time that Father Jack Ash was an associate priest at St. Augustine's in Covert. St. Augustine's is across the street from that Mexican place, Casa Margarita, and Jack was getting a lot of drunks at the door and he was tiring of it. One night the doorbell rang before dinner, and he thought it was just another drunk so he answered the door with a huge butcher knife in his hand. But when he opened the door, it was Monsignor Linguini and Sister Dymphna. They had come to see the newly remodeled parish hall. He's still paying for that mistake."

Boniface's laughter turned into a coughing fit.

Chapter 21: The Exorcist

Oh, how strict and mortified a life did the
holy fathers lead…they were strangers to the
world, but near and familiar friends to God.
— Thomas à Kempis

On Monday, I left for Cainbrook to visit Father David Gregory. I arrived at Our Lady of the River rectory at noon and found Father David watering his flower garden. He invited me into the rectory and we sat in the enclosed front porch that served as a sunroom. The walls were covered in brown paneling and the carpet smelled of mold.

"How is your prayer life, Martin?" He sat in a rocking chair.

"Well, I've been faithful to Morning Prayer," I said as I sank into an oversized, red vinyl-covered easy chair, "but sometimes I skip evening prayer. During the day, I try to read the breviary. In the seminary they teach us we're not to try and pray the entire office all at once, but rather pray the hours as they come."

"So instead of praying evening prayer when you can, don't pray it at all?" He leaned forward.

"I don't think that's what they're saying." I was frustrated with his impatience.

"You know," David began rocking again, "when a priest stops praying, it won't be long before he quits being a priest. The day you toss your breviary aside is the day your troubles begin. The lifeblood of the priest is prayer. A lot of the men who've left the active ministry over the celibacy issue had ceased their discipline of prayer long before they left the ministry."

That was his opinion. Some of it may be true, but perhaps things weren't that black and white. "I don't know if it's just the celibacy thing," I proffered.

"You're right. They lack obedience as well. There's enough priests moping around like the walking wounded claiming they're not getting their needs met. Balderdash. There's just as many single and divorced folks out there dealing with the same feelings of loneliness, and they're not pouting about things.

"You haven't heard confessions yet, Martin, but let me tell you, even happily married men have feelings for other women. But like any choice in life, once you've made your choice, then you've got to stick with it come hell or high water." He closed his eyes and slapped his right hand down on the rocker's armrest. "Sexual tension is just something a priest has to get used to. The day I stop having sexual feelings is the day you can bury me. So, for God's sake, man, if you decide to become a priest, then be the best priest this diocese has ever seen. And do it for the right reasons. A priest chooses the road not taken." He looked at me intently. "You are familiar with Robert Frost's poem, aren't you?"

"No."

He shook his head. "*Two roads diverged in a yellow wood, and I—I took the one less traveled by, and that has made all the difference.* You're a deprived child. Graham Greene believed that seminarians should be required to read good fiction in order for them to understand the human condition. He thought seminaries relied too much upon dry theology and systematic theology. What do you read?"

"I once read a novel by Andrew Greeley."

"Some would say that he doesn't count."

"Well, I really don't like fiction."

"At times fiction can be truer than the truth," he countered.

"I do read the gospels." I sat straight and made eye contact. "And the lives of the saints."

"My! Imagine that—a candidate for the priesthood who reads the gospels and has a devotion to the saints. Be careful with whom you share that information. That's the kind of thing that can get a guy turned out of formation these days."

"Seriously? That hasn't been my experience at St. Albert's. There are other things a guy can get kicked out for."

"Oh, from what I've read, the life in seminary is so stilted and artificial—and unnatural—far worse than when I was in. Many of the men they're accepting today are walking time bombs. Next thing you know, they'll be ordaining homosexuals. Oh, well, you didn't come here to hear me blabber and blubber." He stood and motioned me to rise. "Let's go to lunch."

We went through the house and out the back door to the carport. "Before we go to lunch, I need to make one stop. Mrs. Busseron has been sick and couldn't get to Mass this weekend, so I'm going to bring her communion."

Father David's old, white Mercury cruised quietly as we made our way to the Busserons. The Busserons' home was a two-story brick at the end of a cul-de-sac shrouded by oak and maple trees. We drove down the teardrop driveway to the front of the house. We both got out and walked up the steps to the double doors. Father David rang the doorbell, and the housekeeper answered. I followed David into the house, and the housekeeper led us upstairs to Mrs. Busseron's bedroom where she was propped up in a king-sized bed.

"Thank you for coming, Father—Oh, Martin Flanagan. I saw your mother at the country club two weeks ago. She's so proud of you, you know."

"That's what I hear." She had never quite said so to me.

Father David produced a prayer book from his pocket and prayed several short prayers. After the Our Father, he reached into his pocket for his pyx, opened it, and held up the host before her. "The Body of Christ."

She opened her mouth and David placed the host on her tongue. She closed her eyes, and he prayed the *Ave Maria* in Latin. As she opened her eyes, he traced the cross in the air above her forehead and turned to leave.

We got back in the car and drove to The Pigeon-Toed Moose Café. The parking lot was only half full, and David parked his Mercury in one of the spaces near the front door.

"Hello, Father." One of the middle-aged, red-haired waitresses waved to David as we entered. He nodded to her as he pointed me to a booth. It was his favorite, two booths away from the door with a view of the entire restaurant. As we sat, it seemed the entire clientele of the restaurant turned a collective head our direction; crusty old men in overalls and ball caps and leathery skinned women in t-shirts looking forlorn as they smoked, argued, ate, and drank. It was as if the people were anxiously awaiting someone important, but each time the door opened, they were disappointed.

The images of Elvis, Jesus, and John Wayne stared through thick cigarette smoke. The air vents were clogged with dust and grease, and the spinning ceiling fans only distributed the smoke evenly throughout the restaurant.

David continued our previous conversation after he ordered his coffee and perused the menu. "I never thought I could be so angry at the Church."

Two older men seated opposite us stopped talking as if to listen to David's words. One of the men was bearded and wore a blue and green bandana about his neck. He wore jeans and black cowboy boots. The other man was wearing a blue work uniform with the insignia of a welding firm emblazoned above his heart.

The waitress returned to take our orders. She was impatient with me as I studied the menu. I was torn between pork tenderloin and fried chicken; I ordered a cheeseburger and fries and iced tea.

"I'm convinced Bishop Numbnoddle over in Wheatfield doesn't want priests," David continued, as he worked to light a cigarette with his silver lighter. "Rather than encouraging vocations to the priesthood, his solution is to close parishes. For years he and other bishops have gone around telling everyone, *the Church is the people, the Church is the people*, but then what's he do when he doesn't have a priest for their parish? He closes the place. In one place he sold a church to some Protestants, and in two other places he had the churches torn down." Father David held his cigarette between his index and middle finger and took a long drag.

"Can he do that?" I asked. A heavy-set woman in an oversized, gray jogging outfit two booths away sat staring at us. She had big, rust red hair and was reading a romance novel; on the book's cover was a muscle-bulging hulk of a man entwined in a suggestive embrace with a long-haired blonde woman with incredible cleavage.

"He did it, didn't he?" David removed the cigarette from his mouth, forcefully exhaling a plume of smoke. "His latest move was to close three parishes and build a new church because he has lost so many of his priests. And he wonders why he's lost the confidence of his people. I wouldn't be a bit surprised if Linguini and Munchin don't try it here. Mark my words."

At that, David bemoaned the lack of faith among his brother priests. He also asked me about the missing pews at Saint Patrick's but, before I could recount the details, the waitress served our lunch.

"Cheeseburger and fries for you, sweetheart," the redhaired waitress announced as she placed the food in front of me. "And the pork tenderloin for you, Father. If you need anything, let me know, Honey."

Father David looked at me and raised his eyebrows with a grin. "Honey? I didn't know she cared." He said the blessing. I dressed my burger, salted my fries, and sweetened my iced tea. I wanted to ask Father David about his vocation and thought for a few minutes exactly how to formulate the question.

"Martin, you're quiet. Is there something on your mind?" he asked as he sipped his coffee.

"Father David," I asked between bites, "how did you know that you wanted to be a priest?"

"You mean, how do I *know* that I want to be a priest?"

"Yes. I've never heard it phrased that way."

"Listen." David pointed at me with his fork loaded with two fried potatoes on the end of it. "Every morning when I wake up, I choose to be a priest." He took a bite and swallowed. "My brother has been happily married to his wife for thirty years, but he never wears his wedding ring to bed. Every night he takes it off and puts it on his nightstand. And every morning upon waking, he takes up the ring and quietly renews his marriage vows to his wife. So, you see, Martin, it has to be that way for a priest as well."

David put the potatoes in his mouth and drank some coffee. The waitress returned and looked him in the eyes. "More coffee, Father?"

He nodded and she poured. A busboy at a nearby table raised quite a din as he hurriedly clanged about, forcing cups, glasses, plates, and saucers in an already overloaded bus-cart. Father David reached in his pocket for his pack of cigarettes. He tapped the pack in his palm, pulled a cigarette out, and put it in his mouth.

The heavy woman with the romance novel two booths away scooted out of her seat, stood, and approached our table. Her novel was nowhere to be seen.

"May I ask you a religious question, Father?" She noisily chewed her gum and looked exclusively at David while he worked to produce a lighter from his pants' pocket.

"Yes." David straightened in his seat as he flicked his lighter and lit the cigarette in his mouth.

"I was always told that things happen for a reason," the woman began. "Well, I've been thinking about that. My cousin's fiancé was killed in a car wreck. Was that meant to be?"

"I don't believe in fate, if that's what you're asking." David took a drag off his cigarette and placed it on the table's ashtray. "Then, again, God isn't up there rolling dice with the universe, either. Things don't necessarily happen for a reason, but I do believe that we can find reason in everything that happens."

I folded the end of my paper placemat and ran my thumb along the crease as the woman listened to David.

"God didn't cause that tornado to kill those people in Florence so he could teach us how precious and fragile life is," he explained as he reached for his cigarette. "That would make God out to be Moloch, who demanded human sacrifice to appease his anger.

"God didn't do that anymore than he inspires serial killers to teach us to love one another. But if that's a lesson you learn from tragedy, so be it. So, out of terrible suffering, like the death of one's fiancé, new life *can* come forth. Can, not must. God gives us a free will. The answer rests in how we choose to embrace the pain in our life." He paused, took another drag off his cigarette, and returned it to the ashtray. "Recall that Christ was crucified but rose again on the third day. Even out of crucifixion, resurrections are possible—if we are open to them. Suffering can lead us into a deeper trust with God."

The woman was still chewing her gum; seemingly bored by the time David had stopped talking. "Well, thanks, Father."

"I think she wanted the short answer," I said, looking up at David as she left the table.

"It's that way with the Church, too, Martin."

"How's that?" I drank some coffee and toyed with the saltshaker.

"As the spouse of Christ, the Church must also suffer and die in order to experience new life—just as her Savior did."

The noon hour was waning and many in the lunch crowd were emptying out of the restaurant when two young men in their late teens or early twenties entered and stood at the doors. The men were dressed in black trench coats with silver chains, bright yellow rosaries, and large gaudy silver crosses dangling around their necks. Their hair was multi-colored and spiked, and they wore spiked wristbands and body piercing in their lips and eyebrows.

The waitress took two menus to them and led them past our table. As they walked by, the two men stared at Father David in his Roman collar. As the waitress seated them, one of the men pointed at David. Just as he did, David breathed out the name *Jesus*. He then looked at me with a somber face, made eye contact, and stated quietly, "They're possessed."

No sooner had he said the word *possessed* than both of the men yelled out unintelligible phrases. Tipping their table, knocking their water glasses to the floor and shattering glass everywhere, the two men ran past us and out the restaurant doors yelling, "Die, priest! Die!"

The waitress walked over to our table with a coffee pot in her hand.

"Check, please." David had an ashen look.

She placed the check on the table and stared at Father. "What was with those two guys?" she asked.

Father David ignored her question, reached for his wallet, pulled out a twenty dollar bill, and placed it on the table next to the check. "That should get it. Keep the change." He looked at me and stood. "Ready?" I nodded and followed him out of the restaurant into the noonday summer heat.

"How did you know those two men were possessed?" I asked as I rolled my window down.

"Only by prayer and fasting," he replied with his eyes on the road. "I've been a priest long enough to know. Believe me."

I silently thought about the rumored identity of the diocesan exorcist. Some had said it was Linguini. Others said it was one of the Dominicans from St. Albert's. As for myself there was no longer any need for speculation. There was an eerie silence between us before Father David finally spoke. "They can't stand the presence of Christ."

When we returned to the rectory, Father David went immediately to the church to restore the Blessed Sacrament to the tabernacle.

* * * *

I thought about my time with Father David and the words of the two possessed men. As I drove back to Inglenook, I reflected upon the nature of evil. Until today, I had always considered evil to be an impersonal lack of goodness. Now I wasn't so sure.

When I returned to Inglenook, I stopped at the mall for toothpaste. I also purchased a CD of classical music: Dvorak's *Ninth Symphony*, from *The New World*. I arrived back at Poor Souls before dinner.

Father Boniface was looking for the evening paper. "Who keeps taking the papers?"

Father Kevin had an odd grin as he carried Bubby upstairs. I happened to see several newspapers lying on the floor in the corner behind the recliner in the downstairs sitting room. I went to retrieve them, but as I pulled them up, I saw that they were wet and a large dog dropping was stuck to the front page. Suddenly, Father Kevin reentered the room.

"No, Martin! Those are Bubby's newspapers."

"Yes, I can see that." I went to the restroom and washed my hands scrupulously.

Hyacinth called us to dinner. Father Kevin and I joined Fathers Robin and Boniface in the dining room. She set the food in front of us—pork chops, baked potatoes, and peas. After grace, there was some small talk until Robin began arguing with Father Kevin about his birds.

"Just keep your damned birds in their cage," Robin said. "I found one of them in my sink this morning."

"It was an accident." Kevin dropped his fork on his plate. "The little boogers are smart. Damien figured out how to open the cage door."

"I don't want to hear it." Robin smacked his hand down on the table. "And I don't want to hear that mutt of yours anymore either. She's driving me nuts with that damned yipping and barking. And who painted her nails red?"

"Now, now, Robin," Boniface interrupted, tapping his cane on the floor. "You'd best learn to pick your battles. Just be glad Hyacinth hasn't slipped Cat into your room. Bubby hasn't been bad lately—I just hope she isn't the one hiding my newspapers."

"Well, how about Father Kevin coming off the soccer field and saying morning Mass more often." Robin laughed and turned to Boniface.

"Certainly." Kevin shook his head. "All you have to do is ask."

"Well, then, take them all. In my opinion, we shouldn't even have daily Mass," Robin snapped. "The people aren't getting anything out of Sunday Mass as it is. Why should we perpetuate the myth?"

"*Myth?* My God, man! Where's your faith?" Kevin moaned. "The Mass is a sacrifice. The people need to bring their personal prayer life to the altar of community prayer."

"Try explaining that to the poor souls here at Lost Souls. Besides, they won't sing either."

"How can they sing if they have no song in their hearts?" Kevin raised his arms in frustration. "We must evangelize them. Do they have the Lord in their lives?"

"How the hell should *I* know?" Robin rolled his eyes.

"By God, you'd *better* know!" Kevin said in a near shout. "You're their pastor."

Robin stood and threw his napkin across his plate of half-eaten food and walked out of the dining room. Kevin excused himself and followed Robin down the hall. "Father, we can't just leave it at this!" he disappeared into Robin's office and slammed the door shut. Their voices were dissonant as their argument continued.

"Oh, that was a good one," Hyacinth said as she made her way through the kitchen door with a dessert plate. "*That one*—poor baby—gets his feelings hurt easily."

"Hyacinth, you're judging again," Boniface cautioned.

"No, I'm not," she replied. "I'm stating facts."

"That's no excuse." Boniface coughed and tapped his cane again.

Hyacinth sat down and gave Boniface a tender look. His eyes met hers for a moment before he looked away.

"Martin," Boniface reached for my hand on the table, "do you have the call?"

"I'm still discerning," I said, wiping my face with my napkin.

"So am I." Boniface took a chocolate chip cookie from the plate of assorted treats. Hyacinth held the plate out for me. I picked a piece of chocolate fudge.

"You can have one, too, Hyacinth." Boniface smiled.

"I never met a chocolate I didn't love." Hyacinth set the plate down and took a chocolate candy. She reached for the coffee pot on the table and poured Boniface another cup.

"That's enough," Boniface brought his hand up over the cup. "If I drink another cup, I'll be grinding my teeth all night."

"You grind your teeth all day as it is." Hyacinth sat without expression.

I laughed. Boniface shook his head and finally gave a chuckle. Hyacinth grinned and took his hand. I felt at ease with Boniface and Hyacinth.

They were like an old married couple—without the sex.

Chapter 22: The Pearl of Great Price

"In the tender compassion of our God
the dawn from on high shall break upon us,
to illumine our darkness and dispel the shadow of
death, and to guide our feet into the way of peace."
— Luke 1:78-79

Father Robin had invited me to join him at the Schultz's home for dinner. The Schultz's were wealthy parishioners of Poor Souls. They had a daughter, Margaret Mary, but everyone called her Peggy; she was a twenty-two year old dark blonde. She sang in the church choir. I first met Peggy at the parish festival. I met a lot of the parishioners that weekend. The attention I received was a bit excessive; yet, with fewer numbers of seminarians, I understood why many people felt it necessary to talk to me. But I do remember Peggy.

Her eyes were a cool gray-green, a unique eye color. She was confident and intelligent. The day we met, I felt myself flirting with her. She was wearing a red top, blue slacks, and sandals. I still remember. I don't know why.

The Schultzes lived in an upscale neighborhood, their home a two-story red brick with black shutters and a red front door. Robin rang the bell. Momentarily, the brass doorknob on the front door turned, and Mr. Schultz appeared from behind it. He wore a red cardigan sweater, white polo shirt, and a blue and white striped silk tie. The door opened wide into a spacious white marble foyer with a large winding light oak stairwell and banister.

"Good evening, Father." He shook Robin's hand. "Marvin," he said and nodded to me. I didn't correct him. Mr. Schultz was over six-feet tall and broad shouldered. He had graying black hair, large bristly eyebrows, a thick mustache, and hairy ears. His presence was electric, and he seemed on the verge of anger. Honestly, I wasn't in the mood for socializing, and I certainly didn't want to be intimidated by Mr. Schultz. In the back of my mind, he seemed to be suspicious of anyone in the seminary, especially in light of the recent scandals involving a few priests and altar boys.

Mrs. Schultz entered the foyer as Robin and I entered her home. She had brown hair and was pale and thin like Popeye's Olive Oyl. "Good evening, Father Wood. And Martin. Martin Flanagan, isn't it?"

"Yes, Mrs. Schultz. Thank you."

"Oh, and you remember our daughter, Margaret Mary," Mrs. Schultz said as her daughter walked over from the living room to the right of the foyer; she was wearing an emerald green dress.

"Peggy." She smiled, shaking Robin's hand while glancing at me.

"Peggy," I said, reaching in to shake her hand as well.

"Martin." Her grasp was firm and her eye contact deliberate. I wasn't sure who would break the grip first. She was a beautiful woman.

"Martin, what will you have?" The fifty-something Mr. Schultz regained my attention. I was nearly afraid to answer fearing that I would say something wrong. He motioned us into the room to the left where there was a wet bar and a small refrigerator.

"So, what will it be?"

"Oh, I don't care. I'll have what you're having." I thought he was drinking a soda.

"How do you take your Scotch?" His eyebrows crumpled ever so slightly.

I looked at him and shrugged, unaccustomed to hard liquor. My Uncle Hoot wouldn't have hesitated; he was always three sheets to the wind.

"Straight up, on the rocks, or with a splash of water?"

"With a splash." Uncle Hoot drank it straight from the bottle.

"I hope you like your drink strong," Peggy whispered to me. "A splash of water for dad is no more than a drop."

"Well, maybe a splash of 7-Up if you have any," I suggested to Mr. Schultz. "And some more ice."

Mr. Schultz acquiesced, dropped a few cubes of ice in the glass, and poured in the Scotch. Then he poured in some 7-Up and handed the glass tumbler to me. "With a good Irish name like Flanagan, I'd think you'd take it straight up."

When I sipped the drink, I puckered. By then, Mr. Schultz had taken Robin aside into his den, and Mrs. Schultz and Peggy had returned to the kitchen. I walked to the wet bar, put my glass under the faucet, diluted the drink with some water, added three more ice cubes, and tried another sip. I grimaced.

Suddenly Peggy reappeared in the hall. "What? Too strong?" She looked down her attractive aquiline nose while her perfect teeth glistened in a mischievous smile.

"Yes. I'd rather just have a beer." I smiled her way, as I smelled the sweet rose scent of her perfume.

"My father and his Scotch," she said, rolling her large eyes. "Here." She took the glass tumbler from me and was about to pour its contents down the drain when she stopped. "Wait. My father would die if we wasted his best Scotch." She held the glass aloft and winked. "Down the hatch." She drank the entire glassful. If I had tried that, I'd been on the floor. She put the glass in the sink, opened the door of the small refrigerator under the sink, and produced a beer.

"It's a light beer." Her eyes met mine. "Is that all right?"

"That's fine. I got my fix with the Scotch." Her fingers touched mine as she handed me the beer can. I felt my face grow warm and a chill go through me.

The two of us rejoined Robin and Mr. Schultz in the den. They were lighting cigars. She sat on the divan while I examined a collection of leather-bound books on the shelves. A great globe stood in one corner of the room. Music from the big band era played softly from a ceiling speaker.

"Want one, Peg?" Mr. Schultz held out a cigar to his daughter.

"No, Dad. Not tonight." She blushed and grinned bashfully. I'd never seen a woman smoke a cigar.

Robin and Mr. Schultz began discussing the bishop and the peculiarity of Father Kevin Murphy's sudden appointment to the parish.

"Numbnoddle sent him here from Wheatfield," Robin explained as he puffed on a cigar. "He's originally from New York."

"Yes, well, he was at the club the other day with a couple of Arabs, and he had that damned dog with him, too." Mr. Schultz took a drink from his tumbler. "Of course, they had to ask him to take the mutt outside. He threw a fit. It was our idea to invite him to the club, but I didn't tell him he could bring his mutt and those Palestinian sand fleas with him."

With his last words, Peggy glanced at me with a disapproving look.

"Have you ever figured out why he's here?" Mr. Schultz continued.

"Do we even want to know?" Robin smirked, removing his cigar from his mouth.

"He is one of Numbnoddle's boys—you're probably right," Mr. Schultz said.

"He still has his priestly faculties." Robin took a drink of Scotch.

"Who are those Mullahs Father Murphy hangs with?" Mr. Schultz asked.

"Those are most likely some of his soccer players."

"Soccer players?" Schultz's eyebrows moved down over his eyes.

"Yes, he's coaching a team at Inglenook College," Robin answered.

"I don't understand. He can hang around with Muslims but he can't stand Protestants."

"Yes, yes, I know. The phone's still ringing from the time I let him preach."

"That was *your* idea?" Schultz shook his head. "Good God, don't admit it publicly."

"Don't remind me." Robin closed his eyes and let his shoulders droop.

"What were you thinking?" Schultz drank down the rest of his scotch.

"I wasn't." Robin shook his head and lifted his tumbler to his lips again, finishing the drink with a smile.

"My wife asked him if he would be willing to go down-town and work with the Lutheran soup kitchen. He refused."

"Well, there you have it." Robin glanced at me. "American Protestants treated his immigrant family badly seventy-five years ago in a Catholic borough of New York, and he's never forgotten it."

"Robin, he's out of bounds." Schultz spun the ice in his glass. "You're going to have to sit on him. He's not in Ireland."

"He was born in America." Robin laughed.

"Exactly." Mr. Schultz looked in Robin's empty tumbler. "More Scotch?"

"Sure." Robin held out his glass.

After another drink and some talk about the lack of rain and the baseball season, Mrs. Schultz called out from the kitchen, "Peggy, tell everyone dinner is ready."

"Dinner, everyone," Peggy said as she stood. We both moved at the same time and my right hip bumped her bottom.

"I'm sorry," I said, hoping she didn't think I did it on purpose.

"It's all right." She smiled.

I was attracted to her, though I knew I couldn't do anything about it. I was going to be a priest. Or, at least, I was thinking about becoming a priest.

We all took a seat and Robin said the blessing. Peggy sat to my left. During the course of the meal, talk centered on the parish. My attention was on Peggy.

"I think it's inevitable that we consolidate some of the parishes, or in the least, some of the Mass schedules," Robin said, grasping his wineglass. "If the parishes can't worship together, then can we actually call ourselves Christian? Look at Mass attendance. Fifty-two percent! Lost Souls has the largest attendance of all five parishes in the area. Already Immaculate Heart is without a pastor. Then there's Saint Paul. Deacon Dill's out there and yet one of us has to go out there every Sunday and say Mass." Robin finished his wine.

"You can't just close the parishes and rent out the rectories and convents without the bishop's approval," Mr. Schultz said as he cleared his throat and poured Robin another glass of wine.

I had the same thought.

"And what the hell was Father Frisbee thinking when he had the pews removed from St. Patrick's? Now he's opened Pandora's box by announcing to his parish council that he thinks the Sunday night bingo should be eliminated. Who in the hell would have given him the crazy idea to get rid of one of the best money makers this side of the Alleghenies?"

"You never know," Robin said as he shook his head and smiled, making fleeting eye contact with me. Again, I could have provided a different perspective, but I didn't feel it was either the time or place.

"That bingo cleared five hundred thousand dollars last year alone!" Mr. Schultz exclaimed. "As long as the bingo committee can continue to twist everyone's arm to work the bingo, then Saint Patrick's will be in the black. Oh, and by the way, I have it on good authority that new pews were ordered this week. Old man McNally has offered to pay the entire cost just to get pews and kneelers back in the church."

Robin took another drink and closed his eyes.

"All I have to say is this, Rob, if you do what I think you might," Schultz continued, "you'll get spanked big time. Old Tony Tortellini Linguini—and clams—is going to send you out to the boonies. No more Saturday night symphonies, five-star restaurants, swimming pools, deluxe theaters, or university plays. If he sends you off to the corner of the diocese—there'll be no sign of civilization for miles. Your fare of culture will be the tractor pull, the demolition derby, or the Adams County Turkey Trot Festival, and the closest thing to a five-star dining experience will be a fifty-mile trip to McDonalds."

"I know, I know, Bucktooth Nowhere. But I honestly don't think he would—"

"Don't be so sure," Mr. Schultz waved his finger at Robin. "I hear that Father Jack Ash stirred things up in Possum Prairie. You could be sent there." Mr. Schultz took a drink before continuing. "You know, I asked the bishop once what he was doing to get people to return to the Church and he just mumbled, 'Jesus, Mary, and Joseph,' and blamed parents for not encouraging their sons to pursue the priesthood. He said, 'People are always praying for vocations—as long as it's someone else's son.'"

"If they'd let women be priests, we wouldn't be having this conversation," Peg said looking directly at her father as she sipped her wine.

"Let's don't go there, Peg." Mr. Schultz waved her off.

There was stifled laughter at the table.

* * * *

After dinner and dessert, Mr. Schultz invited Robin and me into the family room. "We're watching *The Thorn Birds.* Colleen loved it when it was on television back in the eighties so I ordered it for her from the video store."

A cassocked priest seemingly lusted after a teenage girl on the screen. I was embarrassed; the music and acting was cheesy. Peggy rolled her eyes and leaned next to her mother whispering something.

"Haven't you ever seen *The Thorn Birds?*" Mr. Schultz squinted at me.

"No," I replied, still glancing over at Peggy. Father David Gregory had decried the film from the pulpit, saying it was a scandalous film, derogatory to the Church.

"If you're going to be a priest," Mr. Schultz explained, "then you'd better watch it sometime before you get ordained."

At that Colleen spoke, "Dear, turn it off. They don't want to watch that."

"I thought you loved this movie." He frowned, holding the remote control in his right hand.

"Not now, Dear. Turn the channel."

"It's a videotape."

"Well, whatever," she said as she left the room. "Just turn it off."

"Okay, what about baseball? Professional wrestling?" Mr. Schultz smiled as he thumbed his remote control and turned to a wrestling match.

At that, Peggy opened the double doors that led outside and walked out on the veranda. The television had Robin and Mr. Schultz's attention, so I followed her outdoors. The crescent moon dangled between the leaves of the trees as soft music played over the outdoor speakers. It was Frank Sinatra.

"So, you decided to join me?" She leaned on the stone banister overlooking the woods.

"Is that all right?" I asked as I leaned against the banister and looked at the moon.

"Sure." She brushed her hair off her shoulders. "How are things at the parish?"

"Fine, I guess." I glanced at her neckline behind the wisps of her hair.

"How long have you been in the seminary, Martin?"

"Just a year." I heard myself accentuate *just*.

"How did you know you wanted to be a priest?" She made eye contact and seemed to move closer.

"I've thought about it from time to time. When I was younger, my brother and I used to play Mass. I was the priest and he was the server."

"But when did you know that you wanted to be a priest?" She touched my right arm.

I wordlessly pondered the question. Peggy was still looking at me as if expecting an answer. Her dimpled cheeks were illumined by the pale moonlight.

"Yes?" She repositioned her left hand on the veranda banister and lightly grazed my hand; I felt the warmth of her hand. "Go on," she said. "I've never been so close to an endangered species before."

"Endangered species?" I smelled her perfume again. Her hand was still next to mine. I couldn't just pull my hand away. That would be rude.

"A seminarian. You guys are a rare commodity these days. Don't you know?"

"Oh, yes, yes. That's funny."

"Then why didn't you laugh?"

"I just did."

"No, you didn't." She pulled her hand away. Peggy's sweetness and beauty—and directness—were disarming. I had seen her at church before, but now under the moonlit starry night of a warm July evening I truly saw her—as a woman.

"You aren't too sure, are you?" She smiled.

"Sure? About what?"

"Being a priest."

"Well, that's why they give us several years to make up our minds in the seminary."

"You still haven't answered my question."

Unnerved at her astuteness, I suddenly recalled the warning from my fellow seminarian, Austin Gerard. *Guard yourself against the wiles of women who will lie in wait to snatch you away from the priestly vocation.* It was crazy that I would even remember Gerard's words. *The temptress, Eve, had offered Adam the forbidden fruit, and he ate the apple to its core.*

"So are you sure?" she asked, persisting.

"I'm *just* a seminarian." I glanced in her direction, noticing her cleavage and round lips, but I avoided her eyes.

"*Just?* What does *that* mean?"

"I don't know." I was perturbed, not so much at Peggy as at myself for not knowing exactly what to think or how to answer her elementary questions.

"I'm not trying to pry; it's just that I'm curious. I would think it's got to be tough to become a priest these days."

"It is." I sighed, briefly imagining myself taking her into my arms.

"Not too many men know what they want these days." She turned away and gazed out into the night.

I said nothing, doubting my own certainty, and not quite sure of her intended meaning. The romantic music continued to play.

"Martin," she said, turning toward me once again, "what is it you want from life?"

The answer was clear: *I have no idea*, but the words never made it to my lips as I stared into the heavens, thinking of a way to answer.

"Oh, there you two are," Mrs. Schultz's voice displaced the silence, allowing me to avoid the question. "Come back inside. It's time for dessert and coffee."

Chapter 23: Hospital Call

Death comes for us all.
— St. Thomas More

On Monday night of the first week of August, I was alone at the parish. Father Robin had yet to return from his day off, Hyacinth was away visiting a cousin, Boniface was out with Monsignor Kelly, and Father Kevin was out, probably playing soccer. About eight p.m. the phone rang. It was St. Luke's Good Samaritan Hospital.

"Is there a priest available?" a scratchy-voiced woman asked.

"Not here. Have you tried St. Patrick's or Saint Sebastian's?"

"Yes, we've called both, and there's no answer at either church."

I was tempted to suggest that she call Immaculate Heart rectory and ask for Father Bill Gallagher, but I didn't.

"What exactly do you need?"

"We've got a Catholic who needs the Last Rites."

"Do you mean the *Anointing of the Sick?*"

"Whatever you call it, but you'd best get over here in a hurry because the family is about to come unglued."

I agreed to go even though I wouldn't be able to anoint since I wasn't ordained. When I arrived at the hospital, I was escorted to the intensive care unit by a bearded, middle-aged orderly in green hospital scrubs. Upon exiting the elevator, I saw several women sitting on the floor moaning. "Those are the man's sisters," the orderly pointed to the two heavy-set women in t-shirts and tight-fitting jeans. "Oh, and here's his wife." The woman, wearing a denim shirt with the American flag emblazoned across it, was crying copious tears and sobbing loudly. The orderly disappeared into the nurse's station, leaving me alone with the woman.

"Ma'am, I'm the seminarian, Martin Flanagan, from Poor Souls Catholic Church—"

"Where's the priest?" she asked.

"Father isn't available, but I came to pray with you and the family."

"We need the priest!" Her bent arthritic index finger was in my face.

"No you don't. I'm here!" a man in a light blue suit coat two sizes too small cried out. "Linda, no Roman priest is going to save Tommy. Listen to your brother for once. Neither one of you's got any faith. That's why Tommy's in there dying."

"Get away from us and quit preaching, Harry," the woman argued.

"Son," the man turned to me, "are you saved?"

"Leave Marvin alone, he's from the Catholic Church."

"You're a Catholic?" he asked me. "Do you pray in tongues?"

"Well, I've never—"

"Well I does. Come on in with me. I'll pray over Tommy."

"No, you leave him be!" Linda grabbed me by the arm.

Harry went into the room and slipped behind the curtain. Suddenly he came out yelling, "Why'd you go put pagan idols on him for?"

"Don't you touch them!" Linda shouted. "Them's going to heal him!"

I wanted to leave.

A doctor then arrived at the room. "What's the problem?"

"My brother is an annoying preacher man," Linda replied angrily.

The doctor shrugged his shoulders, grabbed a clipboard off the door, and went into the room. I followed the doctor in to see Tommy. The sick man was covered with runes, crystals, amulets, rabbit's feet, tarot cards, rosaries, and crucifixes. A clear plastic pyramid sat atop his forehead covering his eyes, and several lit votive candles had been placed at different points near his body along the edge of his hospital bed. The doctor cried out, "My God, we've got oxygen in use up here! Get rid of these candles!" he began blowing the flames out. "Get rid of this superstitious crap! This is a hospital, not a voodoo house!"

Linda stormed in, crying loudly, "NO! Why'd you mess it up! It took me an hour to get the energy fields just right! You've ruined his karma!" She fell to the floor and began collecting the assorted items.

"Why don't you take the family to the chapel?" one of the nurses asked me as she ran into the room to assist the doctor.

"And keep the family out of here!" the doctor called out.

I walked halfway down the hallway with Linda and the two women. Two other men who reeked of cigarette smoke joined us.

"The doctor suggested we go to the chapel—" I explained and nervously thought of something to do with them once we were there.

"No, we're staying up here." They ignored me. "We don't need no slick priest man telling us where to go."

Suddenly an alarm sounded, a blue light flickered on the wall, and a voice came over the intercom, "Code-Blue, ICU, room 402. Code-Blue, ICU, room 402." That was Tommy's room.

The family scrambled to their feet, ran back to his room, and stood in the hall. I rejoined them in hopes of maintaining some semblance of order. A tall, clean- shaven, black security guard appeared from the end of the hall and stood guard at the door of the room. "The family needs to limit the number of visitors," the deep-voiced, uniformed officer spoke directly. "Only the wife and immediate family will be allowed on the floor. The rest of you may go downstairs to the chapel or else meet in the cafeteria." Only Linda and her brother, Harry the preacher, remained.

"Go with the chaplain," said the guard.

I joined the family members in the elevator but once we were at the cafeteria one of the men told me, "Just go away, we don't need you none. We got enough of it from Hypocritical Harry."

I was relieved to leave them, but I prayed for Tommy, knowing that things didn't look or sound good. When I stopped at the front desk to tell the receptionist that I was leaving, she asked me if I would mind going to the seventh floor. There was another Catholic family who had just requested a priest to be with a dying member of their family.

I thought of the irony in being called on for two dying Catholics in such a short period of time, but then again, maybe not. Deaths often seemed to come in threes.

Jotting down the room number, I returned to the elevators. When I arrived on the seventh floor, things were quiet. Almost too quiet. When I got to the room, I looked in before entering. There was a low, soft murmur of words. *"Hail, Mary, full of grace…"*

A pale, elderly woman was in the hospital bed while three women stood next to her, praying their beads and holding the woman's hands. I slowly entered the room, removed my brown, wooden rosary from my pocket, and began praying along, "*Holy Mary, Mother of God, pray for us sinners, now and at the hour of our death. Amen.*" One of the women turned at my reply. She was a gray-haired woman in her sixties wearing a white cotton blouse and a navy skirt. The other two women turned, nodded, and gave me bittersweet smiles. They then turned back to the sick woman. The second woman was dressed in a red jogging suit and had long, gray-streaked black hair. The last woman was slightly younger, in her forties, and wore a green cowl-necked shirt and blue jeans.

Nearing the end of the rosary's prayers, the three women wept and held each other as their loved one struggled to breathe. Her difficulty was increasing with each bead of the rosary. Beginning with the last prayer to end the devotion, I watched as the dying woman opened her eyes and gasped for air, as if attempting to speak. The women all began calling to her and reached for her hands. "Celeste, Celeste, we're here, sweetheart!" Celeste raised herself up on her bed, reached out toward the end of the bed, and tried to speak. It sounded as if she was trying to say "Jesus."

The woman in the white shirt and navy skirt looked at me and called out, "What's she see?"

"I don't know," I replied as I stepped closer to the women.

"She must see the Lord," the younger woman said as she squeezed Celeste's hand. "Do you see Jesus?" Celeste lost her strength and slowly fell back to her pillows and began gasping for more air.

"I'll get the nurse," the woman in red said as she left the room.

The two women then stood silently by, each holding one of Celeste's hands in theirs. They were still clutching their rosaries tightly.

The older woman then turned to me as I approached her. "I'm Mary. Are you a priest?"

"No, I'm Martin Flanagan. I'm a seminarian assigned to Poor Souls' parish. No priest is available."

"Celeste is my sister. She's been in a coma since her last heart attack two weeks ago." She reached out and took my right hand in her left.

"I'm sorry," I said as I watched Celeste and stood next to Mary.

"I'm Collette," the younger woman spoke. "Celeste is my aunt."

"Collette's my daughter," Mary explained. "A Father Kevin Murphy anointed Celeste the other day."

Celeste's breathing became more and more labored. Slowly, the rise and fall of her chest became less and less visible. Mary let loose of my hand and hovered over Celeste and began praying again, this time in Latin.

Ave, Maria, gratia plena, Dominus tecum...

The other woman returned at that point and joined in with the prayer. Celeste inhaled and her chest rose slightly only to slowly collapse as her air exhaled noisily. Celeste's chest collapsed as a slight smile overtook her face while the air escaped her lungs. The women continued to hold her hands while she exhaled.

As the rigidity of Celeste's body eased, the tension in her neck and face relaxed. I waited for her to inhale again and watched for her chest to rise. It did not. The women were still praying when I spoke. "Ladies, I think she's gone."

Just as I said the words, a nurse walked into the room and went over to Celeste's bed. The nurse delicately held

Celeste's hand and looked at the women. "Celeste's with the Lord." All three of the women smiled through tears and hugged each other and kissed Celeste's hands and face. The nurse wiped away a tear. "She's at peace now."

All three wept, bereaved at their loss, yet also happy for Celeste's freedom from the pain. Mary reached over and pulled me close as she stepped up close to Celeste's body. Mary stroked Celeste's sweaty hair and face. "We loved her so much. The Lord gave her to us and now He's called her home." Mary wept again. The three women talked about the wonderful times they had with Celeste while she was alive and how happy they were that she was now in heaven with Jesus and all the angels and saints.

The nurse then encouraged the women to say their goodbyes. Mary told her, "We already said our goodbyes. We loved her in life; we will not abandon her in death." I wondered why I was even there. Unlike the previous family, this family was at peace in the face of death.

As I made my way back to the rectory, I wondered how I would die. *Will loved ones surround me? When will I die?* My father had died alone.

In the seminary, Father Hugh had once said that every time he experienced a death, the more he wanted to live each day of his life to its fullest. I began to understand the scripture passage from the psalms, *Lord, make us know the shortness of our life that we may gain wisdom of heart.* I prayed I would never share my deathbed with the shallowness of superstition.

Chapter 24: Revelations

Hell is full of good intentions and desires.
— St. Bernard of Clairvaux

With Father Kevin Murphy away on a retreat, Father Robin decided that this was the weekend to reveal his plan, his vision for the Inglenook community. He mounted the pulpit that Saturday evening, which was unusual. He was in the habit of walking up and down the main aisle of the church as he delivered his homily, or what seemed like a comedian's monologue. However, tonight, he read from a prepared text.

I observed the parishioners from the back of church. There was a lot of fidgeting in the pews. A couple of men stood up and moved toward the back of church. Robin explained how everyone would notice a change in the bulletin and detailed the plans to consolidate the living quarters to Poor Souls and the parish office to St. Patrick's.

I wondered what the bishop and Monsignor Linguini would say or do once they found out what Father Robin was doing. My vocation director, Father Samuel Good, had told me to follow the advice of my pastor and not try to change things, but was I wrong to keep this information to myself?

After Mass, several parishioners sought out Father Robin. All those who spoke to him complimented him except one elderly woman. She held Father Robin's hand and looked at him sternly. "Bishop Munchkin's lost his mind. This will never work."

"I'll remember that." Robin chuckled and returned the woman's hand. "Thank you."

She started to walk away, but turned back and said, "You ought to put a stop to it!"

"I'll do what I can," he said with a nod.

On Sunday morning, Robin repeated his same homily and met with similar approval, but according to him, it was the ones who didn't say anything that really worried him. He asked me if I had heard anything negative after the Masses. I hadn't. "Give them time to absorb it, I guess," I said.

"Well, you're no help." Robin walked to the sacristy to disrobe.

I returned to the rectory to tend to Father Kevin's birds and Bubby, the dog. Reluctantly, I had agreed to feed the birds and take care of Bubby while Father Kevin was away for his retreat. Father Kevin had warned me that Bubby might be upset over his weeklong absence, though he didn't give any specifics as to how Bubby might express her displeasure.

To my horror when I went to check on Bubby, I discovered that she had pooped all over the living room floor in front of Robin's easy chair. I grabbed a roll of paper towels and a bottle of cleaner from the kitchen in order to clean up the mess.

Boniface complained all night about the stench. "I'll be damned. This is a rectory, not Noah's ark!"

I began to despise Bubby. Hyacinth suggested that she could cook Bubby, serve her to Father Robin, knock the two birds on the head, and serve them up ala Cornish hens.

* * * *

On Monday morning, a ringing noise sounded in my ears.

Finally realizing I wasn't dreaming, I answered the bedside phone. I squinted in the morning sun and glanced at the digital clock: 6:40 a.m.

"Martin?" A strong male voice resounded on the other end of the line.

"Yes." I worked to not sound groggy. I recognized the voice, but at such an early hour, I couldn't place it with a face or name.

"Martin, this is Monsignor Michael Linguini. Is Father Robin in?"

"No, Monsignor. Today is his day off."

"Oh, really? Do you know where I can reach him?"

"No."

"You have no emergency number where I can contact him?"

"No."

"That's convenient." He paused for a moment and breathed into the phone. "When does the parish secretary arrive at work?"

"At eight-thirty."

"Very well. Martin, you are to instruct her to call Father Robin—I'm sure she has the number—and give him this message: he is to call me here at the chancery *immediately*. If she cannot follow through on this, then she must call *me* immediately. It is of the utmost urgency. Do you understand? *Immediately*."

"Yes."

"Thank you, Martin." With that, the phone went dead.

I figured that word had reached Covert about Father Robin's plans for the deanery.

When I went downstairs for morning Mass, Boniface was slumped down in one of the kitchen chairs. Hyacinth stood behind him with her hands on his shoulders.

"Martin Flanagan!" Hyacinth's shrill voice pierced the air.

"Yes?" I replied, looking down at Boniface. "Is he all right?"

"Don't give me that. Why didn't you tell us?"

"Tell you what?" I had a gnawing feeling that she was referring to Father Robin's weekend announcement.

"What else would it be?" Hyacinth coldly replied. "Did you know about *that one*'s plans?"

"Some of it."

"Then you knew that I was going to be let go, and Boniface is going to be placed in a nursing home?" Hyacinth asked.

"Now, wait, I don't think—" I stammered; I had not known any of *those* plans.

"That's right, *you* don't think." Hyacinth wrung out her apron. "Who does your thinking for you?"

"Hyacinth, easy on the boy!" Boniface interrupted, tapping his cane on the floor.

"Never mind," Hyacinth continued. "Father Boniface says his chest hurts." Hyacinth put her hands on his shoulders again.

"Oh, why'd you tell him? It's nothing." Boniface shook his head. "I'm fine. I just need some breakfast."

"*That one*. He's a real piece of work, he is. Letting me go and dumping Boniface in a warehouse for the dying. You might as well put him in the insane asylum."

"Speak for yourself, woman."

"How do you know this, Hyacinth?" I returned to her claim.

"I found *that one*'s notes in the trash. This is one time he should've been more careful and flushed them down the toilet." She produced two yellow legal sheets with scribbles and notes. Written upon the top two lines of the second sheet were the words:

Hyacinth. Gone. X.
Boniface. Nursing home.
Sr. Precious Blood to motherhouse.
Convent and other rectories—convert to rental properties.

"Poor Sister Precious. She's lived in the convent for over thirty years," Hyacinth said as she left the room.

* * * *

On Tuesday morning, Father Robin entered the kitchen before Mass. Hyacinth wouldn't even look at him and breathed loudly through her nose before leaving.

"Father Robin," I began, "Did you call Monsignor Linguini?"

"Yes," he answered slowly and in a monotone as he stood at the coffee pot and poured himself a cup. Turning around, he asked, "Martin, have you heard the news?"

"What news?"

"Father David Gregory was killed in a car wreck just outside of Cainbrook." Robin was calm as if completely unaffected by the news. "It's in this morning's paper."

I couldn't believe his words and was stunned with the ease in which he conveyed the information. "I just saw him less than two weeks ago." A wave of nausea hit me.

"Yes, well, they're not sure if he fell asleep at the wheel or what. One witness says he was run off the road while another says he swerved to avoid an oncoming car."

My thoughts turned to the eerily prescient words of the young men Father David and I had encountered in the Cainbrook Café: *Die, priest, die!*

I needed to be alone and excused myself from the breakfast table. The thought of my own father's death flooded my memory. My aunt crying uncontrollably. Sean's unemotional withdrawal. My mother's relief that he was gone. My own emptiness.

* * * *

Within two days, the funeral plans for Father David had been set. Funeral visitation was at Our Lady of the River in Cainbrook. I accompanied my mother. She wore her large, dark sunglasses and a black dress. Sean came to church about fifteen minutes before the funeral Mass was to begin. Since I was serving as an acolyte and helping prepare for Mass, I only had a moment with him.

"Sean!' I said as I extended my hand, surprised to see him. "Thanks for coming."

"I wouldn't miss Father David's funeral." He avoided eye contact with me as he barely shook my hand. "He's the one priest I respected."

I said nothing and returned to the sacristy where most of the diocesan priests were vesting for the Mass. Bishop Munchin and Monsignor Linguini had just arrived.

At the homily, the bishop honored Father David by calling him "a king among men."

Mother was stoic throughout the Mass. Sean stared emptily into the sanctuary. Even if he had wanted to cry, I knew he wouldn't. The pipe organ played softly as the funeral director and pallbearers slowly rolled Father David's coffin to the rear of the church. Once the white pall was removed, the pallbearers lifted the coffin and carried it to the waiting hearse.

At the end of the funeral Mass, I gathered the holy water pail and aspergillum and made my way to one of the waiting funeral cars. The sun was brightly shining on the windows of the hearse and the other limousines. The funeral director, dressed in a black pinstriped suit, opened the lead car's right rear passenger door for me and ushered me inside. I lifted the end of my cassock, making sure I didn't trip over it, and climbed in, careful not to spill the holy water. The director closed the door, and I looked over at the occupant of the seat next to me. It was the bishop. In the front passenger seat sat the vicar-general, Monsignor Michael Linguini.

The bishop spoke first. "Martin Flanagan."

"Yes, Your Excellency." I straightened in my seat.

"Bishop is quite enough."

"Bishop."

The funeral director walked around the car, opened the driver's door, got behind the wheel, and put the car into gear. A black and white police cruiser with flashing red, white, and blue bar lights pulled in front of the funeral procession.

"So, Martin, how are things at Poor Souls?" the bishop asked as he looked at me.

"Fine, I guess." I was intimidated by his and Linguini's presence.

"You mean you don't know? You've been living there for nearly two months," Linguini said, turning around in the front seat.

"What? Come now, son, do I look like a fool?" The bishop winced.

"I don't understand," I answered, looking at Linguini.

"He's simply asking you how things are at the parish," Linguini said as he looked at me without emotion.

"Things are fine." I avoided Linguini's gaze, preferring to focus on the flickering lights atop the patrol car.

"*Fine?*" Linguini said as he turned around and looked ahead.

"That housekeeper, *the General*, what's her name?" the bishop turned to me and asked.

"Hyacinth," Linguini replied under his breath. "The parish flower."

"Oh, yes." The bishop chuckled and glanced away out the left side of the car.

"So, Martin," Linguini turned around again and smiled wide. "Has the Venus Flytrap bitten you yet?"

"Bitten me?"

"It's a figure of speech, son." Linguini smirked as he turned away.

"You're a bit jumpy." The bishop reached over and placed his hand on my left shoulder.

"Well, I was close to Father David, and his death was so sudden."

"Yes. I know." The bishop removed his hand. "On the subject of pastors, what is our dear Father Robin up to over at Lost Souls?"

"He's doing things without the bishop's approval," Linguini answered for me.

I didn't know what else to say even though Linguini had spoken the truth.

"Mr. Flanagan," Linguini said slowly and evenly. "We know about things. We've seen the new bulletins he had printed for the parish. We also heard about the sermon he gave last weekend."

"Oh." I was stuck. I studied the door handle and the unlock buttons and ashtray.

"Oh?" The bishop snickered. "Is that all you can say?"

"I don't know." I wanted to disappear and be anywhere but in that Cadillac with Linguini and the bishop.

"So much for his promise of obedience to his bishop." Linguini laughed and looked out the window at a police officer saluting the procession. "Here's the cemetery."

Saved by the sexton.

* * * *

As we stepped out of the car, we climbed the hill to where many of the Diocesan priests were buried. The open grave was like a gaping wound upon the earth. The bishop reached for the aspergillum and sprinkled holy water in the grave. He returned the sprinkler to the bucket and led us in prayer.

After the prayers, the sextons lowered the coffin into the ground, and the bishop was given a shovel. He pressed it into the mound of freshly turned dirt and tossed a shovelful atop Father David's coffin. The thud made some of the people attending cringe or start. The funeral directors then quietly dismissed everyone to return to their cars.

I rode back in the hearse with the funeral director. It was a bit morbid, I'll admit, but at least I didn't have to deal with the bishop and vicar-general.

Many things going on in the diocese seemed so political and were conducted with so much hush-hush that it seemed the Church's hierarchy had made it a habit of keeping everything in the dark and acting like the church should be above scrutiny.

In the seminary, I had been taught the opposite—both in word and by example.

Chapter 25: Changes

God commands you to pray,
but He forbids you to worry.
— St. John Vianney

On Thursday morning, Boniface said Mass. As he was about to lift the chalice of wine at the consecration, he clutched his chest and collapsed to the floor. I rushed into the sanctuary with another parishioner, a doctor from St. Luke's Good Samaritan Hospital. He called for an ambulance on his cellular telephone.

Boniface was conscious; yet, his face was contorted, and he clutched the left side of his chest. He complained most about his legs and not his chest. Half of the church, it seemed, was in the sanctuary. An elderly, silver-haired female parishioner wept as she looked at Boniface stretched out on the floor behind the altar.

I ran over to the rectory and got Hyacinth and Father Robin. We quickly returned. Hyacinth knelt at Boniface's side, held his hand, and stroked his head with a wet towel she got from the sacristy until the rescue squad and ambulance arrived. The paramedics placed Boniface on a stretcher, and Hyacinth rode to the hospital in the back of the ambulance with him.

"I told him he should be in a retirement home or something," Father Robin said as the ambulance pulled away from the church. Later that morning Hyacinth called from the hospital to tell us that Boniface had been admitted. He was conscious and seemed fine.

That evening was the regular parish council meeting. Robin began the meeting with a reading from the book of Revelation. "*Behold I make all things new.*" Then without a reading from the previous meeting's minutes, he described his plan for the parish community of the Inglenook deanery. He showed them an architect's drawing of the plans for remodeling Poor Souls' and St. Patrick's rectories. He had another artist's rendering of Poor Souls showing a new baptistery pool in the sanctuary minus the communion rail, statues, and high altar. Then he told the council members that he was going to remove the votive candles in the church and replace them with electric votive lamps that light up after a quarter is deposited into the coin slot. "It's too dangerous to have so many open flames in such an old church."

"Those electric votive lights are tacky, Father," one of the older female members argued.

"Which do you prefer, a tacky candle stand or the smoldering remains of a church?" he asked.

"It depends on what Poor Souls will look like after you're finished tearing it up," she replied as she looked down and reached for her purse as if preparing to leave.

He ignored her comment and pointed at a map of Inglenook.

"How's Father Boniface?" An aged, thin, white-haired, retired professor from Inglenook College leaned next to me. "Father Wood didn't even mention him."

I wanted to answer, but Robin turned at the sound of the man's voice.

"Now all the priests will live here at Lost Souls——" Robin continued.

"*Poor Souls*, Father Wood," the aged man spoke, reminding Father Robin, "Our Lady of the Poor and Forgotten Souls in Purgatory."

"*Poor Souls*. My mistake."

"Listen, Father Wood, I realize you don't like us here at Poor Souls." The old professor cleared his throat. "Sometimes I wonder if you think we're old fuddy-duds who want to act like Vatican II didn't happen——"

"That's not true. Now, as I was saying, all the priests will live here at Poor Souls, and the offices will be at St. Patrick's." He then went on to describe how the other parishes would be reduced to chapels. That was as far as he got before several of the members said that he should take these matters up with the bishop in Covert.

"You had no right to have the pews removed from St. Patrick's church," the aged professor said. "Some of the people down there are heartbroken. You could have at least asked them. And letting Father Frisbee take the blame was underhanded."

"What parish is this?" Robin asked rhetorically. "Poor Souls, isn't it? So let's leave St. Patrick's out of it."

"Excuse me, Father," the professor spoke again, "but you just said that all the parishes were one. So what goes on at St. Patrick's should concern us, right?"

Robin's fist came down on the table hard. "Who's the pastor here?"

At that the professor stood and tossed his council agenda on the table; he walked out of the building.

I was uncomfortable with Robin's brusqueness with the people. In fact, I felt angry and also felt like leaving.

Even Martha Hart was upset. "I hope you're making the

right decision, Father. When I became a Catholic I was taught that the church is the people, not just the buildings."

"We've got to pool resources and consolidate services," Robin countered. "Besides, there aren't enough priests these days."

"So? Ordain more. Men *and women*," Martha Hart replied.

"It isn't that easy." Robin sighed and placed his hands, palms down, on the table.

"Oh, yes. I forgot." Another woman grabbed up her purse and went for the door but not without a Parthian shot. "The church only allows the Holy Spirit to call celibate males to the priesthood."

"I think our meeting is at an end," Robin stood and announced. No one spoke as those remaining filed out.

I followed Robin out of the meeting room. Once back at the rectory, he went into the kitchen and poured himself a glass of Scotch. He ignored me as he went into the living room and turned on the television. He sat watching a program of four angry people exchanging barbs and debating President Clinton's legacy.

I had yet to take Bubby for her evening walk, so I got her leash and went out the back door. When I returned about a half hour later the television was off, but Robin was on his office phone. His voice was raised.

"Well, good. We don't need your complaining anyway." A brief pause followed. "Go ahead, but good luck finding them. I'd look in the city dump. Yeah, I'm sure there's more than one stupid statue out there along with some old pews, too." He slammed the phone down only to pick it up again and make another call.

I moved out into the hall to listen.

"Yes, is this Al? Yes, it is... Well, isn't that something? I was just calling to tell you that I've disbanded the whole council. We need young blood, and I'll get people from every parish… Thanks… Yeah, you bet… Well, why don't you tell me what you really think?"

The phone went down.

I sat in silence, eavesdropping on my pastor, wondering if I should say something. But before I could, the phone was off the hook again.

"That's right. A fresh start… What? Don't try and tell me anything." There was a moment of silence. "Well, Vatican II did happen…. Is that right? You'll have to drive two hours for the nearest Latin Mass. You might find some of those statues I tossed out up there. I hear the people there collect relics. Maybe they'll add you to their collection!"

Down went the phone. "Damn!" Robin said aloud after he had hung up.

I had heard enough and retired to my room for the night. The arguing tone of Father Robin left me uneasy. It reminded me of the tiffs between my mother and father when I was a child. I could never sleep on the nights they fought. I lay in bed thinking about what direction the church was going. I tried to fall asleep by thumbing my rosary beads, praying for Father Boniface, Father Robin, and all the parishes of Inglenook.

* * * *

On Friday morning, Robin rushed through his Mass and left afterwards, not even taking breakfast. Hyacinth cackled as she cooked bacon and eggs. "Well, *that one* sure got his clock cleaned last night, didn't he?"

"What?" I wondered what she could have already heard.

"Martin, don't play dumb on me. News travels fast in Inglenook. Robin couldn't win at monopoly so he grabbed up the game board and ran home like a spoiled brat. *That one* isn't worthy of the priesthood."

Suddenly Bubby ran into the kitchen and Father Kevin followed. "No one's worthy of the priesthood, Hyacinth," Kevin said. "The priesthood is a gift." He knelt down and kissed Bubby's nose.

"And some gifts aren't appreciated, are they?" she replied. "When did you get back from your retreat?"

"Late last night. Oh," he said, turning to me, "Martin, did you know that Bubby crapped all over my bedroom floor? Don't worry, Hyacinth. I cleaned it up. But thanks for taking care of her, Martin. I owe you one."

"You're welcome." I was relieved that I didn't have to deal with that dog and her crap anymore. Of course, I would still have to contend with Cat's hairball vomit.

"Father Kevin, you missed the fireworks." Hyacinth smiled, handing him a cup of black coffee as he came to the table.

"Fireworks? The fourth of July was last month." He pulled out a chair and sat.

"No, I'm referring to last night's parish fireworks. Our notorious pastor, Father Robin, has decided that he's the bishop of Inglenook."

"How's that?"

"Look at the new bulletins." She handed Kevin one of the folded copies.

"What?" Kevin asked. "I've seen them." He took a sip of coffee.

"The bishop never approved any of this!" Hyacinth announced.

Kevin nearly spat his coffee.

"*That one* sure is a work of art, he is," Hyacinth continued and sat with us at the table. "And he has plans to get rid of me and put Boniface out to pasture."

"I assumed this was a decision made at the diocesan

level." Kevin angrily looked up from the bulletin.

"Of course you did. You were supposed to think that because you're just passing through. Old Robin Hood's kept you hidden in Sherwood Forest."

"That's an interesting metaphor." He toyed with his coffee cup, spinning it on the saucer.

"Yes, the Sheriff of Nottingham will be here soon." Hyacinth arranged her napkin on her placemat.

"Who?" He took his hands away from his cup.

"His Highness's sheriff, our venerable vicar-general, Monsignor Lasagna," she said as she looked up. "He's the one who really runs the diocese; he and the Fair Lady Chancellor, Sister Dymphna."

"But—" Kevin began.

"Mark my word," she said. "And to add to the mix, Father Boniface is in the hospital." She then explained what had happened.

"Is he all right?"

"We think so," Hyacinth said and turned toward me. "Which reminds me, Martin, will you drive me to the hospital today to see Father Boniface?"

"Yes. I have communion calls anyway," I answered. "We can go to the hospital first and then I'll bring you back to the rectory before I make the other calls."

* * * *

After breakfast, we drove to St. Luke's and visited Boniface. He was seated in a wheelchair and looked as normal as he ever did. "I'm much better. They said I probably just had indigestion," Boniface smiled. "Too much popcorn or something. As for my legs, they say I've got poor circulation. They say my blood sugar and cholesterol levels are too high."

"Now, don't go blaming my cooking for your poor health." Hyacinth took a seat on Boniface's hospital bed.

"I think I need a second opinion." He caressed the armrest of his wheelchair with his left hand.

"When do you think you'll get to come home?" Hyacinth asked.

"Monday or Tuesday. My right hip is really bruised."

"Good. That will give me time to clean out those rats' nests of yours."

"Now, don't go messing with my stuff. I know where everything is. If you move it, I really will have a heart attack."

I gave Boniface communion and let Hyacinth have some time alone with him.

* * * *

As we returned to the parish, Hyacinth turned to me and said, "He's my buddy, you know."

I nodded as I looked ahead into traffic.

"Answer a question for me, Martin. How are you doing?"

"Fine. I guess," I replied as I approached a stop.

"You guess?" She bristled, still looking in my direction.

I turned toward her briefly before looking back to the road ahead. "I don't know."

"What's up with you and that Schultz girl? I saw you light up like a firefly the other day when she sang at the nine o'clock Mass."

"What?" I kept my gaze straight ahead. Peggy was one of the cantors in the choir.

"Martin. I may be old, but I'm not blind." Hyacinth shook her head as we pulled up in front of the rectory. I let her out and chose to take lunch at the *Pancake Palace* alone. After lunch, I returned to my regular communion calls. I stopped at Viola Pitts' home. It was brief as usual.

When I arrived at Mabel Murphy's, she wanted to talk. "How's Father Boniface? I heard that he fell during Mass on Monday."

"Yes, he did." Classical music was playing softly in the background.

"Was it a heart attack?" she asked, handing me a cup of tea on a matching saucer.

"They don't think so. I've just come from the hospital, and he should be home by Monday or Tuesday."

"Well, good. We need good priests like him. Sometimes I don't know what's with our church." She shook her head and sipped her tea. "One of the ladies from the altar society called me this week and told me that one of her priests yanked out all the pews at St. Patrick's. He's gutting the place, she says. I never thought she'd stop crying."

"The pews will be replaced." I tried to sound reassuring.

"But they have to sit on folding chairs in the school cafeteria." She replaced her teacup on its saucer.

"It's only temporary," I said, distracted by a huge gaudy tapestry of the Last Supper hanging on the wall of her dining room.

"Then I also heard that the bishop's going to close half our parishes."

"That's not true." I looked at her again.

"Well, that's what she told me. She even said that Father Robin Wood was going to get rid of the communion rail at Poor Souls. He can't do that. I knelt at that communion rail when I received my first communion sixty years ago."

I made no response, though I could appreciate her sentiment.

"So, enough tittle-tattle, how are you?" she asked.

"Fine."

"*Really?* You look tired."

"A priest friend of mine, Father David Gregory, died this past week in a car wreck."

"Oh, dear, that's right. These days I can't remember

from one day to the next. The memory's the first to go, you know. I saw it on the news and in the paper. Were you two close?"

"Yes. He was my pastor at Our Lady of the River, and he was the priest that encouraged me to enter the seminary."

"I'm so sorry." She closed her eyes and bowed her head slightly. "I'll keep both of you in my prayers."

"Thank you." With that, I opened the prayer book and prayed a psalm and a gospel passage. We prayed the *Our Father* before I gave her communion.

I then visited Timmy Wimm at the nursing home. The thirty-some year old man had been in the nursing home for half his life, a teenage victim of a drunk driver. Timmy was helpless as he sat in his wheelchair. His hands and fingers were withered and curled, hardly functional. His eyes were crossed, and he wore a child's bib to catch the drool that perpetually dribbled from his mouth. The one thing he could do was smile. When I brought the Eucharist out of my pocket, Timmy opened his mouth wide. His tongue was a discolored pasty yellow and his breath foul. I focused my thoughts on prayer. The man folded his hands, interlocking some of his fingers as he closed his eyes in thanksgiving.

He was a man, cut down in his prime, who still had the faith of a child. The daily vesture of tragedy and death surrounded me. I drove to the Snake River Dam and stood on the levee as the waters flowed by.

By the time I returned to my car, I was in tears.

Chapter 26: Fly Away

'Tis mad idolatry to make the service
greater than the god.
— *Troilus and Cressida*, II, ii, 56

On Saturday morning, I went to Mass. While Father Kevin celebrated Mass, I sat in one of the front pews of the church and heard Bubby's toenails clacking against the sacristy door. Kevin continued to pray the Eucharistic Prayer undisturbed while the dog pounced on the door. Suddenly a loud bang sounded against the wall and Bubby appeared in the sanctuary, victoriously jumping at Kevin's feet just as he elevated the chalice in consecration.

Initially, I expected Kevin to do something with Bubby, but he did not; he continued with the Mass as if nothing was happening. Several of the parishioners were whispering among themselves, and a few were giggling. I reverently came forward into the sanctuary to corral Bubby since Kevin was completely oblivious to the distraction she was causing. Coaxing Bubby into my arms wasn't easy. She would get close and then back off. After the third time, I reached out and grabbed her by the collar. She yelped and whined. Then she growled, barked, and tried to bite me. I was thoroughly humiliated and feared that some of the people might think Bubby was mine. I dragged her away first to the sacristy and then back to the rectory. By the time I returned to the church, Mass was nearly at an end.

Immediately after Mass, Father Kevin chastised me for distracting people during the prayer. "In Steubenville, some children turned over the votive candles, and they caught the church on fire. But did the priest stop Mass? No. He kept on praying. One cannot stop Mass for trifles."

"Trifles?" I had half expected him to thank me for what I had done.

"You know what I mean."

"Not really," I inadvertently rolled my eyes, "but I'll just take your word for it."

"Well, never mind trifles; there's something I must discuss with you. This morning before Mass there was a man in the confessional impersonating a priest by hearing confessions. One of the ladies said he smelled of whiskey and another one said the man used to be a priest. So, Martin, what's with this rumor I've heard about a priest who used to be here at Poor Souls but left the priesthood for a liberal nun? Is this the man?"

"Well, I don't know all the particulars, but I've been told there was a priest who married a nun."

"Don't you ever let a woman become a trifle to you, or else you'll lose your vocation like that priest did. Look at what happened to Adam's race after Eve succumbed to the serpent's temptation."

"Adam was *with* Eve when they fell from grace," I reminded him of the scriptural account.

"Likely story," he harrumphed.

I said nothing, but thought of Peggy Schultz. She didn't seem to be a trifle. Not that I was necessarily thinking of abandoning the call to the priesthood. Nevertheless, Father Kevin's suggestion equating women with trifles and blaming *The Fall* on Eve didn't sit well with me.

"Martin," he said as he removed his priestly vestments, "you need to get some exercise. Why don't you come with me sometime and play soccer? You could even join our team. Ishmael, Josef, Abram and the others would be glad to have you."

"I'll think about it." I only said it to appease him.

"Please do. If you don't exercise, then your cholesterol levels will go through the roof, and by the time, you're forty you'll be a heart attack waiting to happen. It will also help you deal with pent-up emotion—and other things like that."

I went to the library that morning and perused some of the classical music selections and looked at the new, nonfiction books before taking lunch at a fast-food restaurant.

* * * *

Upon my return to the rectory, Father Kevin was frantic. One of his birds was missing, and he was looking everywhere.

"Damian's gone!" The birds, Cosmas and Damian, were named for the twin Arabian brothers, Saints Cosmas and Damian who were martyred for their Christian faith.

Father Kevin eyed Hyacinth standing in the kitchen doorway caressing her fat tabby in her arms. Cat opened his mouth in a wide yawn, his tongue outstretched and teeth showing. Kevin pursed his lips and narrowed his eyes as he glared at Cat. "You'd better have nothing to do with this." Kevin disappeared upstairs again.

Hyacinth put Cat down and called me into the kitchen. "Have you seen Father Robin today?"

"No. Why?"

"Look in the garage." She nodded to the kitchen's access door.

Opening the door into the garage, I saw Father Robin's car. "His car's here." I shut the door and returned to the table.

"Yes, I know." She nodded again and motioned for me to sit down. "Sit. I have something to tell you."

"What's wrong?" I sat at the head of the kitchen table wondering if Robin was sick, or worse, dead.

She sat opposite me. "This morning, not long after you left, Monsignor Linguini and the Chancellor, Sister Dymphna, came and got him."

"Is he all right?"

"I don't know. All I know is that when he answered the door, those two weren't happy. They gave him a few minutes to pack some of his stuff, then he got in Linguini's car and they drove away. They left a note for Father Kevin. He is to take all of the weekend masses."

"Did they say where they were taking him?" I asked as I saw that the coffee pot was nearly full.

"No, but I did hear Linguini tell Robin that he was being relieved of his priestly faculties."

"That's not good." Removing a priest's faculties was usually only done for a serious breach of pastoral responsibilities or violation of Canon Law—or both.

"That's a relative statement." Hyacinth straightened her back and sat erect. "It serves *that one* right."

I leaned back in the chair. "Does Father Kevin know?"

"He's read the note from Linguini, but he's out there losing his mind over that damned bird."

"You haven't seen it, have you?" I asked as I looked at the curtains above the kitchen sink, scanning for any sign of the bird.

Hyacinth hesitated, closed her eyes and frowned. "The note?"

"No, Father Kevin's bird."

She sighed and looked around as if she was about to tell a secret.

"Well? Have you?" I hoped that Cat hadn't eaten cockatiel for lunch.

"Don't tell Father Kevin, but right before Linguini and Dymphna got here, *that one* was chasing one of the birds out of his room. Both birds were flying around in the house. One of them was downstairs and flew past me here in the kitchen. I'm not sure if Father Robin nailed it with his newspaper or if it got out when Linguini propped the front door open to help carry Father Robin's luggage to the car. The dumb thing could have flown out the door at anytime. It could be anywhere—dead or alive."

I shook my head and laughed even though it wasn't funny.

* * * *

The vocation director, Father Samuel Good, called me that afternoon because of the unusual situation that was unfolding at Poor Souls. "Martin, you are to remain at the parish for now. Father Frisbee will likely be named the Parish Administrator until a new pastor can be named. Just keep your wits about you. Things could be worse. If we were to move you, it would only add to the instability of Lost Souls."

"*Poor Souls*, Father," I corrected him.

"Oh, drat. Sorry." Samuel sighed. "Poor Souls."

That weekend, Father Kevin had all the masses, but neither mentioned nor explained Father Robin's absence to the parish. He preached on the gospel message, *to whom much is given, much will be demanded.*

* * * *

On Monday, Father Boniface was released from the hospital and returned to the parish. The bishop had also called him and scheduled a visit for Thursday night.

Father Samuel called me again on Tuesday morning. "I just called to make sure you understand that you are expected to be present for the dinner with Bishop Munchin and the vicar-general, Monsignor Linguini."

Somehow, I sensed that the dinner could prove most interesting.

Chapter 27: Dinner with the Bishop

Alas, how many bad priests there are,
how many who are not holy enough!
Let us pray, let us suffer for them....
— St. Thérèse of Lisieux

After Thursday morning's Mass, I returned to the rectory kitchen for breakfast. Hyacinth was making preparations for dinner with Monsignor Linguini and Bishop Munchin. She had set the dining room table with the best china and old silverware and was now busily pulling out all kinds of pots and pans.

"What's with all the noise?" Boniface entered the kitchen as Hyacinth knelt on the floor in front of the open cabinets rummaging through the cookware.

"I'm preparing *Baked Bishop ala Linguini*," she said, straightening up with a large pot in her hands.

"Poor pun, Dearie." He shook his head and tapped his cane.

"What does he want with you anyway?" Hyacinth asked Boniface as she placed his scrambled eggs and bagel on the table.

"I'm not sure. Maybe he wants to name me a monsignor." Boniface laughed as he reached for his fork.

"If that's the case, there's no doubt he wants something else. And if I know this diocese, Linguini's behind it." Hyacinth took the coffee pot off the burner and poured herself a cup. "He's probably fishing for a new pastor."

"Won't Father Robin be back?" I asked, standing at the counter holding out a mug for her to fill.

"Oh, no. Father Robin has obedience issues," Boniface said as he sat at the head of the table and drank his coffee.

"Well, we knew that." Hyacinth sighed noisily and replaced the coffee pot.

"He's been sent to a Cleveland psychological institute for therapy," Boniface added. "I guess Pittsburgh and Baltimore had no vacancies."

That was the first I had heard concerning Robin's whereabouts. I fixed myself a bowl of cereal and sat at the table.

"Ah, another dysfunctional priest." Hyacinth pulled out one of the kitchen chairs and sat.

Father Kevin Murphy, just returning from Mass, entered the kitchen. "Oh, Hyacinth. I won't be here for dinner with the bishop tonight."

"Why not?" Hyacinth asked as Boniface and I looked on.

"I have a soccer game. Sorry." Kevin vanished up the back stairs.

"You're going to miss out!" she called up the empty stairs.

Hyacinth finished her breakfast and coffee. She stepped to the refrigerator, opened the door, leaned in, and pulled out an unopened bottle of Chardonnay. Walking to the kitchen drawer, she pulled it out, produced a corkscrew, placed it on top of the bottle, and worked the cork out.

"Hyacinth," Boniface said, raising his voice. "It isn't even nine in the morning. And you don't even drink."

"I do now," she said, pulling down a wineglass from one of the cabinets and pouring herself some Chardonnay. "You're not the one preparing dinner for His Highness and his lackey. But let me tell you, this is going to be one special dinner."

As soon as Boniface and I finished, Hyacinth shooed us out of the kitchen. "Now, go on, get out of here both of you. The kitchen is closed!" She locked the door behind us, but called from the other side of the door, "Here—you can either skip lunch or go out and eat." She slipped a twenty-dollar bill under the door.

"Forget it." Boniface pushed the bill back under the door with the end of his cane.

From behind the door, I could hear her murmuring and muttering under her breath. The words *monsignor* and *bishop* and *that one* could be heard every few minutes erupting in different levels of frustration. "Silly men in their fancy dresses think they're so high and mighty. They don't have to cook or clean, do laundry, or earn a living like the rest of us. Think they're lone rangers. Well, I'm no Tonto."

"You can't talk to her when she's like that," Boniface said as he shook his head.

"I guess it's dinner with Linguini and the bishop," I replied.

"You mean *His Highness*, the pointed hat, and his sidekick, Fatso Spaghetti-O," Hyacinth corrected me from behind the door, laughing out loud.

We left her alone.

* * * *

All day long Hyacinth worked in the kitchen with the door locked. As the sun waned, the door opened and a *very* friendly Hyacinth emerged; the bottle of Chardonnay was empty.

She disappeared upstairs to prepare herself for the guests. When she returned she was wearing a light blue evening dress with her hair pulled back from her face. She also was wearing an excessive amount of perfume.

When the bishop and vicar-general arrived, they joined Boniface in the living room for a cocktail. I stayed in the kitchen examining all the different bowls and plates Hyacinth had used in preparing the meal.

Promptly at half past six, Hyacinth rang a small dinner bell and announced that dinner was ready. The dining room, with its china, crystal, silver, linen napkins, silver candlesticks and lit candles, was inviting. Boniface sat at the head of the table with the bishop to his right. Hyacinth winked at me as she took a seat to my right, between Boniface and me. She announced, "This is a *very special occasion* for *two very special people.*" Monsignor Michael Linguini sat next to the bishop, directly across from me.

"Flattery will get you nowhere, Hyacinth," Bishop Munchin said as he placed his napkin on his lap.

"Oh. In this diocese I've always heard that flattery will get you everywhere." Hyacinth looked down.

The phrases *very special occasion* and *two very special people* triggered my memory as I wondered if I had just been served crow.

Meanwhile Linguini reached for the bottle of Merlot. "Do you have any white wine?"

"No," Hyacinth answered, "we ran out this morning."

Linguini returned a puzzled look at her and laughed as if slightly amused. He then poured the bishop and Boniface a glass of wine. "We're here to honor Father Boniface, or I should say, the *Monsignor*." Monsignor Linguini poured himself a glass, lifted it, and tilted it toward Boniface. "Here, here." Linguini clinked glasses with the bishop, but he didn't drink the wine.

"I don't have that title, son," Boniface said to Linguini while looking at the bishop.

"Well, it's high time we made you one." The bishop sipped his wine.

"Well, it's high time that you all came to dinner," Hyacinth interrupted. "I've always said that one day you'd both have to eat crow. He should have been made a monsignor years ago," Hyacinth argued. "Why now? What do you want from him?"

I stopped chewing and looked at my chicken on the plate—or what I thought was chicken—and turned to Hyacinth at my right.

She leaned towards me, smiled, shook her head, and whispered, "Not to worry. You're okay. Yours is chicken. Only those two buzzards are eating—well, you know. Crow."

I looked over at the plates in front of the bishop and Linguini; the portions of meat appeared to be darker and had a different texture. I recalled the day I helped Hyacinth collect the downed crows, and I worked to contain a laugh. *My God, she did it!* I wanted to yell out.

"Actually, we want to rename *you* pastor of Poor Souls," the bishop said to Boniface, ignoring Hyacinth's whispers. "Then, in exchange, I'll name you a monsignor."

Boniface immediately objected to the idea of his being renamed pastor. "Is the well getting that low, bishop?"

"The well's not low." The bishop sighed, clanking his knife and fork down to the plate. "It's completely dry."

"Actually, bishop," Linguini interrupted, "there is no well." His gaze was focused on the painting behind me.

"I don't know what I'll do," the bishop continued, ignoring Linguini's comment. "We might as well reclassify parts of America as mission territory."

"What about Father Robin?" Boniface asked, taking a sip of wine.

The bishop put his hands on the table, smoothing out the tablecloth.

"*Your* Father Robin is a very disturbed man," Linguini asserted, straightening himself in his chair, and taking a drink of ice water.

"*My* Father Robin?" Boniface asked. "Don't you mean *our*?"

Neither Linguini nor the bishop replied as they exchanged glances. The lag in the conversation gave everyone a chance to eat. I looked at the bishop's and vicar-general's plates and nearly threw up.

The conversation began to revolve around President Clinton and his continual political problems and alleged sexual indiscretions. About that time Hyacinth's golden tabby, Cat, sauntered into the dining room, his tail aloft behind him.

"Hyacinth," the bishop said as he wiped his mouth with his napkin, "this is absolutely delicious. What is it?"

"Crow," she answered in a measured voice and sipped her wine.

"Quit." The bishop stopped chewing and laughed as he looked around the table.

Hyacinth shrugged her shoulders as she replaced her wineglass to the table.

"It's *chicken cacciatore*," Linguini said with a shake of his head and a roll of his eyes.

"I'm telling you, it's crow," Hyacinth retorted. "Don't you think I know what I cook?"

"Why not serve pigeon?" Linguini's eyes met hers across the table as he faked a laugh. "I hear it tastes just like chicken."

"I thought about preparing *Pigeon Piccata*, but a bishop and a vicar-general are above eating flying rat—even the likes of you two birds. Why, I won't even let Cat eat pigeon. So I decided upon *crow cacciatore*." Cat then hopped upon Hyacinth's lap and mewed.

"Wherever did you find her, Father Boniface?" the bishop asked as he wiped his brow, still chuckling.

"Okay," Boniface smiled at her, "ease off, Hyacinth."

"All right. I'm just happy they're enjoying my *Chef's Surprise*."

"I will admit it does have a rather gamy taste." The bishop chased another bite of bird and pasta with his wine.

"*Gamy*." Hyacinth smiled wide and took a drink of red

wine. "I like that, bishop. I *really* like that." She repeated the phrase, "*Gamy.*" She fed Cat a slice of chicken from her plate.

"The meat is darker," Linguini said, examining the fowl at the end of his fork.

"Yes, I serenaded the birds in a dark sherry." Cat jumped off her lap and walked around the table.

"Don't you mean you *marinated?*" Linguini asked.

"That, too." Hyacinth clapped her hands as the bishop tried to offer Cat some of the meat from his plate. "No, Cat!"

The bishop and vicar-general both stared at Hyacinth with puzzlement.

* * * *

It was time for dessert. Hyacinth removed the dinner plates and returned with chocolate pecan pie and coffee for everyone. The talk had returned to Boniface being renamed pastor.

"Boniface, your being renamed pastor will only be temporary—" The bishop nodded.

"Oh, hell," Boniface said, "everything in this diocese is temporary. And I am not monsignor material, and I will not be bribed into being named one."

"That's telling him, Boniface," Hyacinth said, standing behind her chair between Boniface and me.

"What's wrong, Hyacinth?" the bishop asked. "Don't you like the way I run my bishopric?"

"About as much as you liked dinner," she answered, looking at the lit candles on the mantle.

"Why, I loved your dinner," the bishop replied.

"Well, then, we're even." Hyacinth returned to her seat. "Even?"

"Hyacinth, please," Boniface said, touching her arm.

"Yes, bishop, you've made a wreck of the office of bishop." Hyacinth took a drink of her merlot and held the glass near her face.

"Do I get the feeling I'm not welcome in my own house?" The bishop bristled at her tone.

"*Your* house?" Hyacinth grimaced as she returned her glass to the table.

"Yes, *my* house." The bishop sat straight in his chair and placed his hands firmly upon the table.

"Since when have you ever lived here?" she asked. "Have you ever swept or mopped these floors?" She stared into the hearth.

"The bishop could evict you from this house in a moment's notice," Linguini said as he slowly placed his untouched wine glass next to his plate.

"But then, where would I live?" She smiled and looked directly into Linguini's face.

"I have no idea," Linguini replied, adjusting the collar of his shirt.

"Perhaps I could rent a room at the bishop's house." Hyacinth giggled. "I hear there's plenty of room in that mansion of yours."

"Off to the kitchen with you," Boniface said, pointing to the door with his cane.

"Yes, anymore out of you," Linguini clicked his tongue, "and you'll be joining Father Robin in Cleveland."

"What for?" Hyacinth asked.

"I don't know yet," Linguini rolled his eyes, "but I'll think of something—perhaps alcoholism." He looked at me as if he regretted his words.

"Well, some people are a hell of a lot nicer if they drink," Hyacinth said, retreating to the kitchen.

"Now I know why they call her *The General*." The bishop chuckled.

"If you say no to being named a monsignor, Boniface," Linguini interjected, returning to business, "then we might be forced to put the likes of a Father Jack Ash here."

"I don't need you or a title to tell me who I am. I know who I am." Boniface raised his voice and pointed at Linguini. "And I, for damned sure, don't need purple socks to let others know how important I think I am." He looked at Linguini out of the corner of his eyes.

"Is that what you think I think being a monsignor is all about?" Linguini raised his voice and leaned on the table toward Boniface.

"I wouldn't be a bit surprised," Boniface replied, relaxing in his chair. "By the way, Jack Ash is a decent guy."

"Horsefeathers!" Linguini champed. "He's a child and has the faith to match."

"At least he has faith," Boniface snickered. "I thought we were all to have the faith of a child."

Suddenly the bishop gasped as if in great pain and held his stomach.

"What's wrong, bishop?" Linguini's face was ashen as he turned to him.

"I've got to go to the john." Munchin slumped in his chair, clutching his stomach.

"Here." Linguini stood and helped the bishop out of his chair. "Let's get you to the bathroom in the hallway here."

"Oh, I wouldn't use that one," Boniface warned, shaking his head. "It's been clogging lately. Use the john upstairs. It's the first door on the left at the top of the stairs."

"No, no, this one's fine," the bishop sighed, taking small steps while at the same time appearing to be hurrying.

"I don't need him messing up the stairs," Hyacinth called out from the kitchen before appearing from around the corner in the dining room. "Besides," she whispered, "he'll be lucky if he makes it in time as it is." She smiled and looked at Boniface. "It's amazing what a laxative and a little syrup will do."

"What?" Boniface exclaimed. "You poisoned him?"

"I made two pies." She looked at me. "One for us and one for those two buzzards."

At that, a disgustingly loud noise of bodily function came from the front hall.

"Oh, too bad," Hyacinth cackled. "His Highness had an accident."

Boniface ate the remainder of his pecan pie and took a last sip of his coffee before pushing away from the table.

"I guess dinner's over, huh?" Hyacinth asked as she stood and began clearing the plates. I collected the silverware and linen napkins, making myself useful while Boniface blew out the candles on the table and the mantle.

The downstairs toilet flushed.

"Michael!" The bishop cried for Linguini. "Monsignor!" The bathroom door opened wide and with it came the sound of gurgling water.

"Oh, oh." Boniface grimaced at me in the mirror. "That's not a good sound."

Linguini called out, "Quick! We need a plunger!" he rushed into the dining room. "The toilet's overflowing, and the bishop is still in there."

Hyacinth appeared from the kitchen closet and held out the handle of the plunger to the vicar-general. He took it and returned to the hallway bathroom and the bishop. The two began arguing.

I went into the kitchen, keeping myself busy, happy to help with the dirty dishes rather than with the plumbing.

After about ten minutes, Linguini came in asking for bath towels. "Oh, and Father Boniface," he whispered, "could the bishop borrow some of your underwear and a pair of trousers?"

A few minutes later Linguini was in the hallway on his cellular phone speaking with the Chancellor, Sister Dymphna.

"I'm not sure, Sister. We're leaving for Covert now. Just meet us at the hospital within the hour."

Linguini then walked into the kitchen and announced that he and the bishop were leaving. Nothing else was said about naming Boniface a Monsignor or renaming him the pastor of Poor Souls.

The humiliated Bishop Munchin avoided everyone as he hurried to the car with his vicar-general. As Boniface closed the door, he and I observed a stack of stinking towels lying on the wet bathroom floor.

"I'm glad Linguini didn't get sick," I said, watching the vicar-general help the bishop get into the luxury car.

"Don't worry," Hyacinth said as she stood in the hallway between the kitchen and the dining room. "It'll hit him on their ride back to Covert."

"Hyacinth, that's—that's—" Boniface pondered aloud, pounding his cane on the floor as the two of us made our way back to the dining room.

"Ingenious?" Hyacinth laughed, removing her apron.

"Wicked would be my word." Boniface breathed out, shaking his head. "Border-line criminal."

"Oh, you're just jealous it wasn't your idea, party-pooper." She returned to the kitchen, still speaking. "You two birds just ought to thank me that you didn't have to eat crow."

Chapter 28: Absence

"What are you looking for?"
— Jesus to his disciples (John 1.38)

Because of Father Robin's removal from the parish, the administration at St. Albert's Seminary and the Vocation Director, Father Samuel Good, thought that Sister Regina Claire ought to visit me. The two of us were already scheduled to meet after Christmas, but now seemed a more appropriate time. When she arrived, she was dressed in her plain white Dominican garb, her hair covered with her veil.

"So, Martin, you've been through a lot," the diminutive Dominican said, glancing up at the yellowing curtains of the sitting room's bay window and the closed French doors.

"I liked Father Robin, but it seemed that he wanted to make too many changes too quickly and without the bishop's approval."

"Are you still at the dry cleaners, working hard to remove stubborn stains from other people's clothing—even your pastor's?" She held both her hands aloft with palms outstretched. "As it is, reality is sullied, smeared, soiled, and besmirched. I think you need to continue to grapple with the reality that human nature is incomplete and flawed."

"Yes," I countered, focusing my eyes on one of the brass

doorknobs of the French doors, "in my own life there's so much that is murky and perplexing—"

"And redeeming," she added, folding her hands upon her lap. "Recall what the author Flannery O'Connor said, 'Sometimes the nature of God's grace can only be made believable by its absence.' Many a quiet evening she would read Thomas Aquinas's *Summa Theologiae* before going to bed."

"I'll bet she slept well." I recalled my own academic bout with Thomas Aquinas and his writings. "He's a sure remedy for insomnia."

"So, were you avoiding your pastor, Father Robin?" Regina Claire refocused the conversation.

"Not really." I looked down at the floor. "I don't think so."

"Did you go along with his plans to consolidate the parishes?"

"No, but I didn't try and stop him either." My eyes followed the different geometric patterns in the parquet floor.

"Why not?"

"Because Father Samuel Good told me to observe things here at the parish and not to try and change things." I looked up at her.

She rolled her eyes slightly. "So you were avoiding conflict?"

"Not exactly, Sister." I squirmed in my chair.

"But you did avoid conflict." She brought her right hand up to her chin and placed her right elbow on the armrest of the chair.

"Yes." I sighed slightly, hoping she didn't hear me.

"Did you think that if you had raised the issue, then you'd have suffered for it?" She extended her right hand toward me.

"A little," I answered, "now that you mention it."

"Do you believe your survival in the Church depends upon your compliance?" She peered out the window.

"Not exactly," I answered, following her eyes. "The Church isn't a business per se."

"I used to believe that myself." She coughed and regained eye contact. "Martin, it seems that you know more of what you don't want than what you need."

"I did expect that my business background and marketing degree would help me in the parish. Priests ought to know something about business. They are, after all, selling a product: Christianity."

"Do you really know what you want, Martin?" She leaned toward me, her hands together again. "You're conflicted. You know what's right and you know what you ought to do but, because of your family background, you seek to placate others. You learned to survive by pleasing your father. And you're still doing it. You seek the approval of the fathers in the church.

"You never complain though you may want to. In a way, you're a people pleaser. You want to stay within the framework of the Church's tradition and submit to its authority. The Church has a bad habit of putting things off and not embracing change."

At that comment, I recalled an American missionary who came to our parish when I was in college. He had spent twenty years of his life in China and had been a scientist before becoming a priest. Something he said stayed with me: "One can be an intelligent person and a believer at the same time."

"Are you an observer or are you passionately involved?" Regina Claire cleared her throat, evidently aware that my mind had wandered.

"In high school, I went on a retreat. I must have been a junior. I came back home on fire for the Lord. The only person who seemed to understand what I had experienced was Grandma Buckner. My mother thought I was light in the loafers. When I went to Mass with her the next weekend, she told me I sang too loud."

"Do you feel the fire now? Have you lost your passion? Are you depressed? Or do you feel like you're just going through the motions?" Regina Clare asked.

"I'm not sure." My business mind and marketing background gave me cause to ponder whether I ought to have even pursued the priestly vocation.

"Do you have compassion for the parishioners? Or are you disengaged from the parish?"

"As I've said, I sometimes wonder whether I truly have the call."

"If you believe you have a call, then that is reason enough to discern the call to priesthood," Sister Regina Claire assured me. "If Jacob, Moses, David, Jonah, Peter or Paul could receive their calls despite their sinfulness, then Martin Flanagan can have the call. Moses murdered a man and had a speech impediment."

I thought of Father Baxter, one of the older diocesan priests in Covert. He had a lisp and stuttered through his Mass, even tripping over the familiar words of the consecration. If Father Baxter could be a priest, there was reason enough to continue in my studies.

"King David committed adultery with Bathsheba and conspired to murder her husband, Uriah the Hittite," she continued speaking as she unlocked her fingers and briefly looked out the front window and checked the time. "The prophet Jonah was a prejudiced man and was initially disobedient to his call, but after the ordeal with the fish, he relented. He was the most successful prophet, yet his story ends with him still prejudiced and angry with the Lord for allowing the Ninevites to have a change of heart.

"Throughout the gospels, Saint Peter had foot-in-mouth disease and eventually denied knowing the Lord three times.

Saint Paul once persecuted the Church, even overseeing the stoning death of Saint Stephen, the first martyr.

"Yes, Martin Flanagan, you have the call. Of that, I have no doubt. However, it is up to you to discern where exactly in God's vineyard you are being called. And having a priest with a business degree might not be such a bad idea."

Sister Regina Claire had been the one responsible for requiring the third year seminarians at Saint Albert's to take a master's level business management course.

"You will bring many gifts to the priesthood, Martin, if you pursue ordination. But remember, if you wouldn't make a good husband or a good father, then you have no business becoming a priest." Her words were exact and to the point. I appreciated her wisdom even if some of my fellow seminarians did not.

I wondered whether I really wanted to be a priest. Those who were discouraging the continuation of the priesthood claimed it would cease to exist in its current mode and proclaimed that there wouldn't be any priests left in the twenty-first century. There were others, just as vocal, who believed that this period would soon pass and give way to a springtime of the faith. I didn't know to whom to listen or whom to believe. All I wanted to do was to bring the love of Christ to the broken-hearted and share the light of the gospel with a darkened world.

I had been filled with zeal for Christ after my weekend retreat in high school, but now the fire had gone out and I was unsure how it had gone out. It seemed to have happened so gradually I never noticed until it was out.

Would the world be better by my giving my life to become a priest?

Chapter 29: Cafeteria Catholic

We have just enough religion to make us hate,
but not enough to make us love.
— Jonathan Swift

After visiting two parishioners at Saint Luke's Good Samaritan Hospital, I stood in the lunch line. As I stared through the glass refrigerator doors looking at various lumps of food and desserts wrapped in clear plastic, I felt someone trying to pluck my wallet from my back pocket. I wheeled about quickly only to see the smiling face of a redheaded man in a priestly collar. It was Father Jack Ash.

"Martin Flanagan."

"Father Ash," I said, relieved.

"You can call me Jack."

"Okay."

"I almost had your wallet."

"I know."

"Are you alone?" asked Jack.

"Yes."

"May I join you for lunch?"

"Sure," I nodded.

We moved through the line.

"What brings you to Saint Luke's Good Samaritan?" I

asked as I nodded to the cafeteria lady and pointed to a tuna salad sandwich. She placed it on my plate.

"Oh, the usual: death, disease, despair."

I shook my head, unsure exactly how to interpret Jack's sense of humor.

"I hear you're looking for a pastor at Poor Souls," he said. "Should I apply?"

"You're asking me?" I momentarily ignored the lady behind the counter who was motioning for me to keep the line moving.

"I just did." Father Jack pointed to a burger, and the lady placed it on his plate.

"Don't you have a parish?" I began moving again.

"For the moment, but who knows with Mrs. Bishop, Lady Chancellor Dymphna or Monsignor Lasagna Brain. Even the possums at Possum Prairie don't like me."

We both got some iced tea and scooted our trays down the rail. I began to reach for my wallet to pay for lunch. "I'll get it, Martin." Jack closed my wallet and pushed it away as he flashed a twenty dollar bill to the cashier. We settled on a corner booth and sat.

"So, Martin, how are things at Poor Souls now that Father Robin has been sent off to the Island of Misfit Priests?"

"The bishop wanted to name Father Boniface temporary pastor," I said.

"So I've heard."

"Then you know that he refused," I said.

"I knew he would even before they asked him." Jack laughed as he took a bite of his burger. "The old pointed hat and Lackey Linguini would've shipped Boniface off to the island as well if the place wasn't so overcrowded. Hell, there's so many of our guys up there, I think there's a wing just for the Covert Diocese. Linguini and Dymphna even sent one of the basketball coaches and a religion teacher up there for rage disorder in hopes of teaching them conflict resolution and the art of consensus building."

I took a bite of my tuna sandwich as an older man and woman glared at Father Jack. The man was bearded and dressed in a red shirt, blue bib overalls, cowboy hat and boots. The woman's hair was long and she wore a long, plain, dark blue dress. They looked like Pentecostals.

"You watch. In a year or two Linguini will get on his soapbox and put in place all of Robin's plans for Inglenook," Jack continued, oblivious to the couple. "But he'll do it in a way that the people will think it was all his idea."

I didn't want to badmouth the vicar-general or say something with strangers listening, so I remained silent.

"Martin, you're just too kind." He squeezed his lemon slice into his iced tea. "So, what's Lost Souls going to do without a pastor?" Jack smiled between another bite and a drink of tea.

"Father Frisbee is taking some of the masses," I answered. "Father Boniface thinks it's only a matter of days before Father Frisbee is made temporary administrator of Poor Souls."

"Never mind the Frisbee. He'll be the next one tossed. The people at St. Patrick's haven't forgiven him for allowing Robin Hood to destroy their pews. What about Father Chris Studzinski down at St. Sebastians?"

"I haven't seen much of him."

"Yeah, neither do his parishioners. Now who's this Father Kevin Murphy?"

"He's a visiting priest from Wheatfield."

"Oh, one of Numbnoddle's rejects. God only knows what he did. Can he say Mass?" He picked up his glass of tea and swirled the ice.

"Yes." I twirled my glass on the tabletop.

"How about confessions? Can he hear confessions?"

"Yes."

"Hmmm." He drank some of his tea. "And what about Father Bill Gallagher? I hear he's still around."

"He is——in town, that is." I was taken aback at how apprised Father Jack was on the Inglenook deanery.

"Then Bill's still staying at Immaculate Heart?"

"What?" I tried to act surprised.

"Don't give me that." He put his tea down. "Is he still there?"

"I think he is."

"You *think* he is?"

"I *guess* he is."

"I wish you *knew*."

"I don't want to get him in trouble."

"He's already in trouble——canonically speaking. He *contracted marriage*. It sounds like a disease, doesn't it? Civil marriage is a contract," Jack asserted. "A sacramental marriage is a *covenant* according to Canon Law."

I drank some tea and nodded.

Just then, Jack's pager beeped. He took it off and looked at it. He smiled. "Speak of the devil, it's His Highness——or else the Sheriff of Nottingham, Linguini. I have a meeting at the chancery today. They want to make sure I'm still coming. I tell you, I can't tell where Bishop Munchin ends and Linguini begins, his head is so far up the bishop's ass."

The older couple came over to the table at that point and engaged Father Jack in conversation.

"Father," the man began by removing his hat, "you anointed our nephew last year when he was in the hospital. The doctors didn't expect him to pull through. Well, by the next day, the boy began to get well. Within the week, he had completely recovered. It was a miracle."

"Oh, do be careful," Jack said as he stood. "I'm no miracle worker. It was the grace of the sacrament. Never underestimate God's grace."

They continued talking about their nephew and his incredible recovery before leaving us to finish our lunch.

As we cleared our table afterwards, Jack said, "I'm sure we'll do this again sometime, Martin. In the meantime, I've got to get back to Covert." He stood and picked up both trays.

"Thanks for lunch, Father."

"No problem. Take care of those lost souls."

Chapter 30: Infirmity

To me, fair friend, you never can be old,
For as you were when first your eye I eyed,
Such seems your beauty still.
— William Shakespeare, Sonnet 104, 1.

When I returned to the parish, red and blue lights flickered in front of the rectory; an ambulance was in the driveway, and two black and white police cruisers and a fire department rescue truck were in the street. I went in and saw two paramedics working on Father Boniface. Hyacinth was in tears. I found my way through police officers and firefighters to her. I put my arm around her shoulder and stood in the silence holding her. She was still trembling from finding Boniface on the floor. It appeared that he had suffered a heart attack.

Where would the parish be without Boniface?

As the paramedics placed him on a stretcher and prepared to take him to the hospital, Hyacinth took one of them aside. "Is there anything I can do?"

"Yes." The reply came from the medic who was hooking telemetry to Boniface's chest. "You can pray."

Hyacinth said nothing; she took my hand and squeezed. She rode to the hospital in the back of the ambulance with

Boniface while I followed in my car. At the hospital, we waited in the emergency room all afternoon and into the evening. About six o'clock I offered to take her to dinner. She said she wasn't hungry, so I went to the cafeteria alone. I bought her a cup of coffee and returned to the emergency room. About seven o'clock a nurse informed us that Boniface had apparently suffered a series of mini-strokes in the days leading up to his heart attack.

In the days following the attack, Boniface was incoherent, groggy, and heavily sedated. He remained in intensive care. After a week, he was moved to a regular room. His condition was improving, but the stroke had left him powerless to walk. The doctors confirmed that his memory had also been affected. He didn't know Father Frisbee or me. Saddest of all, he couldn't place Hyacinth. "I think we've met before, but I'm not for sure," he said to her, repeating himself several times.

He could recall nearly everything that had happened to him from the time he was a child to the time he went to college. He knew he had been to Europe, but he didn't know why. He had studied at a Belgian seminary. Hyacinth tried to hide her tears.

Every day she would go to the hospital and stay with Boniface. Every night I would step off the elevator and walk to the intensive care's waiting room to take her home. The scene in the waiting room was much the same from day to day and night to night. People would be lying on the couches under blankets, sprawled out on the floor, or sitting in chairs surrounded by empty coffee cups and plastic soda bottles that littered the floor and tables.

As I drove her back to the rectory, she didn't talk much about Boniface; it seemed too painful. Instead, she told me about the families in the ICU waiting room whom she had gotten to know. She told me of all the miracles that occurred in the waiting room. A family member had been in a car accident or a loved one had suffered a heart attack and the family had rallied to his or her side. She observed old grudges melt away as past grievances were forgotten or forgiven and estranged siblings, cousins—even spouses—were reunited in the face of suffering and death. Out of the depths of their personal tragedies, new life sprang forth.

Boniface's ordeal had even seemed to thaw the relationship between Hyacinth and the bishop. One evening when I came for her, she surprised me by telling how Bishop Munchin had visited that afternoon. "He was the soul of kindness. It almost makes me regret the time I made the old fart eat crow." Her eyes shined with emotion.

A week after Boniface's attack, he was moved from the intensive care unit to the rehab unit on the third floor of the hospital. Hyacinth began staying all night in his room, sleeping on a pull-out couch. The night shift nurses let her stay even though hospital regulations only permitted spouses and grown children to remain through the night. Some of the nurses and a couple of the doctors thought Boniface was an Episcopal priest and Hyacinth was his wife.

Two weeks after his hospitalization, Boniface was released from the hospital. Monsignor Linguini came for a visit and said that the diocese had yet to determine whether Boniface should be moved to Covert or remain in Inglenook. According to Hyacinth, the bishop had made arrangements for him to be moved to Covert's St. Joseph Retirement Village. When Boniface was well, he had made it known that he would like to retire at St. Albert's Priory, but due to the circumstances, the bishop had decided to place him in Inglenook's Iroquois Manor Nursing Home. Hyacinth didn't complain; Boniface would still be close, and she could continue to visit him. So, for the moment, Boniface would remain in Inglenook.

Every day I would drive Hyacinth to Iroquois Manor, which was about seven miles from the rectory. She said she missed him, likening it to a death. Except he was still alive. The nursing home was clean and well staffed; the fluorescent lighting made things bright, but it all seemed so unnatural. I felt like I was back at my Catholic grade school's basement cafeteria; I even smelled some of the same smells.

There will always be some things about nursing homes that trouble me. Every day when I arrived at Iroquois Manor, I would see an elderly lady in the front lobby stretched out in a wheel chair-quasi-easy chair. She looked uncomfortable as hell. Her neck was bent and her head sidewise, her body contorted at different angles, looking as if she was trying to curl up in the fetal position, her hands together and tucked under her chest. It seemed she had experienced a seizure and was dead, rigor mortis already setting her face and limbs. I found myself watching to see if she really was breathing. Worse still was that it seemed the nursing staff was oblivious to her existence. The workers all walked around her as if she was just another piece of furniture. "Am I the only one who can see this woman," I once asked Hyacinth. The morbid thought crossed my mind that the woman really was dead, but since the staff loved her while she was alive, they had hired a taxidermist to stuff her after she died.

The waiting was the hardest part; waiting for Boniface to begin remembering again. Nothing was guaranteed. The nurses and doctors said he might never regain his memory. One of the doctors had bluntly said Boniface would never be the same. I knew that Hyacinth had begun to realize that she had lost her old Boniface.

* * * *

One afternoon, Hyacinth and I went to see Boniface. When we arrived at his room, he was sitting in his wheelchair watching Sesame Street.

"Father Boniface, I brought you some of your favorite cookies," Hyacinth said as she revealed a dozen macaroons.

"Have a seat, Dearie." He smiled at Hyacinth and moved his wheelchair to face us. "You too, son." He motioned towards me, while taking a cookie. "You are my son?"

"In a way," I stammered, feeling sorry for his loss of memory.

"How are you, Boniface?" Hyacinth reached over and held his hand.

"I'm ready to leave this damned hotel. It has the damnedest room service. They wake me up at all hours of the night to see if I'm sleeping, then they wonder why I'm so cross in the morning. They always want to give me a bath even though I haven't done anything to get dirty. Of course, there's this one real cute nurse that I wouldn't have minded getting in the tub with, but this morning she gave me an enema. That's not exactly what I had in mind. What the hell kind of a hotel is this? They won't even let me smoke a cigar."

"It's good to see you, Father Boniface." Hyacinth smiled and glanced in my direction.

"Dearie, why do you keep calling me 'Father'? You're old enough to be my mother. I'm not old enough to be your father."

"You're a priest, remember?" she replied, looking out the window.

"That's what they keep telling me. I asked one of the young girls here this morning—she's been giving me a bath—I asked her if she'd marry me and she said she couldn't marry me because I was a priest. I told her I didn't want to be a priest anymore, but that didn't change her mind. So, maybe you'll marry me, Dearie. You come and see me every day. Who knows, maybe we're already married. We're not, are we?"

"No, we're not married." Hyacinth blushed and shook her head.

"Well, then, let's get married." He slapped his wheel-chair's right armrest.

"I can't marry you. You're a priest." Hyacinth looked at him slantwise.

"Oh, yes, that's right."

Hyacinth closed her eyes and softly sighed.

"I don't feel like a priest," Boniface said, clearing his throat. "Whatever that is."

"It's not that easy." Hyacinth began to cry and reached for the box of tissues. She started to get up.

Boniface took her by the hand. "Oh, don't go. I like it when you visit me. I was telling the concierge this morning that you were my wife. Are you sure we're not married?"

"I'm sure, Boniface."

"And who are you again?"

"Hyacinth. We've known each other for nearly thirty years."

"Oh, that's right. Did I ask you if you'd marry me?"

"Yes, you did."

"Did you say yes?"

"No. You're a priest."

"Oh, that's right, but what if I don't want to be a priest anymore?"

"You can't do that."

"See, they won't let me do anything. I want to check out! Take me downstairs, son," he said to me. "There's a tobacco shop right off the hotel lobby. Those thugs down the hall keep coming in here and stealing my cigars and whiskey. I think the bellhop took some of my luggage to the wrong room. I can't find anything. I even lost my wallet. The maid says she's been looking for it."

He paused and went for another cookie.

"When's the train coming to take me to New York? I need to get to Penn Station or I'll miss my train."

Hyacinth looked away, daubing her eyes with a tissue and wiping a tear from her right cheek.

Boniface looked up again. "Why can't priests marry?"

"I don't know," she replied with another soft sigh.

"Are you sure we're not married, Dear Heart?"

Hyacinth took his left hand in her right. "Not anymore."

"Well, then, let's get married again, and this time we'll both remember."

"Okay," she said through her emotion, "but just this once."

Chapter 31: Business

A slight error in the beginning
is a great error in the end.
— St. Thomas Aquinas

I learned on Friday morning that Monsignor Linguini would be back at Poor Souls for the weekend. As scheduled, the Monsignor returned to Poor Soul's rectory on Saturday afternoon to take all the weekend masses. That afternoon, he went to the church to hear confessions, but he immediately returned.

"Back so soon, Monsignor?" I asked Linguini as he stepped back into the rectory.

"I thought Father Kevin wanted me to hear confessions, but he's already in there."

"No, he's not," I answered. "Father Kevin took Bubby out for a walk a while ago, and he isn't back yet."

"Then who is in the confessional?" Linguini's face blanched.

"I have no idea," I said, though I knew almost without a doubt that it had to be Bill Gallagher. I prayed he would be out before Linguini returned. Linguini moved quickly out the door and toward the church. I followed him to the sacristy and watched as he opened the priest's door on the confessional only to reveal an empty chair. He appeared frustrated as he peered out into the church before vesting for Mass.

Linguini deviated from the gospel commentary during his homily and explained Father Robin's situation to the congregation. "Regarding Father Robin's condition; he has been taken to a Cleveland institute for psychological evaluation. We must keep him in our prayers. In God's providential care, he may be able to return to his priestly duties relatively soon. However, as for returning to Poor Souls, I do not believe, nor does the bishop, that it would be proper or advantageous for him to return to Poor Souls or any parish in the Inglenook deanery.

"Father Wood, as your pastor, had no right to announce the changes he planned to enact. He had no right to disband both the parish finance commission and the parish council. He had no right to act without the bishop's approval or permission. Each of the parishes in this deanery will remain independent. Father Kevin Murphy will also remain in residence here at Poor Souls.

"Meantime, Father Frisbee of St. Patrick's has been named the temporary parish administrator here at Poor Souls, and the bishop has yet to make a pastoral appointment for Immaculate Heart parish. These are indeed difficult times for the Church."

With that being said, Linguini stepped aside, returned to his high-backed presider chair, and sat. From the parishioners' postures and reactions to Linguini's words, it appeared the congregation gave a collective sigh of relief.

After Mass, Martha Hart cornered Linguini. "Monsignor, I'm convinced miracles are taking place in this parish."

"Young lady, I'd be careful the way you casually throw around the word *miracle*."

"Why? Don't you believe?"

"Of course I believe. Who are you?"

"Martha Hart."

"I don't know you. Should I?" He looked at his watch as if annoyed and in a hurry.

"No. Now as I was saying, miracles are taking place here at Poor Souls," Martha persisted.

"And what are these miracles?" Linguini pinched the bridge of his nose.

"One woman went to confession this afternoon, but then when another woman went in the other door for a face-to-face confession, there was no priest seated in the chair. Right after that a man knelt down on the other side of the screen, and the priest heard his confession. Then I saw you come into church to hear confessions, but you stopped when you obviously realized a priest was hearing confessions. When you came back a few minutes later, you pulled back the confessional curtain but there was no priest in the confessional. How do you explain?"

"Are you sure you're not imagining things? Besides, that's pretty lame material to pass off as a miracle."

"Then you must have imagined the same things."

"Thank you, Ma'am," Linguini said, dismissing her with a perturbed look. "I'm sure there's a logical explanation."

"Maybe there's a priest who can bi-locate. It's been done before. Padre Pio could bi-locate. Maybe there's a holy confessor in this diocese—"

"I'll believe *that* when I experience it myself," he said, interrupting her. "Well, I have to go now."

"Oh, before you go, Monsignor, will you bless this rosary for me?" She held the beads out to him.

He took the article in his left hand and with his right hand traced the sign of the cross over it while mumbling the blessing before handing it back to her.

"Thank you, Monsignor." She nodded as she placed the sacramental in her purse.

"You're welcome. Have a nice day." He walked away from her and disappeared into the sacristy.

I finished extinguishing the altar's candles and turned out the lights when the last person left the church. Linguini left the church without saying goodbye.

* * * *

The next morning Monsignor Linguini was back for the

morning masses. After the last Mass, I walked with him to the rectory.

Hyacinth came downstairs as we walked in. She was wearing her light blue dress, the one she wore the night of the dinner with the bishop. "Monsignor, will you be staying for dinner?" she asked.

"No!" Linguini tersely replied. "I don't care to be fed rat poison again."

"Now, that's a rotten way to talk about my cooking," she lamented.

"Well, it was obvious you poisoned the food the last time I ate here. I thought the bishop would die. I was sick all night myself."

"It wasn't rat poison. Had it been, you'd have been the first to die."

"Well that's comforting. Perhaps it was crow after all. I thought you were jesting."

"Look, Monsignor, are you staying for dinner or not?" Hyacinth began putting on her apron. "I've got to know."

"No. I'll pick something up at Giuseppe's Deli. And I'll be staying at the Starlight Hotel again tonight if anyone needs to reach me. Besides," he put on his biretta and nodded to me, "it smells like a zoo in here. Dogs, cats, birds—who knows what else?"

"I smell a rat," Hyacinth whispered as she passed me.

"Oh," Linguini continued speaking on his way out the door, "if you should see Father Kevin Murphy tonight, tell him I must see him tomorrow morning."

"Thanks for the warning," Hyacinth said once he was outdoors.

Chapter 32: Occult

"In the name of Jesus Christ I
command you, come out of her!"
— Acts 16.18b

On Monday afternoon of that week, I received a phone call from a frantic woman who said she needed a priest. "Three years ago my first husband shot one of the sheriff's deputies, and he's been in prison ever since. My second husband left me when he found out I was pregnant. I got an abortion, hoping he'd come back, but he still left me. I've got three kids—four, two, and nine months. Now my boyfriend's in trouble with the cops. It's the devil, Father. I need an exorcist."

"I'm not a priest, but I can have one call you." I twirled the phone cord around my finger as I listened. She seemed histrionic, her obsession with the devil disproportionate.

"You've got to come over. I need an exorcism. My whole family's possessed. My house is possessed."

I tried to explain to her that only a priest could perform an exorcism, but she persisted. Taking down her name and address, I called Father Frisbee at St. Patrick's but the secretary said he had been called to Covert by the bishop. Father Chris Studzinski at St. Sebastian's was gone for the week, so there was no use calling him. I was tempted to call Immaculate Heart's rectory to see if Father Bill Gallagher might take the call, but I didn't.

Returning to the kitchen, I explained my dilemma to Hyacinth and Susan, the parish secretary. "There's no priest in town. What should I do?"

"Where's Father Kevin?" asked Hyacinth as she swept the floor.

"He's at a soccer tournament in Toledo," I replied.

"Holy Toledo." Hyacinth looked up from her sweeping. "Well, then I say, go ahead and go. It'll be good practice for you. Just take along a crucifix and some holy water."

"Hyacinth, I am not an exorcist," I protested.

"Christ was. He'll be with you." She bent down with the dustpan in her left hand.

"Oh, go on, Martin," Susan, the secretary interrupted. "Sometimes all it takes is the presence of someone who can bring the comfort of religion." Susan poured herself a cup of coffee. "This poor woman sounds more troubled than possessed. It can't hurt."

"Father Boniface would have sent you," Hyacinth added, sweeping the dirt into the pan.

In the end I relented and decided to go, but in the back of my mind I recalled a story Gerard Austin had told of a young priest who had gone on a simple pastoral call and found himself face to face with a young man possessed by demons. His hair grayed overnight, and he had to go on a sabbatical for a year at St. Vincent's Archabbey, the Benedictine monastery at Latrobe. Of course, Gerard Austin was given to exaggeration, especially regarding the occult or the supernatural.

It was a bleak, midsummer day, the winds warm and strong, a portent of an impending thunderstorm. Nearing the house on Elm Street I found myself smiling as I recalled the horror movie that took place on Elm Street. My own imagination fed my fears as I tried to convince myself that it was only an odd coincidence.

Three twenty-nine Elm. The house looked appallingly out of place in an otherwise decent, middle-class neighborhood. A rusty chain link fence surrounded the dilapidated, paint-chipped white house. The yard was cluttered with empty beer cans and whiskey bottles, old newspapers, two broken bicycles, and unraked leaves. There were two gnarled trees in the yard—quite dead—with no leaves, the limbs dangling down like the limp arms of a crucified man upon his descent.

I parked my car across the street in the mud. The other houses on the block were relatively nice with kempt lawns. Before I stepped out of the car, I reached for my bible and a six-inch crucifix. I glanced at the aspergillum in the pail of holy water and, for a moment, considered grabbing it, but didn't.

As I got out of the car and walked toward the house, a barefooted woman with shoulder-length blonde hair stepped out of the house and stood on the sagging, paint-chipped porch. She was wearing cut-off jean shorts and a short red blouse that was unbuttoned and untucked; it revealed both her cleavage and belly button. She had a shapely and attractive body except for her face. Her right cheek was bruised, and her left eye was black.

She had an inner sadness that was revealed in her eyes. For a moment or two, I had the same feeling when Father David Gregory and I saw the two possessed men at the restaurant.

I stood at the gate. Several cats lounged on the porch, and just as many dogs ran loose in the yard. Their droppings were everywhere, and the smell of animal excrement was atrocious.

She spoke first. "Are you the priest from Lost Souls?"

"I'm the seminarian." It was odd that she would call Poor Souls *Lost* Souls. Her German shepherds began barking and snarling at me.

"I'm Tammy." She brushed stray hair from her face.

"I'm Martin," I answered as I opened the gate and walked toward the house.

"Yeah, I *know*. Martin Flanagan."

What did she mean by that? I wondered. And *how did she know my name?*

The dogs continued barking and jumping on me. They likely smelled Bubby or Cat on me.

"Come on inside." She held the screen door open for me.

"Thank you." I followed her inside.

"You know," She turned towards me, making eye contact, "Lost Souls sounds like my kind of church." She adjusted her blouse, which only revealed more of her cleavage and tummy. "I haven't been to church in years." The scent of a sweet, cheap perfume filled the room. "Well, I told you some of the problems," she began. "My grandma was into witchcraft, you know. My first Christmas, I can remember she gave me a planchette."

"A what?" I asked as I tried not to look at her breasts.

"It's like a *Ouija* board. Then she taught me tarot cards as a kid. I guess I've never really gotten over it. I hear voices at night. The board once told me I'd die in 1994. So, I guess I'm living on borrowed time. Maybe I'm dead but I just don't know it. My mother was a medium. I tried the craft for a while. Us girls dancing naked in the cemetery and—well, you know—orgies, but it got old, if you know what I mean." She smiled wispily.

I felt the blood rush to my face and my ears felt warm; I

wished I hadn't come.

"Oh, look at you. I'll bet you're still a virgin." She gave an intriguing smirk, eyed me below my belt, and then glanced back into my eyes. "I'm surprised you believed that I lived on Elm Street. And, yes, I do have nightmares, but don't expect to see nobody with fingernail scissors jumping out at you."

I looked around at the surroundings. There was a baby sleeping in a crib in the corner of the front room. The house was dirty. The curtains were stained brown from smoke or grease and hanging crooked over the window. The smell of cigarette smoke permeated the place, and old newspapers, tabloid magazines, and scratch-off lottery tickets littered the floor.

"This is my boyfriend's mess," she said, following my eyes. "He never cleans up after himself. He brought a whore in here the other night, and they screwed all night. I was high in the bedroom. He didn't think I'd find out—"

"On the phone you said you felt the house was possessed," I interrupted her, hoping she would focus on why she had called. "That's why you called the church."

"The place *is* possessed. My mother told me it's an old Mohawk Indian curse. She held a séance and the spirits told her that some settlers killed the Indians who lived in the woods here. The neighborhood kids are forever finding Indian arrowheads."

That wasn't exactly what I wanted to hear. "Should we pray?"

"I suppose, but God don't hear my prayers."

"God will not refuse anyone's prayers."

"He does mine. You heard what I said. Just pray."

I began praying from memory, opening with the Lord's Prayer, a Hail Mary and a Glory Be. She put her head down and kept her eyes closed. I wondered why she would believe that God wouldn't hear her prayers.

I looked about for any sign of religious symbols in the house and saw none. I took the crucifix and held it out to her. "Would you care to have this for your house?"

She opened her eyes and beheld the crucifix. "Oh." She took it and placed it on one of the sofa pillows as if not sure what to do with it.

I thought of the holy water pail and aspergillum. "I've got something in my car. I'll be back." I went back across the street and grabbed the pail of holy water while avoiding the mud.

"This is holy water," I said as I returned and opened the screen door. "I thought we could bless your house."

She had her baby in her arms. "I'm not a Catholic."

"Oh." I had assumed she was a fallen-away Catholic. I wasn't sure I was right in doing it, but I took the sprinkler out of the pail and splashed water in a couple of the rooms uttering the sign of the cross under my breath.

When I returned to the front room, Tammy had unbuttoned her blouse all the way and both breasts were revealed as the baby rooted for its dinner. I turned away. She hesitated to cover herself, though she eventually did. She winked at me as she conspicuously held her left breast out before giving it to the child. "She's hungry."

"What's her name?" I looked away again.

"Madonna."

"That's a name for Our Lady."

"That's what the nurse at St. Luke's said when she was born, but I named her after the *real* Madonna."

I believed it was time for me to leave, and in my mind, I questioned whether she had truly desired for me to come for the reasons she gave. Gerard Austin's words of warning resounded in my mind. Beware of the temptress. Again, I wished I hadn't come.

"I'll let you be, Tammy, but I'll let Father Kevin know that he should contact you."

"Oh, that won't be necessary. I got what I wanted."

I made haste to leave her house and pushed through the screen door.

"Oh, Martin, where exactly did you want me to stick that crucifix?" The right side of her mouth smiled as she showed the end of her tongue between her teeth.

"It is usually hung upon the wall." I turned to the door, but made no eye contact with her as I fumbled for my car keys. "Goodbye."

It started to sprinkle rain and the warm wind gusted. A flash of lightning and its immediate crash of thunder startled me as I crossed the street. As I hurriedly unlocked the car door, I heard the sound of a fast approaching car and squealing tires on pavement. I turned to see a police cruiser sliding around the corner of the wet, sandy street. A dirty, scraggly-faced, dark–haired, twenty-something man in a shredded black t-shirt and bleached blue jeans ran down the street and leapt across the fence of Tammy's house. The police officer hopped out of the car, removed his revolver, sought refuge behind his driver's door, took aim at the man, and ordered him to halt and raise his hands. "Give it up!" The dogs began yipping and barking loudly, jumping on the fence.

Immediately after that a light blue, four-door car pulled up, and a man in a dark gray suit brandishing a handgun dropped out of the driver's seat and took aim across the hood of the car. "Police! Freeze!"

I had frozen in the street myself, for everything was happening at once. Quickly realizing the seriousness of the situation, I opened the door and took cover by ducking down across the front passenger seat. I fully expected to hear gunfire. I raised my eyes just enough above the seat to see through the back window. The two officers had entered the yard and subdued the man up against one of the gnarly trees, cuffing his hands behind his back as he resisted arrest.

Tammy was screaming and cursing at the police officers as they wrestled him to the marked police car. From the tone and her words, I heard enough to figure out that this was her boyfriend. Meanwhile the dogs were jumping all over the police officers.

"You sonsabitches," Tammy yelled. "Leave him alone!"

"Ma'am, he nearly killed you last week," the uniformed officer yelled back. "But when we took him downtown you wouldn't file charges. But today, we're the ones filing charges."

"You let him go," she cried. "He's my boyfriend."

"He's under arrest," the officer in the gray suit called out. "He just robbed the pharmacy."

I watched the police officers shove the man into the back seat of the police car. Tammy was still shouting at the police when I started my car. The undercover officer in the gray suit crossed the street and walked toward me. I rolled my driver's side window down despite the wind and rain.

"Who are you?" He was clean shaven and had no eyebrows over his pale blue eyes. His left front tooth was gold.

"Martin Flanagan."

"What were you doing here?" He fidgeted with his gun under his left arm and wiped rain from his face.

"I'm the seminarian at Poor Souls, and the lady called the parish so I came out to visit."

"Is that right? Well, she's a poor soul all right. If I were you, I would stay away from her. She and her witch friends are up to no good." He shook his head and adjusted his gun in its holster under his arm again as he began scraping his left

foot against the ground. "Damn! Dog crap!" He ᵕᵕ
again. "Go on, get out of here. It's going to storm."

The wind blew even harder, and the rain came in tor-
rents. Fierce lightning etched diagonally across the sky; loud
thunder rumbled. As I drove back to Poor Souls thinking
about what had just happened, the storm sirens began to wail.
My windshield wipers were ineffective. When I got back to
Poor Souls, the storm was on top of Inglenook. I made a dash
for the front door. Once I was inside the storm got worse,
and the lights flickered on and off. The next lightning strike
knocked the power out in the rectory. The wind howled
louder, and tree limbs blew by the windows. It was then that
Hyacinth made me go to the basement with her and wait the
storm out.

After the storm, we went outside to survey the damage.
We were lucky. A neighbor's tree came down just missing my
car. One of the men in the neighborhood got his chainsaw out
and began to cut the downed tree into firewood.

After the excitement had died down and the skies
cleared, I sat outside on the front porch and read until the
power came back on about five o'clock.

* * * *

That night's sleep was not restful. There were other
storms predicted, and the lightning, thunder, wind, and rain
came in waves about every other hour. I started at a sound and
a towering, shrouded skeleton took me in its grasp and pushed
me down the front stairs where possessed Tammy from Elm
Street was waiting for me. She was naked. I flew down the
stairs against my will. I tried to get away through the front
door, but when I opened it, five other girls ran in and began
dancing around me. It began raining inside the house as the
wind blew the door open. I tried to speak, but my jaw was
locked shut and my tongue cleaved to the roof of my mouth.

Tammy grabbed me by the arms, and the other girls tried to grab my legs. I jerked away just as lightning lit up the room and thunder shook my bed.

I turned my bedside lamp on, took my rosary off the nightstand, and prayed the beads. Something told me that my assignment was not just about church politics, but was also about the supernatural battle between good and evil. *If I become a priest, what am I getting myself into?*

When morning came, my lamp was still on, and the rosary was still in my hands.

Chapter 33: Peggy

All shall be well,
and all shall be well,
and all things shall be well.
— St. Julian of Norwich

The Schultz's had invited Robin and me to dinner that week and, while I was there, Peggy invited me to join her and her parents to Capitol City on Friday for a visit to the zoo and a musical at the outdoor theater.

On Friday morning before the trip, the phone rang. It was Mr. Schultz. Mrs. Schultz had a migraine headache and couldn't travel. Mr. Shultz didn't want to leave Colleen at home alone, so he encouraged me to go ahead as planned. "Peggy's been looking forward to the musical. The two of you will have a good time."

I agreed to go.

When I picked Peggy up at her house, she was wearing a white cotton top, blue shorts, and walking shoes; her hair was in a ponytail. Her neck showed while a few strands of hair graced her cheeks.

The two of us spent the morning at the zoo, and then we had dinner at a Chinese restaurant at Capitol Galleria. Her hazel eyes were filled with life. Her voice was soft yet firm, the cadence and lilt musical; her smile was most inviting; and her personality made her glow from within.

That afternoon we were at Sherwood Forest Park for the musical, *The Sound of Music*. I had seen neither the musical nor the movie. Peggy had seen the movie. All day long during the car ride, the tour of the exotic animals, and the fine cuisine, I found myself more and more attracted to her.

When the musical began, I identified with Maria Von Trapp. The song *Climb Every Mountain* spoke to me. I had heard it before, but never realized it was a song from a musical. At one point, I saw Peggy looking over at me and wondered if she wanted me to hold her hand. I wanted to, but I was a seminarian, engaged to the Church, and the two of us were not on a date. Going on a date with a woman was a non-negotiable canon.

At intermission, I went for popcorn and drinks and was surprised to see someone from the seminary. It was Ronald Sidney. He was from St. Louis, Missouri. He was a six-foot blonde with round, wire-rimmed spectacles. He always wore comfortable clothing that made him look as if he had just come from the country club golf course. Today was no different. My mind wandered back to the first time I met Ronald Sidney at the seminary.

Sidney's extravagantly decorated room reminded me of the Cainbrook Country Club's lobby or the latest showroom display in an expensive furniture store. There were two old world French chairs covered in crushed red velvet and a hand–carved, gold-upholstered Victorian divan. A parquet floor was dotted with two red, black, and gold Persian rugs. The entire back wall was covered with a full-length mirror, and the left wall was decorated with a fine tapestry that bore a southwestern theme; Renaissance prints in gilded wooden frames hung upon the wall to the right. The five tall windows in the room were shaded by louvered mahogany blinds and flanked by lavish florid draperies. At the end of the room was a king-size waterbed and in the opposite corner a wet bar.

Even though his room was the same size as all the others on his floor in Aquinas Hall, it looked huge. I wondered how he managed to fit everything inside. Classical music played softly from several stereo speakers strategically located in the corners of the room, and the brewed aroma of freshly ground coffee and sweet potpourri candles wafted from the room as I stepped upon the dark red Persian rug that welcomed one across the threshold.

He had the hardwood floor installed when he first arrived at the seminary. His great-grandfather had built a furniture factory in the eighteen forties, and it had been in the family ever since.

* * * *

I made my way through the crowd of people standing around, waiting in line for food or the restroom, and approached Ronald Sidney standing in line at the concession stand. He had his arms around a woman. In fact, his hands were cupped around the woman's breasts.

As I stepped up to him, I recognized the woman. It was Professor Au Courant from St. Albert's, the theologian from France.

"Martin. Martin Flanagan. What brings you to Capitol City?" Ronald nonchalantly repositioned his hands around Au Courant's tummy.

"The Sound of Music?" I said it more as a question than a statement.

"Mr. Flanagan, good to see you." Mz. Au Courant nodded and extended her hand.

"Professor."

"You can call me Jeanne." Her English was rounded off by

her French accent. "We're on holiday from St. Albert's."

"Jeanne."

Ronald Sidney raised his eyebrows up and down a time or two. "Where are you doing your parish ministry experience this year?"

"I'm assigned to Poor Souls in Inglenook."

"Oh, that's right."

"What's this holiday you two are on?" I asked him, observing their physical attraction to one another.

"Oh, well, Jeanne and I are on a sabbatical, of sorts."

"Oh." I wasn't sure what Ronald was saying.

Just then, it was his turn in line. "Well, maybe I'll see you around, Martin." Ronald smiled and turned away to place his order.

"Au revoir, Martin." Jeanne nodded and smiled.

Another cashier was ready for me. I didn't say anything to Peggy about seeing Ronald and Jeanne. I wasn't sure why.

* * * *

That night after the show, Peggy and I planned to drive straight back to Inglenook, but not quite fifty miles out of Capitol City we both became very drowsy. I didn't want to spend half the night anywhere, but I couldn't stay awake at the wheel. Halfway between Capitol City and Inglenook we exited the interstate at Coaltown and tried to find two hotel rooms. Unfortunately, we learned that every hotel was booked, all except for an old roadside motel, *ALLEN'S INN*. It was in terrible shape, a motel in disrepair. Even the sign was partially burnt out.

"Look at the sign." Peggy reached over and pointed.

"What?" I drove up near the entrance.

"*ALIEN'S IN*," she said. The bottom of the second *L* was burnt out and the last *N* of *INN* was completely out. "The *ALIEN'S are IN*."

"Yes, I can see that." I shook my head and started laughing. "Great."

"Hey, you laughed at one of my jokes." She softly elbowed me.

"Yeah." I stepped out of the car and rang the doorbell.

An uncombed, unshaven, snaggletoothed man came to the door dressed in blue pajamas with a banana pattern. "Yeah, what is it?" he moaned. His hair stood on end and was greasy.

"The night manager of the Sleepy Owl sent us down here hoping you'd have a room. All the other motels in town are full." I looked inside his office. It was a garbage pit with stacks of paper and clothes, assorted junk, computer monitors, soda bottles, and empty beer cans.

"Those damned casinos. Damned fools think they're going to get rich by gambling. Dream on." His breath reeked of garlic and onions.

"Do you have any vacancies?"

"Yeah. Now my rooms are pretty simple. Since the motel chains came to town we get overlooked."

"All we need are two rooms," I sighed with a yawn. "We're tired."

"*Rooms?* Don't push your luck—" he burped. "I have only one room left."

"Oh, but my friend and I aren't married." I shook my head as the smell of garlic and onions overwhelmed me.

"So what? Neither are the rest of my customers. And they rent the room by the hour, if you get the picture. It's the nineties."

I agreed to take the room and put the bill on my charge card. When I got back in the car and explained the situation to Peggy, I could tell that she was just as shy as I was. "It's the last room he had." I parked the car and we walked to the room.

When I opened the door to the room Peggy blushed. "Oh, well, it's this or just keep driving. I guess it'll do."

"I could sleep in the car," I offered, closing my eyes.

"Oh, don't be ridiculous," Peggy said. "I'll take the bed closest to the bathroom."

Thankfully. there were *two* double beds in the room so at least we wouldn't be sleeping in the same bed. I cringed to think what Father Hugh or the rector of St. Albert's would think.

Peggy took her purse into the bathroom and took a bath. I was exhausted and planned to bathe in the morning. However, as I lay in my bed listening to the water in the shower, I imagined sleeping with Peggy.

When she came out of the bath she got into her bed. She was dressed in her white top and blue shorts. "I didn't bring a change of clothes," she said. "So don't think I'm gross; I have to wear something. Clean body, dirty clothes. Nothing like it."

"I didn't bring my pajamas," I said.

"I had a wonderful day, Martin," Peggy said as she pulled the sheet and blanket around herself.

"Me, too." I turned away from her, wondering what it would be like to be married. For a while before finally falling asleep, I questioned myself as to why I had agreed to go on this outing alone with Peggy in the first place. I even wondered if Mr. and Mrs. Schultz had arranged it all along.

* * * *

I was awakened in the middle of the night by a loud shriek and bright lights in my eyes. "Martin! Wake up! There's something in my bed!"

I fought to get out from under the sheet and blankets and on my feet. Once on my feet, I grabbed the sheets and blankets off of her bed and shook them out.

"I felt it crawl over my face!" She ran to the bathroom. "I could hear it rubbing its legs together! I think it was a huge cockroach!"

There was no roach to be found. After she was out of the bathroom, I went in and got a drink of water. When I came out, Peggy had already turned the lights out. I inched my way to my side of the room, bringing my glass of water back to my nightstand, and crawled back into my bed.

I started when I bumped into something. It was Peggy.

"What?" she laughed.

"We can't—"

"Can't what?" she asked.

"Sleep together," I said.

"Well, you don't expect me to sleep in a bed that's infested with roaches, do you?"

"Who says *this* bed doesn't have roaches?" I asked without thinking.

"You're right." She jumped up and bounced out of the bed. "Let's look."

"Now?"

"Yes, now." She flipped on the lights. "Get up. Let's strip this bed down, too."

"I'm not sure we want to know what we're sleeping on," I said, fearing what we may find under the sheets.

"Just help me. I'm tired."

"Can't we just sleep?" I yawned.

"Not with roaches. Now, get up and help me."

Together we pulled the blankets and sheets off, examining the brown and yellow stained mattress. We flipped it over but found no bugs. We then remade the bed and crawled back in again. I stayed over on the right side of the mattress. She turned the lights out.

"Good night. Sleep tight. Don't let the bed bugs bite," I said.

"Very funny," she said from the left side of the bed, facing left away from me. She curled under the blankets.

Before I closed my eyes I asked, "Are you sure we should sleep in the same bed?"

"Martin, this wasn't just a ruse to get in your bed, you know."

"Is that what you think I thought?"

"I don't know." She grew quiet and said nothing for a minute.

"There really was a filthy bug crawling across my face," she said breaking the silence.

"Well, I'm not a bed bug, and I won't bite."

"Then you don't have to sleep on the edge."

I scooted closer to her, though I was still facing right, away from her.

"Just hold me close, Martin." She moved closer, turned my direction, and snuggled. "We can spoon. Besides, why should I worry? You're going to be a priest."

"Right." *Thanks for reminding me.* I wasn't completely sure of my answer as I felt the softness of her body next to mine, smelled the fragrance of her freshly washed hair, and felt her breasts against my back. She reached around me with her left arm, and I took her left hand in mine. I prayed the Lord's Prayer silently, but emphasized the words *lead us not into temptation.* I wanted to kiss her goodnight but didn't. She was soon asleep.

God only knows how I finally managed to fall asleep.

* * * *

The next morning as the sunlight pierced through the tacky drapery, I reached for my glass of water. Taking a drink, I felt something large and prickly moving in my mouth. I sat up and spat the water out on the floor, and a huge cockroach crawled away under the desk chair. "Ohhh!" I cried.

"What happened?" Peggy awoke.

"I found the roach! It was in my drink!"

I rushed into the bathroom and gargled, wishing I had a toothbrush and toothpaste. I took a hot shower and let the water run in my mouth. When I came out of the bathroom, Peggy was sitting in the desk chair laughing about the roach. "That must have been the continental breakfast."

"No," I answered. "Breakfast is extra."

Chapter 34: Jesus Wept

Saying the rosary takes it out of me
more than any hairshirt would.
— St. Thérèse of Lisieux

During the first week of October, Father Kevin informed us that he was being recalled to Wheatfield. "Bishop Numbnoddle lost another one. This time it was his vocation director. Now he needs me to take a parish in the diocese. I am to leave tomorrow."

The next day I helped Father Kevin load his van while Bubby ran around in front of the rectory. Suddenly the redheaded Father Jack Ash came walking up the sidewalk.

"Leaving so soon?" Jack asked Kevin; Jack acknowledged me with a wink and a wave.

"Bishop's orders." Kevin looked at Jack.

"We haven't met." Jack extended his hand to Kevin. "I'm Father Ash."

"Father Ash," Kevin nodded with his birdcage in hand, the lone cockatiel peeking out. "I'm Father Murphy."

"You're the one from Wheatfield, aren't you?"

"Yes, yes. That's me."

"Father Jack," I said, grabbing Bubby's collar to restrain her.

"Good to see you again, Martin." Jack nodded, amused with Bubby.

Bubby broke away from my grip and ran toward the street.

"Boy, is Bishop Numbnoddle ever in trouble." Jack shook his head.

"Yes, that's why I'm leaving for Wheatfield," Kevin explained.

"Good luck." Jack patted him on the back.

"Thank you." Kevin carried the birdcage to the van.

Bubby disappeared from my line of sight as a car screeched to a stop. She crawled out from under the stopped car.

"Bubby, Bubby, come here!" Kevin called out. Bubby obeyed.

"Say, you didn't, by chance, lose one of your birds?" Jack said as he looked into the birdcage.

"Why, yes, nearly two months ago. Why?" There was a glint of hope in Kevin's eyes as he patted Bubby at his side.

"Well, if you look directly above your head in this maple tree, you'll see a green and yellow parrot," Jack continued, pointing upward. "I don't see a lot of them here in the eastern U.S."

Father Kevin put the cage down in the back of the van and looked up in the tree. "It's a cockatiel, not a parrot."

"Whatever," Jack snickered, looking up into the tree.

"They're not indigenous to the states. They're Australian," Kevin replied, with a smile.

I saw the bird on the limb. It was Cosmas. Or was it Damian? I couldn't remember. Kevin climbed the tree and worked his way to the bird. Unbelievably, the bird didn't move. Father Kevin, in his priestly collar, black pants, and dress shoes, crawled out on the limb where the bird was

perched and coaxed it with clicks and whistles and some sunflower seeds.

"Damien, come to Dada!"

Father Kevin was nearly weeping as he retrieved Damian
and returned it to its cage, reuniting it with Cosmas.

Father Jack returned to the rectory, and I followed. Hyacinth met us in the foyer. "I get rid of one collared mutt only
to gain another? You just better be house-trained."

"I resemble that remark. And, yes, the rumors of my being named pastor here are unfortunately true. His Highness
and Macaroni Crony are desperate. Either that, or I'll inflict
more punishment on the people of Possum Prairie. Maybe it's
both. It wouldn't surprise me if His Highness removes my faculty to hear confessions. Say, Martin, there you go. Since Bill
Gallagher's not hearing confessions these days, you can sit in
the confessional and hear them. It'll be great practice for you
as a seminarian."

Hyacinth rolled her eyes at Jack as Cat came down the
stairs. Cat looked at Jack, arched its back, reared its tail in the
air, and hissed.

"Oh, it's so good to feel welcome." Jack bowed reveren-
tially to Hyacinth. She harrumphed and picked up Cat; the
two went upstairs.

* * * *

Jack worked at settling in as the new pastor of Poor Souls
and learning the names and faces of his parishioners. One afternoon two of the elderly ladies of the altar society, came to
see Jack. I was in Jack's office going over the lector schedules.
One of the ladies was wearing a pink pantsuit; her gray hair
had a blue tint. "Father Jack. The statue of Mary in the church
is weeping blood," she said. "It's a miracle."

"If you stare at an ugly hunk of plaster long enough you're
liable to see anything." Jack smiled.

"Father! I can't believe that you'd say something like that," the other woman replied. She wore an oversized sweater with a pattern of butterflies all over it. "Our statue of Mary is so beautiful."

"She is?" Jack let his jaw hang open slightly, as if actually questioning her. "I prefer the genuine article."

"Don't you pray the rosary?" the woman in the butterfly sweater asked. "All the saints loved the rosary."

"It wasn't Saint Thérèse, the Little Flower's, favorite prayer—and it's not mine either," Jack explained.

"*It is mine,* and I think you owe me an apology," the butterfly sweater continued.

"For what?" he asked.

"For being sacrilegious toward the statue of Mary," the butterfly sweater woman bristled.

"I can't condone idolatry; it made God's top ten list."

"Idolatry?" the pink pantsuit lady said.

"Yes," Jack stated. "Worship of an idol is a sin against the commandments. We do not worship statues."

Both women were silent as their faces fell. They stared at me as if expecting me to say something.

"It'll be okay," Jack said. "It just sounded like you all are a bit too focused on a piece of plaster."

"She weeps." The one in the pink pantsuit reasserted.

"So do I."

"Do *you* weep blood?" the butterfly sweater asked.

"No, thank God. At least not yet, but then I haven't been here long enough."

"Well, I never—" the butterfly sweater replied.

"What are you going to do about the statue?" the woman in pink asked.

"Probably nothing, other than wash the blood off." Jack turned away from their stare.

"Come on, Mildred. Let's go," the pink lady said. "We know when we're not welcome."

"Father," butterfly lady continued, "I'd suggest you go take a look at the calendar. October is the month of Mary." The two women hurriedly left his office.

Jack shook his head. "Half the world is either starving or on the brink of war, and they're focused on a bloody statue." He looked at me with serious eyes. "I'm hurt. Our statue of Mary in the foyer isn't bleeding. Why should theirs?" He closed his eyes, crossed his arms, and laughed. "Jesus wept."

Later that afternoon I went into the church to examine the statue of Mary. She wore the traditional blue gown. Red, plastic rosary beads dangled from her folded hands. A candle wreath was stuck around her head for a crown. Tiny white roses encircled her protruding heart that was pierced through with a black dagger.

I saw no tears in her bright blue eyes.

Chapter 35: Canonically Speaking

Why do you not practice what you preach?
— St. Jerome

The following day Father Jack waved me into his office again. He was on the phone and motioned for me to have a seat. Then he put the caller on the speakerphone and put his index finger to his lips.

"I don't care!" a loud, male voice boomed. "You will remove that man from Immaculate Heart's rectory!" It was Monsignor Linguini.

"Don't tell me—the *Rubric Rats* or the *Latin in the Liturgy* crowd reported him." Jack laughed though he was perturbed. "Then, again, maybe it was the *Cuffers*."

"It doesn't matter how I found out. I know. And so does the bishop. Bill isn't a priest. He violated Canon Law."

"Yes, he is. *A priest forever in the order of Melchizedek—*"

"Don't quote scripture at me. Bill Gallagher is no longer an active priest."

"Yes, he is, Rigatoni."

"According to Canon Law, Bill Gallagher can't live in that rectory."

"Why not?"

"Because he violated his priestly vows and is therefore no

longer a functioning priest!"

"Monsignor Macaroni, I hate to be the bearer of bad news, but a lot of the boys have violated their vows in their rectories, and they're still living in them and they're still functioning as priests."

"Evict him, Jackass. Or else I will. Don't force *me* to do it."

"What if I don't?"

The phone slammed down.

Jack laughed out loud. "I believe we were cut off." He smiled and picked up the phone to dial. "I'd better call him back, Martin, and hope we have a better connection this time." He giggled like a schoolboy making prank phone calls as he looked at me. "Pull up a chair."

I sat with the feeling I was committing a venial sin, guilty of something, but not sure what.

"Yes, Monsignor Linguini, please." Jack paused, his eyes looking out the window. "Yes, this is Father Jack Ash. The vicar-general and I were just speaking, but we were cut off." He put his hand over the phone and whispered with a wink. "This is too much fun."

It was a minute or so before Monsignor Linguini came on the line.

"Yes, Monsignor, this is Father Ash. It seems we were cut off." He put Linguini on the speaker phone again.

"We did *not* get cut off."

"We didn't?" Jack acted surprised.

"No. I hung up on you."

"You're hurting my feelings, Monsignor."

"Jack, quit being such a smart-ass. And I better not be on that damned speaker phone either."

"Monsignor. Please. I do have some character."

"None that I've noticed."

"Ouch, Monsignor. That hurt."

"Hurry up, Jack, I don't have all day. What do you want? You've got a vagrant who needs evicting."

"Bill Gallagher—a vagrant? Come on, Monsignor. Bill gave twenty-seven years of his life to the Church. Certainly we can help him in his hour of need."

"He should have thought about that before he got involved with that nun."

"She's dead, for Christ's sake."

"You blasphemed. Now you'll have to go to confession."

"I'll let Bill hear my confession before I kick his ass out on the street."

"Jack, I'm ready to hang up again."

"Well, then I'll be brief. Let Bill return to active ministry."

"I can't—he can't. Then all of the priests who left over the years will want to come back."

"Yes, and then we wouldn't have a priest shortage, would we? But I can guarantee that not all of them want to come back."

"Jack!"

"Michael! Must we banish him to the outer darkness, left to wail and gnash his teeth, simply because he fell in love?"

"Fell in love? She was his concubine."

"Monsignor, must you be so dramatic?"

"A rectory is for priests."

"Bill *is* a priest."

"*Was*. He's a whiskey priest."

"Oh, like that's original. You're not the only one who's read Graham Greene."

"Listen. Bill Gallagher contracted marriage."

"But his wife died."

"It doesn't matter. We've also learned he's been hearing

confessions at Poor Souls."

"And doing a fine job at it, I will add."

"Not for this diocese."

"Then another diocese might accept him."

"He cannot be reinstated, Jack."

"Must we constantly strain out gnats and swallow camels?"

The phone went dead again.

"*L'incompetant*." Jack glanced at me with a sad smile. "Well, he told me, didn't he?"

"At least you tried."

"Forget him. Come with me."

"Where?"

"We're going to a rummage sale to rescue some missing saints. It seems one of our biggest angels showed up across town at a yard sale and is being held hostage. I thought I'd go pay his ransom so the ladies of the altar society will speak to me again. Father Robin sure got rid of a lot of stuff in the short time he was here. I got another call two days ago from Dan's *Hot* Used Furniture. There's a fancy prie-dieu down there, and someone called the cops thinking Dan had stolen it from Poor Souls or St. Patrick's."

* * * *

The next day, I accompanied Jack to visit Bill Gallagher at Immaculate Heart, but there was no one there. When we returned to Poor Souls, Hyacinth descended upon us. "Father Jack?"

"Yes, Hyacinth."

"Father Bill Gallagher was here."

"When?"

"Shortly after you left. You just missed him."

"What did he say?"

"Not much. He just wanted me to tell you that one of the

diocesan attorneys called the rectory and threatened to have him arrested unless he vacated the premises."

"I'll be damned. Did he say anything else?"

"That he'd either call or come by again sometime to see you."

"Where's he going to live?"

"He didn't say, but I will say that his color is terrible, and he has a hacking cough. I hate to say it, but he's got the shakes. I'm worried about him."

"Damn. I planned on putting him up here at Poor Souls," Jack said. "He can't go back to living in his car." Jack sighed. "Maybe we should go look for him, but where would we start?" Jack ran his fingers through his red hair.

Chapter 36: The Hairshirt

"No one should judge that he has greater
perfection because he performs great penances.
Merit consists in love alone...without which the
soul is worth nothing."
— St. Catherine of Siena

On a cold, Wednesday afternoon in mid-October, Gerard Austin arrived unexpectedly at Poor Souls' rectory. He was wearing sandals and was carrying a brown paper grocery sack.

"Martin. Martin Flanagan, how are you? We miss you in the seminary. How's the pastoral experience? I love the name of this parish: Our Lady of the Poor and Forgotten Souls in Purgatory." I opened the door and let him into the foyer. "You are offering all your sufferings up for the abandoned souls, aren't you?"

"Well, I really haven't thought about it much."

"*What?* Don't tell me you've wasted all your suffering by forgetting to offer it up?" He pressed his way through the French doors into the living room.

"If I start now, will it be retroactive?" I teased.

"Martin, that's sacrilegious—if not blasphemous."

"Gerard. Lighten up." He was already wearing me out. I

shook my head and sat on the sofa.

"Good old rigid, intolerant, orthodox, homophobe Gerard Austin at your service." He remained standing, studying the walls as if he was conducting research.

"Is that what they're calling you now?"

"No. They've always called me that. Don't you love it?"

"I wouldn't be happy with a reputation like that."

"You should have seen it. Two of the faculty members— one of the liberal Dominican priests and a woman who's on the women's ordination conference—cornered me during my evaluation process. They threatened to have me placed in psychiatric treatment if I didn't begin to show signs of assimilation."

"Well, Gerard, they might have a point. You are a little intense."

"And what's wrong with that? John the Baptist was intense! St. Paul was intense!"

"Yes, and they were both beheaded."

"I have prayed for martyrdom. Haven't you?"

"I can't say that I have, Gerard."

"Well, you should. We need priests who are willing to be martyred."

"I agree, but you don't have to go looking for persecution."

I decided to show him around the rectory. When I took him upstairs to my room, Gerard gasped aloud. "Oh, sweet heavens, Martin. This is terrible!"

"What?" I thought something was wrong and looked around to make sure the house wasn't on fire.

"You've got a *television* in your bedroom." He cradled his face in his right hand.

"It was here when I moved in," I defended myself. "Besides, it's an old black and white job."

"It's evil. And look at that bed. I've seen smaller beds in wedding suites."

"You have? What were you doing in a wedding suite?"

"It's a figure of speech." He rolled his eyes and grunted.

"Well, it's a comfortable bed," I said as I ran my hand along the bedspread.

"You need to shun comfort. Blessed are they who suffer, your reward will be great in heaven."

"Gerard, we're not medieval monks."

"I hope that's not an insult to western monasticism."

"It wasn't. I was simply stating a fact. We are going to be priests for the church in the twenty-first century."

"Yes, and there's going to be a rebirth in spirituality in the Church and her Sacred Tradition."

* * * *

I led him back downstairs to the kitchen where Hyacinth was cooking. "Will you be staying for dinner?" she asked, looking up from a steaming pot on the stove.

"Oh, no." Gerard nodded to Hyacinth, but refused to look at her directly.

"Son, you're as skinny as a scarecrow. Let me fix you some dinner."

"No, thank you, ma'am." He looked toward the window.

Hyacinth walked over to the kitchen window and looked out. "What are you looking at, son?"

"Nothing." His eyes were fixed outside.

"Are you sure?" She looked out again, appearing to follow his line of sight.

"Yes. I'm sure." Gerard kept looking out the window.

"Son, why won't you look at me?" She tossed her large wooden spoon on the countertop and opened one of the lower cabinet doors.

"*Custudiat oculos.*"

"Speak English, son," she said, reaching down for another pot in the cabinet.

"Custody of the eyes," he replied as if disciplining a child.

"Listen, son, I'm old enough to be your granny." She rose and held the pot at his eye level. "If an old broad like me can turn you on, then you'll never make it in a parish. Eventually you'll have to talk to women. They make up half the world, you know. And the way I see things, more women work for the church than men. So, you might want to look me in the eyes so as to give yourself some practice." She poured some water into the pot and put it on one of the back burners.

Gerard was visibly miffed, but still he refused to look at her.

"Does your friend want something to eat?" Hyacinth addressed me.

"Does she have any oat cereal or nuts and some bottled water?" Gerard asked.

"Yes, she does." Again, Hyacinth tried to make eye contact with Gerard. "Would you like some?"

"Yes, thank you." Gerard kept his gaze down.

She turned the lazy Susan and pulled out a box of oat cereal and a bag of pecans. She then went to another cabinet, got a bowl, and poured the cereal, mixing in the pecans; then she went to the refrigerator, removed a half-gallon of milk, opened the jug, and poured some on the cereal. Handing the bowl to Gerard, she returned the milk to the refrigerator. As she closed the door, she grabbed a bottle of water out of the door and handed it to him.

"Thank you," Gerard said with a spoonful of cereal and pecans to his mouth.

I grabbed a red crème soda out of the refrigerator and led Gerard back to the living room.

"How can you drink that rotgut?" Gerard asked as he sat

in one of the straight-backed chairs. "It's got thirty grams of sugar, and it'll take rust off of a truck bumper or eat through the acid on the posts of a car battery."

"I'll make a note of that," I said in a serious tone.

"Martin, you've changed." He stopped nibbling. "You've got an attitude."

"Really? How so?" *This could be good*.

"You're more direct."

"I guess being out in the real world and living in a parish will do that to a guy."

"Well, speaking of the unreal world, have you heard about Father Short?" Gerard asked as he resumed eating.

"No."

"Well, we always joked that he was *short* on brains, but he went off the deep end. He announced to his class that he was leaving the faculty of Saint Albert's to study witchcraft and marry another witch. A *male* witch."

I wasn't that shocked knowing Father Short. "He didn't seem too interested in Jesus," I said, offering my thoughts.

"His homilies were nothing but psycho-babble," Gerard added.

Gerard then began describing his experience at Metropolitan Mary Seminary. "They sent me up there for two weeks for a Sexuality Sensitivity Seminar in hopes of brainwashing me and curing me of my rigidity and homophobia. I got to play with clay as they encouraged me to shape the clay in an expression of my unfulfilled sexual desires. Then they told me to go to my room, remove all my clothing in front of the full length mirror, and tell each of my body parts individually how much I loved them."

"Come on, Gerard. You don't expect me to believe you, do you?"

"No, but if it makes you feel any better, that's when I

left."

"What did you tell them when you got back to the seminary?"

"They sent me to the diocesan shrink. The first thing he asked me was why I hated my homosexuality. Imagine *me* a flame. Then he asked me whether I stood in front of the bathroom mirror and masturbated while lusting after my mother."

"What!"

"That's when I walked out and drove straight to the chancery. When I got there, Father Samuel and Sister Hilda tried to prevent me from speaking to the bishop, but the bishop heard me arguing with them and he stepped out into the hall. He called me to his office, but he didn't believe me either. Now I'm on an emotional, psychological, and academic probation of sorts. *Wellness Probation* is what they're calling it.

"Father Samuel, or Sammy, or Smells Good—whatever his name is—he doesn't want me studying for our diocese, you know, so I've been looking into some strict religious orders. But anyway, when I returned to the seminary, I went to one of our communal penance services, and we all sat around in the sanctuary and were encouraged to confess our sins out loud to one another. When I wouldn't say anything, Mz. Au Courant decided to begin confessing my sins for me. There were a couple of other guys who wouldn't say anything either, and others began to confess their sins for them, too. That was convenient. 'Oh, here, let me examine your conscience for you.'

"Then we were to write our sins—real or imagined—on a piece of paper and were invited up around the altar. One of the priests had placed a small backyard grill on top of the altar, and we were invited to place our papers on the blazing charcoal fire. The chapel fire alarms went off, thank God. We had to evacuate."

"Gerard, I've got to hand it to you, that is hilarious."

"Sad, you mean."

"If it were true, yes."

"It is true. And there is a conspiracy, I'm telling you."

"And Bill Clinton's the Anti-Christ." I laughed.

"No, he's not," he said, waving his index finger at me. "He has not the competence, but as for his wife, Hilary, that's a different story."

"Hey, I come from a long line of Democrats." I squinted in his direction.

"I'm sorry." His brow furrowed.

"There's nothing to be sorry for."

"Then I'm embarrassed for you."

"You're an agitator, Gerard."

"And you're milk toast."

Maybe not anymore, I thought to myself, wanting to avoid any further controversy with Gerard.

"I know, I know," Gerard said, as if uncomfortable with the silence, "you're going to tell me to just give them what they want and then, when I'm ordained and sent to a parish, I can be a real priest."

"Well, I don't know if I would have said it like that, but—"

"Oh, Martin, don't you know what's going on? Bishop Maurus at St. Anselm's has kept his seminary on track and risked the wrath of the liberal establishment by dismissing professors who won't teach orthodox Catholicism."

"That's old news," I said, taking a drink of the red crème soda.

"So I take it you haven't heard the rest of the news from St. Albert's?"

"No." I half expected it to be a rumor about Ronald Sidney's holiday with Mz. Jeanne Au Courant.

"Father Hugh's witch hunt is over. Unfortunately, his investigation was a few years too late. I suspect that he offended one bishop too many. They may have threatened to pull all their men out of St. Albert's. Father Hugh himself may be turned out and be forced to look for another priory or another religious order.

"Some of the bishops defend their fair-haired boys from any legitimate criticism. Meanwhile, an orthodox straight, like me, who is intolerant of evil, has to watch his every word lest his forehead gets "homophobe" tattooed on it.

"Of course, some guys have nothing to worry about because they don't stand for anything. I certainly hope *you* stand for something, Martin." He glared at me. "Well, you *do* stand for something, don't you?"

"Yes," I answered, though I had more questions than answers about the Church—a church that was quite clear on what she stood for but seemingly not so sure in standing for those stands.

"Father Michael," Gerard sneered in an effeminate voice, "or *Mike* as he wants to be called, is always asking us, '*Are we willing to sacrifice the Eucharist and the preaching of the Gospel in order to maintain an antiquated mandatory celibacy?*'" I considered it a good, well-reasoned question, almost Thomistic in its logic. "It's open heresy," Gerard flailed his arms, pacing back and forth, before I could respond. "People were burnt at the stake for less. Father Mike tells us that daily Mass has become too routine, and it takes away from the Sunday celebration. Then he tells us we ought to reinstate resigned and laicized priests who left to get married."

"I could see some value in reinstating some of the priests who left," I agreed, nodding my head, "especially those who left to get married and are still practicing their faith."

"Oh, Martin, you mustn't talk like that! That's heresy.

There is no vocation shortage. God is calling, but men just don't want to hear His voice."

Father Jack Ash appeared in the doorway. He was wearing a light green polo shirt and blue jeans. "Austin, isn't it? I believe we met at the seminarian's cookout last summer. I'm Father Jack Ash."

"*Father.* Gerard Austin." He held out his hand and gave a slight bow to Father Jack.

"Oh, now don't go kissing my ring, Son. I'm not a bishop—nor am I ever likely to be named one. Thank God."

"You're a priest of God."

"And so are all Christians. You were saying that God is calling, but *men* just don't want to hear His voice. Some of us would say you're right—but what exactly is God saying?"

"Many are called, but few choose to heed his call," Gerard replied immediately.

"Could it be many are being called, but the Church refuses to admit their call?"

"Father, you can't say things like that."

"Oh, really? Well, I just did, didn't I? Honestly, how can you be so *certain* of everything?"

"I believe."

"'*Lord, help my unbelief,*' is the second part of that passage," Jack said. "Our faith is ultimately a mystery. If we knew everything then we wouldn't hope, would we?" Father Jack moved up the stairs. "Gerard, you're welcome to stay for dinner if you'd like."

"Thanks anyway, but I have plans."

Jack had gone upstairs.

"Pray for him," Gerard whispered. "He's a liberal modernist. He's got the look and the sound in his voice." Gerard bowed his head and closed his eyes for a moment. "You just ought to be thankful you'll have Father Joseph next semester,"

Gerard continued as if Father Jack's words hadn't even been uttered. "The only negative thing you'll get from Father Joseph is second-hand smoke."

"How do you know I'll have *him* again?"

"Are you serious?"

"Yes."

"Professor Mz. Au Courant left the seminary."

I wasn't given to gossip but there was a part of me that wanted to blurt out the details of seeing Ronald Sidney with his arms around her at Sherwood Forest, but I didn't.

"Mz. Jeanne Au Courant—some of the guys were hailing *Au Courant* as *Jeanne d'Arc*—and her class of Theological Deconstruction makes Father Mike and Father Short look like Cardinal Ratzinger and the pope. Au Courant worked at destroying the very foundations of Christianity and marriage— *the Repressive Patriarchal Regimes*, as she called them.

"The only good thing about her was that she was a visiting professor." Gerard began talking even faster. "Some visitor she was. She came in there with her bizarre post-Christian ideas in an attempt to destroy the Church. She was beyond women's ordination. '*We don't need priests, male or female. We need to get beyond clericalism altogether,*' she said. Of course, she also said, '*we need to get beyond Scripture.*'

"One class period she made us all get down on our hands and knees and crawl around on the floor, coo like babies, and explore our surroundings and one another so that we could *get in touch with the child within.*" He let out a cry of disgust, as his face grew red.

"The last week she was there she had all of us male students lie face down on the floor while she and the female students walked on top of us. *How does it feel, men? This is how women feel every day.* Even Ronald Sidney was mad about it."

"Not for long." I laughed out loud thinking of Ronald Sidney and *the professor*.

"What's that?"

"Oh, I just meant that Ronald isn't one to hold a grudge."

"Have you heard about him?"

"No." Technically I wasn't lying. Ronald had offered me no explanation beyond his being on holiday or sabbatical with Au Courant, whatever that meant.

"Well, he left the seminary. No one knows where he is. Not even his bishop or his family."

I volunteered nothing.

"Which reminds me, Martin," Gerard reached inside the brown sack he had been carrying when he arrived, "I was looking at my bookshelves the other day and found a couple of books you need for your library." He handed me an old leather bound tome entitled *The Martyr's Way*. "Here, Flanagan," he said, turning around. "You know, your name is from the Latin word 'martyr.'"

"Yes, that's what they tell me." I paged through the book. Some of the chapters were intriguing. *The Penitential Life. The Path of Suffering. Self-Flagellation and Midnight Scourgings. Perpetual Fasting.*

Gerard reached in the sack and produced another book, equally as tattered. Its title read *How To Evangelize Unwashed Jews, Heretic Protestants, Heathen Infidels, Assorted Pagans, and Other Unbelievers.*

I handed the books back to him. "Thanks, but are you sure you don't want to keep these?"

"They're yours. I have copies of my own."

"I don't know when I'll get around to reading them. I've got a year's worth of assigned reading to catch up on from our theology classes."

"You'll never make it as a Carthusian or a Cistercian monk."

"I don't know who they are, but you're probably right. I'm not going to become a monk."

Gerard insisted I keep the books and I did to placate him. He stayed for a while longer and told me to beware of beautiful women who will attempt to lure me away from the priestly life. I never did tell him about encountering Ronald Sidney and Mz. Jeanne Au Courant on holiday. Neither did I say anything about my trip to Capitol City with Peggy Schultz nor the specifics about our trip back to Inglenook—including the detour at *Alien's Cockroach Inn*.

After Gerard left, I laughed on and off the rest of the evening thinking about what had happened to him December last.

Two weeks before Christmas had marked the opportunity for us seminarians to go to the woods and chop down a tree for the seminary courtyard. Gerard had been in charge of securing the Christmas tree and got me to volunteer for the *Christmas Decoration Committee*. He decided that we would pick one of the largest trees the Dominicans had seen in years. It took nearly the entire day to pick the tree, cut it down, and transport it to the priory. Gerard informed our *Decoration Committee* that decorating would begin the following morning.

The next day, as everyone was filing out of the chapel after Morning Prayer, down in the courtyard a half-naked, emaciated, hairy-backed man with a towel wrapped around his waist and flip-flop sandals on his feet was plucking socks and underwear off of the Christmas tree in the center of the courtyard.

Ronald Sidney opened one of the windows in the hallway and called out to the man. "Hey, get some clothes on, Tarzan!"

It was then that I recognized the toweled man traipsing around in the snow, hopping up as high as he could to grab his underwear. It was Gerard Austin. I could tell by his emaciated frame and the old tattered scapular around his neck.

Ronald Sidney hollered out the window again, "Gerard, what happened?"

"Is that you, Ronald Sidney?" Gerard called out, squinting up at the rows of windows. He yelled, "I was taking a shower and when I went back to my room I found it ransacked! All my drawers were empty! I found a note telling me where I could find all my clothes! Don't think that I don't know it was you, Sidney! I'm telling Father Hugh!"

"Brother Hairshirt!" Ronald called out from the set of windows to the courtyard, "Judge not, lest thee be judged!"

"It's refreshing to know you know some scripture, Sidney!"

"You best get in before you get frostbite, Granola Bar, or else you'll have no choice but celibacy." With that, Ronald Sidney closed the window.

Many of the seminarians were gawking out the open windows, howling in laughter as Gerard struggled to reach his underwear and socks. As everyone watched, Gerard jumped up to grab a pair of his briefs, but when he grabbed a branch, the tree toppled over upon him. As he came down, his towel fell off. Gerard fell face-first in the snow as the tree dropped on his back. Gerard's bare buttocks aimed straight up as he wriggled out from under the Christmas tree, scrambled to his feet, grabbed his towel, and wrapped it around himself again, all the while scooping up his stolen clothing.

"Happy Winter Solstice, all you flaky Liberals!" he cried out to a thunder of applause.

I fell asleep laughing.

Chapter 37: Hot Water

"Today you will be with me in paradise."
— Luke 23:43

That evening Hyacinth returned late from visiting Father Boniface at the nursing home. I was at the kitchen sink when her cab pulled in the driveway. She paid the driver and quietly unlocked the back door.

"Hyacinth," I said, "how about some hot cocoa? I just boiled some water."

"Ah, you know the way to a woman's heart: chocolate." She was wearing a white blouse and a light green skirt. As she sat at the kitchen table, I noticed that her eyes were bleary. Had I not stopped her, she would have tried to sneak past me.

"How is Father Boniface?" I asked as I got two cups out of the cabinet.

"The same. His memory will come and go. He was telling stories tonight of his first assignment as a priest. At least he remembered he was a priest."

"Did he remember you?" I mixed our hot cocoa.

"No." She looked as if she was about to cry. "I could have been a nun, you know, but they turned me down."

"How's that?" I brought our cups of cocoa to the table.

"Not too many years ago, I applied to the Sisters of Perpetual Penance in hopes I could join their community. After living with them for several weeks, they said I had no marketable skills. Good Lord, I could have helped in the infirmary or been part of their maintenance department. I'd scrubbed more floors than most of their sisters had ever walked on."

"I had no idea you had thought of religious life."

"Oh, yes, but they wouldn't have me. They said I was too conservative. I wanted to wear their traditional religious habit. That's when the Mistress of Novices told me to leave. She said I was applying to the order for all the wrong reasons, searching for a lost paradigm, and experiencing *existential angst*. I just think they thought I was too old if the truth be known. Must watch those premiums on health insurance, you know.

"Father Boniface tried to talk to the Mother Superior, but she said they could tell I wouldn't work out. How about that? I guess I could have applied elsewhere, but after that initial rejection, I didn't try anywhere else. Oh, I thought of the Dominicans or Mother Teresa's order, but I guess it's all for the best. Besides, who would've taken care of Boniface? The church does a good job of keeping people in their place."

Just as Hyacinth stopped speaking, I sensed that someone may have opened the front door and walked in the house. I felt a breeze; it was like someone walked behind me and then into the dining room. Suddenly, the crucifix above the refrigerator rocked on the wall. Then a crashing sound came from the front foyer and hallway. At first, I thought it was an earthquake. We rushed to the front door where we found the white plaster statue of the Blessed Virgin Mary shattered on the black and white marble floor. Neither of us spoke.

I bent down to pick up the larger pieces of the Madonna when the phone rang. Hyacinth went into Boniface's office and answered it, but there was no one on the other end.

"There is more in heaven and earth than you've ever dreamt of in all of your philosophy, Martin." She emerged from Boniface's office. "Come, look."

I stuck my head into Boniface's office and every bookcase had been scraped clean; the books were strewn across the floor. Hyacinth and I worked to restore all the books to their shelves.

"This has happened before," she said. "Boniface could explain why." She stopped as if suddenly remembering that Boniface's mind was no longer the same. She didn't seem to want to talk about it, and I didn't ask any questions.

After restoring the books, we swept the front hall. I recalled the words of the police officer the day of the storm, when speaking of Tammy and her claim of possession: *she and her witch friends are up to no good.*

Sorcery, Satanism, and the occult never seemed more real. I slept with my bedside lamp on.

Chapter 38: Incorrigible Grace

Where there is great love,
there are always great miracles.
— Mother Teresa of Calcutta, at a prayer breakfast

It was getting colder, and autumn was in all its glory. The Church year was winding down and with it came the Judgment Day gospel passages. There were some Americans wringing their hands and biting their nails over the possible impending eschatological crisis of the year 2000.

In his homilies, Father Jack chose to play down the focus on doomsday and emphasized our responsibility of the day-to-day task of loving one's neighbor, friend, or foe. *Whatsoever you do to the least of my people, that you do unto me.*

* * * *

After the last Mass on Sunday, Jack approached me. "Come with me, Martin. I hate going to the hospital alone. We have to make a visit to a little girl, Sarah Christopher. She has cancer and the doctors don't expect her to live much longer. Her family is new to the parish."

At St. Luke's Good Samaritan, I followed Jack through the corridors and up the elevator to the pediatric ward. When we arrived at the room, a petite brunette met us in the hallway. "Father Ash, I'm Sarah's mother, Connie. Thank you so much for coming. Could you hear her confession? She was supposed to make her first confession and receive her first communion this year, but she's been so sick...." The mother was so overcome with emotion that she couldn't speak.

"Certainly, Connie." Jack motioned for Connie and me to go back into the room. "I'd like to just talk with her first."

The frail seven-year-old was lying on the bed with an intravenous tube stuck in her arm. She looked extremely weak and pathetically pale, almost blue. Quite a contrast to the room's bright yellow walls and smiling clowns wallpaper.

"Sarah, I'm Father Jack from Poor Souls," he said, approaching her bedside. "I hear you're not doing too well."

"Oh, Father, I wish I wasn't sick, but I am. I feel like Jesus when he died on the cross. I hope I get better, but I know that if I die, I will rise again. Like Jesus did on Easter. The doctors won't say, but I know I'm going to die. They haven't told me, but I know."

"Yes, Sarah, there is sadness in this old world."

"We will all die someday," Sarah said. "Someday you will, too."

"Yes. I know." He stammered for a moment, biting his lower lip. "What does that mean for you, Sarah?"

"That I'm going to see Jesus." Her eyes brightened.

"That's good, Sarah." Jack took her right hand in his.

"Are you ready, Father?"

"I hope so, honey." Jack turned and glanced up at me. My eyes blurred with tears and my jaw grew stiff with emotion as I thought of myself several years before when I was in a situation like Sarah's. Suddenly, all the feelings I had as a child when I was told I wouldn't live through the night returned.

You know not the day or the hour.

"Father," Sarah's mother interrupted Jack, and took him aside, "our family has a devotion to Saint Jude. We're praying for a miracle." Jack nodded as Connie squeezed his left hand with both her hands. "Will you hear Sarah's confession and give her communion?"

"Yes. Do you all mind stepping out for a moment?" He reached in his sport coat, produced his violet stole, and placed it around his neck and across his shoulders, straightening it down the front of his shirt.

Sarah's mother and I went into the hallway. Not knowing exactly what to say, I made for some small talk. "Mrs. Christopher—"

"You can call me Connie." She was dressed in a red and black pantsuit.

"Connie—"

"My given name is *Cunegunda*." She adjusted the white scarf around her neck.

"Oh, St. Cunegunda was the wife of St. Henry. Patroness of Lithuania."

"My mother was Lithuanian, but no one knows who Saint Cunegunda is, let alone heard of her. How do *you* know?"

"I'm in the seminary."

"Well, what do you know," she said, moving toward the wall as a nurse pushed a gurney by. "It's good to know that some of the diocesan tax dollars have been put to good use." Connie grinned.

We stood in silence for a few minutes peering in at Father Jack and Sarah as they talked. I offered to get Connie a cola but she declined. Walking to the end of the hall, I got a drink of water from the fountain. When I returned, Jack put his hands upon the girl's head and traced the sign of the cross on her forehead. Jack turned towards the door and waved Connie and me back into the room.

Jack then returned to the child's bedside when her mother was back in the room. He anointed Sarah on the forehead and palms with the holy oil and then gave her holy communion. Jack bowed his head and quietly prayed. Connie looked on with a bittersweet pride, seemingly happy for Sarah's sacramental union with the Lord, yet sad for her being so closely united to his Cross.

I recalled my own anointing when I was a child. The rheumatic fever had made me so sick I was vomiting when Father David came to my bedside. I had asked him if I would die. My father called the sacrament the *Last Rites*. I thought I would die afterwards just like my Aunt June had died after receiving them. However, Father David comforted me with a measure of hope.

Connie then looked up into Jack's misty eyes. "Tom can't get back until tomorrow."

Jack took her hands in his as she buried her face in his chest. He then held her close as she sobbed.

"Mama, don't cry," Sarah spoke softly. "There are no tears in heaven."

I stood in silent reverence as Jack comforted Connie. Father Jack taught me more in five minutes than I had learned in an entire semester's worth of lectures on pastoral counseling. After Jack had said his goodbyes to Sarah, we left.

"Damn, I hate it when it's like that," Jack wiped away a tear from his right eye as we walked down the corridor toward the elevator. "Come on, Martin. Let's go see an old friend upstairs on the cancer floor. That should really cheer us up." Jack bowed his head as we entered the elevator.

"Who is it?"

"Bill Gallagher."

"Father Bill?"

"Yes. He's been diagnosed with pancreatic cancer."

We got off on the sixth floor and entered the oncology unit. I was relieved but anxious about meeting Bill Gallagher.

I only wished it wasn't under such circumstances. When we entered the room, a round-faced, black-haired man was stretched out on the bed. His face had a greenish yellow hue, and he had several IV needles in his arms.

"Who's the new guy, Jack?" he asked in a scratchy, tired voice.

"Martin. Martin Flanagan," Jack said as he moved to the side of Bill's bed that faced the window.

"Father," I said, grasping his hand.

"Don't let that pointed head, Linguini, hear you say that." Bill took my hand into his and shook it but held on. He looked tenderly into my eyes for a moment before returning his glance to Jack. "So what's new, Father Jack?"

"Father Lee's back from medical leave after being treated for his sexual dysfunction," Jack said as he stood opposite me on the other side of Bill's bed.

"There was no dysfunction." Bill smiled through his pain.

"That's what I said. What I can't understand is why *Pretty Boy* hasn't been sent off. I mean, how many times has he been caught with his hand in the cookie jar?"

"Not now, Jack," Bill said, still holding my hand.

Jack nodded at me.

"Father Lee's going to work at the chancery," Bill explained. "The bishop and Linguini won't let him go back to a parish. Instead they're going to send him away to study Canon Law so he can return to work in the diocesan tribunal."

"Oh, why's that?" Jack asked. "So he can destroy more marriages?"

"Jack—"

"I know; I'm incorrigible."

Bill turned his attention back to me again and squeezed my hand. "Keep your eyes open, man, and think about what you're doing."

Bill's tight grasp gave me gooseflesh.

"If you've got the call it's a wonderful life, but it's a lonely one. Trust me. Don't enter the priesthood thinking you can run away from love. Until you've been wounded by love, you won't be a good priest. Believe me."

"Ah, the joy of celibacy." Jack laughed and winked at me.

"Be careful, Jack. The grass is always greener on the other side of the fence—and it still needs mowing." He paused to cough. "And don't be thinking that by getting married you can escape a priestly vocation. That doesn't work either. Marriage has never solved anyone's problems."

"Well, there goes my escape plan." Jack guffawed.

Bill slowly let loose of my hand and looked at Jack.

"So, who are you praying for these days, Jack?"

"The pope—as usual. May he rest in peace." Jack closed his eyes.

"No, I'm serious." Bill reached for Jack's hand.

"Seriously? There's a little girl downstairs in pediatrics, Sarah Christopher. She's got cancer, and it's poisoning her blood. Doctors don't give her much time."

"Sarah, you say?"

"Yeah. She's a little sweetheart. I heard her confession, gave her first communion, and anointed her."

"I'll pray for her." Bill bowed his head.

"Her mother has a devotion to St. Jude," Jack explained.

"His feast day is the twenty-eighth of October," Bill said, looking up. "That's nine days from now. I'll pray a novena for her. And I'll ask for the intercession of St. Cunegunda."

"Which one?" asked Jack, clearing his throat.

"You're clever, Jack," Bill beamed. "But does it matter?"

"Cunegunda?" I said unevenly. "That's Sarah's mother's name."

"Yes, and it was my wife's religious name as well." Bill

winked at me.

"God loves you, Bill." Jack nodded and stroked Bill's left cheek.

"At least somebody in the Church does." Bill laughed, but it caused him much pain and he coughed himself windless. When he finally stopped coughing, he took my hand again. "Son, don't feel that just because you're in the seminary you have to become a priest. The seminary won't be your refuge. It can't be. You'll only be there for a while. It's an artificial environment." He continued to clasp hold.

"No matter what, you've got to do what you believe God is calling you to do. Remember, God is the One who calls. So, follow your heart. And don't worry. Whatever vocation you choose, and wherever you decide to serve, God will still love you and be with you."

His words remained with me as Father Jack and I returned to Poor Souls.

Chapter 39: Forbidden Rites

The truths of religion are never so well understood
as by those who have lost the power of reasoning.
— Voltaire

On the thirtieth of October, Father Jack shocked me with the sad news that Bill Gallagher had died. "I was with him when he died. He told me that as soon as he finished his time in Purgatory, he would be in heaven praying for us." Jack tried to smile, but his lower lip quivered.

Jack set things in motion for Father Bill's funeral. He contacted several of his brother priests and made arrangements to have the funeral at Poor Souls. During the rush to put things together, Monsignor Linguini called Jack and threatened to remove his priestly faculties if he were to go forward with the plans for Bill's funeral.

I was with Father Jack in his study when the vicar-general, Linguini, called a second time. "Listen, Father Ash," Linguini's voice came over the intercom, "you are in clear violation of Canon Law and run the risk of excommunication."

"He was a Catholic, for Christ's sake," Jack said as he slammed a prayer book down on his desk.

"He was also a suspended priest."

"Bill was one of us, spaghetti brains. He was a priest—"

"That's right, he *was*, but he contracted marriage unlawfully and was suspended from the ministry."

"Since when is the love between a man and a woman an illness?"

"It isn't, unless a man is vowed as a priest. He renounces marriage for the good of the Church...oh, why am I telling you these things? You know that. I will not tolerate you belittling the bishop or me any longer. You knew that Bill celebrated a Mass!"

"It was in the hospital chapel."

"That's no excuse."

"How was I to stop him? *Once a priest, always a priest.*"

"That isn't a defense! He also unlawfully heard confessions at Lost Souls!"

"*Poor Souls*, Monsignor Linguini."

"Well, now that you're there, it *is* Lost Souls. And I pity the poor souls. They *are* lost with you as their pastor."

"Well, you're the one who put me here."

"You are such an ass."

"At least I work at it. What do you do all day at the chancery? Widen your phylactery and lengthen your tassels?"

"Listen, Jack. Your insubordination has gone far enough. You're a rebellious, defiant, disrespectful, disobedient, insolent...priest!"

"What's wrong, Monsignor, did you run out of adjectives? You didn't quite exhaust the thesaurus. You forgot *mischievous*."

"That's it. I've had it. I will personally publicly humiliate you by having you removed as pastor if you allow Bill's funeral to go forward and take place in the church."

"You wouldn't do that."

"That's right. The *bishop* will."

"No, he won't. Who would you send here? No one's fool enough to take Poor Souls."

"You're probably right, but don't think that I don't know you've got those little old ladies believing that the Virgin Mary appeared on the hillside."

"Oh, give me more credit than that! You know I'm not superstitious. Those pious blue-haired ladies conjured up Mary themselves. In fact, they're angry at me because I don't believe that one of the statues here is bleeding from the eyes."

"I'm bleeding from the eyes just talking to you!" Linguini said.

"Then I wouldn't be a bit surprised if Mary didn't appear just to show you up, Monsignor. Come to think of it, why wouldn't she appear here? It's as good a place as any. I'm beginning to like it here at Poor Souls. The place is starting to grow on me."

"Don't try and change the subject, Jackass. You will not—you cannot—have Bill Gallagher's funeral!" Linguini's voice was strained and hoarse. "He is not to receive a Catholic burial!"

"Who are you to judge?"

"Bill judged himself when he broke his vows."

"Well, then, you and the bishop will have to come down here personally and remove his coffin from the sanctuary because that's where it is."

"Over my dead body!" Linguini yelled.

The phone line went dead before a busy signal hummed on and off.

"He'd better be careful, Martin." Jack turned the speakerphone off. "Someone's liable to take him up on his offer."

Chapter 40: Miracles

*It is a heretic that makes the fire
Not she which burns in it.*
— *The Winter's Tale*, II, iii, 113

Father Bill's funeral took place on All Souls Day, November second. It started snowing the night before, and by daybreak, there was nearly half a foot of snow on the ground. Despite the inclement weather, the church was full of people, standing room only. A contingency of nuns from Sister Cunegunda's order attended, and fifteen priests con-celebrated the requiem Mass.

After Mass, a group of priests said they thought they had seen Monsignor Linguini in the back of the church during the funeral Mass.

"Do you think?" Jack wondered aloud.

"Gentlemen." Linguini's voice sounded forth as he stepped into the sacristy and nodded to Jack. "I drove through the snowstorm to get here."

The priests were silent.

"Bill was a friend of mine, too," Linguini said before turning to leave the sacristy.

The body of Bill was being taken to Coaltown where he was to be buried next to his wife, Cunegunda.

* * * *

A few days after Bill's funeral Mass, the little girl with cancer, Sarah Christopher, and her parents, Connie and Tom Christopher, came to the rectory. "Sarah's had a miraculous recovery," Connie announced with tears as she entered the foyer. Sarah didn't look sick at all. "It all began on the twenty-eighth," Connie said.

"The twenty-eighth?" Jack repeated the date as he opened the French doors and seated the family in the living room.

"Yes," Connie said as she sat next to Tom on the sofa.

"That's the feast of Saint Jude," I reminded them as I stood near the doors. Meanwhile Sarah found her way to her daddy's lap.

"On the second of November—the day of the big snow—her color returned," Connie continued, "her pain went away, and she got up and walked on her own. The doctors took her in for testing and found no trace of the cancer. They have no medical explanation."

"It's a miracle, Father," Tom spoke, choking back tears. "You heard her confession and anointed her the week before."

"Now wait a minute, Tom, don't go spreading a rumor that I worked a miracle." Jack sat on one of the easy chairs across from the sofa. "I've got enough problems with the bishop, and I don't need him thinking I'm trying to upstage anyone by performing miracles."

"I didn't say *you* had worked the miracle, Father Jack. The Lord works miracles. You just happened to be the broken instrument through which he worked it."

"Thanks for the vote of confidence," Jack whispered.

"Your entire priesthood's a miracle, Father," Connie assured him.

"The bishop and vicar-general would quite agree," Jack snickered.

"And isn't that the way God works?" Tom continued. "Father Jack, you're a broken instrument, but then so was Saint Peter. Look at all that the Lord accomplished through him."

Jack stared across the room as if suddenly remembering something. "It *is* a miracle." He waved little Sarah over and took her in his arms.

* * * *

After the Christophers departed, Jack turned to me. "They're right. It is a miracle worked through the intercession of three saints."

"Which ones?"

"Saints Jude, William, and Cunegunda."

"How's that?"

"The second of November was the day of Bill Gallagher's funeral Mass."

Chapter 41: Memories

When he shall die, take him and cut him out
in little stars, and he will make the face of
heaven so fine that all the world will be in love
with night and pay no worship to the garish sun.
— *Romeo and Juliet*, III, ii, 21

In November, the group of ladies from the altar society came to Father Jack claiming to have seen a vision of the Blessed Virgin Mary on the hillsides on the north side of the churchyard.

"They said they told Monsignor Linguini about it two weeks ago knowing I wouldn't believe them," Jack explained over dinner. "So far he hasn't done anything about it. So they thought they'd try me. So what do you think? Is it a sign?"

"I have no idea," I replied as I cut into my baked chicken.

"You know, I've heard that before," Jack shook his head and took a bite of his baked potato. "Anyway, I caution against these apparitions. We don't need thousands of people making pilgrimages to the parish, trampling all the grass, hunting for something that they could just as easily find if they'd just read their scriptures or went to Mass. Besides, Monsignor Linguini isn't amused by these kinds of things. He probably still thinks I've put the ladies of the parish up to it."

I went to the church to pray. I paused in front of the statue of Mary. Artificial pink carnations had been placed at her feet. I imagined tears in her eyes.

* * * *

For the thanksgiving holiday, Mother invited me home. On Thanksgiving Day, I attended the parish Mass before leaving for Cainbrook. I arrived home an hour later than I expected due to freezing rain.

"Hurry and help me slice the turkey," Mother said as I opened the back door. Mashed potatoes, stuffing, cranberries, pumpkin pie, and all the trimmings covered the buffet table in the dining room. It was too much food for just the two of us.

"Sean should be here soon," Mother called out as she put on her oven mitts and removed the yams from the oven.

"I didn't know he was coming," I said.

"He's supposed to be in town to visit a friend." She looked up from the casserole.

"Who's that?"

"Brian Small." She placed the yams on the buffet table.

"Brian Small was arrested for attempted murder," I reminded her. "He's in jail."

"Yes, I know. Your brother was going to visit him." She paused as she closed the oven door. "Listen, Martin, quit picking on Sean. He's your brother."

"I know, Mother, but—"

"No buts, Mister. It's a holiday. And the last time I checked, *visiting the imprisoned* was still one of the corporal works of mercy."

"I'm sure that's why Sean is visiting him."

"Don't be so sure of yourself, Martin," she said as she removed her oven mitts and put them in the top counter drawer. "You need to show some mercy and Christian compassion. You're going to be a priest someday."

I didn't try arguing with her. She was right, but I didn't want to hear it.

"Now help me set the table and make sure you set for four."

"Who else is coming?"

"Sean might be bringing his lady friend." She walked back into the kitchen and returned with a bowl of steaming vegetables. I set the table and waited as Mother went into the den and put on some old albums of big band and jazz. Glen Miller, Artie Shaw, and Benny Goodman sounded throughout the house over the ceiling speakers.

As we sat down to dinner, she paged Sean on his beeper. "I've paged him three times already. Maybe he's on his way."

All the food spread out in the dining room reminded me of our many family gatherings of years past. Where were all our relatives now? At one time, this house was alive with laughter and song. Some of the relatives, like Uncle Hoot and Aunt Anna May, had died. The others had distanced themselves from our side of the family after Father's funeral. Actually, the others were already distant owing to Mother and Father's separation; but for the funeral, everyone came round one last time, or for one last feeding, as Mother called it.

* * * *

Mother decided that we should go ahead and eat. "The food is getting cold." She made the sign of the cross and prayed the traditional meal prayer, "Bless us, O Lord..."

"Sean's not coming, Mother," I said in between bites of turkey and potatoes.

"You don't know that." She held her wine glass out toward me, indicating she wanted some.

"Well, he's not here." I took the bottle of white wine and filled her glass.

"Maybe if you weren't so judgmental of him he would

have come!" She sipped her wine.

We hardly said anything the rest of the night. She went into the living room and watched reruns of "I Love Lucy," and I went for a walk and went to bed early.

The next day mother had a card party with some of her lady friends. I returned to the parish.

* * * *

Since early November, I had been practicing with Poor Souls' choir every Tuesday night in preparation for the Advent and Christmas seasons. I saw Peggy Schultz and her mother every week at choir practice; they were both in the choir, but there wasn't much time for socializing since the choir director was a rather eccentric and strict man who demanded discipline. That didn't bother me but there was something that did. The one downside to singing with the Poor Souls' choir was having the misfortune of having to breathe one of the member's noxious fumes as a result of terrible flatulence.

One evening, the Tuesday after Thanksgiving, the choir director had finally had enough of the odor. "Whoever in hell is breaking wind, would you please stop?" he shouted. "I can't breathe! Or else go outside and pass gas."

* * * *

The icy grasp of winter was around the throat of November and with it came the confirmation from Monsignor Linguini that Father Boniface would never return to Poor Souls. Father Jack and Hyacinth would now be responsible for the arduous and lugubrious task of going through Father Boniface's belongings.

There was more than thirty plus years of accumulated possessions and assorted junk. "Rummaging through Boniface's stuff is ghoulish," said Hyacinth.

* * * *

One Tuesday evening following choir practice, I entered

the rectory and went upstairs. When I got to the top of the stairs, the attic door at the end of the hall was open and the light was on.

I made my way up the narrow flight of stairs into the attic. It was cool upstairs, yet not completely uncomfortable. Once at the top of the steps, I saw Hyacinth kneeling down amidst cardboard boxes, crates, and stacks of papers. She was sifting through the contents of one of the boxes of Boniface's affects.

"Good evening, Martin." She wiped her teary eyes and blew her nose before looking up. The wrinkles in her face were accentuated by the lamplight.

"What are you doing?" I asked, knowing exactly what she was doing.

"I'm not sure. It's like Boniface is dead, but I know he's not. In a way, I feel like I'm robbing his grave. I don't think he'll ever be his old self. His mind keeps slipping further and further into the past. Today he went off on a tirade against Nixon and the war in Vietnam. It's enough to make you cry."

In her hands was a cardboard box marked *memories*.

"I never knew he cared that much. These boxes are full of little things that I gave him over the years."

I walked over to her and knelt down next to her.

"Look," she said, holding out an old ticket stub towards him. "It's a ticket stub from a show we saw in Covert. *The Sound of Music*. I remember it like it was yesterday."

Taking the stub, I was reminded of Peggy Schultz. I handed it back to her.

"Delightful." She smiled through her tears.

I nodded.

"Just like Boniface." She reached for my hand and grasped hold. "He loved me. All these years he...loved...me." She dissolved into an emotional tumult and pulled me close, clutching tight.

Her tears soaked my shirtsleeve. In the dim light of the single bulb dangling from the ceiling, we sat together in the silence amid Boniface's memories.

Chapter 42: Christmas Epiphany

"The devil can cite scripture for his purpose."
— *The Merchant of Venice*, II, iii, 95

By the end of Advent the sights, sounds, and smells of Christmas were soon all about: wreaths, holly and ivy, tinsel, hot cocoa, sugar cookies, pumpkin pies, gingerbread, Christmas trees, twinkling lights, eggnog, and mistletoe.

The week before Christmas supplied interesting grist for the diocesan rumor mill. There was a scandal brewing at Covert Catholic High, the largest diocesan high school. In the early 1970s, Bishop Collins had consolidated Covert's four Catholic high schools into one school. The principal of Covert High resigned the last day of school before Christmas break over an accusation of malfeasance and extortion. There was already much animosity among the other Catholic high schools in the diocese over the feeling that Covert received most of the funds while the others barely got scraps.

For instance, the members of their basketball team were treated like gods. The diocesan joke was that under the floor of one of the basketball goals was St. Dominic's Rosary, and the holy relic in the chapel's altar stone was Jesus' athletic supporter or the basketball net from Jesus' boyhood home.

Covert Catholic needed a new floor for its basketball court

a few years back, and the project was begun and paid for within a week's time. Meanwhile, the teachers were underpaid, and the school ran in the red every year.

"They've got money." Father Jack raised his voice to me across the breakfast table. "And now they're letting teachers go for no reason."

"They can't do that," I argued, putting my coffee mug down.

"They can in Covert," Hyacinth reminded us.

"Oh, yes," Jack shook his head.

"That's not legal, is it?" I asked.

"It is for our diocese," Hyacinth replied. "Now you know why I poisoned Munchin and Linguini."

"Now I know why they call you 'the General,'" Jack said to Hyacinth.

"Be careful, buddy-boy," Hyacinth eyed Jack out the corners of her eyes. "Don't make me poison you."

* * * *

I assisted Father Jack as his acolyte at the midnight Mass at Poor Souls. On Christmas morning, I left early for Cainbrook to join my mother for Christmas. It started snowing as I left Inglenook, but it was mostly flurries. At Cainbrook, I accompanied my mother to Our Lady of the River. Father Xavier Lax celebrated the Mass. Sean was supposed to join us, but he didn't.

After Mass, Mother and I went to the Cainbrook Country Club. It had been a longstanding tradition in our family to have Christmas brunch at the club. Sean was supposed to join us for brunch as well, but again he failed to show.

George and Ruth, two longtime employees of the club, were dressed in black and white formal wear and stood outside the swinging double kitchen doors. George was in a tuxedo, and Ruth wore a white blouse with a long black skirt. George and Ruth were black. In fact, most of the club's employees were black, except for one redheaded waitress who looked like she moonlit as a dancer at a lounge, and a longhaired white waiter who looked as if he was tripping out on crack cocaine.

Growing up as a member of the country club, I hadn't given it any thought when I was served by blacks, or African-Americans. Of course, some of the members of the club always called them the Negro help. Some weren't as gracious or polite. However, as I became a teenager, it began to trouble me that the black employees, many of whom I supposed had families of their own, were expected to work on Christmas Day.

As an adult, it bothered me that the blacks were still treated as glorified servants. When I finished my plate, I stood and sought out George and Ruth. "Merry Christmas, George. Merry Christmas, Ruth."

"Merry Christmas, Marty," the two said in unison. Ruth gave me a hug and a kiss on the right cheek.

"You know, Marty," George's low baritone voice resounded, "I hear tell you're in the seminary, going to become a priest, you are." He reverently nodded.

"Yes, I'm studying at Saint Albert's."

"Well, I wish you well." He extended his large hand for a handshake.

"Thank you." His hand swallowed mine.

"I used to be Catholic years ago." He placed his left hand on my right shoulder as he stood facing me, still holding my right hand.

"I didn't know that," I replied with surprise.

"Yes," he relaxed his grip and returned my hand. "It was over forty years ago. I just felt more at home in the Baptist church." He paused and cleared his throat. "Well, you'd better get back to your mother. She seems lonely here these days. Your brother don't come round much no more."

"Yes, I know." I turned to see if Sean had arrived yet. He had not. "George, I hope you and Ruth both can spend some time with your families today."

"Oh," Ruth shook her head, "all the kids and grandkids come o'er whenever they can."

"Our family celebrates Christmas during the week, usually," George said. "We're so used to it, it don't matter."

I wished them a Merry Christmas again and made my way toward Mother's table. As I passed the bar, I felt someone grab me between my legs. I turned around quickly. It was Sean. He wore a red sock cap and was dressed in blue jeans, muddy tennis shoes, and a white t-shirt underneath a *NASCAR* racing jacket. He laughed in my face. "Well, well, well, if it ain't the Reverend Martin Luther King Junior!"

"Sean!" I wondered how he had gotten into the club dressed as he was.

"What?" He then tried to goose me with the bottle neck of his imported beer. "It's Christmas."

"You're drunk?"

"It's Christmas."

I tried to move him out of the center of the dining room and get him over to Mother's table. I could see her motioning to me.

"What were you doing talking to the help?"

"George is more than the help," I argued.

"Yeah, he's the chief nigger."

"Sean—"

"Is that nigger your brother?"

"Yes, he is. And he's yours, too."

"That nigger ain't my brother. The only nigger I got for a brother is you, dumbass."

"Sean, stop the racist crap."

"Listen to you, dickhead." Sean raised his voice to Mother's chagrin. "You're such a phony bastard, you fucken hypocrite."

"Yes. I am a hypocrite, but at least I can admit it." Several people stopped eating and glared at us.

"What's that supposed to mean?"

At that, George approached the table holding out a light tan sport coat. "Excuse me, Mr. Flanagan. You'll have to remove your hat and at least wear this jacket."

Sean seethed in anger, but removed his hat and tossed his jacket on the table as he put on the coat. "There." He smirked.

"Thank you," George nodded to Sean and turned to Mother. "I'm sorry Mrs. Flanagan, but rules are rules."

"Sean," Mother pointed her finger down at the table and gritted her teeth, "you're embarrassing all of us."

"Who gives a fuck?" Sean asked loudly. "They can go to hell for all I care. They ain't no better than me."

"Damn it, Sean. Stop it," Mother whispered.

"Hey, Mama, where's my forgiveness?" He spread his arms wide and turned to me with a smirking grin. "And what about Saint Martin the Hypocrite? Isn't he going to show me any mercy? If he's going to be a priest, maybe he can hear my confession."

I looked at him but couldn't say anything I was so angry. It seemed everyone in the club's dining room was staring at our table.

"Judge not, lest thee be judged," Sean said. "Remember? Why worry about the speck in your brother's eye when you have a beam in your own eye? Huh? Love the sinner. Well, you've got to love me, queer boy. You better practice what you preach, big brother." He laughed and finished his beer. Then he put his feet up on one of the chairs. "That holier than thou attitude you put on don't fool nobody."

"It *doesn't* fool *anyone*," Mother said, correcting his English.

"Yeah, that, too," he answered her, and then he looked at

me. "See, Martin, even she admits it."

"Sean, at least speak correct English," Mother carped. "I didn't send you to the best academy in Cainbrook to hear you talk like white trash."

"We are white trash, Mama, so get over yourself, goddammit. You own a damned dry cleaning business. So what? Who cares? Then you pay thirty thousand dollars a year just so you can say you belong to a Country Club. But then," he said, pointing at me with his beer bottle, "your son here, Martin, is going to become a priest so he can milk you out of the rest of your money for a corrupt church."

"Here's your Christmas gift, Sean." I reluctantly handed him the wrapped package. He opened the box and looked at the pullover sweater I got him. He stood and walked back to the club's kitchen.

"Where's he going?" asked Mother.

"I have no idea."

He soon reappeared through the swinging doors and returned with something behind his back. "Here's your Christmas gift, loser." Sean handed me a can of assorted nuts. "Sorry I didn't have time to have them gift wrapped. They ought to remind you of your priest buddies." Then he nodded to mother. "Merry Christmas, Mother. I'll come visit you when Judas isn't around."

With that, he peeled off the borrowed sport coat and threw it on his chair. He put his sock cap and jacket on again and grabbed an imported German beer off of the redheaded waitress's tray as she walked past him. He hurried away, pushing through the club's front doors.

"Merry Christmas," Mother whispered as she cradled her head in her hands.

Chapter 43: Twelfth Night Vaccination

"The path to hell is paved with the skulls of priests."
— Popular saying during the French Revolution.

On the Feast of Epiphany, January sixth, the traditional twelfth day of Christmas, the annual Twelfth Night celebration took place at Poor Souls. The ritual had been around for fifty years or so. All the parishioners would bring their Christmas trees to church to serve as fuel for the blazing Twelfth Night Yule on the church steps. The bonfire celebrated the manifestation of the light of Christ to the world.

In the middle of the evening prayer, while a good number of parishioners gathered about the steps of church, Deacon Dill cried out in horrible pain. His left arm was in flames. "Crime in Italy!" Deacon Dill cried aloud. "Not again!" he had stepped too close to the fire in his liturgical alb.

The male parishioner who was in charge of setting the annual fire lunged at Deacon Dill, pounded him against the red brick of the church, and knocked the flames down. Meanwhile, I grabbed the pail of holy water from one of the servers, removed the aspergillum, and doused the remaining flames.

"I've been baptized in fire and water!" Deacon Dill exclaimed as he shivered in the cold. "Now I'm freezing to death!"

Then he broke wind.

* * * *

After the festivities, I retired for the evening. About midnight I came downstairs when I thought I smelled smoke. When I got to the bottom of the stairs and stood in the foyer, I felt a cold draft and saw that the front door was propped open. There were no lights on but the living room stereo was playing low; Eric Clapton's *Layla* was on. When I stepped into the living room, I could see an orange glow coming from one of the easy chairs. It was a cigarette. That explained the smoke.

"The Italian Cardinals prop the pope up in his chair and tell him what to say," a familiar male voice spoke, though it wasn't Father Jack's. "Maybe the pope is really dead, and they're moving his lips like a ventriloquist dummy." The voice stopped when I walked in.

"Come on in, whoever you are." Father Jack sounded a bit groggy.

"Father Jack?" I asked.

"Martin, we've got company."

As my eyes adjusted to the dark, I could see Father Robin Wood sitting in the easy chair with a drink in his hand. "Good evening, Flanagan," Robin said, removing a cigarette from his mouth.

"Father Robin?"

"Yes. It's me." His wire-rimmed spectacles reflected the bluish light from the streetlights.

"We're in here vaccinating ourselves, Martin," Jack laughed, sipping from a tumbler.

"How's that?" I asked.

"You don't know what the vaccination for celibacy is?" Robin asked.

I stammered, saying nothing as John Cougar's *Crumblin' Down* sounded from the speakers.

"Booze, son. Booze. Plenty of it. And cards. And if you can make a pilgrimage to Vegas, that'll help, too. Of course, the gambling casinos are coming here sometime, so it'll soon be easier for us."

"Father Robin is visiting us incognito. He escaped from obedience school."

"Psycho Rehab." Robin cleared his throat noisily.

I stood in the darkened room trying to think of something to say, but couldn't.

"As I was about to say," Jack resumed, "when Bill Gallagher died I thought I'd be ministering to him, helping him die, but I'll be damned if he didn't teach me how to live." Jack took a drink, his ice cubes clinking in the tumbler.

"Linguini told me I couldn't have his funeral," Jack continued. "But you know what? Linguini came to the funeral Mass."

"I heard." Robin asked, "What did he say?"

"That Bill was his friend. He stood in the back of the church." Jack paused. "It surprised the hell out of all of us."

I started to leave to go back upstairs to bed when Robin turned to me. "Hey, Martin, when the diocesan newspaper asks you to write about why you want to be a priest, don't give us any of that pious bullshit like that crazy seminarian did in last week's paper."

I stopped on the bottom stair knowing of the series of articles about the seminarians. Last week's column was an interview with Gerard Austin.

"Oh, well, what's it going to matter? Nobody reads that rag. The Covert Catholic Courier is good for one thing and one thing only. When Father Kevin Murphy was here, I had him use it to line the bottom of his birdcage. The bishop's face at the top of his weekly column makes a great target for bird droppings." He paused, lit another cigarette, and poured himself more liquor.

"When we were in the seminary in the seventies, while women were burning bras and reading Gloria Steinam, we were burning our cassocks and copies of *Humanae Vitae* and the pope's letter on mandatory celibacy," Robin said. "Jack, do you remember when we were together at St. Augustine's in Covert when the Mormons came to the door?"

"Oh, yeah." Jack followed suit with another drink. "Martin, you've got to hear this. The Jehovah's Witnesses had been knocking on the door every week, and one day another group came to the door—"

"Jack went upstairs," Robin continued, "and he came back down wearing a bloody Halloween werewolf mask and carrying an American flag, screaming about the Pledge of Allegiance and blood transfusions."

"The older guy said, 'We're Mormons, not Jehovah's Witnesses,'" Jack added. "Then they scrambled out the door. An hour later, the cops came by and said the Mormons were going to file a criminal complaint against me. The next day the bishop called me in and made me get counseling."

The two men began laughing. "Don't let us keep you up, Martin," Jack said.

"Good to see you, Father Robin. Goodnight, Father Jack." I made my way up the stairs as the two priests continued their conversation from where they left off. The cigarette smoke followed me upstairs.

"Around here I felt like a liturgical prostitute," Robin's speech was slurred. "I'd say I'm a poorly paid prostitute, but at least they're appreciated for their services. Yeah, you're nothing but a damned liturgical whore. Face it, Jack, they come here to get their weekly spiritual fix—God forbid if it lasts more than an hour. Jack, you're nothing more than a glorified host dispenser."

Jack guffawed.

"Hell, the church is a corpse," Robin continued, more somber. "All it needs is someone to bury it. The sooner the better. I think I'll retire and take a wife."

John Lennon's *Imagine* wafted up the stairwell behind me.

Chapter 44: Unfinished

I always wanted to become a saint.
— St. Thérèse of Lisieux

That Sunday was my last official day at Poor Souls. Following the ten o'clock Mass, Father Jack had doughnuts and coffee in the old school's basement so that the parishioners could bid me farewell before I was to return to St. Albert's Seminary for the spring semester.

Amid the small talk and shaking of hands, I looked around to see if Peggy Schultz and her family were anywhere in the crowd, but I didn't see them. After the doughnuts were gone, the crowd thinned. I shook a few more hands and accepted several cards before putting on my parka and leaving the building. As I went up the steps and walked under the archway between the old school and the rectory, I saw Peggy in a black cashmere coat with a gray rabbit fur collar, purple sock cap, and purple mittens walking out of the church toward the school. Once she saw me, she hurried to me.

"There you are," she said coming over to me. "I almost missed you."

"And I you," I replied, not sure it came out right. "Thanks for coming."

She was now standing opposite me. I smiled. She came

close and gave me a kiss on the left side of my mouth. Our lips met. She pulled away slowly. "Don't forget us," she said.

"I won't." What else could I say? Her warm, wet kiss was still on my cold, chapped lips. Did she mean us as in she and I, or us as in the Schultz family, or us as in the parish of Poor Souls?

"What was that for?" I asked.

"After all, we slept together, but we never kissed. It's the least I can do." Peggy grinned and adjusted her purple hat. "I've got to go."

My lips were still tingling.

"Goodbye, Martin."

For forever or just for now? She got in her car, started the engine, waved, and drove away. I waved to her as she turned the corner and went out of sight. "Goodbye," I breathed out. My breath disappeared into the wintry air as quickly as it had appeared.

* * * *

I returned to the rectory, packed my belongings, and prepared to return to St. Albert's to begin my next semester of studies. I had much to consider if I was ever to become a priest. In my luggage, I packed a framed picture of Father Jack Ash with the Christopher family. Little Sarah was beaming with a smile.

As I took my belongings to the car, Hyacinth stopped me in the foyer. She hugged me and kissed me on the cheek. "I'm going to miss you. Keep in touch. God bless you."

As I brought my last suitcase down the stairs and out to my car, a local television news crew van pulled up in front of the rectory. Monsignor Linguini had parked behind the news van and was just getting out of his car. He followed the female reporter and cameraman up the sidewalk to the rectory. The cameraman was filming as the female reporter turned to vicar-general Linguini and held the microphone to his face.

"The bishop has appointed me to lead the investigation," he explained. "Of course, the Church is slow to accept any alleged miraculous claims. There have been over eight hundred thousand alleged apparitions of the Virgin Mary, but only seven have ever been approved; of those seven, no Catholic is obliged to believe in any of them. Mary's message is simple: Be open to God's Word and do whatever her Son Jesus tells us to do."

I could see Hyacinth pulling the curtains back from the living room windows and observing the spectacle.

Suddenly, Father Jack came up behind me. "You know, the Jesuit theologian Bernard Lonergan once said, '*The Church always arrives on the scene a little breathless and a little late.*'" He motioned to Monsignor Linguini.

Jack then took my suitcase from me. "Here, let me get that for you." Then, placing the valise in the trunk of my car, he closed the lid. "The media wants to interview me, too. You'd better leave while you can, or else they'll be interrogating *you* for the six o'clock news."

He held out his arms and we embraced. Then he opened my driver's door for me.

"Yeah, I'd better be getting back to St. Albert's." I got into the car, shut the door, and rolled my window down.

"Not all the good priests leave the active ministry, Martin. I'm still in, right?" He winked. "Seriously, a lot of us priests are happy. Sometimes when we get together we're just a bunch of old bachelors who love to whine and bitch. What we need to do is learn how to preach like the Protestants.

"As for the priesthood, if I had to do it all over again, I would still go to seminary and be ordained. I'm actually happier in the priesthood than I ever thought I'd be.

"See you around, Martin." He grinned and placed his

hand on the roof of my car. "It's been real."

"You can say that again."

"*That.*" Jack laughed. "Say hello to Father Hugh for me." He reached in the car and shook my hand.

"Will do."

"Just don't mention Peggy Schultz. That could give him a heart attack. *Ecclesia semper reformanda*—the Church is always in need of reformation." He let go of my hand. "And remember, there's always a place for you at Poor Souls." Jack turned and slowly walked up the sidewalk toward the rectory.

Putting the key in the ignition, I started the engine, turned the heater on, and slowly rolled the driver's door window up. Jack's words surprised me. Had he seen Peggy and I kiss?

I turned on the car stereo and listened to Franz Schubert's *Unfinished Symphony*. I realized that I had more questions than answers concerning my own vocation. My six months at Poor Souls had certainly raised more questions than it had answered, which was probably a good thing. I, like Schubert's symphony, seemed unfinished.

* * * *

The twin spires of Poor Souls had no sooner disappeared from my rear view mirror than St. Albert's Seminary greeted my return. Walking under the seminary archway, I read the words etched in the stone entrance above the main doors: *God Alone*.

ABOUT THE AUTHOR

John William McMullen, a student of philosophy, theology, and history, holds a Master's Degree in Theological Studies and is a Theology Instructor at Mater Dei High School in Evansville, Indiana. He is also a College Philosophy Professor, Third Order Benedictine Oblate, a member of the St. Thomas More Society of Southwestern Indiana, and has authored five other novels, one novella, several short stories, and numerous political and religious articles. He is currently working on another novel. He may be contacted at:

jmcmullen@materdei.evansville.net

or polycarpmac@yahoo.com

*For your reading pleasure, we invite
you to visit our web bookstore*

WHISKEY CREEK PRESS

www.whiskeycreekpress.com